Percy B. St. John

The Young Buccaneer

Percy B. St. John

The Young Buccaneer

ISBN/EAN: 9783337182649

Printed in Europe, USA, Canada, Australia, Japan

Cover: Foto ©Andreas Hilbeck / pixelio.de

More available books at **www.hansebooks.com**

CLARKE'S
STANDARD NOVEL LIBRARY.

N LIFE.

Picture

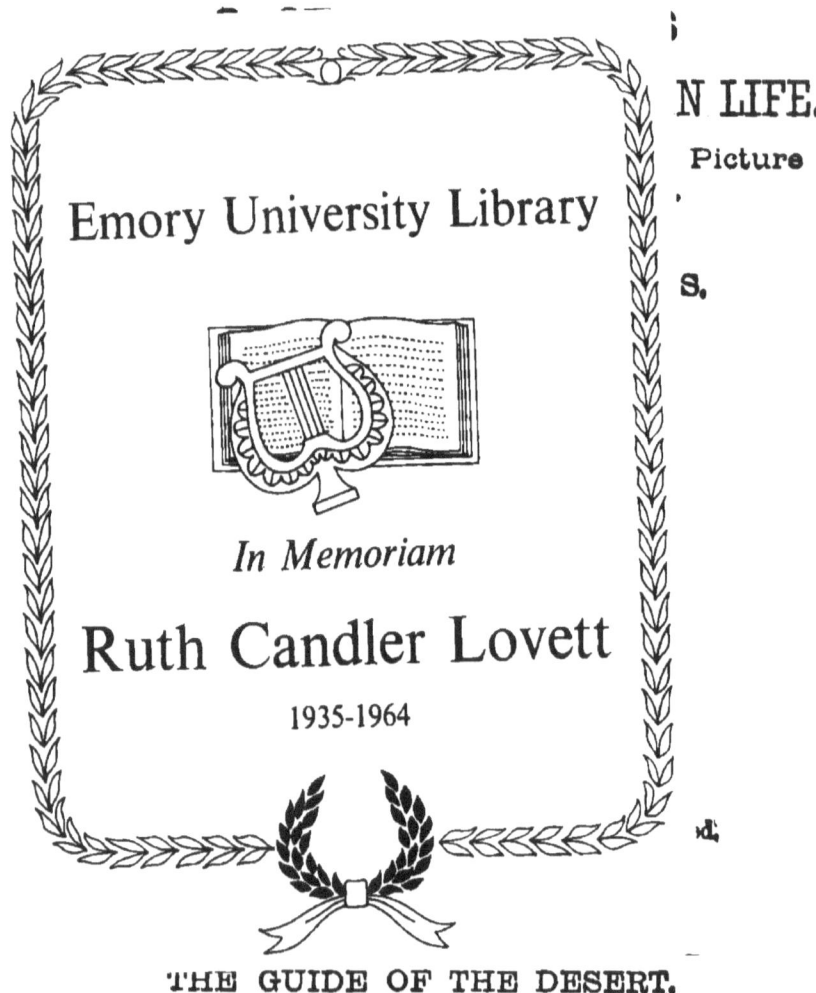

Emory University Library

S.

In Memoriam

Ruth Candler Lovett

1935-1964

LONDON:
CHARLES HENRY CLARKE, 13, PATERNOSTER ROW

CLARKE'S
POPULAR RAILWAY READING.

Crown 8vo, Picture Wrappers, Price One Shilling each

————o————

————

LONDON:
CHARLES HENRY CLARKE, 13, PATERNOSTER ROW.

CLARKE'S
STANDARD NOVEL LIBRARY.

---o---

GUSTAVE AIMARD'S
NOVELS AND TALES OF INDIAN LIFE.

An Entirely New Edition, with New Picture
Wrappers, Post 8vo, Price 2s.

---o---

THE TRAPPERS OF ARKANSAS.
THE BORDER RIFLES.
THE FREEBOOTERS.
THE WHITE SCALPER.
THE ADVENTURERS.
PEARL OF THE ANDES.
THE TRAIL HUNTER.
PIRATES OF THE PRAIRIES.
TRAPPER'S DAUGHTER.
TIGER SLAYER.
THE GOLD SEEKERS.
THE INDIAN CHIEF.
THE RED TRACK.
THE PRAIRIE FLOWER.
THE INDIAN SCOUT.
THE LAST OF THE INCAS.
QUEEN OF THE SAVANNAH.
THE BUCCANEER CHIEF.
STRONGHAND, a Tale of the Disinherited.
THE SMUGGLER CHIEF.
THE REBEL CHIEF.
STONEHEART- a Romance.
THE BEE HUNTERS.
THE GUIDE OF THE DESERT.
THE INSURGENT CHIEF.
THE FLYING HORSEMAN.

LONDON:
CHARLES HENRY CLARKE, 13, PATERNOSTER ROW

THE

YOUNG BUCCANEER.

BY

PERCY B. ST. JOHN,

AUTHOR OF "THE CORAL REEF," "THE SNOW SHIP,"
"THE SAILOR CRUSOE," ETC., ETC.

LONDON:
CHARLES H. CLARKE, 13 PATERNOSTER ROW.

THE YOUNG BUCCANEER.

CHAPTER I.

NED DRAKE AND DIRTRICK.

WERE we to dive into the secret history of English boys'
hearts, we should find that, while few had not at one time
wished themselves Robinson Crusoe, scarce one had ever
wished himself a pirate ! The very word is abhorrent to
the natural instincts, and only the utterly lost, no matter
what may have been their social scale, have so disgraced
the bravery and honour of this great maritime power.
But the natural tastes of islanders have always directed us
towards enterprise by sea, and hence the fascination with
which we regard the adventures of privateers in pursuit of
our enemies, or the somewhat doubtful exploits of bold
buccaneers, like heroic William Dampier.

In the present instance we have to introduce one less
known to fame, but scarcely less worthy of being followed
in his wild and chequered career.

At a time when the police of the seas was somewhat
more carelessly kept than it is now ; when, despite the
men-of-war which kept watch and ward near every shore ;
despite the revenue cutters that haunted every port—
smugglers did a rare trade, and the business of slavers was
at a premium—the coast of England afforded facilities for
the fitting out of lawless cruisers, which, since the introduction of steam, can never occur again.

No more can a taut schooner lie hidden in some creek,
or swash, or gut, awaiting such a wind as shall enable it,
by means of its light draught, to choose its own time, and

run forth while its royal enemy is bearing up to windward;
no more dare the crews of such craft to use violence with
coast-guard men, or tars who are sent to board her—the
romance of smuggling is at an end.

But at the time of which we speak, it was very different.
Then, under a mistaken system of policy, as injurious to
ourselves as to our neighbours, the temptation to smuggling was so great, the facilities so wonderful, and the
sympathies of the masses so universal, that though every
point—north, south, east, and west—had its contraband
cove, bay, cavern, or ruin, scarcely ever were they betrayed;
while some, though their haunts were known, defied the
most earnest researches of the minions of the law for
centuries.

The officers and owners of the brigs and schooners engaged in thus violating the laws, fitted out, rigged, supplied
their vessels in the most frequented harbours, perfectly
certain *there* they had nothing to fear, the shore sharks, as
they were popularly designated, preferring to secure a
cargo to running the idle risk of capturing a perhaps innocent, and certainly empty, boat.

It would be difficult to point out, at this distance of
time, any one spot more notorious than another for these
illegal practices, but there was no more active smuggling
carried on than at the mouth of the Thames, whether on
the coast of Kent or the opposite shores of marshy low
Essex ; an assertion which was, moreover, true within a
very, very few years ago. With what is done now, it is
not our province to treat.

Somewhere near where the Nore Light rides, a guardian
angel on the waters, whispering notes of happiness and
home to the homeward-bound mariner, and speaking,
trumpet-tongued, the solicitude of a paternal Government
for its hardy, salt-water sons—lay at anchor, on a certain
night, a taut, smart, and well-looking brigantine, that any
sea tyro could have told by daylight, had reefed all its studding-sail gear, crossed its royal yards, put on its chasing
gear, probably put its powder on board—in a word, was
ready to take its departure at any moment.

What it waited for was a mystery, as the wind was fair. But it is not given to all to solve the secrets of other men ; and had the captain or skipper of the *Ocean Girl* been asked his reasons, the questioner would most probably have received somewhat of a stern answer, especially if the officer had much in his appearance as warlike as the brigantine, which carried twelve carronades and a swivel.

It was eleven o'clock, and the quiescent ocean to the eastward seemed, in the murky light, something like a vast prairie, except that there was more sound upon the waters than would, perhaps, at night have disturbed the vast plains of the extensive West. On board the brigantine they seemed to keep but a harbour watch, no one being visible on deck until the hour we have spoken, when three individuals might have been seen moving along the deck. Next instant a boat that towed astern was hauled up, and all entered it.

The bow of the vessel was seaward, denoting that the tide was running up, which was of advantage to the light skiff, its way being in that direction. The crew that entered it appeared to consist of two men and a boy, the latter seating himself in the stern sheets, while the former rowed in the direction of the Kentish shore, or rather that portion of it which belongs to the Isle of Sheppey.

The youth, who steered, was wrapped in a boat-cloak, and appeared to assume to himself all the incipient airs which belong to midshipmen, when those young gentlemen, instead of being educated lads, taking wine after dinner, with a handsome mess service and wax tapers, were wont to gnaw hard salt junk, mouldy biscuits, washed down by rum and bilge water, the whole scene illumined by a greasy dip, that dropped upon a table-cloth of no particular colour.

The boy was, perhaps, thoughtful. Well he might be ! He was an orphan, utterly ignorant of his own history, nurtured in a nest of smugglers, by a singular accident well-educated, accustomed, ever since he could walk, to things contraband and illegal, and now, something told him, about to enter on some enterprise more desperate

more venturesome and illegal, than any yet which it had
been his fate to see.

Edward Drake—such was his name—had been brought
up from his earliest infancy by a woman known as "Old
Meg," from whose hands he had passed into those of
Joseph Gantling, the smuggler, captain of the *Ocean Girl.*
At seven they made him useful ; at nine he fractured his
legs, by a fall in the hold, so badly that the coarse seaman
was glad to leave him ashore for some time. Three months
was the time agreed on, but it was extended to three years,
from the fortunate accident, to Edward, of the smuggler being
unable, during that interval, to show himself in England.

The lord of the manor, Sir Stephen Rawdon, had him
taken in hand ; and what with the baronet, himself a sailor,
his daughter Loo, and the mild curate, Edward had a fine
time of it. All saw his natural parts and talents, and
were determined to come in aid of them. During the
years that intervened between nine and twelve, Edward
received the education of a gentleman.

Then came Joseph Gantling, his uncle, a blunt, burly
sailor fellow, who claimed him, rather authoritatively Sir
Stephen thought, and the boy returned to his vessel. But
as the skipper never treated him cruelly—on the contrary,
with tenderness, respect, and even forbearance—the sailor-
lad had little to complain of. It is true that during his
three years of schooling his free-and-easy notions had been
somewhat staggered, but two years now of free-trading had
again somewhat blunted his sensibilities, while awakening
in him that adventurous spirit which is so glorious a mainstay of our royal and mercantile navy.

With these preliminary remarks and explanations we have
sought to pass the time while pulling from the brigantine
to the heavy and sombre cliffs, to the foot of which Edward
was steering his frail and fragile bark. The bay he had
selected appeared a most unpropitious spot, being land-
locked on every side but that by which they had entered,
and from which they could see nothing but that vast expanse of waters that stretched in that direction to the
shores of the Continent.

The boy, having guiled the boat into a small creek, cast aside the cloak by which he was guarded against the night breeze, loosened his dirk, examined his pistols, and then leaped lightly ashore.

"Smoke your pipes, my hearties. If any long-legged chaps come near, give 'em a wide berth," said the youth ; and then walked away with the pride and authority of an admiral.

"Ay, ay, sir!" replied the gruff sailors, who, lawless and rough as they were, loved, almost as much as they admired, the daring boy who had been their leader and associate in many a perilous adventure and hair-breadth escape.

The young sailor—or, as we may at once call him, the Young Buccaneer—though very slight, was tall for his age, and, if not entitled to any privileges of manhood, appeared, at all events, to claim them ; for, now that his cloak was removed, he could have been seen in the careless undress of a naval officer, with a red sash round his waist, in which were stuck, in addition to his dirk, a brace of somewhat large pistols.

He seemed thoroughly aware of the path, which lay up the cliff, and was so steep and rugged that no one but a person utterly reckless of his safety would have followed it, unless confident of himself. To any one else, in that dark night, the danger would have been appalling, what with the darkness, the perpendicular nature of the precipice, added to which was the sullen roar of the sea dashing against the rocks below.

About half-way up, the youth halted as if to reconnoitre ; nor did he do so a moment too soon, as might be discovered by the angry way in which he was addressed.

"What lubber's brat is that?" asked a gruff voice. "Is it egg-stealing you are there, at this time of night? Advance, and if you *can* open your jaw-tackle—let us have the word."

"What will three oar-blades of a row and a pistol-shot bring?" asked the boy, in laughing tones.

"A broadside, you powder-monkey. But where's your

three oar-blades of a row in a cockle boat like yours?" continued the irate sailor.

"The officer having left it," said Edward Drake, with dignity, "there are but two men ; but if you don't let me pass, Dirtrick, I must give you a rap on the head to teach you manners."

"Ned, by Gom !" cried the other, laughing. "Law, how these boys do grow, and how cheeky they get !"

"Dirty Dick !"

"Sir !" said the other, respectfully.

"Do not talk in that way to your superior officer."

"I won't, sir—beg pardon, sir."

"That'll do, Dirtrick," continued Edward, giving his hand to the sailor with the air of a prince. "Is the skipper within ? "

"He is, Master Ned."

"I will go in, then. If there's time, I'll come and have a yarn."

And speaking thus, the young buccaneer turned a dark corner of the rock, and disappeared.

The sentry reseated himself, took an extra bite of "baccy," and looked out once more upon the channel of the great river. His was a history which, from sympathy, connected itself much with that of Edward. The man—a stout, under-built, awkward sailor of forty, did not even know his country. His face had something Dutch in it, with a Spanish complexion. He spoke little but English, while he was an excellent and admirable sailor. His name was Dick—from his complexion called Dirty Dick by his enemies, Dirtrick by his friends. This appellation, having rather a foreign sound and look, satisfied the foundling, who to many good qualities united one characteristic not very useful in his profession, that of sterling honesty and sound simplicity.

But if his moral qualities made the sentry somewhat of a butt on the part of his companions, his great physical powers, on the other hand, necessarily made him respected, especially as they were never brought into play except in dire self-defence, or to protect the weak and oppressed.

CHAPTER II.

THE CAVERN CABIN.

THE young officer of the *Ocean Girl* had entered one of those many resorts of smugglers, and often of worse characters, which then were to be found, not only upon the coast, but in forests and deserted quarries. The dealers in contraband availed themselves gladly of everything like a safe retreat—the subterranean passages of old castles and ruins, the vaults of a church, an empty house, the stable or the vicarage, were all one to them, so that they were out of the way. But caverns were preferred, as in most cases the knowledge of them was confined to the smugglers, who handed it down traditionally from father to son.

The one to which we now introduce our readers could many a tale have unfolded had those bare black walls been capable of speech; not more, perhaps, than many a ruined tower that once held its head on high to the world, like some tall bully, but more of a peculiar character. It was a secret to every soul on the island except the smugglers and their associates. Originally it had been natural, but art had improved it. It exists no longer: big ships now riding at anchor where it stood. So rapid, in certain parts, are the encroachments of the sea.

The yawning mouth of the cavern gave, however, no idea of its vastness, for as you went farther in it became higher and more arched. On the pathway were huge masses of flint, lumps of stone, scattered about as if by accident, but, in truth, acting as indications for the initiated. The youth walked steadily forward, as if familiar with the place, until he was in total darkness.

He then halted, and gave a shrill whistle.

Scarcely had the echoes died away within the vault, when a rough door opened, a man appeared holding a torch, and the lad passed through to descend six or seven rude steps into a large apartment provided with a fire, tables, chairs, and tenanted by half-a-dozen rude sailors, in Guernsey frocks, red caps, and high boots, whose countenances were certainly not recommendatory of their characters.

At one end was a small, well-made door, while to his left could be seen a hollow, containing the commencement of a spiral staircase that led upwards to the summit of the cliff. Such was the renowned smugglers' cave of Sheppey Island, which for centuries was the retreat of contraband dealers, spies, and political outcasts, and which, within the present century, the remorseless waves have utterly destroyed.

Nodding familiarly to the rough assembly around him, Edward Drake passed through the public room, and knocked at the small door on the opposite side.

" Come in !" said a deep, commanding voice.

Edward entered, and pulled the door behind him. Any one who had not been accustomed to the place, might well have rubbed his eyes, and asked himself if indeed he were not dreaming, so startling was the change from the rough cavern to the apartment in which he now stood. It was the perfect facsimile of a ship's cabin in shape and furniture, and of a ship's cabin, too, of the superior order, its equipments bearing every mark of wealth and luxury.

The lamp that swung from the ceiling was of silver, and of a suspiciously sacerdotal shape, while around were cut glass, mirrors, plates, and even hangings, which but half concealed the two standing bed-places.

But despite the ornamentation of this fantastic abode, few would have looked long at it, while tenanted by one every way so striking as its sole inhabitant. He was about five feet eight in height, tall enough for symmetry, the very standard for strength and agility. His face, which was rather regular than handsome, was marked by bold and haughty characteristics. The love of power could be traced in every line, a firm and determined nature in the compressed mouth and well-formed chin, while the grey and wicked eyes told of one who, whether for ill or whether for good, having once formed a purpose, rarely was turned from it.

From good he sometimes was, from evil never.

His costume was that of a naval officer, of no particular navy—it might have been borrowed from a theatrical property man, or it might have been made by a fancy tailor. However this might be, it become Joseph Gantling well, showing off his firm and well-proportioned figure to advantage.

Before him on the table were a chart, a pair of compasses, a bottle, some glasses, and a pipe, like a true sailor, the buccaneering smuggler being fond of his tobacco, of which, on shore and on board, he had the choicest that could be found from York River to Spanish Main, from the Mediterranean to Latakia.

The young officer stood still, waiting his captain's pleasure.

"'By the pricking of my thumbs, something wicked this way comes,'" he said, lifting his head, with a light laugh. "Sit down, Ned; I want a long and quiet talk with you. There's the grog, and there's the water; there's a pipe, and there's tobacco."

"Thank you, sir," he cried; "I will wet my lips with nantz, but no tobacco. I'm a counter-blaster."

"Ay, ay, boy!" said the skipper; "just as you will. But now to business. The night is far gone, and we may have to sail early. I want you to take in every word I say; listen, and remember. But, Ned, as you and I may differ, I want one promise—agree or not to my proposals, and 'tis the same between us—but, ay or nay, on your solemn word, under *no circumstances* will you reveal what I shall say."

"On my solemn word, all that passes shall be a profound secret," replied Edward.

"'Tis well—spoken like a man. Now hearken. I am a rough sailor. I have, when my blood has been up, closed my ears to the voice of mercy, and seen blood shed without blanching. I have defied, and ever shall defy, the laws which forbid me from exchanging my tea, spirits,

silks, and laces for other people's money. Men fear me,
the mother hugs her child with awe at mention of my
name. I am to the world a smuggler, a pirate, a corsair—
what have I been to you?"

This was said hoarsely, and with deep emotion.

"A kind and good father," said the boy, warmly.

"No! no!" exclaimed Gantling, with a slight shudder;
"not a father, but a friend and protector."

"Well, sir, a generous protector."

· "Even so let it be. You have seen me rough, brutal,
and violent; making my very crew shiver with fear.
Did you ever fear me?"

"Never."

"I like your frankness, Edward. Well, forty and odd
years make a great change in a man. Much as I love my
sea-boat, that sits the waters like a swan, and cuts them
like an arrow, I am weary of this life, and would end it."

"Sir!"

"Think not I am going to sell my brigantine, buy me
a lust-hause, like a Dutch Meinherr, and settle down into
a beer-swilling, tobacco-smoking old fogie. Not I! I
dream of something better. What say, boy, to one more
cruise that shall bring us more grist to the mill than any
we have ever tried, and then away to some island of the
sunny south, known to me, and known as yet to none
besides; where Nature asks not even for our labour, but
gives in rich abundance to all who will take? There, my
boy, with this vessel and a chosen crew, we should be
kings, sea-kings, with thousands to obey our will, from
greybeards to girls dusky as night, but night with all her
stars, their sunburnt blood mantling such clear nut-brown
skins as—well, never mind. You shall see my coral
beauties, I call them mine, as, wrecked there once, I have
left a memory or two behind."

"Where is this island?" asked the youth, half fascinated.

"Under the burning sun, my lad, many months from
here. That I consider settled. Never did I see such a
land, never so gentle and amiable a people—naked, they

used me well; but with a ship at my back and wealth to
give them, all they set store by in the land is our own,
Ned. I will be king, you shall be my heir."

Edward laughed, but at the same time the gleaming of
his eyes showed that he liked the idea.

"I was once," continued Joseph Gantling, speaking
now between his set teeth, "I was once in the service of
my country. Why or wherefore I left it, it boots not to
tell. I left it, and though still I am an Englishman, and
love my native land, I loathe and abhor her tyrant rulers,
who—no matter what they did. When I think of it my
blood boils, my cheek is coral red, and I feel that I must
go mad, or be avenged."

"Avenged!" said Ned Drake; "how can you be more
avenged than you have been? If depriving them of
revenue is any satisfaction, you have done that to a pretty
tune."

"The theft of a hen-roost or a brood of lubberly tur-
keys affects them as much," continued Captain Gantling
bitterly; "*but I have them now;* I can now make the
hearts of some in high places bleed; I can—I can—" he
gasped, "revel in *their* gold; I can hold in my hand lives
dear to my very enemies themselves; I can have such
vengeance as shall make all England rue the day she
raised her hand against one who—no matter—no matter
—will this restless tongue never wag like other men's?
Now comes the question—Wilt aid me, boy?"

"I must know more," said Edward, quietly.

"Know more!" cried the skipper, while a blood-red
spot burnt upon his cheek. "How dare—"

"I dare do anything but obey orders blindfold!" exclaimed Ned.

"True! true!" muttered Gantling. "Chip of the old
block. I must wholly trust him, or not at all."

"The best plan."

"I will. To-morrow or the day after, or when it suits
our noble rulers, a vessel, a large East Indiaman, sails
past here on her way to distant parts. She is richly
freighted, boy; she carries out treasure untold; she takes

men of mark and rank and name, and noble women, and joyous, light-hearted girls—and, and—mine enemy."

" Well, sir ?"

" Well, sir," repeated Joseph Gantling, with an oath, " you would weary a saint. That ship, cargo, crew, and passengers will be mine. I mean to have them all."

" What to do with ?" asked Ned, quietly.

" To do with—the ship to burn, the treasure to keep, the crew may do as they please, the passengers to sell, mine enemy to slay," cried the captain, wildly.

" And the young women, sir ?"

" We shall want wives in our new kingdom, as perhaps all may not care for dark skins and dewy eyes."

" Then, sir," said Edward, coldly, rising, " seek some other accomplice; for not only will I not be yours, but ere you start on this fell enterprise, I shall leave the brigantine."

A lioness shorn of her cubs looked not more fierce or remorseless than Gantling at this word.

" You young whelp!" he cried hoarsely; " leave the brigantine ?"

" Yes, sir. But listen. I have been brought up by you. I have, with every fresh hour of my life, learned to love and admire the life of a free rover of the seas. But, while ready to aid you in winning this ship, in gaining this treasure, the fight once over, I must have your solemn pledge that no human life shall suffer, and that passengers and crew shall go where they list unharmed, even if you put them on a desert and abandoned island."

The corsair thought deeply as the other spoke. He was not all bad. Real or imaginary ills had driven him to a course of life which usually blunts every noble sympathy, and gives full swing to hate, ambition, guile, arming a man's soul against himself as much as against the great mass of mankind. Those who were aware of his early history, said that what he might have been few could say; and yet his early exploits were such as to give promise not only of greatness but much nobility of character, ere he knew himself a villain—guilt's worst instrument, driven forth to war against mankind.

"You have spoken of your bolder deeds," exclaimed the lad; "you have, I know, fought many a king's ship and conquered—but what of that?—no life taken in cold blood rests upon your soul."

"Who said it did?" replied the captain, in a hollow, hoarse tone; "who dares say it?" he added, rising and pacing the cabin, with hurried tread, upcast eye, clenched fist, and flushed cheek; "but with you, Edward," he continued, "I will *not* quarrel. There is a spell about you which makes me do your will, when another, if he had all hell to back him, would not make me move. What ask you of me?"

"Life for crew and passengers."

"And mine enemy?"

"Let me judge between you."

"You!" cried Captain Joseph Gantling, retreating to the doorway with surprise and evident alarm; "no—my enemy is my own. You spoke of some desert island. It may not be convenient to dispose of them any other way—but you shall have your will, Ned; mine the ship and treasure, yours the passengers and crew."

"On your oath as a man?"

"On my oath as a man."

"That is sufficient," said Edward Drake, who now freely helped himself to a glass of grog. "What is to be my duty?"

"You see, my lad," observed the skipper, lighting his pipe eagerly, as if to change the current of his thoughts; "I've already six friends on board; but now they've signed articles, I almost wish I hadn't sent them. It's Jabez Grunn and his lot."

"I thought you had started that ruffian for good," said Ned, with a flushed cheek.

"A smuggler is not quite his own master," observed Captain Joseph; "these lads were dangerous ashore, so I contrived to get them on board the *Duke of Kent*. Still, I know, I cannot trust them; but you I can, Ned, so you must join the ship."

"I see—how can that be—as cabin boy?"

"As passenger if needs be," replied Gantling; "but of

that we will devise as we go along. Now it is time to roost. I have a watch set."

" But the skiff ? "

" Was sent away as soon as you entered."

No more was said on either side ; the skipper, slightly heavy with grog, turning in to sleep ; Edward Drake to doze and think of the wild, adventurous, and hazardous undertaking on which he had embarked.

It must have been noted that we speak of days long past, when, in the opinion of most persons, the unlawful trader was a kind of hero, and reprobation lavished only on the merciless and sanguinary pirate. This distinction had double weight with one who, like Edward, loved the sea, and had been educated in the very hold of a smuggling vessel.

When he dreamed, it was of rich Spanish galleons, hard fighting on decks slippery with blood, and then of dusky maids, with coral lips, fanning him after unwonted exertions.

CHAPTER III.

THE STERN CHASE.

THE early morn was pregnant with life, the sweet and balmy air, and the gay sunshine, made the faint greenery of the trees look cheerful and pleasant, while the merry birds sang on every wooded slope and broke the solitude of covert and thicket. A balmy breeze came kindly over the waters from the northward.

Captain Gantling and his young officer were now on the summit of the cliff, to which they had ascended by means of the spiral staircase already alluded to, and which terminated in a hut of clay and shingle, which was erected against the broad back of an ancient look-out tower, and which answered the purpose of an ale-house, though seldom visited except by the smugglers and their friends.

Captain Gantling stood at the very edge of the cliff looking down upon his vessel which lay at anchor at some distance, and yet not so far but that any one might have been struck with the order and symmetry with which the tall spars rose towards the heavens, from the black mass of the hull, and with the rigging that hung in the air, one dark line crossing another, until all design seemed confounded in the confusion and intricacy of the studied maze.

" Isn't she lovely ? " said Captain Gantling, who on all matters connected with his ship was warmly enthusiastic.

" She is," replied Edward, whose looks, however, were directed up the Thames, watching, with interest, the many vessels, small craft, and sail-boats that dotted the water, there white sails floating in the distance, like sea-gulls' wings, now dark and gloomy looking, just as the flashing sun shone on them or not.

" Yonder, in a line with Crowstone," continued Edward, "is a tall brig, which methinks carries his Majesty's pennant."

"Where away ? " cried the smuggler, in an eager, anxious voice.

" Between the Crowstone and Leigh heights."

The captain took a long and careful survey, after which he closed his telescope with a crash.

" 'Tis the man-of-war sloop, *Thunder*," said he, hotly ; " 'tis time we were under weigh. I want to lose no spars in the work we have in hand. Follow as quickly as you may."

In another moment, skipper and youth were within the hut, from which they descended the spiral staircase, bade every man in the cavern accompany him, and then scrambled down the lofty cliff towards a creek, where lay a boat able to contain all. Eight men were soon at their oars ; Ned steering, and the captain keeping a jealous eye upon the distant royal cruiser, which though, perhaps, only out for an ordinary sail might be in chase of their own vessel, which, disguised as it was, might still by some keen and meddling eyes, have been recognized as the daring brigantine *Ocean Girl*, the dread of every one, the oft chased and never captured buccaneer.

"With a will!" said the captain, as the men bent to their oars, "the fellow shows long arms and plenty of teeth, as I can make out old King George's pennant on her topmast head. He is altering her course too, though he cannot see us: pull! pull for your lives!"

As he thus spoke, the eight-oared cutter had darted through the mouth of the retired creek where she had been lying, to find her passage almost cut off by what neither of them had noticed—two heavily-armed boats that darted round a point screened by trees, and the officers and men of which at once began cheering.

"There has been rank treachery here," mused Captain Gantling; "some of the asses on the island whom I have offended—or can Sir Stephen have suspected?—impossible! Pull, all those who would not be in irons in an hour."

Not a word was spoken more. The chase was a stern one, and had. circumstances allowed, might have been a long one, but this the proximity of the ship prevented, as in twenty minutes, if not captured, they would be under her guns. But another danger had to be avoided, While the royal cruiser was coming up with wind and tide, the *Ocean Girl* was lying at her anchors, without the smallest proof that man existed within the mass of black and inanimate hull.

. "Is Darden asleep or drunk?" said the skipper, hotly. "I must waken him up—or we shall have to fight, willy-nilly."

The distance between the cutter and the man-of-war boats, which had crept down so cunningly towards the suspected vessel, was slightly lessening every moment. The royal boats were admirably manned, and flew over the surface of the water with a speed which showed their numerical strength and their alacrity.

They meant to capture the buccaneer, which had been betrayed to them in a way that Captain Gantling and Edward Drake little suspected.

"Surrender!" suddenly shouted an irate officer of marines, who commanded one of the boats; "surrender, or I fire!"

"Fire!" responded Gantling, aiming a musket at the speaker.

This brought a volley from the boats, while at the same moment a column of white smoke was seen issuing from the bows of the cutter, and then almost before the report was wafted to their ears, they saw the shot skipping from wave to wave, tossing the water in spray, and flying to a considerable distance beyond them.

The smugglers smiled grimly at the passing ball, while the captain kept his eyes on the brigantine, still so mysteriously silent. So quiet and motionless was she, that any one who knew nothing of the matter, might have thought her a fixture in the sea, or some marine monster rising from the ocean, where such beings are popularly believed to exist, darkened by the fogs and tempests of ages.

But soon Captain Gantling gave a cry of pleasure.

They were not asleep on board. He clearly saw all her boats out of the water, while the cable, instead of stretching in a long declining line towards the water, was nearly up and down, ready for tripping at a moment's notice. every sail and yard was in its place, not a single rope was wanting; in a word, the *Ocean Girl* was equally ready for fight or repose, while for action she was quite ready; her boarding nettings were braced to the rigging.

The man-of-war boats still made superhuman efforts; but those in the cutter were equally alive, and in five minutes more the whole party were on board; the boat hoisted up with incredible activity, and the captain and his men greeted with shouts and cheers that rang across the waters, and reached the pursuing sloop, which now had a serious cause of delay, in taking in all her boats.

"Make sail, Darden," said Captain Gantling.

With these words he descended into his cabin, followed by Edward, who alone shared it with him. It was in some things similar to that in the cave, though the presence of four dark cannons detracted from the other appearances of luxury and wealth. There pistols, too, and sabres, half-pikes and boarding axes, stands of muskets round the masts, which showed that even in the very mouth of the

C

Thames, and in daily proximity to royal cruisers, he had thrown off the mask, and stood revealed for what he was, a ruthless buccaneer.

The very audacity of the act had hitherto been his safety, as merchant vessels had taken him for a government ship, while he had so truly answered the signals of one or two men-of-war as they went by, as utterly to disarm all suspicion.

He soon found out how it was his true character had been betrayed. A cockney sailor named Moss, had two days before asked leave to visit his wife and children ; and on being refused, had sullenly demanded his discharge, which had been sternly denied, until they came to a more secluded part, when it was faithfully promised him. The man made no remark, but appeared to have swum off to some ship, which taking him up to London, he had, out of revenge for his detention, and the loss of his share of prize money, betrayed his comrades.

When the captain and his young ally, having armed themselves, went on deck, the vessel was under a cloud of canvas, running to the eastward along the warp, with the royal cruiser not three miles behind, with every sail she would draw out. The *Ocean Girl*, a few minutes ago all bustle and activity, was now tolerably quiet, as in an incredibly short space of time she had been loaded with canvas that made her masts bend again like whips. The wind was steady, without puffs or fitful gusts, and when they had made a good offing to the eastward, would be fair.

"This is very annoying," said Gantling, in a whisper to Edward ; "I must either fight this fellow, give him the slip, or lose all chance of the treasure ship."

"King George will hardly forgive man or boy who should dare to fight one of his cruisers at the mouth of the Thames," said Edward Drake, pointedly.

"It would be all the greater glory. Nothing would give me more delight than to let the spectators on yonder shores see me tear down yonder flaunting flag, and replace it by my own," said the captain, with a hot and fiery flush.

"I thought you were an Englishman."

"Hush! hush!" exclaimed Captain Gantling, in a low husky tone; "talk not to me thus; a pirate has no country."

And he turned away, leaving Edward, accustomed as he was to the chief's manner and abruptness, somewhat astonished at a sentence which went to his very heart; he who adored his native land, and would gladly have served it, had he not thought himself excluded for ever from all pardon, by reason of his bringing up.

The cruiser had evidently been selected for its swiftness; the *Ocean Girl* was a splendid sailer, but for once it had met its match.

"We shall have to fight," said the commander, in a low tone.

"I hope not, sir," replied Edward; "for then adieu to treasure ship, to our bonnie cruiser, and the dusky girls with the coral lips."

Now Drake was but a boy, but the education he had received had made him more advanced than his age would warrant. He knew Captain Gantling well, and therefore urged no prudential motives to make him careful, bu rather laid before him the very baits the power of whie' he had earned to himself.

"That's what I'm thinking about, Ned; but see ho he hugs the wind, and keeps to windward; the fellow will fetch the Blacktail beacon—then I expect he'll let go her hold, keep a good full—let the vessel go through the water."

"It is a beautiful sloop," cried Ned, who was by nature an admirer of all that is lovely, animate or inanimate.

"Yes, carries a precious press of canvas; if she goes on like this, we must knock a few cloths out of her bolt ropes, when we may gain on her. I believe she goes quicker than we do."

"I am sure of it," said Ned.

"Curses light on her! what is the meaning of it?" cried Gantling. "We must give him the long swivel, Ned. Tell the men to get it ready; let them at sails and masts."

"Ay, ay, sir."

In a very few minutes the outer gun was ready, and the crack shot of the *Ocean Girl*, of all others, Dirtrick, was taking aim. Then an immense body of smoke belched from the muzzle of the cannon, followed by a sheet of vivid fire, and Edward, leaping on the hindermost gun, saw the chips fly, and one sail fly from its bolt ropes. Then the foretopmast bent, and fell steadily over the side.

At the same moment the drum of the royal cruiser was heard rattling across the water, beating to quarters, but the buccaneer made no response, cracking on all sail, until his tall spars and cloud of canvas were lost in a dense fog, that came rolling and spreading like a cloud over the German Ocean.

CHAPTER IV.

ABOARD THE "DUKE OF KENT."

WE must now momentarily leave our hero and his vessel, to introduce those upon whom Captain Joseph Gantling intended to carry out his designs, the nefariousness of which Edward Drake scarcely understood. However manly his feelings and emotions, he was but a boy, and hardly able to realize the abominable intentions of the buccaneer towards the crew and passengers of the *Duke of Kent*.

This was a splendid vessel, built for the Indian trade, and about to be sent out partly on special service—that is, with an amount of valuable treasure on board, which, as far as people in general knew, might have been a cargo of black diamonds from Newcastle, and partly to convey to India certain important passengers and public functionaries, who objected to the delays and wearisome life attendant on a convoyed fleet, when good sailers are compelled to wait for the merest crawling butter tub.

The *Duke of Kent* was a large vessel, well armed, powerfully manned, and in every way fitted out with a view to the comfort of its passengers, as well as their defence. It was war time; but a large and well-provided Indiaman considered itself good enough for most French frigates, so that on this point little emotion was felt.

What, then, had such a vessel to fear from a brigantine which, however rapid a sailer, however well equipped a buccaneer, must succumb to the mere weight of metal of so large an opponent? But the Government, in despatching a royal cruiser in search of the *Ocean Girl*, did not even think of the Indiaman. Captain Gantling was never very verbose, but to his crew he was always silent. The deserter knew nothing, then, of the buccaneer's intentions, and could only report his presence in the estuary of the Thames.

As for the six men who had been so treacherously sent on board the *Duke of Kent*, they were all able seamen, discharged, as appeared by the buccaneer, at their own wish, after serving several years. None on board the *Ocean Girl* expected that their fellows had been detached, at double wages, upon a desperate enterprise.

It was the day after the slight encounter between his Majesty's sloop *Thunder* and the *Ocean Girl* that the Indiaman prepared to take her departure. The sailing of a large ship was not then such an every-day matter as it is now, so that the wharves were crowded with boys and other idlers to watch its progress, while the vessel was not itself free from incumbrances, such as friends and relatives of passengers are always thought when they are in the way of captain or crew. Even the seamen themselves ran in every possible direction but the right one, until at last, when the huge fabric was hauled out into the stream, there were clear decks and an orderly ship's company.

The wind was fair, and as even the most delicate could not be supposed to feel the hideous *mal de mer* before Gravesend, the poop and quarter-deck were crowded by passengers, chiefly military, naval, and civil officers, their wives, and, in some instances, their children; while about a dozen cadets and as many young ladies stood, the former in listless conversation, the latter collected round their chaperones, or, as Jack said, "the chickens crept close up to the old hens, as if there had been hawks aboard."

In this way the voyage commenced, the ship being now wholly under the command of the pilot, though the worthy skipper, Captain Fred. Dunbar, never kept his eye off her head, the navigation of so large a vessel in a crowded and tortuous river being matter of serious consideration.

In this way, having started easily, they got to Gravesend in one tide, and then anchored until the turn, when they procceded by moonlight, and finally took up a position right in the mouth of the Thames, about a mile to the N.E. of where the daring buccaneer had lain.

The next day, at early dawn, the Indiaman took her final departure, running to the eastward until clear of all the banks and dangers which surround the mouth of old Father Thames. The wind by this time was light and uncertain, with occasional puffs, so that good watch was kept, the more that two hours in the afternoon watch it became overcast and foggy. The huge vessel now forged slowly ahead, the captain by no means desiring to commence a voyage by a collision, or to allow an enemy's vessel to creep upon him unawares.

The passengers still kept the deck, as during the day the sea had every moment been getting smoother, and the wind less and less.

In an elevated position, that enabled her to command a view of a circumscribed circle, stood a young lady, who might have been twelve, or who might have been fourteen, but who, no matter what was her age, was excessively pretty, wore charming golden curls, a Leghorn straw hat, and never seemed happier than when prattling to a stout, florid, handsome man of nearly sixty, whom she addressed by the name of "pa," and who, from his dress, bluff manner, and, above all, honest and fearless conntenance, any man of penetration would have taken for a British sailor, which he was, being no less a personage than the admiral sent out to relieve one invalided home.

"Is this the way we are going to travel, pa?" she said, we verily believe for the twentieth time, which, considering she was the only child of a widower, brought her no rebuke, but a patient answer.

"You know, my dear, that we cannot command the weather," replied the admiral, mildly. "To-morrow, perhaps, we may go quicker than you could wish."

"Father!" suddenly exclaimed the girl, "what light is that yonder, nearly in front of us?"

"Eh—what!" cried the officer, rising.

The girl pointed to where a light was rocking on the water, in a somewhat unnatural and rapid manner.

"Some coble or other at anchor. Captain!"

"Admiral!" replied the skipper, stepping forward, and looking in the direction of the light.

"Why, what on earth can the fellow be doing there?" said the captain, who gave at the same time a whispered order to the man at the wheel. "He can't be at anchor, nor does it appear a vessel lying-to."

They were now within about fifty feet of the light, at which everybody was now looking with some anxiety and curiosity. There was scarcely a breath of wind; the huge Indiaman surged but slowly forward, and not a word was spoken.

"Ship ahoy!" said a feeble voice.

In an instant, at a sign from the captain, the helm was put down, and the vessel hove aback. A boat was then put out with all the precision and rapidity of a man-of-war. Six men rowed, while one of the mates steered. The huge vessel now stood still, except a slight sidling motion, and the boat disappeared in the gloom.

*   *   *   *   *   *

Nothing could have been more opportune for the captain of the *Ocean Girl* than the fog, which kept silently rolling down upon him, to turn day as it were into night, and to render the sea upon which he sailed one of the most dangerous in the world. Usually, nothing is more abhorrent to the feelings of a sailor, especially on a dangerous coast, than one of those remorseless clouds of vapour, which wrap him round in darkness, hiding from him rocks, lighthouses, cliffs, aud even the companion ship, that may be sailing within twenty yards in fancied security.

But now the event was all-important, and the buccaneer, without even reducing sail, which, under the circumstances, would have been the act of a prudent man, kept on his course for several hours, until he thought he might safely change his course, which he did, boldly heading for the Thames once more. The tack was changed, and scarcely was the sheeting home, when, sharp upon a wind, the *Ocean Girl* cut through the head sea, as with a knife. She was a beautiful sight always; but now she was like a bird that was frightened, and had spread her wings in flight.

Towards evening, the fog still continuing, and the coast of England being in almost dangerous proximity, Captain Gantling determined to lie to. This was done, and most rigid watch kept. For some time there was, despite the wind, a heavier fog than ever, cold, damp, and yellow; but soon after the sun had set blood-red or angry, the vapour lifted.

The night was very dark, but with their glasses the captain and his chief officer swept the horizon from the deck, while Edward ran aloft, and did the same there.

"Be-low!"

"What is it?"

"Here she comes with the wind," roared Edward, and came down by the run.

In an instant all hands were making sail, even royals and sky-sails fore and aft, and before twenty minutes, the studding sails were set; but still the royal cruiser, which had been at anchor on the tail of the sands, came down upon them head over head.

Captain Gantling swore a round oath, and then gave orders to his lieutenant, who at once bade the men pass the buckets up to one watch aloft to wet the sails. The buckets were whipped up to the mast head, and this manœuvre was continued until a drizzling rain came on and rendered it unnecessary. It was pitch dark, without a moon; every light was put out, even the binnacle lamp, and a star being chosen as a guide, the schooner was steered by it. Before dawn the cruiser was hull down, and the fog as often happens, an hour after became as thick as ever.

The buccaneer now headed once more for the coast of England, as near as he could in the direction of Deal or Dover, and kept on at a slow and steady pace, reefed topsails and bare yards aloft, until a dip of the lead told him he was nearly on the track of outward-bound vesels. The fog now was, as the sailors say, fit to be cut with a knife, and it was necessary to be wary. The brig was put head to wind, with the foresail aback, after which Edward Drake and Captain Gantling held a conference, which, however, referring to matters already decided upon, did not take up much time.

The long-boat was put out, and in it was placed a couple of stout, air-tight water casks, some planks and a pole, with two large ship lanterns. As they advanced, the barrels were lashed together, the planks nailed on top, and when about two hundred feet from the brig, was cast adrift, with an anchor attached, which soon brought up this singular buoy with a round turn. The pole with the lighted lanterns was then erected firmly, and the trick was ready to be played.

Edward, in the jacket and trousers of a ship boy, now clambered on the singular craft, and was there left, his arms round the pole, looking very far from the miserable being he ought to have been under the peculiar and painful circumstances of the case. He had a knife, a stone jar of beer, and some bread and meat, upon which, as the long-boat moved away, he commenced an attack.

"I hope now," said Gantling, with a grin, "you are well armed at all points. But whatever you do, don't take in too great a reef of drink; you'll be rather too heavy a sailer. Drop anchor, and keep watch."

"Ay, ay!"

And thus these two parted, never to meet again, until —but we must not divulge the secrets of the prison-house until our narrative requires it.

Edward ate his bread and beef, drank his beer, and then crouched upon the tossing raft, rather impatient to be removed, as the berth was neither comfortable nor safe. Had there been a heavy sea on, he must at once have been washed overboard, but as it was, the vessel rose and fell with the motion of the billows.

Hark !

What sound is that ?

There is no other like it, and Edward knows it ; it is the swash of the salt sea waves under the bows of a vessel coming down upon him ; there she looms in the fog—full sail upon the deceptive light upon the treacherous buoy.

"Ship ahoy !"

"What ship is that ?" roared a hoarse voice. "Answer, or I'll blow you to the devil. Answer, I say !"

Ned saw the bows, saw them sheer round, as when a ship prepares a broadside.

Utterly bewildered at this singular turn in his fortunes, he rose to his feet, gave one despairing cry, and plunged into the boiling waters, just as the roar of the cannonade was thundering through the air.

CHAPTER V.

"COME ON BOARD, SIR."

WHEN Ned Drake plunged headlong into the water, just as the swash of the sloop was heard through the fog, it was with a perfect conviction that there was no other way of saving his life. His reasoning faculties had been sufficiently sharpened by his peculiar and somewhat dangerous course of life, to make him aware that the trick they would have played upon the Indiaman had recoiled on themselves, and that the enemy they so much dreaded, had discovered the whereabouts of the smuggler, instead of their enticing the Indiaman into their clutches.

But for the moment every other consideration vanished before that of escaping scot free. Edward was, as every English youth, no matter what his occupation, should be, an excellent swimmer. He revelled in water like a dog, and never was more happy than when floundering about, or practising all those efforts of the art which are to be acquired only by practice. In the present instance, the young officer of the buccaneer craft dived, coming up only to the surface when imperiously called to it from want of air, of which having breathed sufficient for his purpose, he went down again.

At length, however, feeling exhausted, he ventured to remain on the surface, and look around in search both of the raft to which he had clung, and the sloop which had fired a broadside at it. But not a trace of either was to be seen. Edward Drake was alone on the water, with nothing but his physical powers to promise him immunity from death.

But the youth, without once giving way to despair, knew well enough, that however long and protracted the struggle might be, the end must be the same— an ocean grave. The distance from land was beyond the means of any ordinary swimmer, as, though savages, born and bred, as it were, on the water, have been known to struggle on for days, no such hope could he entertain. Besides, he neither knew which way was the shore, nor which way was the open sea, to which it might be wiser to make than the land, in the hope of being picked up by homeward or outward bound vessels.

Under any circumstances, however, the chances were formidably against him, and it required a stouter heart than is possessed by many boys of his age to enable him to struggle at all, when by merely raising his arms in the act of clasping them, he might have sunk to rise no more. Ned Drake, however, calmly took every precaution, kept his arms down in the water, and, without losing his presence of mind, began to reflect as to the wisest course to be adopted.

He looked about for the sun, but that luminary was wholly concealed by the yellow, dense, and drizzling fog which enveloped all nature.

But hark! is not that the sea washing against some solid substance close at hand? Certainly, and there it looms high and black. It is the sloop once more under easy sail, returning on its way to discover the mystery of its broadside against a vessel, which, ere the echoes had died away, had vanished into thin air. As the sails could be made out in the fog, Drake saw that she was lying-to, and drifting with the tide.

" It's very strange," said a voice, so near that Edward quite started, "how she got away. Surely, she could not have sunk bodily."

" I hope not, for there's an end of the prize-money. If we could only pick up a bit of the wreck, or save a sailor, we might learn something; but, egad, it was like a scene in a pantomime. Well, we must wait till this cursed fog clears up, when the matter may be cleared up too. Haul aft the main sheet."

At this critical moment, when the sloop was about to get under way again, Ned had clutched a rope which hung from the gangway, and by which officers held when ascending to the deck, and by means of this was about to climb up, when his quick eye caught sight of something a little astern, which awakened in his bosom both a sense of hope and thoughts of the mission he had undertaken. Without an instant's hesitation he dropped into the water, and, striking out, was a moment later clambering on to his raft, the cause of so much bewilderment to his Majesty's dutiful servants.

The raft, however, was in somewhat of a pitiable state. The wooden bucket, in which his provisions had been placed, was upset; his grog was spilt, the lashings were loose—so that, in case of the slightest squall, all must go to pieces, and he be once more cast into the sea at the mercy of wind and waves.

There was another misfortune. His lamps appeared to have suffered severely from the collision, having been put out, and, in all probability, the oil spilt. Without these could be relighted, all hope of being taken off by either buccaneer or Indiaman was at an end.

With a trembling and anxious heart, Ned Drake lowered the lantern by means of a pulley and rope, and putting them on his tiny deck, examined them carefully.

They were not much damaged, the lights having been extinguished rather by the violence of what the French call *roulis* than by any actual contact with the enemy's vessel, which, indeed, though passing almost over the decoy—by which means it remained unseen—had not been struck.

Ned Drake would not have been an English sailor boy if, in the ample pockets of his trousers, there had not been a knife, tinder box, and matches, by means of which, in a very few minutes, he had trimmed and relighted his signal-lamps, which were then hoisted to the mast-head of the peculiar little craft, which now supported the fortunes and the hopes of our young hero.

Gladly would he, after his swim, have renovated his body by means of some of those creature comforts which had originally been provided him, but this was impossible; his bread and meat were, no doubt, within the all-devouring maw of some monster of the deep, while his beer and rum were so commingled with the briny ocean, that not the ablest chemist that ever taught an admiring audience could have traced its presence.

There was nothing then left for him but to bend to circumstances, and wait upon that precarious tub-supported deck for such fortune as awaited him—capture by the sloop of war, safety from the buccaneer, or success and good luck on board the Indiaman and treasure ship. These reflections made the young sailor think somewhat seriously of other things ; and it seemed to strike him, in that hour of peril and doubt, that perhaps the enterprise upon which he had started was not either the most honourable or the most proper upon which a youth might be engaged.

But then, said sophistry, what has society, or govern-

ment, or the good people done to me that I should,
having fallen into the hands of a contraband dealer,
think much of what I am about to do to them ? He
fancied that there could be no life more delightful to a
youth of high spirit and mighty resolves than that of a
buccaneer, a skimmer of the ocean, who only differed from
the legalized privateers that swarmed on every sea, in
wanting a commission from the king, a formality which,
while dispensing them from control, left them to roam
where they would, and act as beseemed them best.

Visions, too, of that island, rich with hopeful fruits,
where eternal summer reigned, and where they were to
rule as monarchs, with an indistinct notion of the import-
ance of cherry lips and flashing eyes to the sum total
of human happiness, passed through his mind, it is true,
in an odd, dream-like way, but still sufficiently to influence one to whom the ideal of happiness was hitherto
action, plenty of fighting, and plunder, with something of
physical gratification in the end.

Thinking thus deeply, there fell a greater gloom upon
the scene, and to the thick darkness of the fog was super-
added the cloak of night. Ned Drake began to shiver,
and to fancy too that he had entered upon a lane which
had no turning. Luckily, as yet there was no sea on,
though there was a bit of a breeze which, with the tide,
made ·the raft bob up and down with an uneasy but by
no means dangerous motion. Which way the water was
running it was impossible to say, though that it was moving
fast could be made out by the constant wash of the water.

Trifle as it may appear to those on shore, who, unless
utterly without means, have something always at hand
to eat, Ned was getting hungry and faint, so that he knew
the moment the sea rose, he should be powerless to hold
on. This was terrible, especially as the Indiaman and all
other vessels appeared to have resolved themselves into
phantoms. Even the buccaneer had deserted him, though
he had believed Captain Gantling would make a push to
find out what had been his fate.

It was in reality a fearful position, and Edward began

to feel his head getting dizzy, and his senses gradually leaving him, when a sound familiar, and not more familiar than welcome, reached his ears. It was his last chance, however, for he felt keenly that if this failed him, he must yield to the terrible impulse to sleep which was coming upon him, and then die.

The noise was that of a heavy body—a large vessel, as a matter of course—forcing its way slowly through the water against the tide.

It was at no great distance, and if any proper look-out were kept, as a natural consequence his bobbing lights would be seen. Still he would not wholly trust to that, so, raising his voice, he hailed the passing sound. For some minutes no reply came, and then it was wafted on the breeze, through a ship's trumpet, indistinct and muffled —*Who calls?*

"Ship ahoy—boy adrift!" he replied.

Some hoarse answer was made, and then he heard the well-known and welcome sound of a boat being hoisted and lowered. Next minute it was in sight, dashing right at him, with the huge bulk of the Indiaman looming up behind.

"Where away?" says one.

"This way, mates," replied Ned, who was now roused by hope.

But the men now saw the lights, and bore down upon him. Very few minutes elapsed ere he was hauled on board.

"My eye," said one of the men, "if it ain't some outlandish reefer, Where do you hail from, eh?"

"British Channel, just now," replied Ned, "faint, tired, and hungry; so pull away, and don't talk."

"Cuss my eyes, Bob," remarked one, "when this young bear comes forard, with an old blue shirt on and a Scotch cap, we shall make him pay his footin' for his imperence."

With these words they reached the side, where the men ascended, Ned, from force of habit, remaining last, as claiming the highest rank. He then clambered on deck, to the crowd who were surveying him with eager eyes, caught sight of a naval uniform, and spoke.

"Come on board, sir," he said, and fainted.

CHAPTER VI.

A STARTLING DISCOVERY.

Now, if Ned Drake had been the most artful boy in all
creation, this way of speaking, just as if he had been on
duty, and had returned to report himself, following the
said dramatic tableau by a second, that of fainting, he
could not have insured for himself a better reception.
All inquiries were thus stopped, and all idea of sending
him ashore before they left the channel was adjourned,
until the skipper was able to judge if he could bear it.

When Ned came too, he was far better off than he
deserved to be, for he was lying on a couch in the ship's
best cabin, with a pretty girl bathing his forehead with
aromatic vinegar, and a stout, portly gentleman, in undress
naval uniform, looking on. A servant was preparing tea
very quietly.

Ned looked round with a dreamy stare, and then pointed
to a water-bottle, as if he was faint, but the little girl
handed him a glass of wine, which he drank hurriedly.

"And now, my lad," said the stout gentleman, cheerily,
"have some tea, and then, perhaps, you will tell us what
you were doing off the Goodwin Sands on a couple of
old water casks."

"Sir Stephen! Loo!" he cried, and then fell back, muttering to himself, "*The Lord have mercy on my wicked
soul.*"

The little girl clapped her hands, laughed, and then
gave him her hand to rise.

"Didn't I say it was Edward Drake?" she continued,
as, pale, ghastly, and scarcely able to stand, the young
buccaneer allowed himself to be placed at the table, where,
glad to avoid questioning, he appeared to devote himself
wholly to the business of the moment.

The plot of Captain Gantling, his evil intentions to
the ship, his allusion to an enemy—and he was aware the

pirate disliked, if he did not hate, Sir Stephen Rawdon—flashed through his mind with lightning-like rapidity; but there came staring him in the face, at the same moment, certain fatal words.

"*On your solemn word, under no circumstances, will you reveal what I shall say?*"

"I thought Loo must be mistaken," said Sir Rawdon, kindly, when he saw that our hero was mending a little, "but now I begin to know my old pupil again. Egad, sir, it was a queer way to come on board.'

"It was, sir," replied Ned, sadly; "and the best thing you can do is to throw me overboard again."

"Why?" said Sir Stephen, while Loo opened her great eyes and stared.

"Because you know the character of the craft to which I belong—to which I belonged," he added, with heartfelt emotion, "and which, if Providence offers me but a coal barge in place of it, I will leave."

"Is not Captain Gantling your father?"

"I hope not, sir," said Ned, "though he has been very kind to me; but something tells me he is not my father. But I was going to say, I was put there to serve one of his purposes, and I have given a promise not to explain."

"Well—well—my good lad, you need say no more. I am going out to take the command of the Indian fleet, and if you really desire to abandon the unlawful course you have hitherto followed, why I will take you as a midshipman myself—so say nothing about the smuggler on board. Leave all explanations to me."

"You are very kind, sir."

"Not at all. Loo, here, always liked you—you are her pet; so, as you have need of rest, stay with her. I will speak to the captain. When you are tired, there is a berth there ready for you."

Ned Drake remained with Loo, quite bewildered, for though at any other time he would have delighted in the prattle of his old friend and favourite, Louisa Rawdon, yet now his thoughts were far away; and, pleading fatigue and

D

exhaustion, he was soon glad to avail himself of the offer
of the admiral, and retire to a state-room, there to give free
scope to his pent-up feelings.

All his desires for an adventurous life—all his dreams
for avenging his supposed father's wrongs—all his fantastic
visions of a lovely island, covered by exquisite verdure,
and peopled by dusky angels, with a royalty in perspective,
had vanished before the kindness shown him, not so much
by Sir Stephen as that manifested by little Loo, his playfellow and companion for three happy years.

A dozen trifling circumstances now darted across the
tablet of his memory, one of which, in particular, was a
revelation. When Captain Gantling found that his adopted
son—he never claimed him as more—had been kindly
treated, housed, and educated by the temporarily retired
admiral, his rage at first knew no bounds. As soon as he
got his youthful charge away, and discovered how he had
been used, he at first, while cursing Sir Stephen, heartily
added—"Well, he had but the right to, any way ; but
I've a rod in pickle for the old curmudgeon he little sus-
pects. But I must wait—I must wait."

But now Ned Drake was a man in feeling, and determined, whatever happened, to be no mere tool in the hands
even of one of whom he personally had no complaint to
make, and whom, therefore, he would not betray. At the
same time he was resolved, unless the buccaneer showed
some legal right to detain him, to leave him, but to leave
him openly, and in a way that became a sailor. How this
was to be done he could not say, though he shrewdly suspected the *Ocean Girl* would not be long in giving him the
opportunity.

He would then tell him his determination to defend Loo
at the peril of his life, and if he would not abandon his
designs, consider himself absolved from the fearful oath
which hung now with such a leaden weight on his spirits.
It was difficult for him to explain the sudden revulsion of
feeling which the sight of the playfellow of his happy
youth had brought about, but the fact was patent to his
heart.

Even Captain Gantling had educated his *protégé* to tell the truth, and his three years' residence under a clergyman's tuition had fixed this one great cardinal virtue on his mind. He could not, therefore, reveal that which he was pledged not to tell, but he was resolved to foil whatever might be the evil intentions of the buccaneer towards Sir Stephen and Loo, for he was now certain that this was the man of whom he spoke as *mine enemy to slay*.

As to the treasure the ship contained, that he cared nothing about. His education had taught him to consider it a matter of cleverness to outwit the Government, nor was he likely in those days on Sheppey Island to learn any very different notions. ' He would confine himself, therefore, to saving human life, and let everything else take its course, though how he was to act in any case, without putting his new friends on their guard, he could not tell.

But no matter what he risked, were it his body or his soul, he would not have the father of little Loo injured.

With this resolution firm in his head, he went to sleep, to dream uneasily, but at length to awake refreshed and resolute. He found when he rose some clean things, which the admiral had provided, and which his purse had easily commanded from the cadets, midshipmen, and merchant reefers on board. When, therefore, he appeared at breakfast, it was in a span new blue jacket and anchor buttons, a cap with a gold band, and white duck trousers, which nondescript uniform became him well.

Very little allusion was made to the events which had brought our hero on board, but the conversation turned very much on the lad's early life, of which, however, the young buccaneer knew very little. The smuggler chief had often asserted that Ned was not his son, even alluding with much earnestness to the fact, though he would often say he was all the more bound to protect him.

Except those parts he had visited in the free-trader—in war times less looked down upon than now—he knew no land but Sheppey.

" I feel as if there I had taken root and grown," he said, with a smile. "Even old Meg of the Red Cow, who brought me up to seven years, is in my mind but a part of the island."

" You never had an inkling of your origin, your parents, whence you came, or anything of that kind?" asked Sir Stephen.

" Never," replied Ned, and then he faltered, "except once, a strange and unaccountable assertion."

"Speak it, boy. You have strangely come under my care, and I will do everything in my power to serve you."

Ned Drake then related that on board the smuggler was one Dirtrick, a sailor who had always been a favourite of his, and who returned the liking. When he was younger, this man was often fond of telling long-winded yarns to the youth, which often turned upon persons unlawfully deprived of their position and fortune.

"Ah, Ned," he would say, "there's many folk in this world as sails under false colours. I know some as might have to haul down their flag if *you* had your rights ; but all in good time ; he knows—he knows"—and he would point to the skipper—"but don't say a word as I said so, or, Master Ned, he'll cut my throat."

"Master Edward Drake," said Sir Stephen Rawdon, with much feeling, as he shook his head, "we must find this Dirtrick, and we'll make him tell what he means. We'll find a father for you, and in the meantime, why I'll be a father to you, so come on deck, and show yourself with Loo."

And this was the man the young buccaneer had leagued himself with pirates to capture and destroy.

———

CHAPTER VII.

THE CONFEDERATES MEET.

THE morning was fine, and the wind being fair, there was a very large proportion of the passengers on deck to whom Ned had formally to be introduced, as an old acquaintance of the admiral's, who had unaccountably been found floating about the Downs on a couple of water-tight casks. This was enough for all present, and old and young, ladies fat, ladies thin, young and pretty, cadets, mids, all were glad to consider Ned one of them, though, as he murmured to himself, if they knew he was a pirate, they would have gladly headed him up in one of those very casks, and pitched him back again into the sea.

Soon the breeze was pretty strong from the north-east, a perfectly fair wind, which made the three topsails lift and swell, while the passengers looked white and blue, and all manner of colours. Still, they knew not how to mend it, until at last, the wind freshening and the huge hull rolling before it, they gradually got below, or into the poop cabin, leaving the deck to the admiral, Ned, and Loo, who was a capital sailor.

A little later the wind freshened more, so that royals had to be clewed up and furled, upon which Ned ran up the mizen shrouds, stored the mizen royal, and made fast the gaskets. While aloft, he cast a wary eye around, and there, dead to windward, several points ahead, however, was the *Ocean Girl.* He knew her well—a sailor soon recognizes his ship; and coming down, sadly enough returned to the quarter-deck, where he walked like the officer of the watch, every now and then casting a weather-look aloft.

The admiral was reading; Loo was with her governess, a lady-like person, Ned was told, who had not yet appeared in the cabin or on deck; the captain was giving orders to the steward, the first officer was stirring about to see the men clear the deck of all lumber, so that the young buccaneer appeared in command. He was, however, scarcely conscious of the look of things around, being so bent on his own thoughts as scarcely to take note of time or anything else.

He, however, from sheer habit—a habit acquired on board the *Ocean Girl*, where he was often in reality officer of the watch, when Captain Gantling and others were carousing—looked up every now and then at the sails, which once or twice he noticed shivering.

"Mind your helm," he said sharply, without turning round, "steady so—steady—port."

And then he walked on.

"Really you must be removed from the helm," continued Ned; "this will not do. See how the vessel is yawing about—port—steady so."

"Like old times, this," said a deep voice. The young buccaneer turned.

With a flushed cheek and a startled gaze, he saw at the helm a stout, tallish, ill-looking sailor, with great bushy whiskers, penthouse-like eyebrows, and a shock head of hair. He looked at Ned with a half-knowing, half-puzzled air.

"Jabez Grunn," faltered the young man, with a dark frown, but speaking in a low tone of voice.

"The same, your honour."

"Then never speak to me again, or look at me again," said Ned Drake, hurriedly, "or I'll tell all I know about you, and have you under hatches," and with these words he walked away to meet Loo, who was coming out of the poop-cabin.

The steersman glanced at the young midshipman with an angry, but at the same time puzzled glance, taking care, however, to make no further mistake about the helm, which, had it been noticed, might have sent him off the precincts of the quarter-deck for the voyage, a consummation by no means wished by one who desired above all things to have a knowledge of many things which are picked up by a keen ear in such a position.

And such was the first meeting of the confederates on board the *Duke of Kent* East Indiaman.

That day and several others having passed without any further glimpse of the brigantine, they began to feel some little ease of mind. The crew of the ship was large, and apparently well selected ; the armament unusually strong, the ammunition in abundance, and plenty of persons able and willing to use weapons. Drake, therefore, had little fear of an open attack. It was treachery he desired to guard against, and hence his desire to be on deck in the night time, especially in light baffling winds and calms, when the six vagabonds who had been sent on board in charge of Jabez Grunn might take it into their heads to play some of their tricks.

That the half-dozen pirates were there he knew, having picked them out once when they were all mustered to tea in the dog-watch, and when, as if in boyish curiosity, ho stole a glimpse at them under the foot-mat of the fore course ; but they took no notice of him, advised by Jabez Grunn, who could not make out whether the young reefer had retained his old dislike of himself, or was playing a deep game.

The young buccaneer understood fully why they were neither attacked crossing the Bay of Biscay, or even while running along the first part of the coast of Africa. There were too many English cruisers about, bull-dogs that barked too sharply not to be awakened by the guns of an Indiaman and pirate brigantine.

Still, as something might happen at any moment, he ever kept a keen and sharp look-out.

Every evening, as the yellow setting sun was to be seen on the edge of the water, with the wind out west as yet, he would gaze round first to windward, then to leeward, to all appearance in examination of the weather, but in reality on the look-out for *that vessel*.

On the track they were following, the direct road to India, there were naturally many came in sight, but Ned Drake regarded them not. He could have picked out that brigantine from a thousand others, and almost every

evening had good reason to believe he saw it, far off to
the nor'-west, a white speck against the grey sky, with,
on many occasions, a land cloud aloft, in which, every
now and then, it was completely lost.

It was like sailing in company with the Flying Dutchman, now that the young buccaneer began to understand
his feelings. What with the *Ocean Girl* ever in sight, and
the six ruffians among the crew, the position was trying indeed, as indeed it deserved to be, all of us having sufficient
natural sense to restrain us from entering upon an enterprise such as that of Ned Drake—a kind of wild cruise
into No Man's Land, as it were.

Every day the young buccaneer became a greater favourite with the passengers, while to Sir Stephen Rawdon he
was clearly a matter of deep and anxious interest. Loo
looked up to and worshipped him as if he had been something superior to the rest of mankind. Under ordinary
circumstances, this would have delighted Ned Drake ; but
placed as he was, every act of kindness was a dagger planted
in his heart. His health suffered, and though the breezy
ocean and the fast warming sun kept him brown and rosy,
he was thin, and evidently eaten away by the canker-worm
of care.

Young as he was, with such a heavy responsibility on
his mind, the effect was depressing indeed. He was not
old enough to call sophistry to his aid. He had given
a solemn promise, and without warning Captain Gantling, he felt bound to observe his oath. *Honour among
thieves* is an absurd and ridiculous saying, as there is none,
petty larceny pilferers and others of their kidney always
betraying one another when they can get anything by it.
Here were, however, no mean thieves in question, but men
who, at the peril of their lives, filled their purses, chiefly
from their national enemies, but on a pinch, not much re-
garding what flag flew at the gaff.

It was particularly of an evening, when Sir Stephen and
the elders were smoking their cheroots and fighting their
battles over again, that Edward and Louisa were alone,
when the mates were walking the weather quarter-deck in

shipshape style, six steps and a look to windward, that the boy and girl—they were scarcely anything more—would move aft to the lee quarter, and leaning over, watch the waves, talking all the time in the low tone of voice which seems to become the hour and the scene. As yet no heavy weather had roused them from a sense of complete security.

The *Duke of Kent,* one of the finest Indiamen afloat, though well loaded, was lighter than the fat homeward-bounders, laden with spoil of Araby and Ind, and as under everything she could draw, she heeled over to port, they looked down into the watery deep, and, roused by the thoughts which come over us naturally when away from land, spoke dreamily of the lovely country they were going to, and of the mysterious life that awaited them.

" I could live ever thus," would Loo say, in her laughing, merry way; " it is really so nice."

" Wouldn't you like just a bit of land, to grow violets and roses?" replied Ned, with a smile.

" Well, I might, you know. Have you ever read ' Paul and Virginia?' "

" Never."

" I must lend it to you. It is a charming book. They are on an island—not on a desert island—but that I *should* like. Why, fancy you and I and papa shipwrecked—wouldn't it be jolly?"

Now, whether Ned Drake thought the word somewhat out of place in a young lady's mouth, or from what reason we will not say, but he did not reply, and as he clutched the bulwarks with his ten fingers, his teeth chattered, and his face was ghastly pale.

A desert island!—shipwrecked! Who had suggested this?

" You are ill," suggested Loo, anxiously; " You look like that night in the Channel, you know, when you came on board."

" A spasm—'tis over. I will walk forward," said Ned, moodily, and left the girl alone without another word.

The next day was very fine, and any one could see with half an eye they were advancing towards the tropics, where, what with the heat and other reasons, too long to give in detail, calms are so common. This was the hour the young buccaneer dreaded. If while old occan slept, and the crew of the *Duke of Kent* kept a kind of anchor-watch, with their heads on their pillow, or, what was worse, a watch of treachery and death, the buccaneers crept on the doomed ship, and mastered it, what would be his position ?

A cold, dreadful shiver passed over his whole frame, as, with his heart in his mouth, he walked the deck.

There had been rain in the night, and the sea looked hot ; the breeze, though still in the same quarter, was lighter, the water bluer, but certain signs in the clouds, known only to the initiated, plainly indicated that there was more wind coming. This, however, was no consolation, as a brigantine like the *Ocean Girl*, would always outsail an Indiaman, though, if she carried on too long, she might run the risk of being capsized.

A thrill passed through the bosom of the young buccaneer at this thought, and yet, though it would end all his difficulties, he could not say he wished it. The man Gantling he owed a deep debt of gratitude to, even though he was a pirate, for personally he had been kind, though looming in the distance, from this same No Man's Land of the future, he began to foresee reasons for disliking him, perhaps of a darker nature than he had yet imagined. Then there was Dirtrick, whose fidelity to his person was unimpeachable.

After breakfast the weather began to change. The clouds banked dark to leeward, the sea was blacker, while some stray birds, an albatross, a stinkard or two, with some lazy gulls, began to waken up, as if they snuffed the storm. A regular school of porpoises tumbled and rolled about.

Ned Drake strolled forward to the heel of the bowsprit, carelessly to all appearance, but in truth to have a glance round in search of the vessel which haunted his waking thoughts, his night dreams, and floated before him at times, not on the blue waves, but in a red sea of blood. He cast a wary look around, but detecting nothing, resumed his careless mien, looked through the head-boards into the pile of white foam that frothed up as she plunged, and then was about to move aft when he heard words which made him pause.

"That ere cussed young reefer," said Jabez Grunn, with a fearful oath in addition to his nautical epithet, "gets over me. What is he here for? Is he a spy on us, or has he cut and run?"

"Cut and run, most like; he's hand and glove with that blessed old tyrant of an admiral what guv Gantling such a lift once."

"Very like. We'll have a puff from east'ud afore long. This wind's nigh dead, and if that spindle-shanks goes aloft anywhere near me, —— me if I don't pitch him right overboard. Right or wrong, he'll be out of the way."

"Reef topsails," shouted one of the mates.

At the same moment everything fluttered.

"Mind your helm, Jones," called out the first officer; and then, seeing that she would not lie her course, and that the forward sails were aback, the men were set to work trimming sails; and while the wind was freshening, and the topsails flapping, and the booms heading, Ned Drake walked aft with a pale stern face, that boded no good to the pirate crew.

CHAPTER VIII.

THE WEATHER EARING.

IT would be impossible to conceive any position more difficult or trying than that in which Ned Drake was placed. Bound by every tie of gratitude and affection to Sir Stephen Rawdon and Louisa, who twice had contributed to save his life, the youth had also to remember one who, whether father or uncle, had been uniformly kind and affectionate. Whatever the motive might be which actuated him, there had been a strange tenderness about this man's manner, as if he were a holy relic of the past, or a tender remembrance of one he had once loved or injured.

But duty was paramount; and Ned's duty, he felt, was to defend those who not only had been instrumental in saving his life, but had opened up a pleasant prospect of existence. The midshipman was at an age when, in healthy temperaments, love is in the mythic state; and yet so mysteriously are all our sentiments linked, that no doubt something of the more energetic feeling he was to experience as a man, already made his young heart beat.

At all events he felt that, no matter what the consequence, Loo was to be shielded from harm.

How was it to be done? In all probability Captain Gantling's scheme for taking possession of the East Indiaman was connected with a surprise, in which the six biggest ruffians of the vessel were no doubt implicated. It was manifestly impossible to remain always on deck, while the only other course which remained, that of betraying his oath, he resolved to defer until human life was at stake.

All this, however, did not tend to the promotion of his health. The sickly complexion which his narrow escape from starvation and drowning had left upon his countenance, did not pass away; and he who usually trod the deck with double zest under a tropical sky, was sullen and apathetic.

Though the extreme liking he had for the society of Loo made him unwilling to change his costume, he often felt inclined to go forward and help the men in their varied occupations, for no life is less idle than that of a sailor. A landsman fancies after he has been a few days on board, that the vessel will get in sea trim, and then the tars will have little to do but walk about with their hands in their pockets. A circumnavigation of the globe would soon undeceive them; on the last day the crew would be as busy as on the first.

The business of the day commences with the turning-to of the morning watch at daybreak, washing down, scrub-

bing and swabbing the decks, filling the scuttle butt with
fresh water, coiling up the rigging, then breakfast, after
which the studding-sail gear is to be rove, or the running
rigging to be examined, or the standing rigging to be overhauled, or chafing gear to be made, while, when everything
else fails, the men are set to scrape the rust from the chain
cables, as the song has it:—

" Six days shalt thou labour, and do all thou art able;
" And on the seventh, holystone the decks and scrape the cable."

But Edward Drake had no occupation, and though he
began to be fond of reading, yet in his present state of
mind he could scarcely be said to fix his attention on any
book. Loo was a good part of the day with her governess, and Sir Stephen, the young reefer was at times rather
shy of. There remained, therefore, few amusements, and
one of these was to clamber up the rigging, ascend to the
top-gallant mast, and thence survey the horizon on the
look-out for the *Ocean Girl.*

The wind continuing light, they made very little progress ; and each day, so alike is the sea in fine weather,
one day with another, that they seemed scarcely to make
any progress, but to be floating about on the same spot
eternally, like the Flying Dutchman trying to weather the
Cape.

They were in the trade winds, running pretty free, when
one afternoon, while at tea, there came an alarm that a
slaver sail was in sight, giving chase. All went on deck.
Ned himself had a face as pale as marble, and it was only
by lingering behind to take a glass of wine that he
restored his equilibrium, and joined his friends without
exciting suspicion.

It was a clipper-built brigantine, with a black hull,
which was heading directly for them. If Ned had not
known who commanded her, and what she was, a trium-
phant twinkle in Jabez Grunn's eye would have told him
as he stood listlessly steering. There could be no mistake
in the character of the vessel. It was a privateer, pirate,
or slaver, the last to be most feared of all, as the practi-
tioners in the trade of human flesh, which certain polit:-

cians in this country now ignore, in order to excuse their culpable sympathy with slaveowners, were the worst ruffians on the seas.

Everybody was looking out ; and as everybody—the six ruffians excepted—was equally anxious to get away, while the officers and passengers were discussing the merits of the pursuing vessel, the men were busy throwing water on the sails. There was no doubt that, whatever she was, she was an ugly customer.

By directions of the skipper, the East Indiaman was kept dead before the wind, the best point for a large square ship, while she, a clipper, was surfleet on a wind. The pursued vessel carried royals and skysails fore and aft, with ten studding sails, the brigantine having only a gaff trysail aft.

"What do you make her out ?" said the Admiral, quietly.

"Armed—full of men—shows no colours."

"Hem !" replied Sir Stephen ; "a pirate, I suppose ; a French privateer, which is all the same. Of course, Dunbar, we can beat her off."

"No doubt ; but with my responsibilities I do not choose to lose a rope or spar. I shall crack on as long as she does not overhaul us too close, and escape if I can. If not, we must fight, when there can be no doubt we shall give a good account of ourselves."

At this moment, every eye being on the pursuing vessel, Ned approached the man at the wheel.

"Beware !" he said, earnestly. "The moment there is danger, I shall betray the character of yourself and your associates. So no trickery."

And before Jabez Grunn could reply, he was beside the Admiral. It was quite evident that the privateer was gaining ground, though very slowly ; so that without any unnecessary parade, the gentlemen began to get their arms ready, while the word was passed forward to do the same. Fortunate indeed it proved that there was no moon, and that the night was unusually dark for that region. As soon as evening came, orders were given to have no lights of any kind, the mates steering alternately by the stars.

As a natural consequence, the course was altered, and next morning not a sign of the vessel was to be made out. This, however, did not raise the spirits of the young midshipman, who, well aware of a permanent conspiracy on board, could obtain no peace of mind. A couple of boatloads of privateers, seconded by the mutineers, would suffice to capture the Indiaman any dark night.

And now the days got hotter and hotter, and the sea bluer and bluer, and the night came sooner and sooner, until there was no twilight, which indicated an approach to the tropical belt of the earth, and there was a slack, slimy mill-pond. This was what Ned both dreaded and expected. The surface of the water was as dead as a mill-pond, save that there was the ever-pleasant heave or ocean sign, which came from the horizon to the vessel in one lazy coil, with the ship steering round little by little. The sails hung flapping on the yards, and the heat was so great that occupation was out of the question.

Ned, however, kept a keen look-out, expecting every now and then to see the buccaneer come slowly but surely along by the aid of her long sweeps. He felt sure she was always in sight, and that, though they were like babes lost in a wood or a fog, she ever hovered about. Edward Drake remembered some previous captures in these waters, and shuddered.

One night, after several days of calm, and a very sultry twelve hours, the vessel rolled excessively on the black heave of the swell, and Ned, who was standing on a carronade, turned sharply round to the Admiral.

" We're going to have some wind, sir, with a shift," he said.

" Why, you young powder-monkey," laughed the Admiral, " what do you mean ?"

" I'm only a boy, sir," continued Ned, pointing to where a smooth, round-backed swell came out of a dirty thick jumble of a sky ; " but I've seen that wild look before in these latitudes."

" And then, Master Edward?" said Sir Stephen, more seriously.

" There came a storm, as there comes now."

As he spoke, there fell a heavy drop or two of rain, there was heard a long-drawn sigh in the canvas aloft, then came a clapper of two or three carronades, as the sails hit against the yards, and then the rain fell in whole sheets and bucketfuls.

"You are indeed a sailor, Master Ned," said the Admiral. " You must look alive, Dunbar."

" Away there, furl royals, and close reef topgallant-sails !" cried Dunbar, addressing the first officer.

" Ay, ay ! sir."

And Edward, though he had made up his mind to interfere no more in the working of the ship, by a kind of instinct which seems part and parcel of the nature of an English sailor boy, ran up the rigging, while the rain poured faster and faster, until the scupper holes could not let the water out. It was now so dark that no man could see his hand, and, while the heavens sent down their deluge, Boreas began to stir ; and before a man was out on the yards it blew strongly. Still, it was nothing serious, and man after man was at work at reef points and garbets.

Reefing, be it known, is by far the most exciting part of a seaman's duty. Once the halyards are let go, there can be no skulking. It must be done. If one is slow, another climbs over him. The first aloft goes to the weather earing—the second to the lee.

Edward had run along the foot rope until he reached the extreme point of the yard-arm ; where, as in old times, when he was officer of the buccaneer, he began to sing out to the men in true seaman fashion. The position cannot be better illustrated than by a very simple explanation. Every boy, who has not had the opportunity of going to a seaport town, knows that the yard is a cross beam, thicker in the middle than at the ends, which supports the sail. Well, in order to furl or reef, it is necessary for two men to sit astride on the narrow end, with no support but the frail wood, and a foot-rope, on which the reefers stand. There, forty or fifty feet above the raging sea, they sit, see-sawing like boys at play, now one up, now the other down, just as the rolling waves dash them.

Just as Ned began to haul, the rain ceased as suddenly as it began—a common event in the tropics—and it became lighter,—light enough, in fact, to make out the horizon.

"Yoe-oh!" said Ned.

"Yoe-oh!" responded a hoarse voice from the lee earing. The lad knew it; it was that of Jabez Grunn.

Now Ned was brave enough; but many a brave officer and general, who would meet any enemies in the field, has shuddered with horror at the idea of being shot in the back by his own men; and Edward, who would have headed a party of bandits with enthusiasm, had no idea of being murdered by a ruffian seaman pushing him off into the dark and seething waves.

The question now arose, whether the Yankee Dutchman had recognized him or not. His voice was rather shrill, and this, of itself, was enough to betray him. At all events, he determined to act in self-defence. The mates below kept roaring to the men to clew up and furl; which, with the wind and the hubbub of the vessel, rendered any calm or collected action impossible.

All was done, and the men began running down the rigging, to be in readiness to perform any other manœuvre necessary to the snugness of the ship.

But, skulking flat against the rigging, Ned distinctly saw Grunn, his glittering eyes fixed upon him, like those of a cat upon a mouse. Now, to hail the deck in that clamour was impossible. In fact, he could not have been heard. His thin treble would have sounded scarcely so loud as the cry of a sea-mew. Safety, then, depended wholly on himself, as in the stormy life to which he had devoted himself it generally does ; hence the fearless self-reliance of the noble profession, which turns timid boys (apt to allow others to think for them), into active men.

He moved slowly along the yard, with his feet on the

E

foot rope, as if intending to reach the spot in the rigging where it was connected with the mast. Jabez Grunn descended a little way, evidently intending to waylay Ned on the maintop ; but, the instant the brave boy saw him move, he fell, as if accidentally, his feet only remaining fast, to all appearance caught in the sail, but in reality lightly clinging to the cordage on which he had just been resting.

In this way he swung, head downwards.

The astounded seaman began to believe that he was about to be saved from the commission of a crime, and uttered a gleeful oath.

Ned heard him.

" Not yet, Grunn !" said Ned ; and, as the vessel lurched, he caught at the rigging with both hands, clung with the tenacity of a cat, let go with his feet, and, despite a heavy jerk, secured his position, and was on deck before Grunn had recovered from his astonishment.

Then Ned, aware that everybody was too busy to notice him, walked aft, reserving to himself the pleasure of an explanation with the ruffian sailor at a later period.

Indeed, the elements were now too active for men to think of anything else. The gust was upon them, rushing on with a vanguard of foam ; the ship bounded like a race-horse under the whip ; the topsails flashed full, and soon away she went over the huge waves like a frightened steed, the white foam rising on every hand, and two men grinning and tugging at the wheel, and yet scarcely able to grind it down.

Ned forgot everything else in the excitement of the moment, for now he was happy.

CHAPTER IX.

"THE OCEAN GIRL."

It was not long before top-gallant sails had to be furled, and the yards lowered on the caps, so stiff was the tropical squall,—less dangerous since captains study the glass, but then, unhappily, often fatal, through carrying on to the last moment. All, save those on duty, had left the deck, including the Admiral. But Ned, scarcely yet recovered from the excitement of the attempted murder by Grunn, and, scenting the storm as the war-horse does the battle, kept in an obscure position on the quarter-deck, holding on to a larboard backstay.

He was never tired of watching the different phases of power exhibited by Nature. On the present occasion, collision, even on the wide ocean, was added to the other dangers of the deep ; for a huge mist, capped with black clouds, came driving towards them, hiding the heavens, and completely obscuring the stars.

It was followed by a blast, to which the first gust seemed but child's play.

At this moment the door of the round-house opened, and the voice of the Admiral was heard, addressing Captain Dunbar.

"Has anyone seen the juvenile ? Egad, he has got a quick eye ; we should have been all snug before the gale, if I had taken his word."

"Here I am, sir !" said Ned, coming forward.

"Why, where have you been ?"

"Aloft, on the main topsail yard. Took the weather earing," laughed Ned.

"Born to be a sailor !" replied the Admiral. "Dirty night, Dunbar ! come in, and have a glass."

And with these words, skipper and reefer entered the cabin, where Edward was then highly complimented on his

E 2

perspicuity and devotion. Captain Dunbar declared that he had seldom seen so severe a gale in those latitudes.

"But," said he, "to-morrow we shall be in the doldrums again, and very likely, even before an hour, we shall be bowling along under easy sail.

"I hope so," replied the Admiral, laughing, "if it is only for the sake of my crockery."

Captain Dunbar laughed, finished his glass, and went out. The other, trusting to him like unto a second Providence, went to bed, nor rose till morn, when the gale had subsided into little puffs of air and light squalls ; which, in their turn, were followed by another dead calm. All the new, or, as they have it, green passengers, were now for bathing ; and even the ladies thought the sea looked beautiful. It was tempting, hot as it was on deck, to look down upon that blue and smooth surface, in which you could see your face.

"Where's the objection ?" asked a pompous soldier officer ; "I can't see it."

"I can," said Ned, laughing.

"Where, *sir ?*" replied the infantry captain, with a strong emphasis on the word *sir*.

"There, captain," continued the young reefer, pointing to a little black horn, above a huge green body, which sailed about with a kind of patent screw behind. "That fellow, I firmly believe is the same who ate poor Ikey Joues, an old shipmate of mine.

Upon which, without noticing the laugh, Edward walked forward, having, at the same instant, discovered that there was a sail in sight, at no great distance. The young midshipman's eyes were good, and, at a glance, he had recognized the brigantine ; but at the same time he fancied that he detected flags signalling.

It must be recollected that in these utter calms the ship, losing all way, ceases to obey her rudder, and keeps moving round and round, at the mercy of the waves, like a cat settling herself in her bed. The haze was so great, that no one whose senses had not been almost preternaturally worked upon, would ever have detected the presence of a strange vessel. The heat was intenser every moment, and all hands were idle.

Ned had a small pistol in the right-hand pocket of his trousers, which he had asked as a loan from Loo. With this he felt the strength of a giant, and walked forward coolly in defiance of the whole six ruffians who were herded against him.

The general crew were below, or asleep. One man at the wheel, and a look-out or two, seemed quite sufficient watch in such weather; but five of the six buccaneers were collected together in a group at the foot of the mainmast.

Where was Grunn?

Ned could not see him, but he had a very good guess as to how he was employed. As soon as he was near enough, he leaped into the mizen-chains, and looked up. There in the fore-top was the huge Dutchman, busy with some red, blue, and green handkerchiefs, signalling as hard as he could to the brigantine.

"Come down out of that," said Ned, quietly; "come down out of that, Jabez Grunn."

The huge mass of bloated flesh and matted hair that answered to this appellation, looked eagerly down, with a white and scared look, and seeing who it was, he muttered some fearful curse, put the handkerchiefs in his pocket, and slid rapidly down the rigging to within a few yards of where the daring young reefer was ostentatiously playing with a cocked pistol.

"Jabez Grunn."

"Sir!"

"The first time I again see a glimpse of treachery, I shall no longer be able to keep silent, so beware."

"Ay, ay, sir."

"And, Jabez Grunn, allow me to give you a very serious piece of advice."

"What is that, sir?"

"Never threaten to murder a reefer, when he is sitting on the hammock-rail, listening to you. I have now some orders to give."

"Yes, sir."

"I am going on board the *Ocean Girl*. Do not attempt to come with me yourself, nor venture to allow any of your gang to enter my boat. When I return I will bring you orders from Captain Gantling."

"Thank ye, sir," said Jabez, who was bursting with rage and fury.

Ned said no more, but, like the island monarch he was destined to become, walked away as unconcerned-looking as if he was without care or trouble; though certainly his trouble just then was greater than ever he had known before. More and more the complications of his fearful trade struck him with dismay, and he asked himself over and over again, why he ever should have fallen into the clutches of one so cruel and vindictive.

The Admiral was expecting him to lunch, and, not sorry to escape the presence of the great body of passengers, who appeared to him a constant source of remorse, he entered the cabin, and sat down in company with Loo and the governess, a most lady-like and efficient person.

All were so used to what they called the old-fashioned style of the young reefer, that his gravity scarcely excited a remark; and when Mrs. Watson and Loo retired, Sir Stephen was not particularly surprised when Edward demanded the honour of a brief and private interview.

"Sir Stephen," he began, "I am but a boy in years, but during my brief career I have had to endure that which has made me almost a man."

"Your foresight about the storm quite proves that."

"But, sir, sadder and more terrible experiences have done much to age me. Therefore, my generous preserver, when I ask something of your forbearance, believe I have a reason."

"I will."

"Will you honour me by looking from this stern-port— there, where my finger points? You see it. Sir Stephen Rawdon, that is the brigantine of Captain Gantling, the buccaneer, of whose crew I am one."

"Gad, boy, I see—the same that chased us. But this has a long, pale sort of hull, with a broad streak of red, without ports, and is log-rigged."

"Admiral, the chameleon has many colours."

"I understand you, boy. What is it you wish?"

"I would die to serve you and Loo—I beg pardon, Miss Rawdon—but I ask you, without demanding any explanation, to allow me to go on board that vessel. When I return, perhaps my lips may not be so firmly closed. On my honour as a gentleman, and my faith as a Christian, my intentions are good."

"I believe you," said the Admiral, gravely, taking up a glass and examining the pirate craft; "a wonderfully light sparred vessel. Have I not seen her lately, lying off Sheppey?"

"You have, sir."

"There seems to me some memory in connection with this Gantling. Knew you him ever by any other name? Nay, answer not if 'tis displeasing. Poor lad, you have had sad trials on board that vessel, and 'tis a great wonder you did not leave your truthfulness behind. You shall go on board, and when you return I will tell you a story which may assist your recollection."

With these words he put down his glass and went on deck, where he mentioned that Ned was anxious to leave the Indiaman for an hour, and have a row in the dingy to the brigantine, at which everybody was now looking.

Captain Dunbar laughed, and declared that he did not know where, on such a hot day, Master Edward would get his crew, but the dingy was at his service, and he had no doubt two of the boys would volunteer.

Edward thanked them, and while the boat was getting ready, he retired to his cabin, and wrote a few lines, which he hastily placed in Loo's work-basket.

"*If the boat returns without me, I am a prisoner, never an ingrate.*"

Then having secured both pistols, he started upon his bold and daring adventure, actuated by as pure motives and as noble a conception of duty as any hero whose name has come down to us.

The boys were in the boat, quite hearty for the trip, it being a change to them from ordinary duties. The sun was very hot, and the pull a long one, though whether it was a light air, or the effect of the haze, could hardly be made out. Still, with their loose white trousers, blue shirts, bare arms, and natty caps, they looked quite equal to the work.

Ned let himself down the side by a rope, and jumping into the stern sheets, took hold of the yoke lines, and was about to shove off, when the chorus of a well-known voice arrested him.

"Good-bye, Edward ; don't be long. Only your boat's such a cockle-shell, I'd come too."

"Not for worlds," thought Ned ; and then he added aloud, "You are better off on board."

He was right; for as the dingy was urged forward by the oars, and went slowly and rippling over the water, it was so close to the waves, so stiflingly hot and sultry, they could scarcely breathe. There was, however, a long glassy swell over the whole hot, hazy, sullen-looking sweep of water, but as yet not a breath of air, whatever gale might be stirring up the waves at a distance.

The boys were willing and strong, and bent to it with a will, but it soon became hard work to make head against the waves. Ned sat pale, taciturn, and thoughtful. He could not look to his interview with Captain Gantling without emotion. He had always liked—almost loved the man, and it pained him to thwart him, even when his design was so evil. He knew that his whole heart and soul was set upon this enterprise, as leading to that other Arcadian dream, connected with coral lips and scant drapery, about which Ned somehow didn't seem to dream quite so much.

Personal fear for himself he had none ; and even had he apprehended violence, it would not have made him pause. There was before the eyes of the boy buccaneer a vision of right, which even his ill-directed education taught him was paramount. Before it, and his deep regard for his kind patron and playmate, all considerations of the peril—all ideas of wild and lawless glory—vanished.

And now as he neared the vessel, and saw her on the rising swell, rolling as helpless as a cask, now one gunwale, now the other, dipping into the heavy waves, and saw that nothing but the wave anchor-watch was kept, he wondered what Gantling was doing, and where he awaited his coming.

There was, however, not much time for thought, as in a few minutes more the boatman had dropped his oar, and pinned his boat-hook into the rudder chains. Then a line was dropped, and the boat hauled up to the side.

Ere he knew what he was about, he was once more on the deck of the *Ocean Girl.*

"Glad to see you, sir," said Dirtrick, touching his cap, "the skipper awaits you below."

"All right, Dirtrick," replied the young midshipman; and then he added in a lower tone, "if there is any row, let those two boys go—and stand by."

"Ay, ay, sir," said Dirtrick, with a queer, rollicking, fishy sort of glance.

And Edward Drake, with an erect and haughty mien, strode towards that cabin, which contained the present arbiter of his destiny.

CHAPTER X.

A STORMY INTERVIEW.

NED knew the way too well to require any guide, and in another moment he was at the foot of the companion-way, knocking at the bulkhead in which the door was cut.

"Come in," said the deep commanding voice of Gantling.

Ned obeyed, and as he turned the handle, a flood of light fell upon him. The cabin was no longer so peaceful-looking as before. The disguise which, in case of disagreeable visits, had been affected off Sheppey, was thrown off here; and though the apartment was much like most cabins, its mixture of the luxurious and the martial was, to say the least, singular. There were two dark cannon in the room, which, by the judicious removal of all unnecessary gear, could be changed, in a very few minutes, into a well-appointed battery.

The walls literally bristled with muskets, pistols, sabres half-pikes, boarding axes, and all the manifold implements of marine warfare, and in the midst of all this Captain Gantling sat with his bottle, glass, and pipe, smiling grimly at the scene around, as if proud to be monarch of all he surveyed.

" Ah, Ned, so it was you. And pray to what do I owe this unexpected pleasure ?" he said, in rather a thick voice.

" It remains to be proved, sir, whether it be a pleasure or not."

" Ah ! what have we here, my Lord High Admiral ? Speak out, I am ready to answer," laughed Gantling, grimly.

" As my object is to ask questions, I am glad to find you in the humour. Is the *Duke of Kent* the vessel you intended me to board ?"

" It is, and very cleverly you have done it."

" Is Sir Stephen Rawdon, who, with my old friend, Loo, his daughter, is on board, the man whom you call mine enemy ?"

" He is," replied Gantling, now with a truly savage gleam in his cruel grey eyes.

" Then I beg to say he is my friend, and that I will defend him at the peril of my life, and in defiance of the wicked oath which you compelled me to take," said Edward, with calm-spoken words, but a heaving breast, and flashing eye, indicative of his deep emotion.

" Boy," cried Gantling, whose passions were aroused, and whose face indicated the tempest within, " but for that man,

I had no need to have been a buccaneer. Instead of dreaming of sovereignty in the sunny isles of the south, where dusky beauties welcome you with open arms, and perpetual summer creates a paradise on earth, I should have lived honoured and respected in my own land. But it was not to be. I had to leave my profession, dishonoured. I was broke—and by them. From that hour I have vowed eternal enmity to both—one still lives."

"And the other?" gasped Ned.

"Look not at me so," said Gantling, with a shudder; "none can say that innocent blood rests on my hands. He had the same chance as I had, and shot at me. He missed —I did not—and he died."

"Of whom do you speak?"

"'Tis past now, boy, and not worth mentioning. Even this duel was turned against me. They said he would never have met me on an equality; that I had waylaid and murdered him, and that after death I had discharged his pistol. So they hunted me down as an assassin, drove me away, an outlaw, from my native shores, to return a scourge and a terror. Yes, I had my revenge to the full."

"You have been tried, doubtless," said Ned, in a colder tone than he usually adopted to his old officer; "but these details just now can be of no interest to me."

"No interest to you!" laughed Gantling, savagely; "who knows? If you were less obstinate, they might be."

"Captain Gantling," continued Edward Drake firmly, "even if these details personally concern myself, they must be adjourned."

"Must, sir—and why?" asked Gantling, with a menacing look.

"Because unless I have your solemn word, and that I think I can trust to, that nothing more shall be attempted against Sir Stephen Rawdon and his daughter, immediately on my return I will have Jabez Grunn and his lot put in irons, and the guns double-shotted, to give you a warm reception."

"Mad! mad! stark, staring mad!" said Gantling, wildly, as he strode the cabin, with fierce and angry steps. "Put Jabez in irons! double shot the guns!"

"I am not mad."

"And you talk thus to me! Will you allow me to ask you who you may be?"

"Naval Cadet Edward Drake, of the Admiral's flag-ship *Bellerophon.*"

Gantling stood back aghast. A livid pallor spread over his face, his lips quivered, his eyes seemed ready to start from his head, while his fingers mechanically felt for his pistols. Edward faced him, also pale, but firm and re-solved. There was not one atom of fear in that manly atti-tude. Like Nelson, he knew not fear.

"And pray, sir, is there any other remark his Majesty's naval cadet wishes to make to Joseph Gantling," he asked.

"Yes! I have to complain that Jabez Grunn has once already attempted murder on my person, and I have every reason to believe he will put a pistol-ball through my head, the first chance he gets."

"Indeed! As that is a pleasure I reserve to myself, and intend to enjoy shortly, I will trounce the fellow for daring to forestall me."

"Captain Gantling," said Ned, "a truce to idle threats. Have you no memory of our old friendship? Cannot you give up this one scheme, and repair many evil deeds of the past by this one generous action? The world is all before you where to choose. Your island kingdom, with its flowery harvests and hopeful delights, awaits you. Why go there red-handed?"

"Will you go with me?" hoarsely cried Gantling.

"No. My association with Sir Stephen has re-awakened the slumbering echoes of conscience, and I will, cabin-boy or captain, follow my career honestly."

"And begin by betraying the one who has brought you up from childhood," pursued the buccaneer.

"Human life is sacred, and my duty plain. But why not release me from my wicked oath, instead of forcing me to

break it; whieh, having warned you onee, I shall do as soon
as I go on board."

"Whieh you never shall, spawn of Satan! whelp of a
vile brood!" cried Gantling, beside himself with passion.

At the same moment he drew a pistol, eoeked it, and
levelled it full at the boy's heart.

"On your knees, beg my pardon, and renew your oath!"
he sereamed vehemently.

"Never! Dye your hand in blood, if you will; but
death before dishonour!"

"Die then!" bawled Gantling.

He pulled the trigger, the cabin was filled with smoke,
but when it cleared away, Ned stood white, but undaunted,
in the same position, his lips muttering a prayer in-
audibly.

"*Nein! nein!* none of that—*donner* and *blitzen*—none
of that—*hagel* and *wetter*, you forget who is—*nein! nein!*"
cried Dirtriek, who had struek up the pistol; he whispered
in the captain's ear, "not father and son."

"Devil! out of the way—how dare you eome here?"

"*Blitzen* and *donner*—you called loud enough. But
what is the matter?"

"Ask Captain Gantling," said Ned, coldly.

"Yaw! yaw! I see—quarrel—both hasty, make it up,
smoke a pipe in the *lust haus.*"

"Never. No more conneetion for me with Captain
Joseph Gantling. Open the door; the wind is rising, and
I must go."

"That I did not kill you," said the buccaneer, with a
fearful oath, I am glad, for many reasons. But, by heavens,
you must think me a fool to let you go. No, you are on
the ship's papers, and no flimsy commission of King George
avails with me. Here you have eome of your own accord,
and here, my young bantling, you will remain, to erow as
mueh as you like; but you do not thwart my plans."

And pushing Dirtriek before him, he went on deek.

Ned was eonfounded, but ever ready at expedients, he
rushed to a narrow open port.

"Are you there, boys?"

"Ay, ay, sir."

"One moment."

With a pencil he wrote these words on a stiff sheet of paper ·—

"*Grunn and the men who shipped with him are pirates. I am a prisoner. Avoid St. Helena, and sail to the westward. Make Juan Fernandez in preference.*"

"Here, boys, give this to the Admiral."

"Now, then, cut off that boat," cried the stern voice of Captain Gantling; "the young reefer who had the impudence to come here, is a runaway cabin-boy of mine, and I mean to keep him."

The boys made no reply, but pulled away with a will, Ned Drake watching them with a dreamy sort of interest, which seemed· wholly centred in others, and not at all in himself. He could hear the lazy swash of the water, and could see the Indiaman not more than three-quarters of a mile off, her black bows dipping, as she rose out of the swell, and through the vapoury haze he could make out the signal to return.

There were evidently signs of wind; and as a vessel like the brigantine would soon feel it, she was not long before she began to move. Then Edward made out the boat being lifted up quickly by a whip from a boom end, and then a great confusion reigned on the Indiaman's decks.

Men ran aloft, sails were let fall, and every preparation made, he fancied, for a chase.

Two minutes later there was a flash, then a report, and a ball came whizzing along the surface of the water. Then came a furious tramping overhead, and Ned heard the buccaneer giving his orders for flight. The Indiaman, prepared with heavy guns, crowded with sailors and soldiers, over a hundred of whom had embarked at Gravesend, was not to be lightly faced by the brigantine.

As soon as the changing position of the vessels hid the *Duke of Kent* from the sight of Ned, he closed the port, and lay down on a couch, the apartment being amply lighted by means of a massive silver lamp, that doubtless came from some Roman Catholic cathedral.

Scarcely had he done so when Captain Gantling returned. His face was more calm and serene. All trace of passion had fled, and he was the same collected seaman his people always found him whenever there was any danger.

"So, sir, the Admiral wants to fight for his new officer," he said, with a gay laugh.

"Sir Stephen is strangely attached to me."

"Indeed!" half sneered Grantling; "but harkee, Ned, you and I are now on different tacks, but we need not be savage enemies. Hear me out. I shall try and carry out my plans in spite of you; my making you a prisoner releases you from all engagements. Do what you can to serve your friends—so will I to serve my designs; but hang it, don't let us altogether forget we are messmates and shipmates."

"Captain Gantling, while a prisoner here, I presume you will treat me like a gentleman, and I will behave the same. But of our differences, not a word. Your mind is made up; so is mine. Let us speak of other things."

"That's it."

And the buccaneer struck a slight blow on a Chinese gong, which, with many other similar nicknacks, was suspended from one of the beams of the upper deck, within reach of his hand

A cabin boy appeared.

"Let us have supper—quick. The wind is freshening, and I shall be wanted on deck soon."

The serving youth retired, and soon returned with one of those dainty suppers which the man of the world knew so well how to order and enjoy; being in this like to most men of genius, who dine when other men eat. The two things, gastronomically considered, are as different as a China teacup and a pig's trough. The buccaneer had inoculated Ned somewhat with his taste, and the lad knew therefore the pleasures of a good dinner.

But Gantling did not press him now. He merely put before him delicacies that might have tempted a saint on a fast day; also exquisite wines, not your fiery ports and sherries, but delicate and seductive juice of the grape, that steals softly over a man's senses, and lifts him gently into elysium, without the slightest vestige of intoxication.

And when by slow and insidious degrees he had led him to take a glass or two, when his pale cheek glowed, and his eyes flashed, and his breath was quick, the buccaneer began one of his most entrancing stories of adventure. They were told so well, that they had a charm of freshness and excitement about them, the power of which he well knew over one at Edward's age. It was the better side of piracy, admirably painted by a skilful hand, that had won the boy's former adhesion to the bold career of a free trader, and the captain saw no reason why the same influence should not be successfully brought to bear again.

When he had worked him up to the required pitch, he stopped.

"And now, my hearty—though you are not one of my creed—come on deck : we shall have a dirty night."

They went, and to judge from appearances, they were about to have a dirty night.

The sun had dipped into the sea, the shades of night had gathered over the vast surface of the illimitable waste—nothing could be seen but the chill and gloomy element.

It was more than half dark, with heaps of clouds lengthening out blacker every moment. W..ere the sun had been, high aloft in the heavens, was a small orange-coloured lurid speck, which seemed to look down upon the deepening gloom.

" 'Tis an ox eye," said Ned ; " we shall have a regular tornado."

" We shall, my boy," replied Captain Gantling, sadly ; " and such a pupil as you have been, to desert me ! What a thing it would be, if you were to change your mind. By heaven ! I would resign my command to help you, and obey my bold boy buccaneer."

" It's very tempting, certainly."

" Ship ahoy ! ship ahoy !" said a hoarse voice at some little distance.

" Here we are ; what ship is that ?"
" No ship, but a very long boat : and Jabez Grunn came on board to wring the neck of that cursed young reefer."

CHAPTER XI.

JABEZ GRUNN.

JABEZ GRUNN had seen Edward Drake's departure for the *Ocean Girl*, with undisguised apprehension and alarm. He could by no means unravel the mystery, which made the youth, who had been the pet and favourite of the captain, all at once their enemy. That he was about to oppose their piratical expedition, he felt certain, though his motive was beyond his ken.

The ugly foretopman watched the boat go away, from his usual berth in the rigging, when not employed elsewhere. He distinctly saw the small craft return without the midshipman, and he reasoned, that in all probability the buccaneer and the youth had had an explanation. He hastily summoned his comrades, and in order to be prepared for the worst, they all armed themselves, and while the lads were making their report in the cabin, they hauled up the boat right into the bows. Though the chain slings were all ready to hook into the rings, no one had thought fit to hoist until the report was made.

Each man then took his kit, and dropped it down into the clinker jolly, after which he himself followed.

Creeping up the bowsprit, and lowering himself to where the martingale guy alone stood between him and the water, Jabez Grunn bided his time.

He had not long to wait. He saw the first mate come forward, while the captain, Sir Stephen, and others, stood together on the quarterdeck.

" Send all the men aft," said the first officer to the second.

F

"Ay, ay, sir."

And in five minutes more, the whole crew that could be found, were mustered around the mainmast.

"How many are missing?" asked the skipper, looking round the astonished group.

"Seven, I think, sir. Jabez Grunn and the fellows who shipped with him," replied the second mate.

"Find them, sir. Take ten men you can depend upon, and put these rascals in irons. They are pirates, and have come on board to rob and murder us all."

"Boat ahoy!" roared a look-out in the maintop.

"Where away?" cried the skipper, rushing to the side.

"Stealing away to windward," replied the look-out.

"Come back, or I will fire," continued the skipper. "Out with the guns. The villains have stolen my boat."

All was hurry and confusion for a moment, and muskets were rapidly found, but by the time they were able to take aim, the boat was a dark speck on the ocean, the night having fallen suddenly upon the great deep.

The anger of the captain could only be equalled by the sorrow of the Admiral, who saw the career of his young and hopeful protégé thus cut short. He had some suspicions of the reasons which actuated Drake, having an intuitive belief that the boy himself was honest and sincere. His coming on board appeared part of a great scheme to secure the Indiaman. It was clear, too, that Edward had sacrificed himself on the altar of duty, and had left his friends in order to be of service to them. Poor Loo quite cried, especially when she found the note which Ned had written to her.

A sharp look-out was kept for the pirate, as the crew and officers of the *Duke of Kent* had no fear of her now. That, with accomplices on board, and by a clever surprise, they might have been overpowered, was quite possible; but armed and manned as she was, they had now no fear for the result.

The Admiral's object was to wait until morning, chase the buccaneer, disable her if possible, and then propose a ransom for the lad. Had the vessel been a man-of-war, duty and inclination both, would have made Sir Stephen fight; but the Indiaman was better qualified to defend herself than to assume the offensive.

Meanwhile the pirate runaways had reached out of range, and, in fact, could not be seen. Half-an-hour after their departure it was quite dark, with the heat excessive and uncomfortable. There was not the faintest breath of wind in the heavens above, or on the waters below. The sky was, however, cloudless, while the stars were obscured by a thin mist. The elements seemed temporarily stagnated.

As soon as they were out of reach of the Indiaman's menaces, Jabez Grunn peered about to catch a glimpse of the buccaneer, which could not be far off. The men meanwhile, who had provided themselves with both rum and brandy, took a heavy pull.

"Avast heaving!" cried Jabez: "none of your mutiny here. If we gets drunk, no more brigantine for us. Heave and pall; hand over the wicker this way, old moony-face," addressing a German vagabond.

And having received the wicker-bound bottle, he took a heavy drink, after which he popped the whole under the stern sheets, and bade the men row.

The cool impudence with which he made himself captain seemed to amaze the men, who, however, pulled off their jackets, and began to bend to their work with a will. But though they made considerable progress in the desired direction, the brigantine could not yet be seen.

All, therefore, with one accord desisted from rowing, vowing they'd have a drain, and go to sleep. The atmosphere had by this time become more opaque, and the darkness more intense and horrible.

"Well, just as you likes, you know, my hearties," cried Jabez Grunn; "but if we're took we shall hang, instead of hanging that there cursed young reefer as has blowed upon us."

"You knows as we can't see nothing," replied one, "and it ain't no good a-rowing. So hand over the beaker, and we'll keep a nigger's watch till morning—take in sail, and go below."

"I believe it's all you're good for," growled Jabez, as he plunged his nose into the bottle, and after a heavy draught, resigned it to his companions; "but you see the devil won't have none of you, for there's the brigantine. We're close on board."

And then it was that they were hailed as before related.

"Well, sir," said the buccaneer captain, "what has made you return?"

"I think I have pretty well explained," said his subordinate gruffly; "where's that young thief? I mean to wring his neck afore I turns in."

"Sir, I am captain of this ship. Go forward to your berth. If you have any complaint to make about any of your shipmates, let it be done in a proper way; I will then take notice of it."

With something more like a grunt than is generally heard from the lips of a man, Jabez took his way to the forecastle, where the men were about to take supper. As the *Ocean Girl* was not intended to carry any cargo, except such pretty trifles as silks, ivory, gold dust, and the like, the space afforded to the men was very large. They were in all respects quite as well lodged as the crew of a man-of-war.

Down the centre of the lower deck there was a long deal table, with benches, and this was loaded with provisions. Though, in the interests of all, good discipline was ordered and enforced, there were no restrictions as to food or drink, except that certain petty officers were bound to report any instances of actual drunkenness. As, on board the Indiaman, grog, unless stolen, was a rare commodity, her runaway crew joined in the festivities with great delight, eating, drinking, and then singing to their hearts' content.

But Jabez Grunn, though he put a whole bottle of whisky before him, did not thence become very talkative. He was brooding—brooding, first, over the public affront put upon him by the captain; secondly, over the means of avenging himself.

Now the sea-lawyer, as he was often called by his companions, had long nourished one ambition, and that was, to take Captain Gantling's place. Hitherto, however, he had never any chance of carrying out his views; the skipper was popular, and a good scholarly sailor. Grunn was a hog; but, by dint of talking, of grumbling, and by the assistance of his own intense self-conceit, he had made for himself a party in the ship.

Now there was an opportunity not to be thrown away. They must all know that Ned was a traitor.

"Well!" he suddenly cried, "What about this here young spy? Ain't he agoing to be hung?"

"What spy?"

"This here young Ned Drake."

"But he is the captain's friend."

"But he ain't. The —— young varmint has been and peached. If we hadn't comed away quite premiscuous-like, we should have had the darbies on us afore now. I say as the law of our craft must be put into operation. The young devil shall swing."

"Tell us all about it!" cried one.

Jabez Grunn asked no better; and rising, with a full command of that rough eloquence which is so persuasive with sailors, he told all he knew, and a great deal more, about Edward's arrival on board the *Duke of Kent*, about his reception in the cabin, about his open enmity to all belonging to the buccaneer. He wound up by demanding that he should be put upon his trial as a traitor and a spy.

General approbation followed, and it was determined that an instant demand should be made to that effect, upon the captain. A dozen were balloted for, and, led by Jabez Grunn, who agreed to be speaker, they marched aft.

CHAPTER XII.

THE night was now rather misty than dark. A full and bright moon had arisen, but it pursued its way through the heavens behind a dense body of dusky clouds, which only now and then allowed the borrowed light to penetrate. From the deck of the *Ocean Girl* the Indiaman was still clearly visible, all her sails set, and forging slowly ahead, before a wind so light as to be scarcely perceptible.

There was one figure only on the quarterdeck. It was that of the buccaneer.

He stood with folded arms, leaning on his sword, which, as usual in the times of which we speak, was a heavy cavalry one. He had a brace of pistols in his belt, and others lying openly on the capstan.

From Dirtrick he had just received a report relative to what was going on ; so that he was fully prepared, except that he knew not how far the mutiny had extended.

Dirtrick had retired to leeward, where also Ned Drake sat, very indifferent as to what was going on aboard. His thoughts were far away on board the East Indiaman, with his companion and friend, little Loo, whose society to him was charming.

The men came huddling up behind Grunn, very much like a flock of sheep. The dense mass of the ship's crew could be distinguished forward. From habitual respect to the quarterdeck, a kind of instinct with the profession, the ugly sailor took off his hat.

The buccaneer stood as if perfectly unconscious of his presence.

" Ahem ! a word with you, if you please, sir."

" Well," said Gantling, coldly.

" Me and my mates we've been talking over this affair of Ned Drake's, and we've come to the conclusion——"

"You mean to say that, like the reckless vagabond you are, you have been inciting the men to mutiny. I've a great mind to put a bullet through your head."

"There ain't been no talk of mutiny, sir ; but this young shaver, on duty connected with the ship, has blown upon his messmates, and so we calls upon you to put him on his trial."

"And if not ?"

"Why then we means for to make short work of it ; and if, sir, while we are settling his hash, we has to imprison you——"

"Go forward, sir ; you are drunk."

"No, sir, I ain't drunk ; but I speaks the meaning of all the crew."

A loud shout from the deputation, followed by a cheer from the remnant of the men, indicated that Grunn was right, and that caution was essential on the captain's part.

"The youth shall be put upon his trial," he continued.

"Thank you, sir ; that is quite fair. May I ask when ?"

"To-morrow, if we lose sight of the Indiaman ; which, I am sorry to say, we must give up for the present."

"That we all suppose," cried Grunn, "and all his doing. Is the lubber below ?"

"He shall be put into the dark hole in irons, but the first man who strikes or illuses him, dies by my hand."

Ned Drake, who had heard all, now rose and confronted the crew. His mien was proud and haughty.

"What have I done ?"

"I'll teach you, you —— young whelp," cried Grunn ; "to the black hole with him !"

"Avast there, ye lubbers !" cried Dirtrick, who was leaning on a heavy capstan bar, "if so be as the skipper is going to shove this youngster into the hole, why just keep your ugly paws off, that's all."

And with a mysterious sign to Ned to make no resistance, he led him away, followed by the watchful eyes of one or two of the conspirators, who insisted on seeing the orders of the captain fully carried out. They escorted both Ned

and Dirtrick down the ladder to the berth deck, where,
having seen the former handcuffed, and his feet inserted
into heavy anklets of iron, running along a great bar
bolted down to the deck, they left him, locking the door of
the partition which divided the prison from the part of the
lower deck inhabited by the sailors.

The whole thing was done so quickly, that Ned scarcely
had time to reflect on his true position, ere he was a prisoner, ironed, and in the dark. The situation was horrible
enough, he knew, for it was clear the captain had lost a
good bit of his authority over his men, especially since
the return of Grunn, who would hurry matters to a
climax.

There was, however, one thought which sustained him.
It was the sense of duty. *That* he had stuck to, even
at the peril of his life.

He had not been long in the confined hold before he
began to feel a strange nausea. In those days the proper-
ties of air were little understood, and it never would have
struck Ned, or any one else, that what he wanted was ventilation. It cannot be too generally known that air from
the lungs of animals, when inhaled a second time, acts as
a poison, which is more or less deadly as the oxygen is
more or less vitiated. A man consumes twenty-six cubic
feet of oxygen daily, and generates nearly a cubic foot of
carbonic acid hourly.

Now carbonic acid gas extinguishes light, and produces
suffocation. Being heavier than air, it remains at the
bottom of wells and mines, causing smoke damp. It is
produced in quantities, during the act of respiration ; and
yet a stiff-necked generation, old women, especially, will try
experiments on our chokable powers, by stuffing up chim-
neys, listing doors, and all other contrivances to keep out
cold air.

It is to be hoped the rising generation will be
a little better educated, and learn that a draught is
better than no ventilation, without which health is impossible.

In a small square box, with no air except what crept in

through chinks, Ned Drake soon felt the absence of the healthy, and the presence of the deleterious air. His head ached, his temples throbbed, and he surely must have fallen into a heavy slumber, from which he might never have awakened, had not a sound aloft attracted his attention. He listened with all his power.

It was somebody at work at the hatchway tarpaulin.

This, of itself, was a relief, and when at last the tarpaulin was heard to give, and a slide in the hatchway was removed sufficiently to give air, the sense of relief was wondrous.

"All square below?" whispered Dirtrick.

"No, my friend ; very sick and ill."

"Well, my hearty, it's quite clear to me you'll be sicker if you don't get out of here. Them varmint is dead on to you ; so you see, Mister Ned—what says you, will you go adrift, or will you stop, and chance a trial?"

"What says Captain Gantling?"

"If so be as the skipper takes your part, he'll go by the board," said Dirtrick, quietly.

"Then do with me as you please," replied Edward, "anything rather than this den."

"If you listen to me, then, it may be as we may not speak agin. That ere cursed Grunn, he's getting the men's back up ; they've spliced the mainbrace pretty well, and when they're drunk there'll be a lark. It's dead calm, but a breeze is sure to spring up soon. It's my idea that are Injirman ain't far off; I see'd a light just now afore the futtock rigging."

"Look again."

Dirtrick rose and went to the side.

"She's there. Now, I'll just heave over two empty butts. They're water tight, and such things as is handy. I'll fasten them with a booling-knot to the main shrouds. You watch your opportunity, my lad, and then cut and run."

"But how am I to get free?"

"All in good time," whispered Dirtrick, handing down a basket of provisions, and then pushing the slide, but not quite so close as to make the wretched prison suffocating.

Again was Ned alone. It cannot be said that to him the position was much improved. The *Ocean Girl* was practically without a head, and in the hands of the many, which, though a most sensible government where civilization has sway, is quite out of the question on board ship, where, with wild and unruly men to command, a captain must be a real despot.

Even if he escaped, death only faced him in another form, for out upon that sea alone, cast about at the will of winds and waves, what chance was there of his finding—not the Indiaman, that was a forlorn hope—but any vessel whatever. Still, hope dies last of all, when everything else is gone, and Ned preferred the chance of life to the certainty of a cruel death.

While these ideas were passing through his brain, he heard a sudden rush, a clamour of loud voices, and then, the door opening, a rush of light illumined the dungeon.

" Come out of there, you young whelp !" said Grunn, in a husky, menacing voice.

" I wish I could," replied Ned, so drily as to set some of the men laughing. " I wish I could."

Dirtrick coolly entered with a light, and proceeded to remove the lad's irons ; upon which he rose and walked to the door, where the drunken ex-boatswain of the *Ocean Girl* clutched him by the arm.

" Move on, you ——," grunted the ruffian, using a foul epithet, and lifting his hand to strike.

" I say," cried Dirtrick, " none of that ; a bargain's a bargain ; he's to be tried for'ard—I sticks to my word."

" Well, heave ahead ; a mighty fuss about a young varmint as is only fit for a powder-monkey," growled Grunn.

CHAPTER XIII.

THE TRIAL.

In well-appointed ships of the present day, the lower deck, occupied by the crew, is comfortable and clean ; on board men-of-war the earliest attention of the officers is given to the berthing of the men, without which no orderly discipline can be established. Cleanliness, room, and ven tilation are seen to, the lower-deck guns being run in and housed, while care is taken that the guard and quarter-masters are disposed of in the wings, or anywhere out of the gangways, so that the deck may be cleared easily, and the men who have night-watches may not be disturbed.

On board the buccaneer no order of the kind prevailed. The officers were content to see to their own comfort and security, leaving the men entirely to themselves, so that they were berthed just as their own fancy suggested. Some had hammocks, some standing bunks, some lay on the floor.

In the present instance, all except an anchor-watch were below, so that the forecastle was crowded to excess. Candles were stuck about, and whether the men reclined on the ground, or sat by tables, or near sea-chests, they were all drinking and smoking.

A rude chair was provided for Ned. It was on the top of a large cask, so that, when seated on it, he was in full view of the whole crew, who were about to decide his fate.

Grunn, who by force of impudence and swagger had got into the position of president, took his seat at a long table, round which were the oldest tars, men without much heart or conscience, their souls seared by the life of rapine, lust, and plunder they had so long led. All had rum in abundance.

"What's the report from deck ?" said Grunn, to a pale-faced young sailor, near at hand.

"Officers battened down," replied the man, "and a guard over the gangway."

" Any resistance?"

"They're kicking up a blessed row," continued the reporter from the deck.

"Let 'em kick. Mind they don't kick a hole in her garboard strakes, and go to the bottom."

"What, with all hands, messmate?" asked a gruff old salt.

"No, but I'm thinking the ship 'ud be lighter for the room of them officers," grinned Grunn.

"There's a little wind, sir," said a man, peering down the forecastle.

"Keep her sou'-west, and look out for the Injirman. The court is opened."

And striking his fist heavily on the table, the ugly seaman called for silence, and then in a speech, the coarseness and blasphemy of which prevents it from soiling our pages, he recorded his opinion of the conduct of Ned, which he painted in the vilest and most hideous colours.

"So now, you see, this here young scoundrel's robbed us of that 'ere ship's treasure ; so I says, in the fust place, he's been mutinous, so we'll cut him to ribbons with the cat ; then, as he's stole our plunder, it shall be the thief's cat, with three knots in each tail——"

"One word, you cold-blooded ruffian!" cried Ned, hotly.

"Silence in the court! Then it's my idea he should be keel-hauled afore he hangs."

A roar of laughter from some of the crew showed how much the three phases of punishment were enjoyed in anticipation. Hanging and flogging need no description from us, but keel-hauling may not be understood so readily. A long rope is passed under the ship, from a block fastened to the end of the mainyard. About the centre of the rope the body of the victim is fastened, and several men pulling on one side, the sufferer is drawn right under the bottom, where, if not suffocated, he receives such cuts and injuries as probably maimed him for life.

It is a cruel punishment, but is varied in small fore and aft vessels, by sending the navigator on a voyage of discovery under the bottom of the vessel, lowering him down over the bows, and with ropes retaining him exactly in his position under the keelson, while he is drawn aft by a hauling line until he makes his appearance at the rudder chains.

The punishment is of Dutch invention, but was often used by our old brutal captains and admirals—a coarse, drinking, ignorant set of fellows, without an atom of mercy in their composition.

"Does you all think this young varmint guilty?" continued Jabez Grunn.

"I ask to be heard," exclaimed Ned.

"Silence, you mutinous rascal!" cried Jabez, "or I'll have you put in irons again."

"Anywhere, rather than in your company. Englishmen—for some of you, at least, bear that honoured name—is it your intention to allow me to be judged by a beer-swilling Dutchman, whose sole object is to get rid of his humane and able officers; that, drunkard as he is, he may have the satisfaction of sending you all to perdition in the first gale of wind?"

"Silence, you swab!" roared Grunn.

"No, no!—hear him!—he's a brave boy!" shouted the English party.

"That's fair," cried Dirtrick.

"Silence, you mutinous hogs!—you scarecrows!" shrieked Grunn, who knew that his adherents were in the majority; "is this the respect you owe to the court?"

"Court be jiggered!" observed Dirtrick; "it's my opinion there ain't no court; but if so be there is, why, I say, hear the prisoner at the bar."

"You bargou-swilling son of a sea-cook!" yelled the infuriated boatswain, "sit down, or I'll make you."

"Boo!" said Dirtrick, casting off his jacket, and appearing in another moment with his sleeves tucked up; "come and do it. I say he shall be heard, that's sartin; you say he shan't—let's fight for it."

"A ring! a ring!" cried the delighted sailors, jumping up one and all, and clapping their hands.

"It ain't usual," blustered Jabez Grunn, "for the court to fight a sea-lawyer."

"The court's afraid," muttered one or two of the English part of the crew.

Grunn's eyes were always red and bloodshot from passion and drink, but now they were hideous. His sallow complexion was of a whitey-brown hue, and though really not afraid, he looked sufficiently alarmed to arouse the murmurs of many of the crew.

"No white-livered cur for captain," said one.

"Who spoke?" cried Grunn, turning round with a savage glare upon his face.

There was dead silence. The look of the Dutch ruffian was very ominous, and none cared, just then, to confront his anger. With a grim smile, he began divesting himself of his coat, and as he did so, he showed a power of muscle such as is seldom surpassed in the human frame. He held up his arm and tapped the thick part of it with satisfaction.

"A clear ring, and no favour," said an Englishman, who was used to the whole affair, and who, as a matter of course, was appointed general umpire.

His injunctions were obeyed, and soon an eager crowd of men were moved back in every direction, to stand with glaring eyes and hopeful countenances, over the delightful prospect offered to them. A fair stand-up fight between two grown men was not an every-day occurrence on board ship.

It is not for us here to record such a combat. Poetry, prose, and the nondescript literature of the ring, have exhausted the topic; suffice it to say that they fought like men; that height and weight were in favour of Grunn, to say nothing of practice, his face being seamed from similar encounters; that thrice Dirtrick fell prostrate to the ground, and thrice rose from his "mother earth as a giant refreshed;" in the fourth round the smaller man was more wary, and finally struck his antagonist such a heavy blow between the eyes as to incapacitate him from moving for some minutes.

On this, "time" was called, and Dirtrick adjudged the victor.

"Well," said Grunn, with a malignant scowl, as soon as he was able to resume his seat as judge, "we will hear the prisoner ; it won't save him from keel-hauling, the scoundrel."

"Ha ! ha ! ha !" laughed Dirtrick, who had seen Ned escape twenty minutes before—the fight had lasted over half an hour—"first catch your fish."

"Thunder and blazes," yelled the discomfited Grunn, "this is some infernal treachery of yours."

"I've saved the brave boy——"

"To h—— with the traitor," shrieked Grunn, rising.

Rub-a-dub ! dub !

The ship's drum beat to quarters. Mechanically the men tumbled up, to find the officers, marines, and several of the loyal portion of the crew, armed to the teeth, with a heavy swivel gun pointed at the mutineers.

"Down with your arms !" shouted the loud ringing metallic voice of the skipper ; "Put that man Grunn in irons at once—at the third word, I fire. Once, twice——"

Grunn was seized, some of his own friends being the first to lay hands upon him, and committed, heavily ironed, to the dark and gloomy den to which he had consigned Ned.

"Bring Ned aft," said Gantling, addressing Dirtrick.

"Can't, sir,"—and, with no other apology, he at once explained what had occurred ; adding that Ned must have unbattened the officers.

"He's best away," mused Gantling, and, walking away, he looked over the taffrail into the deep blue water, on which sparkled the reflection of a few stars. "That was his voice—I knew it."

CHAPTER XIV.

NED had watched the progress of the quarrel between Dirtrick and Grunn with intense interest. At first, it appeared to him a mere accidental quarrel ; but one glance from his faithful and attached follower sufficed to let him see what was meant. It was a got-up affair, to enable him to escape. Now, Ned knew those by whom he was surrounded too well, not to be aware that the majority would hail the cry of all hands to punishment with grim delight ; and, as his imagination conveyed to him a very vivid idea of what keel-hauling was, he resolved to make a dash for his life.

For a moment, all thought of the prisoner, who was being tried for his life, was absent from the minds of those to whom the brutal spectacle of a fight was supreme delight. Ned saw this, and slowly and cautiously let himself down off the barrel on to the ground. His task was then comparatively done; as to glide along the side of the ship, where shadowy darkness played, was to him easy ; the ladder, quite in gloom, so that he ascended it, giving one last glance at the scene, just as the two adversaries were striking their first blows.

Such was the excitement caused by the fight, that, the wind being very light and steady, the man at the wheel had lashed the helm amidships, and gone below. The deck was entirely abandoned. The marines, who were all faithful to a man, were secured in the after-hold.

Ned at once determined to release Gantling ; and, without making any more noise than he could help, he unfastened the battens that confined the companion-way, and in a hollow voice spoke down the ladder.

" Mutiny and murder going on ; creep on deck, and be cautious."

Then with a bound he reached the hammock rail, clambered over the side, loosening the knot of his rope, and hid in the main chains. He distinctly heard Captain Gantling and his officers come on deck, and then with a brave heart he lowered himself to his raft; and, parting away from the ship's side, which, heaving and rising slowly to the wind, passed ahead of him, he launched into darkness.

Weary and exhausted, it was sufficient for Ned that he was free; and, with one short, untaught prayer to the Giver of all Good, he lay down and slept soundly.

A chilly sensation awoke him. It was some rain falling, as it often does just before break of day. Ned now examined his raft. It was composed of two butts and four half-hogsheads, water-tight, empty, but well bunged; the whole lashed together by means of a copious and judicious use of strands, spun yarn, and sennit. Not a nail had been used, and yet three planks formed the deck. A twelve-gallon cask of water, not half full, a pannikin, and a small tub of bread, were all in the provision way; but there were two pistols, a cutlass, a spar suitable for a mast, and the means of stepping it, together with a boat's ensign reversed.

Having examined thus far, Ned Drake looked around him; the sea, under the influence of a gentle breeze, was smooth, though the water was broken, and a slight morning haze obscured the atmosphere. In the distance he clearly saw the white sails of two vessels, and, strangely enough, both were coming towards him. Now, our young hero's eyes were keen enough for him to know them both. To the eastward was the buccaneer, under a heavy press of sail; while, to the westward, was the Indiaman.

They were both heading northward.

A moment's reflection explained this seeming anomaly. They were looking for him. Captain Gantling, knowing the time that Ned Drake went adrift, was returning on his way, steering exactly the opposite tack, whilst the Indiaman was either closing up to fight, or was imitating the manœuvre of the other.

G

Ned Drake at once proceeded to hoist his small sail at the mast-head ; with the union-jack reversed ; Dirtrick having taken the precaution to lash a slight pole for the purpose.

The raft, slight as was the motion given to it by the sail, took the desired direction, heading for the Indiaman. The brigantine at once altered her course, and hoisted a signal, which, even at that distance, Ned clearly made out; it was to recall boats. This showed him that one or two were out in search of him.

The Indiaman made no sign, but kept steadliy on her course.

As Ned was going south, with a wind aft, the vessels could only approach him on opposite tacks ; so that it became a mere question of time as to which should pick him up. A raft is not easily steered a point from the wind ; but Ned, as far as he could, kept it inclined to the westward.

It was quite clear, however, that the brigantine had the advantage, and that, close upon a wind, she sailed better than the three-masted vessel. Still, on reflection, it appeared hardly possible for the rival ships to avoid a collision—which Ned felt convinced both would risk for his sake—Gantling, from many mixed motives ; Sir Stephen Rawdon, from pure affection.

However this might be, and whatever the possible result, Ned could do nothing ; he was completely in the hands of an over-ruling Providence. Seated with his feet paddling in the water, and resting on a lower deck of spars, which Dirtrick had passed under the half-hogsheads, as a protection against sharks, Ned took a biscuit or two and some water, for breakfast, watching, now the brigantine, and now the ship.

The two were perhaps a mile distant, when Ned nearly leaped into the sea from sudden terror.

" You —— young whelp, I've got you !" roared the voice of Grunn, close to his ear ; and turning wildly round, Ned saw him—yes, saw him standing upright in the sea, his body, from the waist up, being out of the water.

"Keep off!" cried Ned, recovering himself.

"Not I, you imp of Satan!" bellowed the ruffian; "they've cast me adrift, a —— sight worse off nor you— in a —— beef-cask, damn 'em!"

Ned could not help a scream of laughter, as he saw that the assertion of the ex-boatswain was true. A large beef-cask had been, by means of weights at bottom, and cross-spars at top, made to float upright, and into this Jabez Grunn had been thrust, as Ned afterwards discovered, to look out for himself, with strict injunctions not to come on board without the reefer.

"I'll make your jaw-tackle winch on the other side," cried Jabez, who was paddling close up to Ned, "that I will. I've got a few yards of hawser-laid rope here, and I'll par-buckle you up in this old tub; see if I don't."

"Keep off!" or if you come one stroke nearer, you shall have two ounces of lead," said the young midshipman, presenting both pistols.

The face of the boatswain became livid. Since he had been cast adrift, he had sobered himself by a drink of salt water; now he was both hungry and thirsty; and food and drink, and revenge—sweetest of all—were within his reach.

"Well, you needn't be so hard upon a fellow," said he, with a disconsolate face; "if you were as hungry and as thirsty as I am, you'd be glad to rob a church."

"Keep off, I say," continued Ned, "and I'll see what I can do."

The man had mysteriously advanced nearer to Ned, but now as unaccountably he went to leeward. While conversing with Ned, he had, unperceived, caught hold of the long painter of the raft, which, unnoticed by the young buccaneer, was floating on the surface. In his fright he had let it go, and in a few minutes he was left behind, cursing, yelling, and threatening, with ferocious impotency.

Meanwhile, the two vessels had come within gun-shot, and Ned saw a rapid exchange of signals taking place.

Then both vessels threw their foresails aback, and lay to, at the distance of half a mile.

Ned watched them with intense interest, for he saw that each was putting out a boat ; the brigantine with extraordinary rapidity ; the Indiaman with more of sobriety and slowness.

Ned now lowered his sail, keeping his flag up, towards which he saw that both boats were making.

The whole was inexplicable to him, nor could he make out what were the intentions of either party. Even, however, in this, his hour of anxiety and distress, he thought of Grunn, and how to give him up his raft. Luckily he did so, for there, close to him again, was the ugly seaman, foaming with rage, and swearing that Ned should not be saved, if he were not.

Again the young midshipman presented his pistol, calling out, as he did so, "Boat ahoy !"

"Hurrah !" came from a dozen throats ; and in two minutes more he was on board the pinnace of the Indiaman, Sir Stephen Rawdon himself acting as coxswain.

At the same moment—the other boat being in the act of picking up Grunn—a splash was heard, and a seaman swam wildly towards the pinnace.

"Come back, or I fire !" shouted one of the piratical officers.

"Hold !" cried Sir Stephen, while the sailors held up their muskets, "fire at your peril !"

"I will !" screamed Grunn, snatching a musket from a marine, and taking deliberate aim at Ned.

Next instant Grunn went back—felled like an ox—into the bottom of the boat ; while Dirtrick was hauled into the pinnace, which at once returned towards the Indiaman, without further communication with the crew of the pirate.

CHAPTER XV.

For a while, Ned Drake was so overwhelmed with excitement, that it was not easy for him to give anything like a succinct account of his adventures ; and when he recovered, Sir Stephen and Loo insisted on his taking a night's rest, ere he conversed much. Sir Stephen then explained that the pirate, or buccaneer, (being in possession of the signals appertaining to the East India Service) had signalled that a mutiny had taken place on board his ship, adding that, under the circumstances, they wished the Indiaman to retain Ned, while they would land Grunn and his fellows at the Cape, as runaways, where Sir Stephen Rawdon could reclaim them.

When Ned went on deck, preparatory to seeking his berth, it was midnight ; and the clouds had risen where light had been just before ; a long ragged strip to the westward was opened up, and a clear glaring flame of the sky, as pale as death, shot through it on the horizon. Into this Ned peered anxiously, expecting to discover the buccaneer, despite the gloom. But, though once he saw something like the white wings of a bird on the distant horizon, he could not be sure ; at length he retired ; and, thanks to youth and health, he slept, under circumstances which might have kept an older person awake.

Excitement is the enemy of sleep. Those of calm nerves and serene minds rarely complain of any difficulty in wooing slumber. Those only with whom everything is going wrong—who have dark clouds hanging over their horizon, or whose present is irritating and perturbed—court Morpheus in vain.

Next day, the morning was fine, and promised to be hot ; the ship had a fair side wind from near south-west, which it was easy to see had slackened since midnight. It had rained heavily, the sails were all wet, and coats hung to dry in the fore rigging. She had about five or six knots of headway.

There was a great change in the weather; the water was bluer than ever it had been, lifting in long waves— scarcely a speck of foam, except about the ship; but, instead of having fled before the sun, or sunk below the level, the long white clouds had risen high to leeward, and were wandering away at the top, a sign of more work to come.

But for the present all was well, and the Indiaman was alive from stem to stern; the decks were drying as clean as a table.

The re-united party—Ned and Loo quite delighted to be together again—seated themselves to breakfast, and in a very brief space of time Ned had told his story, to the surprise and admiration of his hearers.

Some little time having elapsed, comments and observations filling up the interval, the baronet seemed thoughtful.

" What manner of man is this Joseph Gantling ?" said the Admiral, in a musing way.

Ned described him accurately.

" Ah, well !" 'tis strange I did not see his face the night he fetched you."

" He was disguised," said Ned.

" I thought so. How far back does your recollection carry you ?" continued Sir Stephen.

" I must have been very little ; but my earliest recollections are of a cottage, near a lawn, with oaks in front, and a park where I played, and which once or twice I crossed, to a big house, where a gentleman would kiss me, and give me sweets ; then he would suddenly cry, and send me away."

" Then——"

" Came darkness, gloom, and night. A wretched hovel succeeded to the cottage, a huge cavern to the great house."

" Well, well. Let us not dwell so much on the past. To change the subject, I will tell you a story."

"Capital!" said Ned, while Loo laughed and clapped her hands.

The baronet smiled, and adding that it was nothing very wonderful, only a local narrative, told it briefly, clearly, and with much animation and some emotion.

It was the regular orthodox "once upon a time," but as we have no space for his amplifications or descriptions, it must here appear in our language.

* * * * *

Many years before, a gentleman of fair estate, strictly entailed, though at the same time it was in his power to control very large sums of money, was left a widower with three sons, the elder of whom was destined for the army, while the second and third were to become sailors. Dwelling on the magnificent estuary of the Thames, then, as now, one of the most mighty highways of commerce, they were passionately fond of the water, and zealously desirous of serving their country.

Rich, and both able and willing to gratify their whims, the father presented them with a yacht, which was manned wholly by lads, among whom was chiefly conspicuous one Harry Greames, the son of a steward of the house, and a great favourite of the family. He was a bright-eyed handsome lad, jovial, full of animal spirits, and much petted and spoiled by both father and sons.

Well, time passed, the young gentlemen were entered as midshipmen on board the same vessel, while Harry joined as a boy; though it was understood, if he showed capacity, he was to be advanced as petty officer, in those days a matter more contingent on patronage than merit.

Three years had elapsed; the second son was twenty, the third nineteen, while Harry Greames was the same age.

Now it is necessary to explain a very interesting part of our narrative. Close to the park and residence of the father was the rectory. Good Doctor Luscombe was a widower with only one child, a girl of fourteen at the time of the departure of the young men. As children, all four, including the steward's son, had been intimate, playing, nutting, and boating together. Now it happened that,

while the baronet's two naval sons were very boyish for
their age; hearty, honest lads, willing to be boys as long as
possible, Harry Greames was far more manly.

Harry made love to Lucy Luscombe, who, a girl full of
romance and vivacity, encouraged him, without any thought
or deference to difference of station. A youthful attach-
ment arose, and as Harry, under the influence of love,
could, he said, do anything, it was settled that his whole
energies were to be devoted to rising in rank, and that as
soon as ever he was in a position to do so, they were to be
married.

So the boys came home, and delighted the father's heart
by their manly appearance and manner.

In honour of their return, a ball was given, to which
Harry, for old acquaintance sake, was invited. The
brothers had passed, and he was now rated as a midshipman, so that he was, at all events, an officer and a gentleman.

The ball was attended by all the beauty and fashion of
the country round, who assembled gladly to do honour to
the two nautical youths; the belles of Sheppey, when a
pleasant day was offered to them, not stopping to inquire
if the said nauticals were younger sons, or heirs to vast
estates.

The second son—number one was present in full uniform—was standing in the embrasure of a window, watching the company, when suddenly a lovely creature, all in
white, with brown hair, a pale complexion, blue eyes—
blue as the ocean near the line—and with pearls in her
hair, attracted his attention. Attracted! riveted; and
hastily advancing, he contrived to be introduced, and to
dance with her.

"You don't remember me?" she said shyly, as they
walked away after the dance.

"Remember!"

"I am Lucy Luscombe."

"Oh!" was the monosyllabic reply.

Nothing further passed at the moment; but shortly after
he induced her to glide with him into the garden, and

there, after an hour's converse, was laid the foundation of a love which lasted their lives.

Youth is ever hopeful, and they separated at early dawn completely fascinated, and, as far as such young people could be, engaged. There was, however, no great disparity between a younger son and the rector's daughter, while the baronet himself, who was sincerely attached to the clergyman, would be more than likely to favour the match.

So both thought.

Next day the young man, wishing to be alone, went out into the park. It is true that he expected to meet Miss Luscombe, but at a later hour. But young lovers take no note of time, and he, unable to conceal his secret from prying eyes, resolved to bury himself in one of the thickets near the path where she must pass on her way to the hall.

A dreamy reverie, full of rosy colours and bright hopes, followed, from which he was awakened by the sound of voices. Lifting his eyes, he saw Miss Luscombe standing in the path, confronted by Harry Greames.

"So," said the steward's son, " this is your truth and fidelity ? One evening has undone the work of years."

" Mr. Greames," replied the rector's daughter, in a calm and dignified way, " when I was a silly girl, my vanity and folly made me glad of a lover in name. I was too young to know my own mind, and I had hoped you had forgotten, as I wish to do, an unfortunate episode."

" Episode !" he cried fiercely ; " I have your written promise of marriage."

" The promise of a child. You will not be so unmanly as to detain it."

" Retain it ? Yes! My wife you have promised to be, and my wife you shall be, and no other man shall claim you. I would wade through blood rather than *he* should win your smiles."

" Let me pass, sir ! Your language is insolent. You forget yourself."

" Forget myself," he said, clutching her by the wrist, " I

wish I could—memory it is that kills me. But beware how you rouse me to madness."

" Unhand her !" cried the voice of the young lover, who, with pale face, dilated nostrils, and clenched hands, stood before them.

" You'd better make me ; two of you could not," said the infuriated Harry.

One blow decided the question, and next minute Harry Greames lay stunned on the sward, while the lieutenant drew Lucy hastily away. Before night, their betrothment received the sanction of both fathers.

Harry Greames came no more to the hall, and measures were taken to have him removed from the ship, as contact with him would now be unpleasant. The baronet undertook to forward his views, but declined all further personal connection with the young fellow.

The two nautical sons now made the most of their leave of absence, being, as a rule, the body-guard of Lucy in her walks through the park. Now that all secrecy and reserve were over, the lovers enjoyed the company of the younger son.

One day they reached the borders of the dark firs. The lovers walked first. The youngest brother came behind with a favourite spaniel, playing with him as he went along. Suddenly a pistol-shot was fired, and with a loud shriek, Lucy fell.

" The assassin ! the assassin !" roared the lover, and the youngest brother, understanding his meaning, bounded into the copse, and, guided by the dog, soon came up with the murderer, whom, after a desperate struggle, he captured.

It was Harry Greames.

The pistol had been fired at the young officer, but by a sudden movement of Lucy, the ball struck her shoulder. She had thrown herself forward to shield the man she loved, from the villain's attempt.

As the wound was slight, an Admiralty order was easily obtained, disrating Harry Greames, and reducing him as a common sailor, and before the mast for five years, without permission to go ashore, or communicate with the land.

The lovers were married, and at the end of the honey-moon they were about to part, when the eldest brother of Lucy's husband died ; and, as a midshipman with twelve thousand a year was incompatible with the rules of the service and articles of war, the young lieutenant resigned. No doubt the young wife supplied the more cogent argu-ments ; but at all events, before a year was out, the hus-band of Lucy Luscombe was a father and a baronet, the fine old gentleman soon following his eldest son.

The youthful heir was two years of age, when, sad to say, his mother died, leaving the ex-lieutenant a broken-hearted man, even to the extent of refusing to see his child, which was put out to reside with a favourite nurse.

When the child was three years of age, the younger brother was at home, trying by his society to cheer the head of the house. He was, however, very gloomy, and moped about as one who cared not for existence.

Then came a mysterious letter from Greames, full of expressions of repentance, and asking the baronet, for the sake of old times and one they had both loved, to do something for him. He had deserted from his ship, and wished to escape to America. As his presence was known in the island, he begged his old patron would meet him at the Craig's Head, after dusk.

The younger brother wished him not to go, or at all events not to go alone. But he was a wilful man, and would have his way.

The younger brother, who loved and esteemed him much, resolved to follow him, and to be near in case assist-ance was needed. He armed himself and went out. Far down in the west, he had beheld the sun sink behind a bank of black clouds, the upper edge of which it stained with blood, as it descended—here flushing into red fringe, there extending into patches of sullen crimson, till the vapour engulfed the last rays, and left nothing visible but the dusky earth and the star-lit heavens.

After leaving the park, the way was rugged, and the moor over which they walked was broken into chasms and precipices, which put their heads in jeopardy every moment.

The wind, too, over these bleak heights swept piercingly cold, and once or twice the younger brother felt the biting points of fine snow piercing his skin ; but it could not be, for the stars still twinkled above, though their lustre had become dimmer.

He could scarcely see before him, he but felt his way down a ravine, where the ground was rough and broken, so that showers of stones slid before him at every step.

At that instant there came the flash of a pistol right in his path, and not a dozen yards before him he saw the gaunt figures of two men on the summit of a cliff. Then, with a loud wailing cry, one fell, and the younger, starting forward, had only time to see the baronet whirled down a cliff.

He followed, although the angle was sharp, and descending, grasped fiercely at the stones, which gave way and slid from him ; he, however, sought to pass his fingers through them, and dig them into the earth, but it was a task of immense and painful difficulty. Still, at length he reached the ledge of rock where his brother lay dying.

By superhuman exertions he clambered with the body up a sloping path to the summit of the cliff, where a cottage gave shelter to the master of all the country round—master for only a few hours.

He lived long enough to exculpate his brother, at once suspected from venal motives of having compassed his death, and to accuse Harry Greames, who, however, fled the country, and was no more heard of. Unfortunately, he stole the child of Lucy, so that his vengeance was complete. The younger brother succeeded to the baronetcy, married, and had one child ; but he held the title and estates only in trust, in case the stolen boy, not having been murdered, should re-appear to claim his own.

  *   *   *   *   *   *

" And now, my dear Edward," said the Admiral, " I need scarcely say that you are the stolen child, your father the murdered man, I your uncle, and the assassin and thief Joseph Gantling, alias Harry Greames."

The youth gasped with surprise, and when the first emotions were over, he embraced his uncle with tears in his eyes.

"And now, my dear boy, we must find this fellow, and by force tear from him the proof of your birth, when I shall be proud to call you Sir Edward Rawdon, and to resign estate and title into your hands."

"No, sir; worthily have you administered them. I will only take them as your heir; and if you will promise to give me Loo into the bargain, I shall be the gainer."

"But suppose Loo does not mean to be handed over in this summary way?" gravely began the young girl.

"My children," said the Admiral, with deep emotion, "you are worthy of one another. It shall be as Edward says. I will keep the estate, and he shall have Loo until the hour when all shall belong to him."

"But the murderer of my father——?" cried Ned, with a dark and gloomy brow.

"Shall have his reward."

CHAPTER XVI.

ON SHORE.

Now that all reserve was over, and the boy and girl were in the light of cousins one to the other, their happiness was complete. It is true their love was as yet purely that of near relatives and friends, yet it was pleasant to converse and talk of the future, without our hero looking forward to a doubtful and uncertain career.

But one thought in his lonely hours, in sleepless watches of the night, when alone on deck, after others slept, absorbed the thoughts of Edward.

It was the hope of avenging his father's murder.

All gratitude, all thought of what the buccaneer had done for him, faded from his view, and naught remained but the burning desire for vengeance.

That they would, some time or other, come up with the vindictive pirate who had stored his hatred against the Rawdon family for years, he was certain ; the exploit was deferred, not abandoned. Even if he were compelled to cruise about for years, he would not give up what to him was now the purpose of his life.

As they advanced over the trackless and fathomless abyss, the young man burned to be at the end of his journey. He had resolved to win his spurs, or rather his epaulettes, before he settled down into an English country gentleman, which, when he married, he fully intended to do.

This impatience it was that kept him so much on deck. About a week after the disclosures made to him by the Admiral, there were none above but the watch. The night was misty, rather than dark. A full and bright moon was up, but it pursued its way through the heavens behind a body of dusky clouds, that was much too dense for any borrowed rays to penetrate. Here and there, however, a straggling gleam made its way through a covering of vapour less dense than the rest, and trickled along the water.

The wind was fresh and easterly, and altogether somewhat threatening.

Edward, who distrusted these dark nights, went aloft, and peered round the whole horizon, as, unless a very strict watch were kept, the pirate boats might steal upon them in the gloom. His glance went slowly to every point of the compass, until it settled on a streak of misty light, into which the waves were tossing themselves, like little sandhills before a whirlwind.

It is true, scarce anything could be seen but a faint tracery against the sky, like a spider's web. Yet did the boy know it at a glance.

It was the buccaneer, going the same course as themselves, and probably trusting to the chapter of accidents for a catastrophe.

Slowly and thoughtfully Ned came down the rigging, and seeing a light in the Admiral's cabin. he went in. He was preparing for bed, but hastily resumed his apparel when the boy gave him the information relative to the vessel in sight.

Taking a powerful night glass, he went out and carefully examined the horizon.

Sure enough, there it was, clear and distinct against the sky, just where the heavens and the water met.

As soon as Sir Stephen had assured himself of the fact, he told the officer of the watch to keep a good look-out, and then summoned the captain to an earnest conference, which ended in a decision to put into Rio Janeiro, where a swift cruiser would, in all probability, be found to put upon the track of the buccaneer.

This decided on, and the night wind keeping pretty steady, all retired, Edward himself feeling a kind of savage satisfaction at the prospect of the career of Gantling being put an end to.

Soon after daybreak Edward was up, and there, far away to the eastward, still could be seen the light tracery of the brigantine, which doubtless kept as far off as it was possible without losing sight of the chase.

But they cared little now. They knew its character, and were quite prepared for him, except that in a contest of mere swiftness they would have been outdone.

They were now looking out for land, the decision to get into Rio Janeiro being come to when very nearly in the latitude of that celebrated port. It was confirmed by the state of the weather. A tremendous storm was evidently brewing, if they were to judge by the well-known and sinister omens. Heavy masses of black clouds began to collect on the eastern horizon, until vast volumes of the vapour were piled upon the water, blending the two elements into one.

Everything which experience could dictate, was done to make the vessel snug ; but it was with no small satisfaction that officers, crew, and passengers saw land, and sailed that evening into the magnificent harbour. As they expected, there were two fast English cruisers in the bay, with whom the Admiral at once communicated.

Their captains were only too glad of a chance of prize money and promotion ; and though it was considered wise to let the severe storm blow over ere they sailed, every preparation was made to start at a moment's notice.

Edward accompanied the Admiral on his visit to the men-of-war, and was introduced to one or two midshipmen, who volunteered to show him the sights of the place. Edward, who had seen very little of the world, and to whom everything of this sort was new, readily agreed, and two young gentlemen from the *Rattlesnake* accompanied him.

He easily obtained permission for himself and Dirtrick, who acted as his servant, to pass the night at an hotel, the more readily that Sir Stephen himself was to dine and sleep at the British consul's.

The youths, of course, made rapid acquaintance. It is the habit of boys so to do, when they are genial and light-hearted, and not setting themselves up for men too early—a great error of the present day. Of course the first thing to be done was to dine. Fortunately, all had money, Ned being treated already as the Admiral's nephew, quite as much as if his status had been proved in a court of law.

This important matter settled, the young middies frankly asked Ned whether he would go to one of the balls frequented by the better class of citizens, or whether he would go to something like a genuine fandango, the latter being the place for real fun.

Boy-like, Ned naturally preferred the latter, and to it they went. There are few who have read anything, who are not aware that a fandango is a dance, and that all of Spanish and Portuguese origin—whether scattered over America, or collected in a public-house in Ratcliff Highway —are passionately devoted to this amusement. The one to which the young officers were taking Ned, was outside the town, and, with them, had the recommendation that it was not likely to be visited by any of their superior officers.

Ned was, however, rather surprised to find that a large portion of the supporters of the establishment were common sailors—many English—while scarcely a reputable person was to be seen even among the dancers. Our hero was a little angry at first ; but his companions, laughing heartily, and bursting at once, despite the heat, into a lively dance, he seated himself in a corner, and looked on.

It was a large room, with small narrow tables to support the wine, which was the chief drink in the establishment. It was lighted by oil lamps that left the corners of the room in deep gloom. Not caring about the dance, Ned called for a bottle and three glasses, to be ready for his companions, when their exertions should incline them for refreshment.

He watched with dreamy eye the whirling damsels, scarcely, however, aware of a figure that passed, for his thoughts were far away; but the entrance of a noisy party of sailors soon roused him, and next minute made him shrink into the deepest gloom of his corner.

He heard the voice, and he saw the form of Jabez Gruun, accompanied by several of the pirate crew.

His heart beat wildly. If they were ashore, the vessel must be in the same harbour as themselves, and might be captured without a struggle. Thoughts of his father, and his untimely fate, made Ned pitiless. The man whom his parent accused as his murderer, doubtless had some sinister motive for what he had done.

Gantling regarded Sir Stephen as his enemy, and very likely meant to make him the supposed instrument of revenge upon him.

The ruffians of the pirate crew seated themselves at a large table near the door, and ordered rum and tobacco, and were speedily immersed in the enjoyment of these creature comforts, always the delight of sailors of most nations and climes. Edward chose this moment to summon his friends to his side, and to explain the presence of his enemies.

" Could we not fetch the police ?" he said.

" No," replied one of the midshipmen. " Better seize the vessel at daybreak. Once in the clutches of the alguazils here, you will see little of them. If you explained

H

matters to the police, they would give them a hint for a
trifle. Wait until you see the Admiral."

Though Ned candidly believed they said this, because
they did not wish to abandon the pleasures of the fandango, he gave way, as probably their advice was correct,
but he qualified it by an engagement to leave early. The
difficulty was to do so without being seen by Grunn, who
might be on shore for some sinister object.

When, however, the two middies appeared a little tired
of their dancing, and Ned suggested supper at the hotel
at his expense, the volatile but good-hearted young scape-
graces at once agreed, and showed him how to leave the
osteria without passing near the pirate crew.

There was a side door through a yard, and this they
crossed, reaching the gloomy and narrow street, or rather
lane, in which the inn was situated. The night was far
advanced, and the sky, the flying of the scud, the lurid
light of the heavens, with the howl of the wind, showed
them what a storm they had escaped. Buttoning their
jackets tightly, they hurried along, for rain seemed inevi-
table, and rain at night, in Rio Janeiro, is both drenching
and unwholesome.

Had the youths not known their way well, they could
never have reached the hotel.

Another danger, however, stood in their way. As they
advanced, now arm-in-arm, now one by one, looking up
at the houses to reconnoitre, they discern a figure coming
along in the gloom of midnight, screened by the dark, by
the clamour, and the shadow of the houses?

It is a man in sailor's garb, who is dogging their footsteps, and who, as they go on, creeps nearer and nearer.

It is Grunn, with a gleaming knife in his hand.

They are in the lighted streets; they near their hotel :
they hear the great cathedral bell strike two, and the man
is within two paces of them—his knife upraised—when
a cry from the hotel window is heard, a cry of warning ;
followed instantly by a flash and a report—that of a pistol.

Edward turned just in time to see Grunn, with a furious
yell, rush down a narrow street, while Dirtrick, who had

been sitting up for him, rushed forth from the hotel, whence he had fired.

A search ensued, but in vain. Not a trace of the villain was to be found.

CHAPTER XVII.

DARK CLOUDS.

NEXT day, on the requisition of the British Admiral and Consul, the port, bay, and offing, were searched; but not a trace of the *Ocean Girl* was discovered. Doubtless the audacious pirate had run into some creek, and landed his men, who by means of a small boat had reached Rio Janciro, and made the atrocious attempt upon Edward.

He, however, was far from believing that Captain Gantling had authorized the attack upon him. There was something in the man's manner towards himself personally, which forbade this hypothesis from obtaining credit with him, while of the intense personal hatred of Grunn he was well aware.

As the storm had blown over during the night, both the Indiaman and the cruisers were ready, the former to pursue its journey, the latter to search the whole coast.

To remain together was useless. A rendezvous was therefore fixed at the café, when all could report progress.

Edward would gladly have volunteered with one of the cruisers, but the wishes of Sir Stephen and Loo prevailed; and he agreed to defer formally entering the service until they had reached their destination.

They parted then, all in high spirits, and hopeful of the capture of the pirate, which could not be expected to escape their joint activity.

We may here remark that the Indiaman, though to all appearance a first-class ship, and fitted out as a man-of-

H 2

war for the occasion, was, what with passengers and soldiers, more like a slave ship than anything else, being
laden with all sorts of careening gear, military and other
stores, and what is more, crowded with bale goods, and
encumbered with merchandise.

A ship of this quality and condition could not be expected to work with that readiness and ease, which were
necessary for her security and preservation in those heavy
seas which she had to encounter.

After separating from the cruisers, they ran down the
coast, until they had nearly gained the southernmost mouth
of Straits La Maire, when, by a sudden shifting of the
wind to the southward, and the turn of the tide, they
were very near being wrecked upon a rocky bound coast,
to which they had approached too near.

For a moment all was wild confusion, and then discipline obtained the upper hand, and by the exercise of
those manœuvres which display human ingenuity and
energy in the highest degree, the vessel was hauled off the
shore, and was proceeding on its voyage, when, by a great
roll of a hollow sea, they carried away their mizenmast,
all the chain plates to windward being broken.

This was followed by hard gales at west, coming on
with a prodigious swell, which caused a heavy sea to break
upon the ship, that stove in the boats, and half filled the
ship with water. The carpenter soon supplied the loss of
the mizenmast by a lower studding-sail boom, but this
expedient, together with the patching up of the rigging,
was a poor temporary relief. They were soon obliged to
cut away their bower anchor to ease the foremast, the
shrouds and chain plates of which were all broken, and
the ship in all parts in a most crazy condition.

All began to regard their position as serious, the Admiral most of all, though he said nothing to discourage
the brave men about him, or to unnecessarily alarm the
women. But when, thus shattered and disabled, they had
the additional mortification of finding themselves on a lee
shore, from the weather being unfavourable for observations, he called a council.

There was but one opinion, and that was to sail to the eastward on the track of outward and homeward bound ships, when they might meet with succour or aid ; or to enter some port, and refit and lighten the ship. The latter counsel would have prevailed if they had known anything of their whereabouts. They were aware of their proximity to land, from such tokens as weeds and birds; but what land ?"

An occasional glimpse of what appeared high mountains, however, settled the matter, and showed the nearness of the danger. But it was too late to avoid it, for at the same moment the straps of the fore-gear blocks breaking, the fore-yard came down, and the greater part of the men being disabled through fatigue and sickness, it was some time before it could be got up again.

But now the land was clearly visible, the ship driving bodily on to it. Every effort was now made to sway the fore-yard up, and set the foresail, which done, they wore the ship with her head to the southward, and endeavoured to crowd her off from the land ; but the weather, from being very tempestuous before, now blew a perfect hurricane, and right in upon the shore, which appeared to render all their efforts fruitless.

And now the night came on, dreadful beyond all description ; and when attempting to throw out their topsails to ·clear off the shore, they were at once blown from their yards.

All this time everybody remained up and dressed. The Admiral and the officers, were busy aiding and advising the men, so that Loo remained wholly in the hands of Edward.

CHAPTER XVIII.

A NOVEL EMETIC.

SHE clung to him with feverish energy, saying nothing, however, but cowering under the bulwarks, where he had taken her for shelter. The night was fearfully, horribly dark, and it was almost impossible to discover anything beyond the ship.

At last, at four in the morning, the ship seemed to strike. Still, though the shock was great, very great indeed—being not unlike the blow of a heavy sea, such as during several preceding days they had often experienced, it was taken for the same; but the whole of the passengers and crew were speedily undeceived by her striking again more violently than before, which laid her on her beam ends, the sea making a fair breach over her.

It required no warning voice to bring every one upon the quarter-deck; indeed, many appeared, who had not shown their faces upon deck for more than two months; one or two unfortunates, who were ill with scurvy, and could not crawl from their hammocks, were instantly drowned.

Edward clung to a belaying-pin with one hand, while with the other he clutched Loo. He had little hope, for the vessel lay in the same dreadful position for some minutes, all on board believing it to be their last moment; no glimpse of anything could be caught but of breakers all around. Next minute, however, a mountainous sea hove the vessel off, though she soon struck again and broke her tiller.

This was a disaster apparently so fatal, that many seemed inclined to give up all hope, and at the sight of the foaming breakers around, felt inclined to cast themselves over in utter despair.

The Admiral sternly addressed them, asking them if they had never seen breakers before, nor heard of men escaping from the most fearful dangers. He then ordered

them to seize the sheets and braces, and thus command
the ship.

As he spoke, the Indiaman ran in between an opening
of the breakers, steering by the sheets and braces, when,
by great good fortune, they stuck fast between two great
rocks; that to windward sheltering them from the violence of the sea to a certain extent.

They immediately cut away the main and fore masts,
but still the ship kept heeling in such a manner that few
imagined she could hold together for many minutes.

The day now broke, and the weather, which had been
extremely thick, cleared away for a few minutes, and gave
them a glimpse of the land. This set everybody thinking
of saving their lives. To get out the boats, now that the
masts were gone, was a work of some time, which, when
accomplished, many were ready to jump into them headlong, without regard to women, children, or sick.

The admiral, captain, officers, and some of the best of
the men, however, armed with cutlasses, interfered, and
those whose sex or age entitled them to the preference,
were first helped in. The men, upon this, grew very
riotous, broke open every chest and box that was at hand,
stove in the heads of casks of brandy and wine, and got so
rapidly intoxicated that several were drowned on board,
and lay floating about the decks for days afterwards.

Edward stood by Loo until she had been lifted into the
boat, when he went down to his chest, which was at the
bulkhead of the ward-room, in order to save some little
matters, if possible. But while he was there the ship
bumped with some violence, and the water came in so
fast, that he was again forced to get upon the quarter-
deck, without saving a single rag but what was upon his
back.

The boatswain and some of the people would not leave
the ship as long as any liquor was to be got at; upon seeing which, Sir Stephen and the captain, with the rest of
the officers, went ashore, without more ado.

When a shipwreck occurs, the first thing that is thought
of is the getting to land; it is the natural and highest

wish to be attained, but in the present instance the change was very little for the better.

On every side a scene of horror—on one side the wreck (on which was all they had in the world to support themselves), together with a boisterous sea, presented the most dreary prospect ; on the other hand, the land scarcely presented a more favourable appearance. It was desolate and barren, without a sign of culture, so that they could hope to receive little other benefit from it than the preservation it afforded them from the sea.

Of course all who were possessed of manly feeling, confessed it was a great and merciful deliverance from immediate destruction ; but there they were, all wet and cold and hungry, the elements to struggle with, and no visible remedy against any of these evils.

Edward, as soon as he saw the head of land they had chanced on, though faint, benumbed, and almost helpless, exerted himself to find some covert, however wretched, against the extreme inclemency of the weather. He was fortunate enough to find an Indian hut not far from the beach, within a wood, and here all the ladies, without distinction, crouched for that night, which was most tempestuous and rainy.

None of those who were saved from the wreck ever remembered such another night.

Even if the weather had not excluded all idea of rest and refreshment, other ideas would have interfered, as they were not without alarm and apprehensions of being attacked by the Indians, for they had made a discovery of lances and arms in another hut.

In this miserable hovel, where he had been admitted that night because of his illness, died a lieutenant ; and of those who went for shelter under a great tree, which stood them in very little stead, two more perished by the severity of that cold and rainy night.

In the morning, the calls of hunger, which had been hitherto suppressed by their attention to more immediate dangers and difficulties, became too importunate to be resisted. Most of them had fasted eight-and-forty hours—

some more. It was time, therefore, to make inquiry as to what sort of sustenance had been brought from the wreck by the providence of some, and what could be procured on the island by the industry of others.

The whole amount of food saved from the ship was three pounds of biscuit dust, reserved in a bag.

Several, however, ventured abroad, the weather being still exceedingly bad ; but they killed only one sea-gull, and picked some wild celery.

The whole of this was put into a pot, with the addition of a large quantity of water, and made into a kind of soup, which was then divided amongst them all as far as it would go. But no sooner had they partaken of it, than they were all seized with the most painful sickness, violent retchings, swoonings, and other symptoms of being poisoned.

This misfortune was imputed to various causes, but chiefly to the herbs they had made use of ; in the nature and quality of which they fancied themselves mistaken. A little further inquiry, however, made them aware of the real occasion of it.

The biscuit dust was nothing but the sweepings of the bread room ; and the bag in which it had been put had been a tobacco bag—the contents of which not having been entirely taken out, what remained got mixed with the biscuit dust, and proved a strong emetic.

CHAPTER XIX.

ON SHORE.

THE weather abating somewhat, it was ascertained that about one hundred and forty had got ashore. A few, however, still remained on board, giving way to drunkenness, and pillaging the wreck. The leader of these was the boatswain.

The Admiral sent out officers in the yawl, with orders to endeavour to prevail upon them to join the rest, but they proved to be in the greatest disorder, and disposed to mutiny, so that the officers were obliged to desist from their purpose, and come away without them.

Everybody was very desirous to take some survey of the land they were upon ; but the general opinion being, that the savages had merely retired to a small distance from them, and only waited to see them divided, no excursions were made from the hut. All the land seen, however, was morassy and unpromising.

They were in a little bay, formed by hilly prominences, some so steep as to be inaccessible.

Nothing was obtained that day but shell fish and wild celery, and that in very insufficient quantities.

The night was exceedingly tempestuous, and the sea, running extremely high, threatened those on board with immediate destruction by the parting of the wreck. They were, therefore, now as solicitous to come ashore, as they had before been obstinate in refusing assistance.

But the captain could not acquiesce with their wishes, it being impossible to send off the boat in such a sea. The drunken and silly fools then fired one of the quarter guns at the hut, the ball of which passed just over the covering of it.

Another attempt was made to bring the madmen to land, which, however, from the violence of the sea, and other impediments occasioned by the mast that lay alongside, proved ineffectual.

Upon this delay occurring, the people on board became outrageous, and began to beat everything to pieces that fell in their way. At last, so great was their intemperate excess, that they broke open chests and cabins for plunder that could be of no use to them. So far in earnest were they in this mere wantonness of theft, that when they were brought off, it was found that one man had evidently been murdered on account of some quarrel over the division of the spoil.

But the chief object of the mutineers was to provide

themselves with arms and ammunition, so that they might be able to carry out their mutinous designs.

They asserted that the authority of the officers ceased with the loss of the ship.

They soon afterwards came ashore in one boat, all crowded together.

The sea still ran very high.

The Admiral and officers held a consultation, and as the mutineers approached the shore, all the good and tried men of the shore party ran into the water, as if to help them, but in reality to rush upon them and disarm them, which in their maudlin state was done without difficulty.

The men were half sobered, and, though still insolent, they all appeared inclined to acquiesce in their defeat, except for the boatswain.

It was ludicrous to see them, with the officers' best suits, which they had rifled from chests and cabins, put over their greasy trousers and dirty checked shirts.

The boatswain was the most marked, being all in laced clothes, and also most insolent ; but the captain knocked him down with his cane, and ordered both him and his companions to be stripped of their finery.

As it appeared quite clear that some time must elapse ere anything could be done towards leaving this desolate region ; and, taking into consideration the incessant rains, and the exceedingly cold weather, everybody felt it impossible to subsist without shelter.

The hut was scarcely enough for the women, so the gunner, the carpenter, and some more, turned the keel of the boat upwards, and thus made a tolerable habitation.

This kind of settlement having been made, with the addition of rude stone walls all around, they made their researches with greater accuracy than before.

They were well aware that even the most desolate shores are seldom unfurnished with supplies of some kind.

They therefore soon found some sea fowl, limpets, mussels, and shell fish, in tolerable abundance.

Still no provision proportionate to the number of

mouths to be fed, could, by their utmost industry, be acquired from the part of the island they had yet seen.

Therefore it soon became necessary to visit the wreck, and from that to take such supplies as could be got out of her.

This, however, was a very precarious fund, and could not last long ; and as no man could rightly say how long they might be detained on the island, the stores and provisions they were so fortunate as to release, were not only to be dealt out with the most frugal economy, but a sufficient quantity laid by, to fit them out as soon as they agreed on any mode of transporting themselves from that dismal spot.

This led to an examination of the boats, which were all more or less injured, so that they would carry scarcely half the number. It became necessary at once, therefore, to resolve on a raft, which might be towed by the boats, and by their means either to reach a more hospitable clime, or to cross the track of other vessels, which might thus save them.

All this time no signs of the Indians were seen, and Edward, who was of no use in any other way, strolled about with a gun, making Loo his companion.

From the stores of the ship she had been rigged out as a boy, as being more convenient ; and it was her delight to follow her favourite and friend.

The long boat was still on board the wreck ; and as soon as the weather abated, a large number of hands were sent to cut the gunwale of the ship, in order to get her out, all planks and beams being saved for the raft.

While the men were engaged on this business, there appeared three canoes of Indians paddling towards them.

Motions were made, and after some time they approached, and proved to be people of small stature, very swarthy, with long, black, coarse hair hanging over their faces. Despite the cold, they had no clothing but a bit of beast's skin about their waists.

They could not make themselves understood, but in return for a looking-glass and some other trifles, they brought in three sheep, which made the people fancy their troubles were nearly at an end, and that food would be plentiful.

Many wanted to make a feast accordingly, out of what had been taken from the ship. But the officers were obdurate. They had erected a storehouse near their own huts, from which nothing was to be dealt out, but in measure and proportion as agreed on by the superiors.

The men seeing this, and finding that the Indians did not return, set to work with a will, modelling the long boat, to make it carry as many as possible, and tow the raft also.

CHAPTER XX.

THE PERIAGUA.

ONE day the sun seemed to shine more brightly than ordinary, the wind was lulled, the weather appeared cheerful and serene, so that Edward and Loo took a stroll farther than usual, in search of wild fowl and limpets. He had a gun, a pistol, a knife, and a horn of powder, while she only carried a basket, in which to collect shell fish.

The pressing calls of hunger had made some of the men very ingenious, driving them to their wits' ends, and proving that necessity is the mother of invention.

Among some of the more ingenious was one Phipps, a boatswain's mate, who, having got a water puncheon scuttled, then lashed two logs, one on each side of it, and set out in quest of adventures on this original and extraordinary craft. By this means he would very often, when all the rest were starving, provide himself with wild fowl, and it was very bad weather indeed which could deter him from putting out to sea when his necessities required it.

On occasions, he would venture far out into the offing,

and be absent the whole day.   At last it was his misfortune, at a great distance from the shore, to be overset by
a heavy sea ; but being near a rock, though no swimmer,
he managed so as to scramble to it, and with great difficulty ascended it.   There he remained two days with very
little hope of any relief, for he was too far off to be seen
from shore.

Fortunately, however, a boat having put off and gone
in quest of wild fowl that way, discovered him making
such signals as he was able, and brought him back to the
island.   This accident nowise discouraged him, for soon
after he procured an ox's hide, used on board for sifting
powder, and called a "gunner's hide." By the assistance of
some hoops, he formed something like a canoe, in which
he made several successful voyages.

Now Edward was extremely anxious to be instrumental
in procuring a useful supply of food, before they took
their departure from this inhospitable climate, where,
from the thick rainy atmosphere, they were not only
deprived of the sun, but were also visited by frequent
tempests.   He had the canoe, or boat ; but on several
occasions he had remarked that whole flocks of wild fowl
flew in a certain direction across the island.

Towards this he now made his way.

They climbed a very steep hill, descended to the other
side, and found themselves in a valley, which was rather
greener and more fertile than the other.

This appeared tempting, and the young people soon
found themselves in a region very superior to any they
had as yet witnessed.   Here they shot several painted
geese, whose plumage is variegated by the most lively
colours ; also a bird much larger than a goose, which the
men called Racehorse, from the velocity with which it
moved on the surface of the water, in a sort of half-flying,
half running motion.

There were also some woodcocks, some humming birds,
a large number of robin redbreasts, and a small bird with
two very long feathers to his tail.   There were also car-
rion crows.

Having collected a large number of limpets, and made a pretty good bag of game, they continued on their way, until across a rapid channel they saw an island covered with wild fowl, which they could neither shoot nor reach.

About a couple of miles up, under cover of the hills, were some Indian huts, and on the beach three canoes, one of which was sufficiently large to have a mast. As they were on good terms with the Indians, Edward resolved to borrow this one, with which to carry back the game he was already in possession of, and, if possible, a good supply more.

The boat was launched, its tiny sail set, and the adventurers—better pleased than they had been for some time —started. The wind was light, and the waves small, but the canoe walked over them truly like a thing of life.

A cry of joy escaped the lips of Loo, as they rose and fell on the waters.

Suddenly Edward half rose, making the boat rock and vacillate greatly, as he seized a paddle, and lowering the sail, tried to make for the shore.

"What is the matter?" said Loo.

"Heaven help me! we are in the suck of a current, and are being carried out to sea."

"Oh, my poor father!"

"Be still; I will do everything I can to regain the shore. Be calm, dearest."

And without speaking, he used his paddle with all the energy of which his arms were capable. But it was of no avail. The remorseless stream carried them on until they were swept upwards along the coast, a long way from where the wreck lay.

This was a fearful calamity; but, if they could only save their own lives, might be productive of good. Should they fall in with a vessel, its crew might be induced to run down to the place where the wreck of the Indiaman lay.

But it was useless to form any illusions. The boat they were in, though built purposely for fishing and tra-

velling in bad weather and breaking seas, could not be
expected to take them far.

They had provisions, but no water, save a small leather
bottle-full each.

Loo, in the first burst of grief, sobbed herself to sleep.
When she aroused herself, she was calm. They were
running along the coast with great rapidity, the sail being
set to keep the boat steady.

" What is to become of us ? " said she, in a low, trembling voice.

" We have no hope, save in Providence ; " replied the
young lad, quietly.

" Shall we ever get back ? "

" Not in this boat: we cannot breast the waves, nor
beat against a steady wind with this cockle shell. We
can only move along at the will of wind and waves."

" You are pale and ill," said Loo.

" I am sleepy."

" Let me steer ; I will wake you at the slightest event,"
she said, eagerly.

Edward resigned the light paddle into her hand, and
lying down, fell into a heavy sleep, which lasted many
hours.

Now began the usual horrors of such a voyage. The
want of water, raw birds, and exposure, soon made them
so faint and exhausted, that it was with difficulty they
could eat, drink, or steer. Loo became lightheaded, sang
snatches of songs, and, if her strength had allowed, would
have cast herself overboard. Edward scarcely knew what
he was about, except that he gnawed at the birds, and
drained his water bottle, and let the boat go as it liked
over the wide waste of waters.

Then came a heavy shower of rain, which both roused
and refreshed them, abating the fever, though both were
still too weak to move.

They were dying of starvation ; but in one of the lucid
intervals of the madness which preceded the final struggle,
both gazed around in amazement. They were gliding
along a soft, pellucid, lake-like sea, and at no great dis-

tance from an island, with bare cliffs of a fine bold appearance.

The wind was shorewise, and Edward feebly adjusted his sail.

Slowly, with a soft breeze, they advanced ; the rugged peaks showed their clothing of timber and verdure ; and, unpromising as was the distant view, a nearer approach revealed many beauties.

Between the high cliffs there were verdant valleys stretching up into the island, each with its rill of clear sparkling water.

Edward felt, if he could but reach one of these, he might be able to save Loo.

His arms were too feeble to row, but, sitting like a statue of death, he directed the course of the stout canoe, which had carried them so many miles.

He saw that the water was deep to the very shore, and he easily found a creek, up which to drive his boat.

He allowed it to ascend as far as it would, until he was stopped by a small waterfall. Here he crawled out, drank from the sparkling stream, and then, reinvigorated for an instant, he dragged Loo ashore.

She was in the last stage of exhaustion. But water had its effect upon her also.

Ned looked around ; there were cabbage palms in abundance ; but these were not to be reached. Close at hand were some fine fat ripe cherries ; a handful of these being picked, they were gently forced into the girl's mouth.

The effect was really wonderful, as they were taken into the system. Anything will support nature awhile, however little nutritious as a whole.

Finding that a faint colour returned to her cheeks, and that she seemed inclined for repose, Edward himself eagerly devoured some fruit, and, casting his gun on his shoulder, he began with slow and uncertain steps to explore the place.

It had large trees, myrtles that attained the size of forest trees, but without scent; and it had peach trees and strawberries also.

I

But what amazed Edward most, was to come across fields of wild oats, and even radishes. He looked about for horses and inhabitants, but not a sign of any was to be seen.

There were figs and poplars, too, and wild rhubarb, and thyme and mint.

Then he started, as a flock of twenty goats rushed by. It was an opportunity not to be lost, and having seen carefully to the priming, he fired, and two fell before his shot.

This was a triumph, and, shouldering one of them, he returned to where he had left Loo, and found her in a calm sleep. Quietly, without noise, he made a fire, and broiled some of the most tender parts of the kid.

Suddenly the girl awoke, and looked at him, without speaking. She had no idea where she was.

" Better, Loo ?"

" Are we alive ?" she asked, in a faint whisper.

" Yes ! and safe on a beautiful island," he replied, handing her some broiled goat flesh.

She took it, not eagerly, not anxiously, but as if to oblige him, and, unable to eat, sucked it. Many persons, half dead with starvation, have been saved thus.

Edward himself soon ate heartily, as strength and appetite gradually returned.

At the end of half an hour, Loo could sit up and listen to details of their voyage. She heard of them with horror and trepidation.

" Oh my poor father ! and where are we now ? "

" I do not know, but I suspect," said Edward Drake, earnestly ; " more than suspect."

" What ? "

" That we are in a place as romantic as dangerous," he added, thoughtfully.

" And where may that be ? "

" On the island where once lived Robinson Crusoe, and which is now used by Gantling to refit. I have heard him speak of it often."

" Would he harm us ? surely not ! "

"Heaven only knows. But I hope never again to be in the power of my father's assassin."

"Father! father! what of my father?" continued Loo.

"Calm yourself, dearest; we are two; we are brave, and some plan must be devised to escape. The island is often visited now, by whalers and others. I am not at all fearful."

Loo shook her head, while Edward rose to make a hut, in which to pass their first night on the romantic shores of the island where Robinson Crusoe vegetated nineteen years.

CHAPTER XXI.

ALONE.

EDWARD was at that pleasurable age of boyhood, when to be the servant and slave of a sister or cousin was in itself happiness. Forgetting all else but his anxious desire to be subservient to her comforts, he began erecting a small hut of such boughs and leaves as were nearest at hand.

The task was not a difficult one, as, by means of his knife, he had only to cut such branches as served his purpose, and, sticking them into the ground, they very soon formed a shelter quite sufficient for an island in such a climate, until the rainy season set in.

This done, he led the poor suffering girl to her repose, and making a large fire to scare away wild animals, he lay down with his gun close to his hand, to seek that rest of which he stood so much in need. But though wearied to the last degree, he awoke several times to replenish the fire, and each time listened eagerly, to know if his precious charge slept. And every time, his anxious solicitude was rewarded by the discovery that she lay in a sound slumber.

At early dawn he awoke, and, going to a sparkling rill, he filled up the gourds with water ; then, cooking some more goat's flesh, he returned to arouse the sleeper.

She was nowhere to be seen.

Alarmed lest some misadventure might have occurred, Ned was about to call her name loudly, when she emerged from behind a rock, fresh and blooming. She had found a secluded nook where she could perform her ablutions, and she was now, comparatively, as well as ever she had been in her life.

A long and interesting conversation now ensued. To make any further attempt at a voyage, in their case, was out of the question, while it was equally painful to contemplate remaining on that island all their lives. Adam and Eve in Paradise would probably have wearied of it, if no society had turned up.

The island had plenty of food. There were goats in abundance, there was fuel, and the crews of the different vessels which visited it as a victualling place, had planted numerous English pot-herbs and vegetables, which were used as preservatives against the scurvy.

There were also several caves in the rocks, which, during the short time it had been a convict establishment, had served as prisons for the unfortunate exiles. There were, also, some ruined huts, and the fallen frame of the governor's house, all of which would afford materials useful for their purposes.

The island was sure to be visited, as it was the common watering-place of whalers and buccaneers, who also often resorted there for weeks at a time, to give their sick time to recover.

But for their anxiety about the Admiral and their friends, wrecked on the miserable Patagonian shore, they might have been tolerably happy, as at their age there is a youthful buoyancy, a romantic courage, which sustains young people against almost all difficulties, and which has so often made a boy-middy do deeds of heroism worthy of a man.

The first thing to be done was to select a home, and, after due consideration, it was resolved to repair the kind of log-hut in which the former Spanish governor had resided. It was two storied, with one room aloft, and two below. The one above was small, and, as it only wanted repairing in the roof, it was assigned to Loo, while one of those on the ground-floor was to be the joint apartment and kitchen, reserving a kind of cupboard for Edward.

The difficulty was to repair it without tools; but necessity is really the mother of invention, so by means of a knife some bark was cut, and placed over the holes which time had made in the ruin, the bark being kept in its place by stones and staves from the other huts.

Then came the question of beds. But in such a climate, during that season, some sweet straw served every purpose.

There remained then, the question of food. They had a few charges of powder, but that could only serve them once or twice. Vegetables existed in plenty, as did cocoa-nuts and palm-cabbages; but, whatever philosophers may say in their closets, such a diet is neither pleasant nor satisfactory.

It was resolved, therefore, to look to the capture of goats as their mainstay : but how was this to be done ?

Few hearts but would have been moved to compassion, mingled with admiration, to see this young couple, so ignorant of the world's ways, devising and planning the means of existence. It is true they did not contemplate a lengthened residence on the island.

After a long discussion, an ingenious idea came into Loo's head. She knew both how to knit and how to net, and she believed too, that by means of an admixture of goat's hair and cocoa-nut fibre, she might make a snare sufficiently strong, to place across one of the narrow passes leading to the hills, and into which it would be easy to drive their coveted prey.

Edward at once set to work to shape two long wooden knitting-needles, as well as all else that she required, and with which she at once began her labours.

Behold them now at work for their living, in a few days after.

They have arisen to breakfast, and have taken their frugal meal. They have collected wood with which to keep up a fire all day, so that passing vessels may know that some unfortunates are on the island.

Loo then seats herself near enough to the fire to re-plenish it, while Edward wanders in search of limpets, oysters, and anything else which may vary their stock of food. He looks, too, to the supply of cocoa-nut fibre, which can only be obtained from the nut in a certain state of its growth. He sees also to the vegetable gardens, where the fences have been broken by the goats. These animals, however, since his arrival, have not ventured from their mountain fastnesses. Had they, their capture would have been easy and certain.

The principal vegetables which the captains of merchant-vessels had succeeded in raising, were scurvy-grass, parsley, carrots, and onions, all of which are wholesome and anti-scorbutic.

The difficulty was to cook them, and at best the process was extremely slow. They were compelled to put them into cocoa-nut shells, to heat small stones red-hot in the fire, and clearing them of ashes, to cast them into the water: by which means, after a time, the requisite heat was gained. As, however, they had no great abundance of occupation, this was perhaps an amusement, and helped to pass the day, which otherwise would have been idly enough occupied.

Meanwhile, however, Loo advanced slowly but surely with her masterpiece. It was not a handsome work: the knots were many and ugly; but it promised to serve the purpose, and both were extremely anxious to try its merits.

Their stock of meal was soon run out, and they desired to renew it. This consideration, however, weighed less with them, than the love of adventure inherent in human nature, and which is as common in girls as in boys, until the hour comes when nature, speaking with its mighty power, drives them into the shade, modest and shy.

A supper of limpets and oysters, somewhat coarse and insipid, made them long for better fare, and it was mutually resolved, that the net was long enough for the purpose for which it had been so laboriously constructed.

It was accordingly agreed to start at daybreak, and try their fortunes in the interior of the island.

CHAPTER XXII.

THE HUNT IN THE VALLEY.

THE morning was bright, the song of birds was pleasant, as hand in hand the juvenile Adam and Eve took their solitary way. Edward carried the gun and the net, somewhat heavy, wrapped up like a haversack, while Loo carried their small supply of food.

They had taken up their station near the shore, close to some woods, through which they now walked, surprised at the abundance and variety of the foliage, no less than by the beauty of the flowers.

Some of the palm-trees rose to a height that amazed the young girl, though to Edward they were tolerably familiar, his cruises under Gantling having taken him both to the West Indies and to the coast of Africa. What, however, brought a smile to the countenance of the young girl was the loquacity and number, as well as the impudence of the monkeys. They did not appear very fearful of the strangers, but made grimaces, chattered, and laughed in a most ludicrous manner.

"If the worst comes to the worst," said Edward, "we can make these brutes our purveyors, ugly as they are!"

"How?" replied Loo, with a pretty little shudder—"nasty creatures!"

"I will show you," said Edward, merrily; "wait a moment!"

The monkeys were grinning, and, to all appearance, talking overhead, very high out of reach. Edward, however, laid down his gun and parcel, and picking up stones, began throwing them at the animals with all his strength, and as rapidly as he could.

The imitative brutes, with infinite chatter and fury, after holding a sort of consultation, began plucking the cocoanuts, and throwing them down so rapidly, that had Ned and Loo not concealed themselves, they might have been seriously hurt. As it was, they only laughed heartily, and, opening the nuts, took a cool drink and a refreshing meal.

Edward took occasion to tell Loo how, in Java, the monkeys meet together in bands, led by some old chief, and, descending at night on the native villages, pillage their poor huts, and even carry off children and young girls.

"There is no place like England," sighed poor Loo; "I wonder if we shall see it again!"

"Of course, and laugh as we tell our children of our strange adventures!"

Now, Loo was a little girl; but little girls are very fond of being thought of as sweethearts and wives, so she looked down, blushed, and made no answer.

They rose, soon after, and continued their journey until they reached the foot of the hills, when they began carefully to look about for a place to commence operations. The hills were not very high, but they were rough and steep, so that they advanced but slowly on their way. At length, by dint of great exertion, they found a valley where goats were feeding, and, peering down so as not to be seen, they examined the place carefully in search of a situation for a trap

It was soon found.

At the further end of the valley, to the left, was a narrow gap, almost closed by trees, and admirably suited for their purpose.

Telling Loo to remain at the other end, and to appear if necessary, he, bending low, crept to the spot, and succeeded in reaching it without being discovered by these timid and shy animals.

He fastened the net securely, and then made a wide détour, in order to rejoin Loo, who awaited him impatiently.

The flock, about twenty, were huddled together, sniffing the air, as if they suspected an enemy.

Both, however, crept slowly on, until they cut off the retreat of the flock, when they appeared suddenly, and rushed at the goats, which went off at a rapid pace in the direction of the trap.

Their hearts now beat wildly, for the whole flock would soon have carried their frail net before them.

Much to their mutual relief, nothing of the kind occurred.

Two kids and a large she-goat were sent to the ground, secured by thongs, their horns and feet being taken out of the net.

The rest of the flock passed round, evidently making for the other end.

It was, however, only for an instant, for, as the kids and goat sent up a plaintive cry, the buck, the patriarch and guardian of the flock, turned, and with fury flashing from his eyes, he darted at the foe.

Loo was nearest, and at her he rushed. She, uttering a shrill cry, ran away.

Edward, who had placed his gun on the ground, snatched up the first thing at hand, a heavy fallen bough, and met the animal face to face. It was a *hand to horn* encounter, in which great dexterity was required.

Leaping aside with a bound, such as few but young sailors can appreciate, he dealt the infuriated brute a severe blow across the back. It shook itself, and seemed disinclined to renew the contest, when again the kids and mother gave their pitiful cry.

The goat reared, and then bending his head low, he rushed forward. Once more the leap and the stick sufficed to check his advance, and then with something of the dexterity of a bull-fighter, Edward plunged his knife into the animal, and finished him by a second blow.

"Are you hurt?" cried poor Loo.

"Not a bit," laughed Edward; "but what a fury!"

Loo made no remark; but she thought that in all probability it was quite natural that the male should defend the weaker.

It was now resolved to skin the dead beast, and take the others home alive—no very easy task, but still it was one worthy of trial.

Edward performed the butchering part, while Loo looked about for flowers, or culled grass for the she-goat, which, however, the poor animal strenuously refused to eat.

As their load was so heavy, they wrapped a good portion of the goat-flesh in the skin, and hid it in a tree. Then they determined to pass the heat of the day under shelter, and return to their hut in the dusk. This necessitated a meal; but Loo could not as yet reconcile herself to eat of the animal, so they were satisfied with cocoa-nut.

So inviting was the cool retreat they selected, so languor-inspiring the outside air, which came balmy and flower-laden, that it was not long ere both were fast asleep.

When they awoke, it was quite dark, and, therefore, in a country they knew not, it was impossible to travel.

A camp in the woods was at once decided upon.

"We can fancy ourselves gypsies," said Loo, laughing.

"Or robbers," said the boy. "I have often wished to see a camp of Italian banditti. It must be fine!"

"Romantic," observed Loo, thoughtfully; "I don't like banditti. They remind me of pirates or buccaneers."

"Like me," said Edward, in a tone of semi-pique.

"If all were like you," began Loo, and then she hesitated.

" Well——? "

" Well, I should like them," cried Loo; and jumping up, she began collecting fuel for a fire, which, almost in any latitude, is pleasant at night, but is always required to keep off wild animals and noxious vermin.

As the trees were thick, a much less complicated hut, than where the trees were thinner and more open, was all that was needed to keep off the dew. It consisted only of a roof composed of branches and leaves ; under this, after some serious talk about their situation, these innocent children slept, like the babes in the wood, until morning came.

They were awakened by the bleating of the two kids and the mother, now much tamer from the unusual deprivation of food.

Loo rushed to pluck grass and delicate shrubs for the she-goat ; and Edward, taking advantage of the animal's secure position, milked a small quantity into a cocoa-nut shell, and handed it with pride to his companion, when she returned.

Loo clapped her hands with delight.

" We will keep her, and have milk every morning," she said, enthusiastically.

Edward proceeded, with a smile, to loosen the goat, that she might rise to her feet, and giving her food, she ate it heartily. As for the kids, there was no necessity to tie them, as, once loosened, they rushed to their mother, and would not leave her. This little event seemed to elate both Ned and Loo, and to make them forget the dangers they had already passed through, or to feel anxious about those which might yet be in store for them.

They took up their march early, leading the goat, and walking slowly across the hills.

At the same instant both halted, as if struck with sudden fear, or, at all events, with some all-powerful sensation.

Each, at the same time, had heard a gun at sea !

CHAPTER XXIII.

A NAVAL ENGAGEMENT.

A GUN at sea! What did this portend?—assistance from friends, or danger from enemies! At all events, it was useless to speculate on the matter ; so both, with one accord, hastened towards the summit of a rock, on which stood a solitary palm, and gazed out.

But for some minutes they could neither hear nor see anything.

There was a red haze under the rising sun, which prevented them from seeing very distinctly, though they strained their eyes as much as possible for the purpose. It was early, too, and the sun itself was low upon the waters.

Suddenly a red flash illumined the sky, and a distant boom followed rapidly. It was a vessel at some distance. Both now, breathless and overcome by mingled fear and hope, seated themselves. They did not speak for some time, so absorbed were they in their feelings.

"I can see her sails," suddenly exclaimed Edward, "just under the sun yonder, like a huge sea-bird's wings."

"I cannot," whispered Loo, as if afraid of the sound of her own voice.

"There, too, is a second in chase, and the one in front is making directly this way," he added.

Loo, this time, was just able to distinguish the vessels as they rose rapidly, both having every available sail set. The atmosphere became clearer, too ; and as the sun lifted itself above the waves, the character of the contending ships became quite clear.

"'Tis the *Ocean Girl* flying before a larger vessel !" cried Edward ; "and yet I understand it not. The pursuer is not a man-of-war ; and I never knew Captain Gantling fly before a merchantman. At all events this may enable us to escape. We must make a beacon fire, and possibly the larger vessel may send a boat."

They rose ; and, with eager and trembling hands, began collecting wood, bushes, leaves, and grass, which they piled round the solitary tree on the summit of the rock.

This operation occupied some considerable time ; and when they looked out seaward again, the state of affairs had considerably changed. The brigantine was not more than a mile off shore, going, with all sail set, much slower than the larger vessel, which was swiftly overhauling the buccaneer.

The pursuing vessel was evidently one of those armed Indiamen which often beat off the largest French corsairs, and four of which, by advancing fearlessly in line of battle, caused five men-of-war, commanded by Surcœuf, to fly.

But now a change took place. Edward was narrowly watching the stern of the *Ocean Girl ;* a strange ripple behind, puzzled him.

" I see it! I see it!" he cried. " It is a trick. The buccaneer has a spar trailing behind, to retard her speed and draw the pursuer within reach of his guns. That man is the genius of evil ! "

His supposition was correct : for, while a heavy spar trailing behind, was hauled in, all unnecessary sails were also taken in, and the vessel stripped to her fighting order.

Then the sound of the drum beating to quarters was heard ; and, changing her course, the pirate fired a gun at the advancing vessel, which sailed on majestically, without making any reply for some minutes, when she also began to strip for the combat.

They were now very nearly within effective distance, on different tacks, neither showing any colours.

Next minute, however, the broad flag of England appeared at the peak of the large vessel, while a pennant waved from the masthead.

The brigantine showed no response, but next instant

a crashing report—that of two broadsides—indicated the commencement of the combat. Round with marvellous rapidity went the *Ocean Girl*—so much more rapidly than the square-rigged vessel, as to give the first fire—a raking one—which appeared to cause some confusion on board of the enemy.

After this, for some time all was confusion and smoke ; the two vessels approaching until they were wrapped in one cloud, the detonations of artillery, and lurid flashes, alone indicating their position.

" And this is war," whispered Loo, shuddering ; " this the way in which Heaven's beautiful ocean is desecrated by selfish man."

" War is a fatal necessity ; but this is not war. Here a pirate, after attacking a merchant vessel, has pretended to fly, and has met with his match. Victory to the trader is life to us."

At this instant the vast canopy of vapour moved slowly to the northward, carried away by the light breeze to which the wind had been reduced by the fierce and continuous cannonade.

The two vessels were locked together, and the pirates were rushing like a hive of bees on board of the Indiaman. From where they sat, no just idea of the carnage could be obtained, but they knew that it must be fearful. All they could make out was the flash of swords, the crack of pistols, and the hoarse shouting of the men.

" The pirate has met his doom," cried Edward, in a low tone.

The *Seagull* had evidently caught a Tartar. For, as the young man spoke, the whole piratical crew were hurled back upon their own deck, followed by the victorious enemy.

But the brigantine slipped from the grapplings and sheered off, lifting sail after sail with marvellous rapidity.

The other did the same, and soon, once more they saw the buccaneer in full flight before the victorious Company's vessel.

At once they proceeded to light their beacon, which in

a moment sent up a dense column of smoke, followed by a burst of flame.

They then watched with bated breath for some signal from the victor,—a single shot in reply.

But none came. Both vessels, cracking on all sail, continued on their way, until they were lost once more on the blue expanse of ocean, fading away like phantasmagoric shadows of the night.

" Gone ! all lost !" whispered Loo ; "cruel, cruel vessel !"

" Yes, but though the trader may not return, the buccaneer will," said Edward, sadly ; " we must keep a good look-out."

And so, slowly and sadly, they descended to their little island home, all their visions of beatitude quite departed from both their minds.

CHAPTER XXIV.

NEW ARRIVALS.

FOR some days they led a monotonous existence. The goat was tethered in some rich grass ground, and after the second day, the kids, which were quite big enough, were taken from her and placed in the paddock-like enclosure where grew the carrots, the tops of which they were extremely fond of ; in this way they obtained a goodly supply of milk. Edward went to the mountains to fetch the goat-flesh which they had left behind, and then quite listlessly they continued their labours for some time.

Though at first they had looked upon a short residence as no great hardship, the sea-fight, having aroused sudden hope in their breasts, had left them terribly disheartened.

It seemed to have snapped the last link between them and society. When would such another chance present

itself? However, youth is fortunately hopeful, and inclined to view the rosy side of questions; and by a
natural law of humanity, they were soon once more, to a
certain extent, reconciled to their fate.

Much time was spent in improving the character of
their residence, so as to guard against the rainy season,
which is very severe. The roof and sides were strength-
ened, not only with bark and staves, but by removing
creeping plants to the walls, which, growing with marvellous rapidity, soon made one bower of verdure of it, while
the tendrils, entering into every chink, served the purpose
of securing their work.

Though no signs of dangerous animals had yet been
seen, the nightly fire was kept up; and Edward never
forgot to replenish it.

One night it had burned low, and he came forth to cast
on fresh fuel. It was very dark, but still, as if wind had
never blown. He took up a large faggot of boughs and
vine sticks, which he cast on.

As he did so, he was startled by the sound of human
voices. Looking seaward, he at once saw a light dancing
on the waters, and the faint tracery of a vessel against the
back-ground of the sky.

It was unmistakably the tracery of the brigantine.

The sound he had heard proceeded from a boat's crew,
who were cautiously coming up the creek—he could tell
this by the slow motion of the oars.

He ascended the ladder which led to Loo's room, and
whispered her name.

"Who is there?" she replied, starting up. "Edward
—help!"

"Hush, in Heaven's name, Loo. Come down. There
is danger nigh at hand. Speak not until I tell you—but
come!"

He was obeyed; and next minute they were leaving
their hut, with no other part of their earthly riches but
the gun. With this in one hand, and leading Loo by the
other, he gained a dense thicket, to which they only
obtained access by crawling on their hands and knees—

and there they halted. Fortunate was it for Loo she had taken to stout male habiliments; she would otherwise have had her clothes torn off her back.

Scarcely had they taken shelter, when there was a rush of human feet towards the hut, a waving high of torches, and then a hearty volley of curses.

"There is the nest, but the birds have flown," said one.

It was the voice of Jabez Grunn.

"We must put our trust in Providence, for from man there is no hope," whispered Edward; "our island is invaded by the pirate crew."

Loo shuddered, but made no reply.

The buccaneers dispersed themselves around, beating the bushes, and venting the most awful imprecations on the fugitives, whoever they might be; but, finding this vain, they returned to the hut, and, making up a roaring fire, they proceeded to enjoy themselves.

Edward and Loo, retreating still farther into the thicket, lay down under the heavy foliage, and were soon fast asleep, despite the awful danger in which they were placed; nor did they wake until it was quite light. Not a moment was to be lost. The pirates were quite still, probably sleeping off the effects of their debauch.

Edward, in his journeys, knew of a rugged hill-side where there was a small rude cavern, and to this he intended making his way, there to conceal themselves until they found out the further intentions of the buccaneers. To reach this spot, they had to pass the station of the goats. These animals they secured, and drove before them, for they were now so tame as to make this quite easy.

But, though to the goats the hill-side afforded no difficulty, to the fugitives it was a most rude and arduous ascent. Danger, however, was behind; and, after much labour and many stumbles, they reached the desired spot.

It was a rude ledge, with some stones about, and in the rear there was a small but gloomy cavern.

K

Nothing grew near it but cacti, which, however, the goats eagerly devoured. When we say goats, we must premise only two, for one fell a victim to the ravenous appetite of the wolves.

A fire of very dry sticks in the cavern was not only not dangerous, but quite pleasant. It gave out scarcely any smoke, and that was lost in the crevices of the rocks. The two goats were secured in a natural pen by the removal of some rocks ; and thus they were prepared for a siege.

As soon as the rage of hunger had been appeased, both crept out to a spot where they commanded a good view of the sea, and at once discovered that Edward's suspicions were correct. The pirates were about to refit after their late engagement. All their stores were being brought ashore, while the carpenters were busy at work at the masts and spars.

This was a fearful blow.

Had they been drawn ashore only from curiosity, to find who occupied the solitary island, they might, after a superficial search, have departed. But as they would now have ample leisure to search the island, it was scarcely possible that Loo and he could escape discovery.

Edward, however, resolved to use every endeavour to outwit them, as he had no desire to return to the hideous slavery which must in future ever be his lot on board the buccaneer *Ocean Girl*.

The fact that Jabez Grunn retained the least influence, was enough for Ned ; besides, how could he trust himself to the hands of the murderer of his father ?

The pirates began their search of the island at once, and Ned could both see and hear them scattered over the island—shrieking, hallooing, and threatening, in the most obscene language, death and destruction to the intruders, if they did not at once surrender. After two or three days, however, this ceased, and all seemed to relapse into quiet, except that all hands were put to work.

Then Loo began to feel ill. The confinement, the want of exercise, and change, and food, told fearfully upon her. Her eyes became unnaturally large, her cheeks pale and wan, and her whole frame shadowy and weak.

Edward saw that something must be done, and that quickly.

The fourth night, after having with great difficulty pursuaded her to remain alone, he saw carefully to the loading of his gun, and began his descent towards the camp of the enemy. His design was to obtain some vegetables, and anything else that fell in his way.

Great caution, however, was necessary, as the pirates would be on the look-out. His only course was to pass through the thicket, and thus reach his own hut, now doubtless used by the chief.

It was close to the thicket.

After a long and tedious journey—but devotion will overcome every difficulty—he reached the desired spot.

The bandits slept at their camp-fires without one sentry. There was a light in the hut, but no sound of voices.

There was a small window at the back, for light and air, and this the boy buccaneer approached with intense caution.

He peered through.

On a rude bench sat Captain Gantling—haggard, worn, pale, his eyes sunk in his head, his cheek-bones protruding, and his whole look being that of one devoured with remorse.

He half dozed, his eyes fixed on vacancy, while muttered words escaped his thin and livid lips.

Before him, on the table manufactured by Edward and Loo, was a small roast leg of pork, some biscuit, and an untouched bottle of wine. These Ned Drake unhesitatingly transferred to the wallet he carried—in this committing a small act of piracy, under the circumstances, quite venial.

The captain put his hand mechanically forward to reach a horn cup of brandy, and as he did so his eyes fell upon the pale and menacing countenance of Edward, one instant seen—then away.

K 2

"More tortures: is he, too, dead?—and comes he to reproach me with my crime?   Will this never cease?"

His eyes fall on the table—he misses the supper, and at once the truth flashes across his mind.

"It is himself.   What mystery can there be?—how came he here?"

And he stepped out, just as the figure of the boy disappeared in the thicket.

"Ned Drake," he said, "come back; you are safe with me, on my word."

"Give me back my father," cried the boy, bitterly, as he darted away under cover of the gloom.

"Great Heaven?" gasped the pirate chief; "how can he have learned—who could have told him?   Mine enemy who has escaped me?"

And he re-entered the hut, to drink more heavily still of the brandy, which was now his only solace.

CHAPTER XXV.

THE PIRATE CAMP.

NED DRAKE felt a stern and savage dislike of the man supposed by the Admiral to have killed his father; and, much as he desired to leave the island, he preferred an eternal exile, to trusting himself within his grasp.   He knew the lawless character of the men he had to deal with, and instinctively he hesitated to put one so gentle and so much loved as Loo, in their power.

The moment he disappeared in the dark and gloomy thicket behind the pirate encampment, he walked hurriedly away.   He had left the young girl in a state of mind and body quite sufficient to excite alarm and anxiety, and he was fearful that she might be desirous to follow him.

It was nearly dawn when he was once again in sight of

the cavern, and there, as he expected, he found Loo, her face haggard and wan, watching for him with intense anxiety. She could hardly believe that he really had returned, after trusting himself near those dreadful men, who excited in her bosom the most intense fear and dislike.

"You surely have not been in the camp!" she cried, when the brave young lad showed his plunder. "What a fearful risk!"

"You would have died, Loo, had I failed"—and, without another word, he pressed refreshment on her, after which the imperious necessities of fatigue induced him to seek repose.

Late in the afternoon they awoke, and had a long conversation. Loo was anxious that they should remain concealed closely until the departure of the pirates took place, when they would be able to return to their home, and wait the arrival of some other vessel of a more respectable character. Edward reasoned differently. He was particularly anxious to know the intentions of the pirate chief. There was something in his manner that closely resembled remorse, and it might be useful to him to know whatever he could pick up by overhearing the captain's conversation with his men.

He resolved, therefore, to start early, and to conceal himself within hearing of the buccaneers, and, if possible, thus to learn their future intentions.

They must know that the island was inhabited, and by this time the captain must suspect by whom.

Would he depart without making an effort to find the fugitive, whose presence must have particularly puzzled him?

"Let me go with you," said Loo, earnestly; "it is so lonely."

"You will only ensure my capture," he replied, gravely: "alone, if discovered, I might escape : but together, it would be impossible."

Loo pouted, and sat down. She was a young lady not in the habit of being contradicted, but at the same time very sensible. She made no further remark, however, but making up a fresh fire, she prepared anxiously to await his return.

Ned only paused for the dusk to fall, and then boldly and fearlessly, he started on his journey.

The way was more familiar to him now, and he reached the spot about an hour after sundown. Creeping through the thicket, he again peered forth.

A very picturesque scene presented itself to his view. The whole crew were at their meals, seated round the little camp fire which had served to cook their repast. They were chiefly smoking; and, as their fierce and begrimed faces were lit up by the flickering light, they did indeed look a lawless gang.

Most naval countries were represented. There were Englishmen, Scotchmen, Dutch, Bretons, and Italians, with here and there a face which bespoke genuine African origin. These negroes—originally victims—become the most atrocious of villains when once corrupted—just as, in gambling-houses, the softest pigeon often becomes the cruellest rook.

They were talking in small groups, but only one excited the attention of Edward Drake.

Close to him, and within reach of his gun-barrel, sat the Captain and Jabez Grunn.

The former had been drinking, but not much; the latter had been drinking freely, but without much impression being made upon his great head.

Close by him there was a third individual, whose face was unfamiliar to Ned : he had been shipped, most probably, at Rio de Janeiro.

He was an undersized, bullet-headed, beetle-browed savage, with hair black and curled like a negro. His lips were thick, his eyes small and restless ; his form was that of a stunted Hercules.

"Grunn," said the captain, in a low confidential whisper, "do you believe the dead ever come back to meet us ?"

"Donner und blitzen !" cried the other ; "they say so.

But I don't know, and don't care. I'm more afraid of a good rope, or a volley of musketry, than of anything from the other world."

"I fear nothing in this world. But last night, wide awake as I am now, I saw and spoke with young Ned Drake, whose vessel must have been wrecked and all hands drowned."

" I wonder you did not see the ghost of all hands," replied Jabez Grunn.

" Do not joke," said Captain Gantling, wearily, " it was as I state. I wish the boy had never come aboard on this voyage."

" So do a good many," observed Grunn, drily. " The Jonah—he has spoiled our voyage."

That has to be seen. When our vessel is once refitted, and again we sail under the true flag, it shall go hard but I get you all ample prize money. It is not that I fear—I had my private reasons for securing that vessel. It is now too late, they have surely gone to the bottom."

" It's my candid opinion that the youngster is skulking about ; and if you will spare me and Jacobs here, see if I don't find the young rascal before we go. The crew owes him a grudge."

" Should Edward Drake be on this island alive, he is my prisoner, and no harm shall be done to him. Leave him to me," said the captain ; "but it is impossible. This hut must be the habitation of some runaway sailor. I shall turn in."

And he strolled away within the hut, the entrance of which he closed.

The two inferior pirates remained alone. These man were united by the bond of intense mutual ruffianism. They had, in days gone by, when on board another vessel, committed crimes which would have made any other men pass sleepless and miserable nights ; but in these true limbs of Satan, conscience slumbered.

" Who is this, and why does the captain feel so hurt about him ? "

" A young whelp whom the captain brought up from

childhood, and who has turned spy. I've missed him twice ; but if so be he's on this here island, I'll be upsides with him this time. What say you, Jacobs—will you join in the haul ? "

"That will I. Pity I haven't got one of my dogs. The thing would be done," said the newly enrolled pirate. " Ah ! them dogs is a fine institution. People talk about sporting, but b——t me if there's anything like a good man-hunt."

" We'll be our own dogs to-morrow. I know this island pretty tidy, and he's an artful chap if he keeps out of my way. Now, if we find him, I shouldn't wonder but he'll leave his bones on the place. I ain't particularly fond of his company on board."

" What will the captain say ? " asked Jacobs.

" I don't care a fig ; he's getting half spooney," laughed Grunn.

" He ain't like old Roberts," said Jacobs—a produce of Ratcliffe Highway—his father a Portuguese, his mother a blackwoman—" those were the times. He *was* like a free-booter. In his days many a rich bark was plundered, and yet no tongue betrayed the secret, for sunken ships and murdered seamen followed each deed of rapine, and that they never reached a port, was falsely ascribed to storm or some maritime calamity ; but he fooled us after all."

"That was some time after I left," observed the bigger ruffian.

" Yes : it seems that crime and cruelty palled upon him ; that some strange fancy for home crossed his brain, so that he secretly determined to abandon a rover's life. We had rich booty in gold, plate, and jewels, which he resolved to appropriate to himself, deserting the ship and crew."

"A pretty scoundrel ! " muttered Jabez between his teeth.

" He and a confederate packed the whole in parcels of convenient size, and going into Cuba to refit, they con-

trived, before the hour of distribution came, to carry all
ashore and sail for England."

"Ha! ha! ha!" laughed Jabez, "it was cleverly done,
and saved the men many a splitting headache and murderous quarrel. Fill, and drink to the success of our man-
hunt to morrow."

The other, nothing loth, willingly consented, and the
orgie continued.

CHAPTER XXVI.

THE HUNT.

IT was with a deadly and sickly sensation at the heart,
that Edward Drake listened to the words of these ruffians.
Had he been alone, he would not have cared so much;
but that Loo should run the risk of falling into the hands
of such monstrous caricatures of humanity, excited in his
mind the liveliest feelings of disgust and fear.

To him she was a sacred charge, and should her father
never survive the sufferings he endured on that inhospitable coast, he would be only too glad to devote his
whole existence to her, in any situation in life in which he
might be placed. Even if condemned to remain all their
lives on that island, he would not murmur, considering, as
he did, the terrible dangers and sufferings from which
they had escaped.

What was to be done?

It was quite certain that, with two such cunning and
resolute ruffians at their heels, they could not expect to
remain concealed in the small cavern in the rocks, as they
would be indefatigable in their search. A move must be
made at once.

While these thoughts were slowly passing through his head, he did not attempt to move. He was listening all the time to the conversation of the pair of buccaneers, in the hope that something they might say would aid him in his plans to escape. He was disappointed, however. Their talk was of their misdeeds and crimes, of which they boasted with that gusto and glee which appertains only to utterly lost humanity. Ordinary criminals, when overcome by drink, or in moments of excitement, may boast of their own wickedness; but in the calm still hours, when conscience pricks, they know themselves to be the rogues and fools they really are.

Fools, because a life of dishonesty is the hardest and most perilous that any man can follow.

By degrees the bandits lay down, and, ere the hour of midnight, they slept as men do who have indulged in potent doses of spirituous liquors.

Ned Drake now rose, and stole into the camp. Had he been older and less generous, his two ferocious persecutors would have been at his mercy. One blow of a knife would have settled the question. But, excusable as the act might have been, such a thought never entered the head of our young hero.

His intentions were very different.

Beside a tall tree that overshadowed a portion of the camp, he had noticed that the arms were piled, numerous large powder horns being also hung from the branches. Stepping lightly and cautiously between the sleepers, he soon reached the spot, and, without the slightest hesitation, he appropriated one gun, two large powder horns, and a bag of bullets.

Having made sure of these, he would not risk recrossing the camp. He determined to make a round: especially as, being loaded, he could not, if discovered, have been active enough in his movements.

As he stepped from under the trees, he noticed a slight movement on the other side.

It was Captain Gantling, who, being unable to sleep, had come out into the open air to smoke.

Ned Drake stood, inadvertently, in the full light of a bright and glorious moon, which, motionless as he was, gave him, if not a ghostly, at least a statuesque appearance. As the captain's face was turned full towards him, he was afraid to move. Hoping the other would soon turn away, he moved not a muscle.

"Away, offspring of the fiend!" suddenly exclaimed the pirate. "Why haunt me thus? Thou canst not say I slew thee. Away, accursed spirit—away!" and as he spoke, he advanced menacingly.

Several of the buccaneers leapt to their feet, and crowded round their chief. Among them were Grunn and Jacobs, who eagerly inquired what had happened.

"I saw him—there, standing still in the moonlight, motionless as a statue, and now he is gone!"

"'Tis the fever, sir," said the big buccaneer, who hardly believed that Ned would enter their camp willingly; "you are not quite yourself."

"Perhaps so," he replied, more calmly. "'Tis true I have been ill; and illness breeds strange fancies. Go, rest; I will watch awhile."

And he did; but no further interruption taking place, he at last retired to seek that rest which is soothing to the body as well as to the mind.

When, however, the discovery was made, that a gun and two powder horns and shot pouches had been abstracted, all doubt was at an end, and Gantling himself was forced to assent to the astounding belief of Ned Drake being on the island. This discovery did more to restore him to an ordinary frame of mind, than all the reasoning of his comrades and all the medicine he had been trying.

Meanwhile, Ned Drake had made the best of his way back to the cavern, which, however, promised no further security, now that his presence was known. Such men as Grunn and Jacobs have all the instincts of the hound, whilst, the island being small, it could by perseverance be searched in a very moderate space of time.

There was, however, no immediate danger. Ned Drake

had examined the neighbourhood pretty accurately, and had secured a path by which to retreat, at the first alarm. It led down a narrow ravine to a mangrove swamp, dark, damp, and infested by water snakes—a hideous class of reptile, but preferable to those who were on their track.

They reposed until after daybreak ; and then, letting loose the goats with reluctance, they peered out upon the stony track by which their enemies were likely to come.

But though they heard occasional shots in distant parts of the island, no one came their way during that day.

This was, they knew, only a respite. Fortunately, the goats, which were very tame, would not leave them ; so that they had their usual supply of milk, which, in the absence of water, was essential to their existence.

Long and weary were the hours of that watch. Both, usually so talkative and ready to amuse each other, were now moody and silent. They looked with horror to the probability of their capture by the ruffian crew, who, though on ordinary occasions obedient to their commander, took occasional lawless fits into their heads, and then mischief was sure to ensue.

All day they sat, retreating to their cavern only when night fell. They made up a small fire and resumed their seats. Neither had any consolation to give—why, then, talk ?

Presently a sudden bleating of the goats was heard, and Ned crept slowly out, satisfied that they had been startled.

The night was dark. The moon had not yet risen, but there was that baffling light which is so common in the tropics, by which he clearly saw two figures at no great distance, on the summit of a ridge, looking about them.

They were Grunn and Jacobs, who were now on the track, and had succeeded in finding some sign by which to trace the fugitives.

They appeared to be making straight for the cavern. No time was to be lost. Putting his finger on her lips, he took Loo by the hand, and crept up the side of the rock, satisfied that the smell of fire would betray the secret of the cavern. The way they had chosen was rude and difficult, but anything was better then falling into the hands of these atrocious miscreants.

In the eyes of Ned Drake, life was too sacred to be taken unnecessarily, but he resolved to use his firearms, rather than be captured. With this determination he loaded the guns carefully.

They were now on the edge of a swamp, quite a quarter of a mile from the cavern.

A loud shout proclaimed that the ruffians had found their late place of concealment, and Ned Drake shuddered as he reflected on the position they would now have been in, if they had trusted to the cavern. But no time was to be lost.

The swamp was filled with mángrove trees, which grew out of the murkey fen in all sorts of shapes, the roots invariably above the water. However, there was no choice but to clamber through them. The buccaneers were already scouring the rocky way by which they had come, but had not succeeded in discovering them.

The trees were so close together that their journey was performed with comparative ease, though the fatigue was great. At length they reached a small mound, where Ned Drake halted with the intention of passing the night.

Under the deep shadows of the trees, in the gloom of that strange spot, the young people seated themselves, with an earnest prayer to Heaven for protection and succour.

Then, in the earnest hope that they were safe, both slept; for youth cannot easily resist the imperious claims of nature.

It was morning when they awoke, though no sun penetrated to that secluded nook.

Hark! what sound is that? It is the cautious-whispered tones of the two pirates. They were close to them, and there was no choice but to make an open run for it. Whispering to Loo to come, the agile boy leaped from root to root, helping her as he did so.

With a volley of fierce oaths and exclamations, the bandits ordered them to stop. The pirates, however, were not so lithe and youthful, so that the fugitives were able to keep ahead of them, without much difficulty. Still, concealment was now idle, and some other course of action had to be adopted.

Ned Drake, in this fearful emergency, had to decide at once.

CHAPTER XXVII.

DEPARTURE.

THE work of refitting continued rapidly. The buccaneers, despite their fondness for revels, were too fond of money and the society of the dashing beauties of the isles, to waste much time. Every hour of daylight was therefore taken advantage of.

Captain Gantling interfered but little. He was really ill, and the fever that heated his blood, filled his brain with many and strange hallucinations. He believed himself haunted by the spirit of the boy, and he regarded the hunt by Grunn and Jacobs as an idle act of folly.

How could a boy whom he had left safe on board an East Indiaman, be on that desert island, where none but whalers and buccaneers were in the habit of calling?

It was thousands of miles out of the track of the transport.

He was thinking deeply over the matter as he walked up and down before his hut. All the rest were busy, and the sound of hammers was heard, mingled with the songs of the light-hearted workers.

Sailors are the most careless of human beings, and

go to work as readily as to fight, dance, or spend money

Suddenly a loud commotion was heard in the thicket, and then two shots from a distance.

All ceased working : while Captain Gantling turned round, and gazed wildly at the thicket, from which, next instant, two boys issued, one of whom he at once recognized to be Ned Drake.

"Am I awake, or is this some vision come to haunt me ? "

"Captain Gantling, I have reasons to fear you, perhaps to hate you ; but I prefer trusting to your clemency, rather than be murdered by that ruffian Grunn."

"It is the boy," gasped the buccaneer. "In the foul fiend's name, how came you here ? And who is this lad ? "

"We are, I fear, all that remains of the Indiaman," replied the youth, evasively.

"Ah, has my enemy indeed perished ! How happened it ? "

"I will tell you presently, captain. Here comes the bloodhound."

"Fear nothing ; go inside the hut. So, Grunn, you've hunted them up ? " said the captain.

"Yes ; and now I mean to do for the young whelp ! Come out of that ! "

"The boy is mine ; and shall never be hurt while I remain in authority ! " replied the captain, coldly.

"This is madness—folly ! The men won't stand it ! " cried Grunn, in a furious voice.

"They will have to stand it ! " continued Gantling, as he caught up a musket, "this is my remedy for mutiny ! " and he pointed the gun directly at the heart of the tall bully.

Grunn muttered some indistinct threat, and turned away to foment, in secret, the mutinous band which he headed, and which were now in a considerable minority.

From that moment no allusion was made by Ned Drake or Gantling to any cause of enmity between them. The young buccaneer knew how frail was his term of life, and how, for Loo's sake, he must keep friends with his old captain. He alone could save them from the villanous crew.

The captain himself dreaded an explanation. His old liking for the boy was very far from being extinguished. It was the more necessary to him, too, because in all that band he had no real friend or companion.

Gladly would he have resumed his confidential intercourse with Ned, but there was an impassable barrier between them now.

At last the vessel was ready for sea; and as no idlers were allowed on board, both the youths received rating as midshipmen. The crew were generally rough, and the captain feared for their safety, if they were allowed to mix with them; each, therefore, enjoyed the privilege of a state room in the officers' department.

Loo was thus isolated, and able to preserve the secret of her sex.

The vessel was now headed for the China seas, there to intercept some of the richly laden vessels, which were the chief prey of pirates and buccaneers. There was no part of the world better calculated for the purpose, there being so many islands, channels, and secret bays, where they could defy detection.

Several attempts had been made by Gantling to win something of the confidence of Ned, but, though the latter was scrupulously polite, and even deferential, there was no farther advance towards cordiality.

Gantling was much changed. He was moody and thoughtful. None of his old cheerfulness remained. He indulged in no more pleasant visions of isles of beauty, but seemed to think that Death had marked him for his own.

He spent much time in writing in his cabin.

About ten days passed; and, though the look-outs never left the mast-head, no vessel had come in sight. The crew began to murmur, and at last the skipper agreed to lie-to, with all sails furled, as the best means of falling in with some unfortunate trader.

Gantling was again confined to his room, and Jabez Grunn ruled the quarter-deck.

It was a calm, dark night, and the brigantine danced lightly on the waters.

It was the watch of the two lads, who always kept together—Ned, in every possible way, easing Loo of all trouble.

At last the darkness began to yield to day. Morning dawned gloomily, and a dense mist hung over the ocean, and shrouded the ship in vapour.

The thickness of the weather made Grunn anxious.

"Go up aloft, you lubber," he said to Loo, "and look if you can see a hole in yon blanket.

Ned turned on him.

"My friend is not a sailor, and cannot go aloft: I will go."

"Stop there, you powder-monkey! I'll let you see who is master."

"I will try," said Loo, in a faint voice, at the same time advancing towards the rigging.

"You shall not," cried Ned Drake, firmly; "the captain said so."

"Captain or no captain," roared Grunn, now in a furious passion, "if you don't stand aside, and let that little whelp obey me, I'll flay you!"

"Coward and bully!" said Ned Drake; "you dare not."

"Trice him up!" screamed the infuriated ruffian.

In a moment Ned Drake was caught by two powerful men, and tied up to the rigging.

"Spare him!" gasped Loo, falling on her knees.

"Hold your tongue, or I'll flay *you* afterwards."

"Ask no favour of the brute," said Ned, with a warning glance.

"A round dozen," said Grunn, addressing the boatswain, who stood ready with his cat.

At that instant, faint sounds, like strokes on a ship bell when a watch is changed, came stealing over the water. L

"Beat to quarters!" cried the voice of the captain, who, pale and shivering, stood on the quarter-deck. "What means this impudent interference with my privileges?"

Grunn muttered something about the boy being insolent, and then untied him.

"It was only to frighten him."

The haze began to disperse, the sun shone out, the morning breeze freshened; for a mile around, the sea was clear, the vapour in huge fleeces rolling off before the wind.

The captain swept the horizon with his glass, and, within a cloud bank to the southward, he fancied he discovered something darker than the mist.

Then another portion of the fog rolled off, and there, not more than two miles distant, and dead to windward, he saw a brig under easy sail. Her low black hull, and raking masts, told that she was anything but a trader.

Every man flew to his post, and sail was rapidly made; but their helm was scarcely up, when the stranger changed her course, and bore down upon them, and the rapidity with which canvas was crowded on her to the trucks, told that her crew was numerous.

No mist now remained, the sun poured a glorious flood of light over sea and sky; not a sail was on the ocean far as sight could range, except the stranger and the buccaneer.

The breeze freshened, and the brig overhauled the pirate rapidly.

Then the meteor flag of England was flying at her mast-head, and a gun was fired across the bows of the buccaneer.

CHAPTER XXVIII.

THE MUTINY.

WE left the Admiral, and such of his crew as had survived the wreck on the unhospitable coast, preparing to attempt an escape by means of a raft. It was their only hope, as doubtless no vessels ever willingly visited that rocky shore. To dwell there for any length of time would have been impossible, for not only were provisions very scarce, but the climate was fearfully inclement.

They must all have certainly perished during the winter months.

At the same time, the voyage projected was a terrible one to contemplate. Anything, however, was better than to die miserably in that desolate region.

The ship had gradually broken up, and the carpenter occupied himself in repairing the larger boat; while, from the wood of the Indiaman a stout raft was made, capable of supporting not only the crew, but the provisions, on which life mainly depended.

Since the disappearance of Edward and Louisa, the Admiral had fallen ill, and much fear was felt that he would never again lift up his head. The surgeon, however, did all in his power to raise his spirits and to restore his health. Bodily, he in part succeeded, but the blow was dreadful; and Sir Stephen brooded over his sorrows, in a way that strangely affected his mental faculties.

A strong sense of duty alone prevented him from utter prostration. He supported the captain, therefore, by his example; and every day, for a certain number of hours, he superintended the works.

The longboat was the first finished, and supplied with a mast, sail, compass, and as much in the way of provisions as its lockers would hold. The main store was to be placed on the raft itself.

This had a mast as well, with two large oars by way of a rudder.

Every possible exertion was made to have all in readiness ere the winter set in, and that season was surely and rapidly approaching.

The longboat was to carry the officers, ladies, and twenty of the crew ; the raft had to support nearly a hundred seamen, besides provisions. It was, however, very large, and buoyed up by all the barrels that could be spared. Still, when all its freight was upon it, it was level with the water. This was of little moment with hardy men, while the sea was calm ; but should the wind rise, it would be painfully disagreeable.

The day was bright, chilly, and sparkling ; the sky was almost cloudless, seaward, as the longboat towing the raft, sailed with a light breeze out of the harbour.

As in one hour the boat would have run out of sight of the raft unless they were attached, this precaution had been taken, the officers having no desire to abandon the men ; on the contrary, they were determined to abide by whatever good or evil future was to befall them, together.

The raft had three masts crosswise, to support the mainsail, close reefed, and this being a very large sail, they moved tolerably fast for so unweildy a conveyance.

The Admiral and captain had determined to steer as much as possible to the northward and eastward, as they might thus fall in with vessels homeward or outward bound. It was, however, soon seen that their probation would be long. It was the evening of the second day before they lost sight of the shore. With a light wind, and an unweildy craft, they did not make a knot an hour.

When properly under discipline, on board a comfortable ship, and with regular rations, sailors are not the most contented people in the world ; but under circumstances such as those we now describe, they are inveterate grumblers. Fortunate if, under the influence of black sheep, they are not something more.

The crew on the raft had no amusement, save conversaion and smoking, the whole store of tobacco having been distributed—a very wise precaution, as nothing pleases a seaman more.

They were divided into gangs or watches, under the command of petty officers. The boatswain headed one, and the gunner the other, each having selected his own party.

That of the boatswain consisted of the black sheep,—the late mutineers, the discontented in the late wreck.

There were about thirty of them who were quite ripe for any mischief.

Four days passed, and the wind rose slightly, becoming also rather unfavourable. The monotony was, however, still dreadful.

"Slow work this," muttered the boatswain to one of his cronies; "a blind sort of navigation. I don't think it bodes any good."

"But what is to be done?" asked the other in a doleful tone.

"Humph!—if thirty of the boys were of my mind, I'd soon see."

"What would you do?" continued the other, peering into his face.

"Well, you know, I'd have that precious boat to ourselves, and leave them as stuck to the raft to their fate—that's what I'd do."

"But how?"

"Humph!—if they'd come quietly here, well and good. If not, force must be used."

"I'm agreeable. This here funeral dodge don't suit me."

"Speak, then, to our best men. Not more than thirty must be in the secret. With that number the longboat will be in good trim."

"It's agreed. When shall we do the deed?"

"The sooner the better. I'll give the signal directly after dark. Let each man drop into the water, and dash for the boat. All who surrender can try their chance on the raft; all who do not—overboard to the fishes."

With this fierce and sanguinary resolution, the men

appeared satisfied ; the lieutenant going away and whispering to his colleagues what was expected of them.

In a couple of hours, the thirty had agreed to do the deed ; possessing themselves of the jolly boat, they might escape with some hope.

The boatswain remained with his back leaning against the mast, smoking, and occasionally moistening his lips with brandy and water, which was given out once a day.

He already chuckled over the probable success of his plot.

It was not his intention to be picked up by any large vessel, or man-of-war. They would all be guilty of mutiny, and punishable accordingly. It was, therefore, his resolve to piratically seize some small vessel, and enter boldly on a lawless career, too common at the time of which we speak.

The police of the high seas was carelessly kept, and the existence of many secret bays and coves, now well known, but then secret and retired, gave every facility to the lawless and reckless.

The great majority of the crew slept. To them this was by far the most agreeable way of passing the time.

Two men sufficed to steer the raft.

The boat was ahead about fifty feet, attached by a long rope, which lashed the water tolerably taut, but really doing very little service. The little vessel seemed to tug on, impatient of restraint, as if eager for liberty.

The boatswain was impatient of delay, but to face the officers in daylight would have been dangerous, had he attacked them openly.

It was about an hour before sundown, and the sea was agitated. Long billows lifting the raft, and making the men cling as it ascended and descended the slope, indicated that the vast ocean had at no great distance been much disturbed.

The sun appeared to go down angrily in a bank of clouds ; and darkness lay on the face of the deep.

Then a man slipped gently into the water, and, guided

by the towing-rope, took his way in the direction of the longboat.

Any one used to his figure, would at once have recognized Dirtrick.

CHAPTER XXIX.

THE ATTACK ON THE LONGBOAT.

AN hour passed : the sailors ate their frugal suppers, and then, after a careless look around, they lay down again to slumber, or sat in groups conversing, chiefly as to the state of the weather.

There was, however, one group, more numerous and careful, which by common consent had separated itself from the others.

It will easily be supposed that this was the band of the boatswain.

They were all armed with knives or handspikes,—the officers in the longboat having secured all the fire-arms.

But as they were about to attempt a surprise, this mattered not.

Most likely those in the longboat slept heavily.

At last the signal was given, and stealthily the whole body glided in the water, thanks to the darkness, without discovery.

But there was a marked difference in the trim of the raft, which was for a moment somewhat lop-sided.

It was so dark that nothing could be seen but the distant sail of the longboat.

This the men took for a guide, and every now and then they lifted their eyes, to see that they were going in the right direction.

The boatswain, a powerful swimmer, kept ahead, supported by one of his fellows, the man who had collected the gang.

"I say, Thompson," said the boatswain, suddenly, "where is the boat?"

"I don't see it," hurriedly replied the other, "what's up?"

"There she is," cried the boatswain—"by heaven she 's making off! She has slacked off the rope. We are tricked."

But at this moment the boat went round, and came dashing in their direction.

"Now then, all at once!" cried the boatswain; "spare them not."

The longboat, with all sail set, was now coming up close to them, and as it dashed in to their midst, every hand was stretched out to seize the gunwale.

Then came a sudden volley, and with a wild shriek the mutineers sank into the water, wounded, dying, or terrified.

The boatswain succeeded in grasping the prow of the boat, and in hitching himself half in, as yet unwounded.

"No, you don't," said Dirtrick, raising a handspike: "you're not wanted."

"'Tis you betrayed us," gasped the boatswain; and, dexterously avoiding the blow, he dragged the faithful sailor into the water.

They sank together—for one moment only, when they again appeared on the surface, clutching one another in a desperate death grip.

Both had knives, and both swam admirably; but they were compelled to let go their hold, for fear of sinking.

Then striking at one another with one hand, while supporting themselves with the other, they each sought a vital part.

"Take care, Dirtrick," said one of the sailors in the boat; "I'll shoot him."

The boatswain turned involuntarily, and seizing his

opportunity, the faithful follower of Ned Drake struck him a blow which effectually closed the struggle. He sank to rise no more.

The survivors of the rebels now turned towards the raft.

The longboat pursued its way until it was close to the raft, upon which the wildest confusion prevailed.

"What means this dastardly outrage?" cried the menacing voice of the captain.

"We don't know, sir," said the gunner respectfully, "no more than you."

"It was the boatswain's gang. He meant to leave you all, after murdering us," continued the captain; "be careful, as I must leave you."

"Don't leave us!" cried a dozen voices; "we will watch them."

"My men," said the captain, "I have made up my mind that, as a British sailor, I am bound to stick by you, and mean to do so,—that is, if you continue worthy of it. There must, however, be no more mutiny, no more attempts at violence. We have a fearful and dangerous journey before us. If once the raft were abandoned, your fate would be dreadful—therefore I say, be careful. If there are traitors amongst you, denounce them. I shall know what to do."

The sail, which had been lowered during this conference, was again hoisted, and in a few minutes the rope was again attached to the boat. All resumed their old positions, except that seven or eight men were missing.

The sharks doubtless could have given an account of them.

For some days things went on very quietly, but the weather began to change gradually. It became intensely cold; and, on the third day, they were visited by a severe snowstorm.

Fast and heavy it fell in huge feathery flakes upon the crouching figures of the men, who began to give way to utter desolation of heart. It hid the boat from the raft, and the raft from the boat; it muffled all sound, it mantled the sails with a white cloak of a pure unsullied colour, and accumulated in mounds and ridges over the cowering bodies.

The wind was light, but it was fair.

It was quite certain that they had drifted too far to the southward, and must now make all the northing they could, to reach a warmer climate.

It must be remembered that they were on the other side of the Line, and that the further they went to the southward the colder it became.

Nothing but the regular allowance of rum and brandy sustained them.

Hitherto no effort had been made to exceed the rations, the stern threat of the captain ringing in their ears.

Now, however, the men began to murmur and to demand double rations. The officers peremptorily refused.

Low murmurs arose on all sides, and men were heard muttering the most fearful and sanguinary threats against their superiors.

The petty officers grew alarmed, and quietly seated themselves, hauling on the rope until the boat loomed huge and ghastly close to them.

"What is the matter?" said a muffled voice from the boat.

"The men insist on having double rations of rum," replied the gunner. "They can stand the cold no longer."

"Give them double rations," coldly replied the old captain.

The men gave a loud cheer, and stood up in the cold, while the petty officers distributed the fiery liquid in tin pannikins.

There being eleven petty officers, the distribution was soon finished.

"Are they satisfied?" continued the stern voice of the captain.

"Quite satisfied, your honour," was the reply ; "only the tubs are empty."

"Exactly !" sarcastically observed the captain, "and will remain so while mutiny is rife. There will be no grog to-morrow."

There was at this a great cry, but it availed nothing, as the boat once more headed them.

All that night the men huddled together under the large spare sails which had been provided, and thus they were tolerably warm, especially as the snow lay thickly over all.

At daybreak the fall ceased, and a warmer breeze restored hope somewhat to them. They had providentially escaped any severe storm.

But provisions and water began to fail them, while the distribution of rum, brandy, and wine was necessarily small.

They were, however, evidently getting into a warmer latitude.

But salt meat, little water, and a small allowance of bread, began to tell upon them ; scurvy broke out suddenly and violently, carrying off no less than a dozen on the first day.

"It's all up with us," said one of the principal malcontents, as the bodies were heaved into the sea.

" Why ?" exclaimed several voices.

"Don't you see them gentlemen yonder," replied he, pointing to some horn-like points that rose from the water on all sides.

" What are they ?"

"Sharks ! We shall all be food for them soon."

"Better make them food for us," said the boy, laughing.

Without another word, he sought out and found a large hook, to which he fastened a good-sized piece of pork. The cord to which the hook was attached was then hitched on to one of the masts, and the bait cast into the sea.

The sharks, however, swam at a respectful distance

in a regular line of battle, as if quite sure of their prey.

About an hour later, however, a great splash was heard in the water, the cord was taut, and the raft shook all over.

"Heave away, my hearties ! here is a prize !" cried the delighted boy ; and in ten minutes more a huge shark was tossing and kicking on the raft, with such violence as to drive off all from its neighbourhood.

There is no animal more tenacious of life than this huge fish, and it was only by a dexterous motion that its tail was cut off, and then it lay quiet and bled to death.

A fire was soon made on the centre of the raft, on some iron plates belonging to the old galley ; and the shark, broiled and roasted, was by no means a disagreeable supper. All who where ill from scurvy enjoyed a slight respite.

CHAPTER XXX.

LAND HO !

BUT again all was gloom.

They advanced with the slowness of a funeral procession ; getting into pleasanter and warmer latitudes, it is true, but utterly unable to make out their whereabouts.

Water was out.

Even in the longboat there was scarcely a drop for the ladies.

Symptoms of insanity began to show themselves amid the crew, who eyed one another in a strange and ominous manner. It was quite certain that should starvation reach its acme, the last fearful resource of poor humanity would be adopted.

There was cannibalism in their eyes.

On board the longboat things were little better. The officers had certainly, by means of their steward, received on board some few of their own private stores, which proved salutary and pleasant, but already one lady and a midshipman had perished.

All were sad and gloomy. The horizon was swept every five minutes, in vain. No friendly sail came in sight.

They had been twenty-seven days at sea, and the hearts of all began to sink within them. They were now in a warm region, and the want of water was all the more severely felt by every one.

The women were merely the skeletons of their former selves; their faces were pale, haggard, and wan. Few complained. The hour for noisy ejaculation had not yet come—in a word, they were not *yet* mad!

It has been well said, that, in a civilized country, "hunger any man can conceive, but thirst none." With every convenience for assuaging the most natural of all human sensations, we cannot realize to ourselves the torturing agony which arises from the want of water.

Here they were doubly tried, for in the words of the homely poet it was—

> " Water, water everywhere,
> But not a drop to drink."

Agonized glances were cast at the sky; hopeless look-outs stood clasping the mast, and yet no hope.

Including the mutineers shot during the attempt to capture the longboat, forty-seven men had been cast into the deep.

What remained for the others but to lie down and die !

"Land ho !"

This cry, from one of the midshipmen who had clambered to the foot of the spritsail, caused everybody to spring to their feet.

A low dark line on the horizon became clearly visible.

What hope again rose in the bosoms of all, who can tell ?

It was just as a reprieve under the very gallows tree.

The longboat was at once cast off from the raft, and all set sail in the direction of, to them, the ocean El Dorado.

Those on the raft uttered curses both loud and deep ; but they availed not. The longboat was scudding, like some hugh bird of the ocean, over the surface of the waters, in the direction of what was doubtless some island in the midst of deep waters.

The mirage in the desert, when thirsty travellers, dying from want, behold a kind of lake, and rush forward to find it but a mist, never excited more hope than did this little plot of land.

It was only four miles off, and yet did it seem a hundred, such was the impatience of the voyagers.

The longboat was soon lost to view, except when something white, like the wings of a sea-gull, fluttered on the ocean.

Slowly and sadly the raft was impelled by sail and oar.

Swiftly and gaily sped the longboat. Soon did its hopeful denizens behold welcome trees upon the land ; trees that spoke loud-tongued of moisture—of water !

There was loud rejoicing on board the longboat ; everybody was again hopeful—even the women forgot their sufferings.

The land was so low, that they were upon it almost before they were aware of it, the striking of the bows first warning them of its unexpected proximity.

" A coral reef, by the Lord !" said the experienced captain.

Those who were only tyros in navigation, knew the full extent of this exclamation.

A coral reef, and therefore an island without water.

And yet many of these extraordinary islands are inhabited by a small population, who make it their perpetual residence.

How this happens, we may shortly explain ; that is, in another narrative.

" But the cocoa nuts !" said a sailor.

No more was said. Everybody strong enough leaped on shore, and with axe and cutlass began to slash at the trees, half a dozen of which soon lay upon the ground.

The nuts were wildly plucked from the trees, and opened. Everybody had one for him and herself.

Here was both meat and drink !

Those on the raft were not forgotten. As soon as the first rage of hunger was appeased, four sailors, with an ample supply of the kindly fruit, one of nature's choicest blessings, were sent to the raft, the occupants of which received the boon with deep gratitude at first, and then with joyous shouts.

Two hours later they were all ashore on the reef.

It was a little more.

One of those extraordinary mountains which rise so miraculously from the unknown depths of the sea, had rescued them from death.

But it was only a temporary boon.

The whole of the vegetation of the island would not keep them a week.

But that was quite sufficient to cure all of the scurvy, which was decimating them : a disease now only known on board a few Scotch ships of inferior quality.

The captain, however, now knew where he was, and publicly announced to the men that in five days more they would be on habitable ground.

This of itself was enough to cheer and rouse the spirits of men who, like all British sailors, were much more easily moved to mirth and merriment, than to sadness.

It was, however, differently fated ; for man proposes, but Providence disposes.

At the end of a week, and just when about to set sail at break of day, a ship startled them by appearing in the offing, not four miles distant.

The recumbent cocoa trees were soon brought into use, and a huge bonfire was made.

Five minutes after, a gun responded to the signal, and the tall ship, a three-master, hove to.

The longboat was at once manned, and Sir Stephen, with his officers and a small crew, set out for the ship.

As they approached, they at once saw that it was a man-of-war, and, thank heavens ! an English man-of-war.

Sir Stephen Rawdon smiled grimly. He could not help thinking that, however humane and courteous the captain might be, he would rather have rescued anybody else than an Admiral.

He determined, therefore, to be very reserved in his communications.

A midshipman who steered, and across whose mind some similar ideas had floated, completely spoiled his good intentions.

" Boat ahoy ! "

" Aye, aye ! " replied the midshipman.

" What boat ? "

" Flag ! " continued the middy.

Sir Stephen bit his lip ; the other officers stifled a laugh.

" Now my joker," said a petty lieutenant, astonished at so big an announcement from the longboat of a wreck, " no skylarking. Make a proper answer. What boat is that ? "

" Flag ! " again said the boy, grinning. " Sir Stephen Rawdon, Admiral of the China seas ! "

In five minutes more the miraculously saved officer was on the deck, and in command.

His flag was hoisted at the main, amid the loud cheers of the men, and the sincere congratulations of the officer whose authority was thus superseded.

As a rule, there is no more generous or unselfish being than the British sailor. The loss of the Indiaman with all on board had been reported at the Cape, but no promotions had been made in consequence.

CHAPTER XXXI.

THE BUCCANEER'S EXPLANATION.

HAPPINESS is relative. The Admiral felt deeply grateful for his escape with his crew and the passengers ; but scarcely had his feeling been indulged in, when other senti-ments assumed sway over him.

The loss of his daughter seemed—now that he had leisure to think of himself—to paralyze his energies.

While there had been something to do, he had held up. But now that he had a cabin to retire to, and could be, as it were, alone with his God, he gave way fully to his deep and overwhelming grief.

The vessel was bound for India—was, indeed, a frigate sent out to reinforce that very fleet of which he was once again the Commander.

A week brought them to the China seas.

They had had fair weather for a while, but now an almost dead calm prevailed.

At daybreak, the sun fell upon flapping sails.

No seaman required to be told that they were near land. The colour of the ocean showed him quite plainly that the water had shoaled, and that it was necessary to keep a sharp lookout —all the more that a thick hazy fog pre-vailed.

There was not an atom of wind, and the ocean had assumed the placid character of a sleeping lake.

The sails flapped, it is true ; but it was only from what the sailors picturesquely call the breathings of the morn.

All was soft, mild, and placid.

The Admiral and all the officers of the ship were on the deck, looking around them and conversing quietly, after their morning meal, principally, it must be allowed, about the wind.

M

A hundred stout and stalwart sailors were hanging on different parts of the rigging, laughing, joking, and speaking to their messmates below, in that low and respectful tone always assumed in the presence of officers.

There was little to do ; but the discipline of a vessel is not consonant with idleness. Officers must find the men something to do, or there would be no commanding them.

The duties of this morning were, however, trivial.

The Admiral, after some few words of course with his officers, stood apart, wrapt in deep thought. One might have fancied him anxious about the weather, from the way in which his quick eye roved from the deck to the light fleecy clouds that floated in the blue vacuum above.

"I think the wind is coming," said the captain, after some hours had passed.

At the same time an officer began to take the altitude of the sun. Having carefully, as far as the haze would allow him, settled this important matter, he announced that it was twelve o'clock.

"Then make it twelve o'clock," replied the captain in nautical phraseology.

The bell sounded at once.

Then the haze began to disperse, the sun shone out, and the morning breeze freshened ; for a mile around the sea was clear, and the vapour in huge fleeces rolled off before the wind.

"A sail !" cried a dozen voices.

The Admiral turned slowly round, expecting to see a merchantman lazily making its way under their lee.

He started and turned pale.

"By heavens ! it is the pirate ;" he cried ; "beat to quarters."

The order was instantly obeyed, and almost ere the tap of the drum was heard, the men were at their stations.

The officers then advanced, and reported that their several divisions were quite ready to engage the enemy : the topmen and sail trimmers were examined and found ready ; the shot flags and stoppers were seen to, the magazines were opened, the arm-chests emptied; while down in the hold, the surgeon began laying out his case of terrible instruments.

"All hands clear ship far astern!" was the next order given, and cheerfully obeyed, though little remained to be done.

The frigate now yielded to the breeze, and increased her velocity; the water gathered under her bows in a little rolling wave of foam, and the chase commenced.

Meanwhile, on board the pirate all was confusion.

Captain Gantling, after instructing his officers to make sail as rapidly as possible, ordered Ned, and his supposed boy companion Loo, into his own cabin.

The buccaneer was pale, but resolute; his very illness seemed to have disappeared.

"Boy," he said, "'tis likely this may be our last fight; I wish that we may be friends."

"How can I be friends with the murderer of my father?"

"I tell thee, boy, 'tis false."

"The Admiral asserts it."

"The Admiral lies!"

"My father—never!" said Loo in an indignant tone.

The pirate turned upon the supposed boy, while Edward drew the trembling girl to his side.

"So!" laughed the buccaneer, "this is the daughter of mine enemy."

"She is my ward, and I will defend her with my life!" cried Ned.

"Silence, boy—I will not harm her. But listen to me calmly. You assert that I am the murderer of your father. I will tell you the truth, and you shall judge between us."

He waved them to a seat. The way in which the flooring bent from its level, showed how the breeze was increasing.

"I was midshipman on board the same vessel as the Admiral and your father——"

"But who was my father?"

M 2

"He was Sir Edward Rawdon, the Admiral's elder brother."

"Then I——"

"You are Sir Edward Rawdon. But of that anon. Your father was a strict disciplinarian, and I, a somewhat light-hearted and merry boy, was fond of shore and of the many amusements it affords. After I had been in the service one year, I obtained a fortnight's leave of absence, during which I went home. I had many friends, and in their company I forgot my duties. That is, I stayed eight days after my time ; and when I rejoined my ship, I found that I was dismissed the service. On my knees, I implored your father to reinstate me, promising that the devotion of a life should repay the favour."

The buccaneer turned away to hide deep emotion.

"But I have heard a very different story," said Ned.

"Wait ! I was spurned, but after a while I was taken into favour again. The rest you know."

"I know that my father had reason for disliking you."

"He may. But why should he have persecuted me? That matters not. I had to join a desperate set of men ; I became a smuggler. One night, when on a desperate enterprise, I met your father. He was walking in his own park, which I crossed to avoid the highway. We came face to face in the moonlight."

"Scoundrel ! what do you here ? " he said boldly.

"My blood was up.

"'Tyrant and slave !' I replied ; 'now is my time for vengeance.'

"My pistol was cocked ; but, as he stood calmly and firmly, my heart misgave me. I could not murder him in cold blood.

"'I could slay you as you stand,' I said ; 'but I will not. You remember I was an officer and a gentleman once. Take this pistol, and let luck decide between us."

"He took my pistol without a word ; and we retired to a distance in the pale moonlight. When about twelve yards apart we halted, facing one another with looks of deadly hatred.

" 'Art ready, ruffian ? ' he said. ' At your answer, I fire.'

" 'Ready ! ' I cried.

" 'Hate nerved my arm, for the next instant he lay dead at my feet. The ball had been merciful, for it penetrated the brain. No sooner was the deed done, than my soul was more in arms against him than ever. Self-preservation, however, was imperious; and, at its dictates, I hurried away. In my hurry, I passed near the house, where, waiting for the baronet, there was a nurse, with a boy about two years of age.

" She was looking out to call the baronet to supper.

" Stealthily I crept behind her, and clapping my hands on your mouth, I hastened away with you, without being discovered.

" Then came rewards for my apprehension ; and for two years was I hunted over England by Sir Stephen— as if he were *not* glad to be a baronet and heir to a fine estate."

" He is not glad," said Loo ; "and will give up all to dear Edward here."

" Is this possible ? "

" I am certain he *would* do anything that was noble and generous," said Edward ; "but while he lives he shall enjoy that which he has thought his own."

" There is little time to lose, boy. I have been ill; and during my illness, strange fancies have come over me— sorrow for my misspent life, and deep regrets for the past. In this packet you will find my full confession, and the proofs of your birth. If Sir Stephen means honestly, they will satisfy him. Ned, through all these years I have loved you, and hoped to have died with you near me as a son. It was not to be. All I now ask is your forgiveness, since I cannot have your friendship."

" 'Tis given ; and now what will you do ? You must remember that Sir Stephen Rawdon is probably a prisoner on those bleak shores whence we escaped."

" The king's ship will seek him."

" Do you, then, mean to surrender ? "

"No: but I will restore you to the cruiser. If we escape, well and good : if not, we must fight."

He then led the way on deck. The wind was now strong and steady : the frigate was coming up with great rapidity.

"Out with the jolly boat !" said the captain sternly.

The officers stared ; but the chief was himself again, and they were in presence of a powerful enemy.

"You will descend into the boat," he continued, "which has a small mast. The sea is smooth. In half an hour you will be safe. They must halt to take you on board ; that time may save us. See you yonder mounds of earth ?"

Ned looked, and made out the points of two rocks.

" *We* can pass between them, but yonder frigate would strike. If we can reach them, we are safe. Farewell for ever !"

They were lowered into the boat, which was at once cast adrift. One glance—he was standing, with pale face and earnest mien, gazing at them—and they were gone.

CHAPTER XXXII.

CONCLUSION.

"WHAT is the vagabond up to ? " said the Admiral to the nearest officer.

"He has put out a boat, which is making our way," replied the officer.

"What on earth can he mean ? He has clapped on every wing, and yet would treat with us !" exclaimed Sir Stephen. "What is to be done ?"

"There are only two hands in the boat," observed one who had a powerful glass ; " and were it not impossible, I should say one was Ned Drake."

"In the name of the most merciful Creator," gasped the Admiral, " who is the other ? "

"A slighter smaller boy," said the officer. "I do not like to be sure, Sir Stephen ; but I think it is Miss Loo."

A loud shout from the officers and passengers of the late Indiaman arose.

"Heave to !" said the Admiral, in a husky voice.

The order was obeyed, and three minutes later the nephew and daughter were in the arms of the enraptured Admiral.

"But the pirate ? " said his captain, touching his hat.

"D—— the pirate !" was the hasty reply. "I beg pardon : set all sail in chase."

"May I speak to you in private, Admiral ? " asked Ned.

"Come this way, my dear boy," replied the other ; and he led him into his state cabin.

Ned told him all that passed between himself and Captain Gantling.

"Hum—not so bad as I thought. Well, duty must be done ; as I must hang him if I catch him, perhaps it will be better if he escapes. Come out, my dear boy."

They went on to the deck, and watched the scene. The buccaneer was now close on a wind, making for a cluster of low islands.

The Admiral's face brightened.

"Captain Howard," he said to the flag officer, "we must take soundings. Yonder fellow has a shallow draught, and can run where we should strike."

The necessary orders were given, and an officer stood by the leadsman to report.

"By the mark, seven"—that is, seven fathoms—was the first cry, which marked ample water.

Five minutes elapsed.

"By the mark, five."

This was also quite sufficient. The next report was looked for with great interest, especially by the crew, to whom the prospect of a fight was particularly pleasing.

"By the mark, four ; by the mark, three !" rapidly followed.

"Ready about," cried the Admiral, quick ! Forward !

All hands 'bout ship—hands by the topgallant clew lines."

In a few minutes the ship had turned away from that dangerous coast, and was running free to go round the islands.

By this time the pirate was in a narrow channel, and an hour later, it was but a speck of white upon the ocean.

Nor was she ever seen by any of our friends more, though they heard such a craft had been sold to one of the native princes of that strange and picturesque region. What became of Gantling, never could be ascertained.

Sir Stephen would not keep the title, though people persisted in calling him by it. Edward served with distinction in the war; and when his uncle was invalided, he went home, took up his residence in Kent, and.——

Well—married Loo, of course.

"Who else would have me," she said, when he asked her the question, "after running about like a distressed damsel with her knight errant?"

"I had some notion of that," smiled Edward, "when I asked you."

For which remark he received a gentle box on the ear, which he did not return—at all events, not exactly in the same way.

THE END.

THE YOUNG MIDSHIPMAN.

An Indian Tale.

BY PERCY B. ST. JOHN.

THE YOUNG MIDSHIPMAN.

CHAPTER I.

IN WHICH OUR HERO APPEARS UNDER VERY EXTRAORDINARY
AUSPICES.

DURING one of those really gorgeous and superb days which
the traveller meets with at times in the Gulf of Mexico, a
small but well-rigged schooner lay becalmed upon its ever-
vexed waters, which spread on all sides without sign of
land to break the monotony of the scene.

It was towards the latter end of the summer of 1835,
or in what is so expressively called the fall of the year—a
period at which calms are of rare occurrence, and in general preceding bad weather. The sky was for the time,
however, of that intense blue which is peculiar to the
tropics, and it was unshadowed by a single cloud, the sun
shining with all its dazzling brightness upon the smooth
but slightly heaving billows, that appeared to bask in a
flood of heat.

It was, we have said, calm ; indeed, not a breath of air
was stirring, and but for the long swell, remnant of wind
past or sign of wind to come, one would have thought that
upon that spot the cold northern, or hot and suffocating
south-easter, had never blown.

The captain, a passenger, and the crew, which was composed of four men, were standing aft, smoking, and were
conversing and speculating on the probable result of all
this delay

" Rather discouraging, Monsieur Grignon," exclaimed
the passenger , "three weeks out from New Orleans, a

dead calm, very little provender, and at least a hundred miles from Matagorda."

"Develeesh provok—ing," replied the Frenchman, shrugging his shoulders; "put tish tam culf is never vid hout de sacre calm. Mais! vat is dat on de vatere? Von *tortue-de-mer*, as I am lif."

Instantly bustle and activity were the order of the day; the boat was lowered from astern and brought alongside, and the captain and crew jumped in, despite the remonstrances of the passenger, who warned them that the wind was about to rise.

"Bah! bah! Monsieur Blake; dere is no vind can come so quick I not see him," exclaimed the laughing and light-hearted Gaul, as he sat himself in the stern-sheets of his boat, "but you keep a look hout hall the vhile."

"Never fear, Monsieur Grignon," answered the passenger; "I see mischief brewing in the south-east, and shall be on the alert."

Four vigorous arms soon bore the dingy to a distance in chase of the turtle, which, about half a mile off, lay asleep on the face of the water—the captain and his men pursuing their object with all the vivacity and thoughtlessness of French sailors, who on sea and land, in all parts of the world, keep up the character of their country.

The young man who remained on the schooner's deck rose with a dissatisfied air, scanned the horizon in every direction, lit an elegant German pipe, and then seizing the tiller, stood ready for any emergency which might happen, well satisfied that his energies would shortly be called into action, though, in reality, he expected nothing save a stiff breeze, which made him attempt no alteration in the craft's canvas.

Edward Blake, such was his name, was habited in the jacket, cap, and well-fitting pantaloons of a midshipman in the English navy, a costume which peculiarly became his stature and form. He was about the middle height, rather more slight than corpulent, though so nicely did he balance between the two as to be sometimes called stout. With a profusion of dark curls, a straight nose, a peculiarly well-shaped mouth, while an incipient moustache of great promise garnishing his upper lip, completed the outline of his personal appearance. His mental qualities it is our province in these pages to develope.

Edward Blake had entered on board an English man-of-war at the usual age. The son of a respectable private gentleman of moderate fortune, he possessed no friends powerful enough to ensure his promotion, a fact which had not come home to him with full force until a few years of naval experience had rendered him more thoughtful than before. The idea having once struck him, however, his temperament being quick and hasty, he became convinced that advancement was hopeless in his native country.

While under the influence of these feelings, he received a communication from a friend who had emigrated to America a short time before, and who informed him that an immediate outbreak was contemplated between Texas and Mexico, a navy was in active preparation, and finally, that if he felt disposed to register himself on the books of the young republic, a commission would be given him, with good pay, and the prospect of rapid promotion.

No more was wanted to inflame the hopes and desires of an ardent and sanguine mind like that of Blake, and at the age of nineteen he quitted his native land on a very brief notice, sailed from Liverpool to New Orleans, where, finding the *Dame Blanche*, Captain Grignon, about to start for Matagorda, he had taken passage, furnished with credentials and letters of introduction from friends in the United States to several of the leading men who had brought about the Texan declaration of independence.

Meeting with contrary winds, and numerous calms ensuing, they had been already three weeks out, and were at the moment we speak of, in lat. 27 deg. 50m. N., long. 95 deg. 30m. W., and consequently about a hundred miles from their destination. The calm to which we have alluded, had already been of considerable duration, the wind having died away on the previous evening, and it being now about mid-day.

Nothing can be conceived more vexatious and annoying than a calm at sea, excepting it be a storm of such a serious nature as to place life in jeopardy ; otherwise I would prefer half a gale of wind to no wind at all.

Whether Edward Blake felt all this I know not, but he sat quietly on the companion, his hand resting on the tiller, now watching the motions of his associates, and now the various signs of a coming breeze, which showed themselves in the heavens and upon the waters. At a considerable distance, the long billows appeared slightly agitated, a bank rose, the smooth shining and silvery appearance of the slumbering ocean was darkened—it was a south-east wind moving rapidly over the face of the deep. In a few minutes a slight air fanned the cheek of the young sailor, the lazy sails swelled, and the craft was gently in motion before the breeze.

Blake now naturally turned his eyes in search of the crew. At the distance of about three quarters of a mile ahead, they were seen pulling smartly for the schooner ; and Blake, therefore, using every caution, steered the vessel towards them, the breeze increasing every instant, until it became a matter of certainty that a storm was about to follow the treacherous calm. The wind, indeed, already blew in powerful gusts, dense clouds began to pass over the face of the heavens, and it was not without great anxiety that Blake neared his comrades, who appeared ready to seize a rope which towed astern, resting meanwhile on their oars in the course of the craft.

Five minutes elapsed, and it blew a strong gale of wind, the schooner labouring heavily, every rag being set, and Blake being obliged to remain at the helm; for to have left it and let go the halyards would have been to have given the *Dame Blanche* to the mercy of the wind and waves. Rising and sinking, and rising and sinking again on the furious and boiling billows, the schooner under her heavy press of canvas may have been said to have flown rather than to have sailed.

Presently a blast more heavy and impetuous than any preceding one, sent her bows under, the masts bending

and quivering like a whip handle, and the vessel appearing to plunge into a deep and awful chasm, to rise no
more. However, as Blake felt the blast diminish in force,
and could see through the dense volume of spray which
played around him, he gazed abroad, and foun l himself
alone on the face of the deep—not a sign, not a vestige
remained of the boat or of one of his companions.

Suddenly an object caught his eye, which, for a short
time, divided his attention, though he did not cease to
watch the helm with the greatest care and assiduity. A
barque, her royal yards sent down, her top-gallant sails
furled, her courses up, her spencer, gaff-topsails, jib, and
flying jib snugly stowed, was seen standing towards him,
close on a wind, under treble-reefed topsails, storm stay-
stail and spanker.

She neared him rapidly, evidently striving to get as
much to windward as possible in order to speak the
schooner ; the captain stood erect on the companion,
holding on with one hand to the cabin, which was built
above deck, and with the other grasping his speaking-
trumpet.

" What is that craft ? " roared he, making himself heard
above the howling of the tempest, as Blake shot under
his stern.

" ' La Dame Blanche,' of New Orleans. All hands
drowned ! " shrieked Edward Blake ; but his voice was
borne uselessly on the blast—it never reached its destination.

In another instant the barque was before the wind, her
spanker and staysail in, standing after the smaller craft.
The intention of the captain was, evidently, to make an
effort to save Blake ; but to the daring and undaunted
young midshipman it appeared that to get alongside the
ship was a useless risk, though with the addition of his
square mainsail, his comrade on the ocean was keeping up
with him.

" Can I help you ? " bellowed the jolly-looking English
sailor in command, having once more resort to his speaking-
trumpet

Blake rose, holding fast the tiller, giving his vessel now and then a dig into some hollow wave to lessen the rapidity of his own motion, and waving his cap in the air, he pointed, with a shake of the head, to the boiling waves between them, and then resumed his former position. A loud and prolonged cheer burst from the British barque, marking their admiration of his courage. The friendly vessel had only kept up with Blake by his manœuvring, and he no longer attempting to remain beside his larger companion, they parted, and our hero was once more alone on the face of the deep.

Hour after hour passed by, when, presently, by the sudden increase of the gloom, our hero considered that night must be coming on. Deep darkness covered the face of the waters, and alone in this raging wilderness of waves the schooner pursued its way.

The howling of the wind appeared more terrible, the clamour of the waves more furious, when, suddenly, a bright flash of lightning poured its brilliant and meteoric light upon the waters, showing the outline of every rope, and the whole features of a wild and terrible scene—a scene which is rarely gazed upon by mortal eyes ; when once gazed upon, however, never to be forgotten.

For Blake there was but one point of attraction, and that was a low jagged black line ahead, which, as flash succeeded flash, became at each instant of time more distinct.

"And now," said he fervently, as he grasped the obedient tiller still more energetically than ever, "I have overcome the raging tempest thus much, but by far the greatest danger is at hand. He alone, who has till now saved me, can bear me harmless through it," and casting a somewhat stern look on high, he gradually allowed his features to relax into calmness and placidity.

The young sailor sent up an inward prayer. What a time, what a place ! Could it be unheard ? "So soon !" muttered he, as dashing amid a species of whirlpool of breakers, a huge crested wave swept the deck, sufficiently betokening his proximity to land ; "so soon—now for it, then."

A tremendous peal of thunder, preceded by a brilliant flash, lit up the heavens, the sea, and the low outline of the coast, which our hero appeared rapidly to near. With a quick and keen eye, he had caught sight of one spot more low and flat than the rest, and for this he determined to make.

When darkness once more overspread the scene, a fire showed itself on the land, a species of safety beacon to the weary traveller. It was faint and indistinct, now it vanished entirely, and then it rose more vivid than ever. Presently the air was illumined by an extraordinary blaze; a column of fire shot up towards the sky, burnt brightly for a few minutes, showing plainly the outline of various forest trees, and then it fell, leaving only the smaller light which had at first attracted Blake's attention. He drew nearer and nearer, until at length, when apparently not more than a couple of hundred yards from the fire, which was now to his left, a violent concussion took place; the schooner grated harshly, and then struck with tremendous force, hurling him to the deck. His head having struck against the bunk as he fell, he became insensible.

CHAPTER II.

BLAKE MEETS WITH A CELEBRATED CHARACTER.

ABOUT an hour previous to the accident with which our first chapter concluded, a very different scene presented itself at no great distance from the spot at which the gallant schooner had happened to arrive, guided by the mad wind, which, having done its worst upon the waters, swept by to scourge the prairie and the forest, to drive man closely within doors, and the wild beasts to their most sheltered haunts.

An extensive grove of trees, somewhat scattered over the surface of the ground, stretched to within a few yards of the water's edge. To the right, about a mile off, was the Sabine river : to the left, the wide and apparently interminable prairie, now screened by the huge and sombre canopy of night. In the centre of the grove was a small hollow, surrounded on all sides by trees, but itself untenanted by any. It was about three yards long and three or four broad, and not more than six feet deep in the lowest portion.

At the nothern end was an opening, whence ran whatever moisture at times poured into it, and to this spot there was a slope from all parts of the hollow. Across it, from the eastern side, leaned a stunted and aged tree, almost touching a solitary and majestic pine which stood directly opposite to it, while dark masses of similar growth rose plentifully in the background. The pine here particularized, had been made to serve the purpose of a back to a blazing pile of wood which spread a lurid glare upon the surrounding grove.

Opposite the fire was a man, sheltering himself from the blast, behind the stunted tree above-mentioned, which had been made the central point of a species of rude tent; in the open entrance of which the individual in question sat quietly and contentedly gazing upon a ramrod that was thrust into the ground before the fire, and on which were spitted various long slices of venison, cut from a freshly-killed deer that hung to the topmost branch of the gnarled tree above his head. Within reach of his right hand was a long, old American rifle, which had apparently seen better days.

Its owner had certainly been younger than he now was, for though there was fire in his eye, and much strength yet visible in his long and sinewy limbs, he was, in reality, fourteen years over fourscore. His garb was half military, half senatorial—buckskin forming by far the most prominent material of his various articles of clothing. If we except a red flannel shirt, which he wore next his dark red skin, his whole dress was of deer's hide.

Close to the old man's feet was a little heap of hot ashes, which the hunter kept constantly renewing, until at length he ceased, as if satisfied with the result of his labours. He then spoke for the first time.

"Cap'n Harry," said he, turning towards the interior of the little tent, and shaking a form which had up to the present time been shaded by his own erect person—"Cap'n Harry, I conclude you've had snooze enough for any moderate man ; open your peepers and chaw. Supper waits ; and I reckon if I were one-eyed enough to jerk it into me, without callin' on you to foller my example, you'd call me the meanest thing on airth—an old 'coon dog barking at the wrong tree."

"Oh, I know you're death onto a deer, Colonel Crockett, but I sagacitate as how it 'ud take two like you to walk into the whull of that buck."

"I'm the yaller flower of the forest, and no mistake," replied the famous hunter of Tennessee, "but it 'ud go beyond the power of my internals to swaller that brute. But git up, cap'n, git up; a volunteer out west should be as smart as a streak o' lightning, whin a fight, a gal, or a supper is in question. When I was out wi' Gen'rl Jackson in old times at Pensacola, Talladago, and Jallisa-hatchee, I know it were a caution if I said no to ere a one."

N 2

"Ah, colonel," continued the individual addressed as captain, rising from his position in the tent, and seating himself alongside his companion, "we all calculate what you were sixty years ago ; he must be etarnally deaf who arn't heard tell of the bay filly. That was like a man who warn't afraid of the gals."

"That I guess warn't so smart as it might ha' been, seeing that wur whin I was arter my first wife, Cap'n Harry," said the old man, laughing, though not without a certain saddened expression ; "but thin have you got the right eend of that story ? I conclude not. So just scrapet him sweet potatoes out of the hole, hand here the ramrod, and while you're digging your teeth into the deer meat, maybe I'll tell you the rights of that anecdote."

"Right as a trivet," replied Captain Harry, "here's the praties, here's the meat, and now, venerable steamboat, go ahead."

"Go ahead I will, friend Harry, in a brace of shakes; but as to saying it 'ull be like a steamboat, I can't promise, since thims an invention I knows little of, and likes less. But do you see, whin I was quite a boy, I reckon not more than three-and-twenty, I fell over head and yars in love. This wur quite nat'ral like."

"Well, you know, Cap'n Harry, I reckon, that it wur all a frolic ; the girl wur pretty," continued the veteran, sadly, "very pretty, and I concluded to have her and she me. So we agreed I should ride over to her mother and ask her consent. I wur a mighty long time thinking of it, but one day I plucked up smart, mounted one of my master's horses, and rode over to whar I heard she wur on a visit to a friend's house. Well, whin I kim in sight of the log, I began to feel mighty cool about the heels, and hot about the head and shoulders, but it warn't to be thought I was a going to go back, so I rides up the yard, whar wur standing a power of boys and gals, and, says I, to mask my love scrape, 'Has any one seen a stray bay filly of my master's?' Well, they all roared, for it seems they all knowed I wur coming, and one told me I should hear inside."

"My heart in my mouth, I went in, and thar wur my gal. So I asked her plump if she wur going back to her mother's, 'cause if she wur, I would take her up behind me. She said, yes, directly, and after a drink of milk and a bite of cake, we started, I a-straddle, and she behind me."

"As I went out of the yard, feeling a little bearish about the knuckles, a fellow calls out, 'Have you found your bay filly now?' I wish I may be shot if I know how I felt; all I know is, I felt all over-ish."

The captain laughed, as he handed a fine large brown potato to his aged associate, which the latter accepted; and his bowie-knife being brought into use, huge lumps of deer were speedily disappearing, proving incontestibly that age diminished few, if any, of his faculties.

Captain Harry Coulter, as Crockett, in the true spirit of American politeness, called him, but as he was oftener denominated Mr. Henry Coulter, and oftener still plain Harry, was a man some six-and-twenty years of age, under the middle size, of stout athletic make, but with a thin haggard face, sunken red eyes, a bitter sneering lip, a complexion naturally fair, but on which climate, dissipation, and, latterly, exposure, had done their work. A brace of pistols and a huge bowie-knife were seen beneath an ample blue cloak, which covered habiliments much less elegant than his outward garb might have led an eye-witness to expect.

His trade, profession, mode of life, and character, are summed up in a word—he was a New Orleans gambler; one of that numerous class of individuals whose baggage consists of a shirt, a pack of cards, and a bowie-knife. For some reason, which he did not choose to explain, he had taken it into his head to visit Texas, and had fallen in accidentally with the celebrated Colonel David Crockett, who had himself travelled from New York, chiefly on foot, though sometimes a wagoner could induce him, by dint of great persuasion, to take a lift.

"Going—going,", said the gambler; "it's a tall tree

that, and casts a glare that might lead an Indian war-party further than would be pleasant."

"If there was any Ingin varmint in these parts," replied the other, without pausing in his meal, " I reckon you wouldn't find David Crockett outlying even sich a night as this, with a fire by his side large enough to roast an ox : he'd burrow in a hollow tree, man, and never mind the cold. But see, Cap'n Harry, that old pine is raaly going."

Of a truth, the sturdy old tree had seen its last days. The fire had eaten half through its expansive trunk, had then mounted aloft, caught the dry boughs, and was blazing in the keen blast, like some huge beacon in time of war. Every now and then the flame heightened afresh, and sent forth myriads of sparks amid the darkness around. Presently a loud crash was heard, the tree bent slowly, and then fell heavily to the ground, the flames being extinguished by the violence of the concussion.

"Bravely," cried Crockett, laughing ; " that was smartly done, cap'n ; that ere log, if pulled up to its proper place, will make a rare good back to our fire for the night, and will burn a first-rate time."

"It's broken in two ; snapped like a bow of pine-wood," responded Coulter, "and here's boughs enough to last a week. Bear a hand here, colonel, and we'll settle the matter in less time than one 'ud take to drink a quart of whisky."

" And that's two 'coon-skins," said the colonel, rising and assisting his companion to place the log in the desired position ; after which he once more seated himself before the fire, and surveyed the handiwork of his friend and companion, with evident satisfaction.

"What's that ?" cried the captain, starting to his feet, as a loud and heavy crash was heard on their right, at the same time seizing a rifle which lay beneath the tent, and rushing out of the hollow in the direction of the sound.

The colonel followed slowly, and when about half way, his companion shouted to him to return and bring a torch.

Crockett wheeled round, and once more approaching the fire, he selected from the heap of wood at its side a pine knot, which was soon ignited at the flames, and then borne aloft, serving excellently well the purpose of a torch. With this in one hand, and old Bet in the other, the great bear-hunter hastened forward in the direction to which his friend's voice led him.

Captain Harry Coulter, on leaving the cover, had observed a dark mass at two hundred yards distance. Close to the grove above alluded to was a narrow gut, leading into one of the lagoons, which communicated with the Sabine lake. On the edge of this bay lay a large two-masted schooner, with her mainmast and foresail set, her bow embedded in the bank, her larboard gunwale under water, her starboard side high above.

The gambler advanced to the water's edge, wrapping his cloak closely about him, and concealing his rifle beneath, for when out of the shelter of the trees, he found the wind furious and cutting in the extreme. Two minutes brought him close upon the devoted craft, over which the mad waves broke furiously.

By the dim light which prevailed, he saw something lying, as it were, in a heap upon the deck, which he judged rightly to be a human being; laying his rifle a short distance from the beach, he clambered upon the planks, and raising up young Blake, he supported him in a sitting posture, until Crockett stood over them both, and threw the glare of his torch on the pallid but gory features of the young sailor. Both the hunter and his companion looked on for a few minutes, curiously and in silence.

"A smart youth, as sure as ever I slayed a 'possum or a bear," remarked Crockett. "But how came he here? I wish I may be shot if I can tell."

"Nor I; but one thing's sure, he's a Britisher. This here jacket is that of a midshipman in the English navy;" remarked Coulter, examining the article of dress with attention.

"Well, I conclude you're right, since you say so, cap'n; but I can't say myself, seeing that service is a trifle beyant me. The youth's only stunned and will soon revive, I reckon. But it's a huckleberry above my persimmon to cipher out how he got here alone."

"Look in the cabin," said the New Orleans blackleg, hastily, as if a sudden thought had struck him ; and fastening the look of a basilisk on the breast of Edward Blake. Crockett assented, and, turning round, moved towards the place pointed out, with some anxiety, as if expecting that the interior would explain the secret of the vessel's presence on that barren strand.

Quick as thought Coulter leaned the young man against the inclined plane formed by the deck, drew forth his bowie-knife, seized upon something which encircled the youth's waist, next his skin, and cut it in twain. Thrusting it into his own breast, he replaced the poniard in its usual position.

"Not so much as a rat to be noosed out hereabouts," exclaimed David, returning from his fruitless search. "This youngster is flower of the forest here. Does he revive ?"

"He breathes audibly," replied Coulter, a little confusedly ; "suppose you take hold of his legs, and we'll carry him to the camp. The fire 'ull warm his blood and pull him up smart."

"Nay, cap'n ; I'll carry thy rifle, the torch, and my own Bet, a load I take it, for one of my years. I reckon you'll carry the lad yourself.

"Humph !" replied Coulter, contemptuously, "I conclude he ain't an elephant, nor an ox neither. Lead the way—I follow."

Crockett shouldered the two rifles, raised the torch—the blaze of which scarcely gave any light, so great was the fury with which it was blown about by the wind—and stepping on shore, he led the way towards the shelter of the welcome hollow. Coulter, tottering under his burden, followed, and a few minutes brought them once more back to their camp.

"I'll be catawampously chawed up by a Florida alligator," observed the gambler, depositing his burden upon the ground, "but though he ain't so very big; he's heavy as lead."

"Why, you see a dead man and a stunned man is much of a muchness—awk'ard to carry, and still awk'arder to bring too ; howsomever, we'll do our best, tho' he be a Britisher, and we raal true-born Yankees."

Without noticing Coulter's sarcastic smile, Crockett proceeded to fulfil his humane intentions. Placing Blake in as easy a position as possible, the old hunter took down a gourd from the inside of the tent, and having first washed the bleeding temple of the young man with water, he bound it up with some rags, carried for patching rifle balls, and then poured down his throat a small quantity of brandy.

Our young friend, who had been severely stunned and slightly wounded, opened his eyes feebly, stared at the fire, and at his companions. Consciousness gradually returning, he sat up and gazed for some minutes in silence on the scene around him. Mutual explanations ensued, and ere half an hour had elapsed, the excellent constitution of the young English sailor gained the ascendancy, and he sat before the fire, eagerly devouring venison and sweet potatoes. Exhaustion from want of food had, more than anything else, retarded his recovery.

"By the way," observed he, suddenly, "in a small locker of the cabin there is a liquor-case, in which are sundry bottles of excellent Irish whisky, which, being my private property, I freely offer you, my kind and hospitable friends."

"Irish whisky !" replied Coulter, with a bright flash of the eye, and, as a nicely critical ear might have it, the smallest trifle of a true Hibernian accent. "Irish whisky is first-rate, and by your good leave, Mr. Blake, I will conclude to light the pine-torch, and make a v'ge to the schooner."

"Darn my grandmother, but it's a smart youth," said Crockett, approvingly.

"Thanks, my good sir," continued Blake, addressing Coulter; "and perhaps while you are about it, you will just put your hand into the lower locker and fist the bread-bag ? "

" Consarn your young skin," again cried Crockett, ' but you're raal juicy. Bread's a rarity in these parts, and I reckon I could scarify another pound of deer's meat, if I had a biscuit or so to crackle with it."

Coulter hurried to execute a right welcome commission, and soon returned with three or four bottles of whisky,, a bag of bread, two or three lemons, and a canister of lump sugar, not forgetting three tin mugs.

" Cap'n Harry arn't lived in New Orleans not to larn something," said Crockett, chuckling ; " he knows a hare skin from a 'coon-skin, and whisky punch from the raw extract."

" I reckon so, Colonel Crockett. But, Mr. Blake, your late friend, Cap'n Grignon, knew what livin was, I can see."

" Colonel Crockett ! " exclaimed Blake, in his surprise, not noticing the levity of Coulter's remark ; " you don't mean to say I am in company with that famous hunter and politician, whose name is as well known in England as is the king's ? "

" As to that I can't say, Master Edward," replied the gratified hunter ; " but Colonel David Crockett I am, and that's the short and the long of it."

Edward Blake did not reply, but gazed silently and with undisguised interest upon the man who, above all Ameri-can celebrities, he had been desirous of knowing, that is to say, historical celebrities ; for while the English language endures, Cooper's fictitious Hawk-eye must ever remain the most deeply imprinted continental portrait ever presented to the imagination.

Coulter, meanwhile, was engaged in the manufacturing of punch, in which he showed that he was no mean adept, and proved himself quite ingenious in the way in which he overcame the obstacles presented to him ; so that a supply of hot punch was soon ready for imbibing.

" Raal spicy," cried Coulter, with an American oath, with which he continually interlarded his discourse, but which elegant universal expletive we spare our readers, since none can say swearing is now an English gentleman's accomplishment. "Raal spicy. I'm bound to get drunk to-night."

Blake looked up, startled at the blasphemous expressions of the reckless gambler. Crockett, however, laid a veto upon drinking as yet.

"Jist take a squint at thim horses, and shift their lariettes to new ground. I'll lay they've chawed up all the grass within reach. Business afore pleasure, and as you conclude to get drunk, it's a caution if I arn't ditto; and then the horses' ud be a case."

CHAPTER III.

EDWARD BLAKE SMELLS POWDER.

At the expiration of a twelvemonth after the occurrences of the events narrated in our previous chapters, which must be considered introductory, night fell upon the skirts of a long strip of forest, as two travellers cantered up and halted upon its extreme edge. The one, in dress and appearance, was clearly a white man; the other was no less certainly an Indian. Both were clothed with extreme plainness.

The aboriginal wore a red hunting-shirt, and leggings of mountain goat-skin, with buck mocassins, while a rifle and a small axe were his only arms. The tinge of his countenance and his peculiar features, alone gave token of his being a native of the wilds, which his accoutrements in no wise demonstrated to be the case.

The garb of the white man was similar, while his naturally fair skin, tanned by constant exposure, was not much lighter than that of his companion. In the stout bearded hunter, of marked features and sturdy frame, few would have recognised the stripling who, under the name of Edward Blake, has already been introduced to our readers.

Disappointed in his expectations of a commission—the navy not being as yet formed—he had started to pass the time on a long journey into the interior, during the course of which we take up our narrative.

Both seemed truly weary from the effects of their day's journey across the wilderness, and drew rein with every appearance of extreme satisfaction, such as is seldom more warmly experienced than when, after hard riding for some ten hours, one prepares to stretch the weary limbs, and, in the very changing action of walking, to find relief.

Behind them was a vast prairie—a very ocean of high grass—one of those picturesque and deep-clad rolling meadows of Upper Texas, stretching away as far as the eye could reach, and over which they had travelled since the morning. Before them lay a narrow opening in the belt of trees—a slight gap or break, leading to some forest path or woodland glade. At no great distance, on their right, and somewhat in their rear, an island of timber contributed to the scenic effect of the whole.

" Well, red skin," exclaimed our hero, " I really cannot advance any further, I am dead beat, thoroughly worn out, and must rest."

" Good ! " replied the Indian ; " here camp."

" I am glad of it," continued Blake ; " and if you would only converse a little more, friend Chinchea, we might pass another very tolerable evening in the woods. Tobacco is plenty, venison in abundance, and I have no doubt you will find water. Three things which, however incongruous to other minds, to one who has seen the elephant, they are of very serious moment."

Chinchea replied not, which, seeing that he scarcely comprehended what Blake said, was less to be wondered at ; but leading the way, and entering within the arches of the forest, they soon found themselves in the centre of a green glade, surrounded on all sides by a dense mass of wood. Not more than a dozen yards across, with tall trees, pea vines and thick undergrowth compassing it about, with a huge half-burnt log as a foundation for a fire, with a very mountain of dry wood piled up in one corner (it being a favourite hunting camp of the Waccos), it wanted but the presence of a rippling stream to render it the very beau ideal of a forest encampment.

"Good camp," said the Indian, with that sententious gravity for which his race are famed, leaping from his steed at the same time, an act in which he was speedily imitated by Blake ; "white man light fire—Indian stake mustangs."

"Agreed," replied the young man, speedily disburdening his weary animal of all trappings save his lariette ; and drawing forth a flint, steel, and a supply of spunk, a species of fungus which admirably serves the purpose of tinder (so provident is nature for those whose necessities call for aid), he proceeded to light a fire.

Blake in another moment was alone in the dark solitude of that gloomy little forest cove, on the very verge of the wild Indian country, with nought to depend on for liberty or life, save the sagacity and honour of his Indian guide.

Disappointed in his hope of obtaining an immediate berth in the Texan navy, Blake, ever venturous and fond of excitement, had started on an expedition to visit the tribe of aborigines to which his companion belonged. Blake was now a tolerable backwoodsman ; sanguine and enthusiastic, he entered into every feature of his new life with a spirit and animation that betokened the zest with which he enjoyed it.

From the huge trunk of an aged sycamore near at hand, whose boughs spread in leafy grandeur far and wide, he speedily drew a handful of dry Spanish moss, which, with dead grass and leaves, formed the foundation of his fire. Twigs, thin boughs, small bits of stray sticks, which cumbered the turf all around, served for the second layer, over which logs were heaped. A spark waved backwards and forwards in the air, and soon produced a cheerful and welcome blaze. This placed below the pile, and gently fanned, speedily kindled the whole mass.

Blake was too intent upon his occupation to notice the return of Chinchea, who glided to his side, and drawing forth several slices of venison, the whole stock of provisions they now owned, proceeded to broil them over the smoky fire. Blake, seated on part of the log against which the fire rested, looked on admiringly. His journey had been long, and without rest or refreshment the whole of that day, which made him regard the Indian's proceedings with a complacency which would have surprised our young Englishman at no very distant period of past time.

While, however, his eyes were thus pleasingly occupied, his active mind dwelt upon the singular features of his position.

Suddenly a cry so unearthly and horrible as to make Blake start with horror to his feet, came full upon their ears.

" What infernal whoop is that? is the forest alive with devils?" cried Blake.

" White wolf," said Chinchea, calmly, turning the unbroiled side of his venison to the fire, and examining it with an appearance of much gusto.

The restless neighing of the affrighted horses prevented the immediate reply of Edward Blake, who stood still, bewildered by the sudden nature of the surprise. Nothing can be conceived more wildly lugubrious, more unearthly or more horrible, than the howl of the prairie wolf at eventide. It booms across the plains, first in a low how! how! how! and gradually rising, it becomes at length fearfully horrible.

" You are right, friend Chinchea," said the young man, after a pause ; " but they do howl most frightfully. If the Comanche war-whoop be more horrible than that, I am in no hurry to hear it."

Chinchea replied not, though a grim smile played round his mouth ; and handing the meat to Blake to finish, he took up a large pumpkin gourd, and went out.

During his absence, Blake, speculating on the relative horrors of an Indian war-whoop and the howling of prairie wolves—very similar in nature to the jackal—finished the cooking of their meal, having during his wanderings become a perfect wild Soyer.

Chinchea returned in less time than Blake had expected, and as he laid his finger in a warning manner upon his lips, Blake instantly knew that something in the forest was of more than common interest, thus to disturb the calm serenity of the Indian.

"Come," said Chinchea, pointing to his arms; "bad man in forest, close by."

With these words, he beckoned Blake to follow him, and silently led the way to the wood pile, whence he, and in imitation of him our hero, took an armful of heavy logs and bushes, which they hastened to heap upon the fire, in such a manner as for the time completely to deaden its brightness. Over this they cast leaves and earth; which done, loading themselves with every article of their baggage, not forgetting the venison, they crept with noiseless footsteps towards the horses. Not a word passed; the white man knew too well the exigencies of the case to waste time in idle questions.

Breathless with excitement, his blood tingling with delight at the novelty of danger, Blake followed the movement of the Indian with his eyes, rapidly imitating him in his every act. Chinchea, as soon as they had laden their horses, again dived within the forest, passing the fire, and entering on what, to the young man's surprise, presented all the features of a beaten bridle path.

"Look!" said the Indian, in a breathless whisper, as, after ascending the side of a somewhat steep acclivity, they suddenly halted. As he spoke, Chinchea caught the young Englishman's arm in his grasp, and pointed through the trees. Blake at once understood the reason of their change of camp.

A small fire in the depth of a hollow revealed a party of no less than thirty men, some Indians, some whites, sleeping or watching. In every variety of costume, scarcely any two Indians were of the same tribe. While some were rolled in blankets, others less fortunate lay on the bare ground uncovered ; a few stood leaning against the trunks of trees, while one who, by his costume, some-what more military looking than any of the others, appeared to be the chief, was supporting himself with his arms crossed on the muzzle of his rifle. The lurid glare of the fire, in that dark and gloomy dell, fell upon the bronzed countenances of the men with singular effect.

It was with little surprise that Blake heard from Chinchea that they were a dreaded gang, commanded by a white man, who roamed about Texas, pillaging, and enact-ing scenes more bloody, ruthless, and horrible, than any of which the Indians were ever guilty.

" Blackhawk," said Chinchea, gravely pointing to the figure we have mentioned as leaning on the muzzle of his gun.

Blake made no reply, save by a slight nod ; he was busily engaged in scanning the features of this very man. They were familiar to him, or, at all events, lived in his remembrance ; that he had seen him before he felt certain, but at so distant a period it seemed to have been, as to leave the impression of its having occurred previous to his departure from England.

" Hist ! " whispered Chinchea, drawing the attention of Blake to other matters.

At the moment that the Wacco spoke, the blaze of the fire they had left burst forth at the termination of a low and dark vista of the forest, discovering itself, however, not to them alone. It was no faint mass of flames—they rose manfully and merrily, the more so from having been previously pent up.

" A camp ! " cried one of the party overlooked by Edward and his Indian guide.

" I see ! " exclaimed the chief, raising his head calmly, and then as soon as he had spoken, relapsing gloomily into his thoughtful mood ; " slip through the trees, and bring word who and what they are."

" It is time to be moving," whispered Blake, turning

towards the place where the Indian had stood, but which was now occupied by his horse only. In the close observation of the movements of the knot below, Edward had not noticed his departure.

Blake, however, was surprised, but not alarmed or distrustful of his guide; and satisfied that his absence was connected with some matter necessary to their safety, he turned his eyes again upon those who had caused so serious a change in their movements.

For some brief space of time, no alteration was manifest in the disposition of the extraordinary gang—their camp remained in its pristine quiet. Suddenly a rush, a sound like the heavy but disorderly charge of cavalry, was heard, and every man started to his feet. The tramp was at that moment plainly upon the eastern side of their camp.

"The horses are loose!" cried the chief, with a fearful imprecation.

"Indians!" exclaimed another.

"A stampede!" put in a third.

A rush then took place towards the coral which contained the horses, some few remaining on the outskirts of the camp.

In a few minutes after carrying out this daring manœuvre, Chinchea returned, and taking the halter of his steed in hand, fell into a cautious trot, in which he was imitated by Blake. In about ten minutes they once more emerged upon the prairie.

"Well, Chinchea," said Blake, "you have stampeded these rascals' nags, and how much farther do you intend going?"

"Camp in wood," said he; "Blackhawk no follow—too busy find horses."

"The sooner the better," exclaimed Blake, for that disappointment about the venison was a serious thing to a hungry man. "Proceed—I follow."

And he listened with intense anxiety for the sound of pursuit, and watched with scarcely less eagerness for the shortening of the distance, which was to be the termination of their journey.

O

At length, pushing away through the bushes and trees for some two hundred yards, another open space presented itself; and before the two men, at the distance of about a quarter of a mile, rose the clear outline of a hill stretching to the right and to the left as far as the eye could reach, rising gradually both on its right and left wings.

Edward felt surprised, and his astonishment was in no degree lessened when, advancing up this acclivity, the Indian guided him towards the very summit of the height. He followed, however, in silence, until at length Chinchea halted on the verge of a deep chasm, of very moderate width, not perhaps more than eight or nine feet.

The wind swept by, cold and chilling at that height above the plain, growling and moaning as it flew to bury itself in the deep gloom of the forest; and Edward was about to ask an explanation of his guide choosing this inclement spot for a camp, when the voice of the Indian made itself heard, in a series of cries, or rather howls, of a most peculiar and startling description.

" Why, Chinchea——"

The young man's speech was cut short by an event which added not a little to his astonishment. Chinchea's cries at first brought no answer, but, after a few moments, they were successful.

" Who calls at this hour?" exclaimed a voice on the other side of the chasm, in good and plain English, spoken with a purity which surprised the young sailor.

" Chinchea," replied the Indian; " Blackhawk in the woods."

" Heaven defend you, then," replied the voice; "I will lower the bridge, and then you pass quickly."

A creaking noise like the turning of a wheel, followed; and a huge black mass, which before had all the appearance of a portion of the face of the rock, came slowly down, and in a few moments offered a passage to the fugitives.

Edward Blake, between astonishment and weariness, was totally unable to speak; and following Chinchea across the drawbridge which had so unexpectedly presented itself, and passing quite silently, in imitation of his guide, two figures whom he met, he was in a few minutes dazzled and confounded by the blaze of a huge fire.

The log-house into which they had entered was of tolerably large dimensions, and composed, apparently, of one room.

To the right of the door was the fireplace, a deep hollow, piled up with heavy hissing logs of wood, which emitted a heat most welcome to the wearied Englishman, and creating a grateful glow in pleasant contrast to the cold he had so recently experienced, while the fragrant odour of the wood was most agreeable to the senses.

Chinchea had led away the horses, and ushered Edward Blake, alone, into this welcome shelter.

"Hush!" said the Indian, gliding in next moment loaded with the bedding, "master house—good man—but no talk of great country over water—bad done him there, he never forgive."

Chinchea then slipped away, without giving time for any questions, leaving our young adventurer still more puzzled than ever.

"My position is certainly a very odd one," thought he; but the buoyant nature of youth came next moment to his rescue; "I have, however, a warm fire, a roof over my head, a supper in prospect; let chance provide the rest."

Two individuals at this moment entered the room, whom we must pause to describe, though Blake did not discover all the minute features of the stranger until the morrow.

The one, of middle height, stout, and of singularly muscular frame, at once attracted our hero's attention. He was a man of about forty-five years of age, in the full enjoyment of the muscular vigour that is incident to his time of life. His face was thin and long, not even the intervention of a moustache serving to break the very glaring character of this defect. His eyes were small, grey, and suspicious in their glances; his nose slightly aquiline; his mouth wearing, on almost all occasions, a bitter and saturnine expression; while the chin, somewhat full and round, gave a look of sensuality to a countenance

which, in its main characteristics, was intellectual. His
forehead was the most remarkable feature about him,
being so high, as fairly to occupy much more than a third
of the whole length of his face. This gave him an im-
posing and majestic air, despite the rudeness of his
garments. His hair was thin and grey, a circumstance
which Edward Blake noted with much curiosity.

A green hunting frock of coarse materials, a common
cotton handkerchief round the throat, pantaloons of deer-
skin, with mocassins, and a wampum belt, were his attire.
A brace of huge pistols, a short cutlass, and a heavy
double-barrelled rifle, were his visible arms.

Behind this remarkable figure, and reaching no higher
than his waist, stood a man of some fifty years of age,
whose appearance was startling in the extreme. Without
any deformity of shape, his extreme littleness was in
itself a defect. Only four feet ten in height, with sandy
whiskers and moustache, as well as hair, with little hands
and feet, like those of a woman, his costume was exactly
similar to that of his companion; his rifle, however, being
of slight and elegant workmanship, and single barrelled.
The expression of his countenance was far from agreeable;
his eye appearing to penetrate your inmost thoughts.

" You have been in danger of the woods, stranger," said
the master of the house, somewhat gruffly, laying by his
arms, and advancing towards our hero, who was seated by
the fire.

" There you go, Philip," said the little man, in a shrill
voice : " always the same. You never saw this man in
your life before—I beg the stranger's pardon—but caution
is the first requisite in life—and you lay by your arms,
while he's studded like an Italian with pistols, knives,
and guns."

Edward rose, his eyes glancing fiercely at the dwarf,
while at the same time he disburdened himself of his
defensive weapons, which, from habit, he had retained.

" Jones, you are mad," said the man addressed as Philip,
turning round with a glance no less fierce than that of

our young Englishman ; "you seem to take every man for a cut-throat."

"I do, until I know the contrary," said Jones calmly.

"Sir, you are welcome," said Philip, turning contemptuously from the dwarf ; "I trust you will excuse the eccentricities of my friend, Mr. Jones."

"Yes, sir, his friend," repeated the dwarf, somewhat testily ; "and the first duty of friendship is caution for those we feel an affection for."

"Sir," replied our hero, with a smile, "I am a stranger, in peril of my life ; and as the Scripture hath it, you have taken me in ; I know too well the gratitude due to your hospitality, to feel for one moment hurt at the jokes of your companion. In fact, I am rather partial to humour and eccentricity, and am persuaded, Mr. Jones and I will, ere long, be very good friends."

"I never joke," said the dwarf, laying aside his arms as soon as he saw that Blake had left himself without a weapon, "Never." There was an ugly grimness about his tone which very strongly supported this statement.

"I rather differ from you there, Mr. Jones, and must say I think you excessively facetious. The idea, now, of taking me for an Italian bandit was rather comic—I, a true-born Englishman."

"There ! there !" muttered Jones, with a look of strange meaning, intended for Mr. Philip ; "you hear what he says—a true-born Englishman. Well, I never ! who would have thought any of the real islanders would have ventured up here ?"

"I was but following a very worthy example," said Edward Blake, with a smile.

"How ?" said Philip, somewhat sternly.

"Why," continued Blake, carelessly, "where two of my countrymen are so snugly located, a third should scarcely have any fear to venture."

"Humph !" said Philip, interrupting the dwarf somewhat fiercely ; "how learned you we were Englishmen ?"

"The fact is—excuse my ignorance," replied Edward, bowing, "I never heard of you at all until about twenty

minutes since. From Chinchea, however, I gathered that
you were my countrymen."

"Our renown is not very extensive," remarked him
called Philip, quietly; "few white men penetrate so far
as the Eagle's Nest, save trappers and hunters, whom we
always welcome. But come, here is Chinchea, and I
suppose supper will be no unwelcome break in the conversation."

This concluded, Blake entered fully into every detail in
connexion with Blackhawk—the position he occupied, and
the number and nature of his forces ; while Chinchea also
added to the stock of information, addressing the master
of the house in his own Wacco dialect, which the other
appeared to speak fluently.

"His design is certainly upon this place," said Philip,
after he had heard both stories, "there being no other
location within fifty miles. However, he shall have a
warm reception ; we are two dead shots—Chinchea is
another ; while you, sir," addressing Edward, "will, I
suppose, lend the aid of your arms ?"

"With pleasure," replied young man, who now began
to believe himself in reality in the thick of an adventure.
"I do not boast much of my shooting acquirements, but a
year's experience in Texas will always go for something."

"You may chance before sundown to-morrow to gather
further experience," replied the other ; "a skrimmage like
this we have before us, is no trifle in a man's existence."

"I shall summon you before dawn," said Philip, "and
would therefore advise your taking rest. Yonder hammock
will, with the aid of your blankets, be very comfortable."

"Many thanks," replied Blake, "but do I deprive you
of—"

"By no means," said the other. "Jones and I never
sleep in this house. We live here and give accommodation
to strangers at times. On the morrow, however, you will
find this but a small part of our residence."

With these words, the two men took their arms and
went out, leaving Blake and the Indian alone.

The latter was soon fast asleep before the fire, and

Edward, though little inclined for slumber, climbed into the hammock, wrapping his blankets round him, having the universal accompaniment of every Texan traveller in his mouth—a pipe of real Virginia—he passed in review the events of one of the most remarkable days of his existence.

This rencontre with Blackhawk, his flight and escape, his arrival in the mysterious Eagle's Nest, the strange character of its inmates, were all matters which crowded at once upon his brain. The manner of the two men puzzled him most of all. He could comprehend neither. It was clear they were anxious not to be too extensively known—above all to Englishmen. Their object it was not so easy to define. Doubts, even fears, crossed the mind of our young hero—but the reflection that he had nothing with him to lose, calmed all suspicion with regard to himself. Still, surmises of the most varied and strange nature entered into his head, to be chased away and followed by others only new, strange, and even absurd.

In the midst of all he fell asleep, and his heated imagination once set to work, with the face of Blackhawk (so familiar to him) and those of Philip and Jones, he dreamed a dream. The dream was—but, it being a record of the past event, which the reader must not learn at present, we are compelled to omit it.

CHAPTER IV.

THE situation of the Eagle's Nest was singularly and strikingly picturesque.

An isolated and bare rock, rose in the chops, as it were, of a narrow valley, and was separated from the sloping hill which fell perpendicular from its crest on the side facing the rock, by a deep chasm, through which rushed a stream, in its depth not unlike a thread of silver—it was so jagged and precipitous on all its four faces, as seemingly to be impregnable. The surface was uneven in the extreme, here a point jutting up, and there a deep hole sinking, and to no one would it have offered any features attractive as a residence, save to one whose principal object was security.

On each side were lofty hills, the branches of a common chain broken by the valley, the mouth of which the rock above alluded to almost closed. Covered by a deep panoply of forest of sombre and dark fir, they were too far distant to render their height of any advantage to a besieger, while the hill, the summit of which approached within eight feet, was so commanded as to be completely useless also to any foe, however daring and bold.

From the skirt of the wood on this side unto the Eagle's Nest, over the glassy plain which swept in a gentle slope upwards to the rock, the distance was about half a mile, its monotony broken only by a grove of fir, not more than fifty yards distant from the habitation, and which presented all the marks of having once reached to the very crest of the hill—the intervening space having been cleared in order to provide logs for building, and also for firewood.

The rock itself was surrounded on all sides by a wall of stone, rude and unplastered, while exactly opposite the spot on which Chinchea and young Blake had stood on the night of their arrival, was the drawbridge, which, when up, served the purpose of a gate to defend the narrow aperture left for the purpose of entry. Behind this, leaving first a small courtyard, was the log-hut occupied by the travellers, while on each side, reaching from it to the stone rampart, were outhouses. Behind this, and perched on the summit of a small table rock, was another edifice.

Like the first, it was formed of huge unsquared logs, without windows, though several loops served for that purpose; its roof was of treble shingle, and was surmounted by a bare pole, that had all the air of a flagstaff, even to the halyards destined to haul up whatever colours the owner of the retreat had a mind to unfurl.

The remainder of the surface of the rock, in all about an acre and a half, was composed of *corals* for the cattle, both horned and other, which owned the sway of the strange beings who dwelt in this sequestered spot.

Young Blake, at an early hour, stood surveying the features of the scene with a zest and interest which increased rather than diminished, as his eye took in all the varied beauties of the landscape, illumined as it was by the rising sun, that over all shed its crimson glories, as it crept slowly upward in the eastern sky.

While his thoughts were busy with the past, and his eyes glancing over the superb landscape which lay at his feet, a slight rustling at his elbow caused him to turn. It was Chinchea.

"Good camp," said the Indian, "better place—woods bad—scalp gone 'fore morning."

"A very undesirable consummation, certainly," said Blake, gravely ; "though whether this be a good camp is a question I have yet to solve."

The Indian grunted, but made no answer ; it was clear he did not understand the meaning of the young Englishman's words.

Blake made no attempt to enlighten him, but scanned him with a scrutinising air.

" Chinchea," said he, " you are my friend."

" Ugh !" replied the Indian, assuming an air of grateful remembrance—the origin of their connexion being
Blake's assiduity in attending him during a severe illness
at Houston.

"Chinchea remembers the day when his white brother
gave him physic in the great village ? "

The Indian assented.

" What is my name ?" asked the young man.

" Blake," replied the Wacco, pronouncing the word
with a strong emphasis on the *a*, and nearly omitting the
e, making it almost Blácke.

" It is," said the other ; and laying his hand on the
Indian's arm, he added, " I have a strange fancy, I know
not why, that my name should remain a secret with these
people."

" No business of Indian to know white man's name ;
Chinchea got no long tongue like squaw."

" But I must have a name. It would be unpolite to
decline giving one," mused Blake.

" Call himself Little Bear," grunted the red skin.

" A very fine appellation, no doubt," said the young
man, with a smile, " but under the circumstances I think
I shall adopt Brown."

" Brown—good," said the Wacco, whose long intercourse with the whites had made him an adept in their
tongues, " when tired call Brown—speak, and Indian call
him other name."

This was said with a quaint gravity that fairly overcame the Englishman ; he laughed outright with a heartiness which searched out the echoes, and brought them
playing back about his ears in merry guise.

" Well, I do not think I shall adopt many more aliases,"
said he ; " but Brown is a good travelling name, it leaves
no great mark behind."

While the young man yet spoke, the voice of his
host of the preceding night hailed him from the door of
the hut.

" Good morning, sir," exclaimed he, advancing as he

spoke, "what think you now of our Eagle's Nest, Mr. ——" he paused.

"Brown—Edward Brown," said our hero, with a slight tremor; "your position is certainly well chosen, and might be defended against vast odds."

"You think so," said the other, with glistening eyes. "I am glad of it, and as I fancy we shall soon try the experiment—hope your words may come true."

"I hope so too, Mr.——," our hero hesitated, imitating the other's manner to the life.

"Philip Stevens," said he, drily, and yet with a smile at Blake's manner.

"There! there!" muttered a voice at his elbow, "what occasion is there for you a bawling out your name in that way. There is no occasion for everybody to know your name, Philip."

"And if they do, no great harm is done," said Philip, fiercely; "my name is not one that I care much to hide. And if I did, in this country we are pretty much our own masters."

"There! there! you are so impatient," said Jones, advancing. "I did not mean anything, and only spoke for your good. Breakfast is ready."

"Mr. Brown," said Philip Stevens, turning to our hero, "the keen air of this lofty rock has doubtless whetted your appetite."

"I am already sufficiently of a Texan never to refuse a good offer," replied Blake, following his host, who led the way towards the log hut.

The Indian all this time had leant motionless against the stone wall, his eyes apparently fixed on vacancy, but in reality watching the countenance of our hero with jealous care. He had divested himself of every sign of civilized garb, and stood ghastly in his war paint.

When the young Englishman set his foot upon the threshold of the log hut, his surprise knew no bounds, though he did his utmost to conceal so very great an evidence of inexperience.

At the head of the table sat a young girl, while four

men, besides his host and Jones, simultaneously took their seats. A vacant place was pointed out beside the first, near Philip.

Behind, occupied in laying the various articles of food upon the table, was a glossy, sprightly, laughing-eyed negro lass, whose healthy appearance spoke volumes for the treatment she received.

" My daughter, Mr. Brown ; Captain Cephas Doyle, Mr. Brown ; my hunters," said Stevens, with a glance of peculiar meaning at the girl.

Edward muttered some incoherent reply, and then the whole party fell to upon the viands, Blake imitating them as much to conceal his surprise as to satisfy his appetite.

Dressed plainly, but in a lady-like manner, of marked beauty, there was a delicacy and grace about this young creature, which astonished and bewildered the Englishman, as by stolen glances he drank every feature of her lovely countenance.

Not more than eighteen, there was a sadness, a gloom about the expression of her face which added not a little to our hero's curiosity. She did the honours of the table with quiet grace, and seemed by no means inclined to open her lips, while apparently from being so used to strangers, she paid little attention to the new arrival.

For some time Blake spoke not at all, the others snatching an occasional moment to discuss the probabilities of a contest with Blackhawk and his gang.

Captain Cephas Doyle appeared somewhat anxious that the contest should take place, and his warm antipathy to everything in the shape of an Indian, not even restrained by the presence of Chmcnea, who calmly and silently glided into a seat beside Blake—caused our hero to survey him a little curiously.

About five-and-twenty, his face was rather broader than is commonly the case with your true Yankee. His eyes were small, grey, and keen ; his nose broad and straight ; his mouth large, with thick lips, while his chin was somewhat overburdened with fat ; he wore neither moustache

nor whiskers, appendages which are rarely to be seen upon
Americans at home, whatever may be the case abroad,
where Jonathan, we know not for what reason, is generally anxious to be taken for anything save what he
really is. His costume was much the same as our hero.

"What is your opinion, Miss Stevens?" said young
Blake, addressing the daughter of his host.

"Well, I conclude no female has much of an idea in
them partiklers," interrupted Captain Cephas Doyle,
hastily; "I reckon they are about ignorant on that
pint."

"My opinion, Mr. Brown," said the young lady appealed
to, without noticing the captain's interruption, "is, that
God made all his creatures in his image, and that while
he has given one colour to one, and to another a different
hue, he has granted a soul unto all. In my opinion, a
man is to be judged by his acts, not by the colour of his
skin."

The captain appeared not to relish this view of the
matter, and continued his argument with the more willing
auditors, or, at all events, with auditors who showed less
distaste for his views.

Edward Blake and Alice Stevens, the ice being once
broken, opened a *téte-à-téte* conversation, which was
speedily carried on with animation on both sides. Edward
was delighted with his companion, whose elegant tastes,
refined language, and sound knowledge, surprised him.
All the accomplishments of her sex appeared familiar to
her, while the rich stores of English, French, and Italian
literature were equally well known. As soon as the
young girl found that her neighbour was one who could
converse like a gentleman; who spoke without using the
backwood slang; whose education had been that of a
scholar; who had travelled much, and observed men and
manners—then all her reserve vanished. So animated
did their talk become, indeed, that they scarcely noticed
the departure of the greater number of their guests from
the table.

"Well, Mr. Brown," said Philip Stevens, a smile

playing upon his generally solemn features, "you and my daughter appear such good friends, that I shall leave you to make better acquaintance, while I and the rest see to such preparations as are necessary."

The two new friends started, nay, even blushed, while Edward replied, as he rose—"Nay, Mr. Stevens, though not a soldier, I am a sailor, and will not be absent when duty calls."

"I am sure of it," replied the other, with another smile, "and will summon you when needed. Meanwhile, my daughter and you can become, as I have said, better acquainted. It is seldom Alice happens upon a traveller who can converse with her—never, indeed, has she seen one who engaged her attention so completely."

This was said with some degree of playful malice in his manner, that forced a reply from Alice.

"Sir," said she, with a slight shudder, and relapsing almost wholly into her former gloom, "it is not often that an educated gentleman finds his way into these parts. Mr. Brown has unconsciously recalled to my recollection so much of my early associations, as to be a most welcome companion."

Edward Blake, *alias* Mr. Brown, bowed all due gallantry, while Philip Stevens, with a slight frown, called Alice aside for a moment, and having held a brief conversation in whispered tones, he left the hut, and these two new friends, *who had met before*, remained alone, utterly ignorant of the wild and mysterious tie which had ever bound their fates together.

CHAPTER V.

PIETRO, THE SCOUT.

ABOUT three miles to the west of the Eagle's Nest, is a spot very different in its characteristics from that which we have just described ; the hills and the wood in this instance being in close contact, the former even nestling over the latter, in an overhanging cliff some fifty feet high. Beside this rise the fir, the sycamore, the cedar, and the oak, their tall heads waiving over the summit of the precipice.

Between the skirt of the wood and the lower part of the rocky height was left a small space, which, being favourable for all purposes of concealment, and being protected from the weather, had often been the retreat of travellers. On the morning of which we have already spoken, it was occupied by a tent, formed by a few poles leant against the rock, and over which a large cloth had been cast. In front of this was a fire, round which several packs formed commodious and comfortable seats. On them were seated three men, of whom one was evidently a man of superior rank, while the others were as clearly his menials.

About sixty years of age, with swarthy complexion, hair as black as jet, eyes large, piercing, and fiery, his costume was that of a Mexican *caballero* of the first rank. His lofty steeple hat of white felt was ornamented with much bullion ; his jacket was striped with various colours, his pantaloons were covered with embroidery, while over all was cast a splendid *poncho*—a Mexican blanket.

"I wish Pietro would return," said the master—speaking in that mixed Spanish and Indian dialect which has, in the present day, been dignified by the name of the Mexican language—"for if he be right in supposing that men of evil disposition are in the forest, the sooner we reach shelter the better."

" Pietro is a clever lad, Don Juan," replied the elder of
the two domestics, " and I warrant me he was not mistaken."

" And yet a distant vapour may have been taken for
smoke," observed Don Juan de Chagres."

" Pietro is too used to the woods," said the old servant,
shaking his head ; " he has been amongst these wild Texans since he was a child."

" True—true ! " said their master, " and the more reason,
therefore, for our taking a meal.   Here comes the signora,
and we will breakfast."

The domestics rose, while their master quietly drew forth
a cigarette, and lighting it, puffed away, as if he fancied it
a necessary preliminary to the coming meal.

The tent opened as he spoke, and there issued therefrom
a young woman, in the full pride of her beauty, not a little
heightened by the fresh air which came murmuring through
the trees.

About two-and-twenty, a brunette, with large, speaking
eyes ; a mouth delicate, small, and rosy ; hair glossy, and
jet as the raven's wing ; her person had all the fulness
and rounded grace of womanhood, with the light airy step
of a girl.   The chief defect, perhaps the only one, in her
beautiful features, was the lowness of the forehead.

Her costume was the usual graceful walking dress of
Mexican ladies, who, though their darkness be like the
embrowning of fruit that tells of the richness within, yet
want the charming skins and rosy complexions of our fair
countrywomen.   The principal feature in her costume was
the *reboso*, or mantilla, which, flung gracefully over the
left shoulder, and passed across the mouth, left nothing
but the eyes visible.   This is all the more necessary, because Mexican female costume is but little without it ; one
garment only, besides the petticoat, being worn, braced
with a sash round the waist.

Taking her seat upon a pack opposite the old man, the
young woman signified her readiness to partake of the
meal which had been prepared, and which, despite the

rudeness of the spot, would have been despised by no traveller in any part of the world.

" Where is Pietro ? " said the lady, addressing the elder domestic, as she sipped her chocolate.

" Pietro is in the woods, signora," replied the servant, "the lad thinks he has seen enemies within the gloom of the forest."

" *Santa Maria !* " exclaimed the signora, with a start, "then why sit we here so calmly ? "

" It would be unwise to move, until we are certain in which direction our enemies lie. There might be such a thing as falling into their very jaws."

" This comes of these wild journeys," replied the signora, with a sneer ; " were we quietly at home in Santa Fé, there would be no such fears."

" There would be worse," continued Don Juan de Chagres ; "your own countrymen, when enemies, are more dangerous than even the Texans."

" *Santa Maria, madre de Dios !* " cried the young woman, as a rustling was heard in the bushes, " what noise is that ? "

" Pietro ! "

As the elder domestic spoke, a young man, half Indian, half Mexican, in the many-coloured garb of the latter country, and armed with a heavy short rifle, large pistols, and a small axe, stepped forth from the cover of the woods.

" What news, Pietro," cried the signora.

" Blackhawk is in the woods," replied the young man, with a slight shudder.

At the period we speak of, the gang of marauders commanded by Blackhawk had, by a series of atrocities of a most frightful character, gained a very widely extended reputation. Now appearing on the border settlements of Texas, now on those of Mexico, this gang defied retaliation by the swiftness of its movements. Indians, Mexicans, and Texans alike, were bent on its destruction, it being composed of outcasts from the three races, who treated all they met with as enemies.

P

" Blackhawk ! " exclaimed the old man, rising.

" Blackhawk ! " almost shrieked the young woman.

" Blackhawk ! " repeated the servants, in a kind of chorus.

" Bring up the mules," cried the master, "we will return upon our steps."

" To advance would be better, Signor Don Juan," said Pietro, who was satisfying his hunger ; " there is a white settlement not three miles ahead."

" A settlement," said the signora.

Pietro assented, and in a few words described the position of the Eagle's Nest.

" Doubtless, the post of these thieves," said the terrified signora.

" By no means," exclaimed the signor ; " I know the owner. It is Signor Filipo Stephano, a brave Englishman."

" Then," said the signora, rising, "let us hence."

The mules, eight in number, with five horses, were now brought up and hastily loaded. In less than a quarter of an hour, the whole party, with the exception of Pietro, were *en route*. Having given ample directions to the others, he remained behind, intending once more to creep within sight of the terrible gang, whose chief had given to it so unenviable a reputation.

Pietro stood in the skirt of the wood, watching the disappearance of his companions, and was about to turn to seek the shelter of the forest, when some sudden and inexplicable impulse induced him to glide beneath the shelter of the rock, and by standing motionless against its blackened and cracked surface, his body seemed to blend with its shadow.

Next moment the face of an Indian peered through the trees in the direction of the retreating party, whose forms were not yet quite concealed in the distance, and then, after a rapid survey of the late encampment, he stepped forth into the open space.

About six feet high, hideous as paint and ugliness could make him, naked, save round the middle, and armed with musket, cutlass, and knife, Pietro at once recognised him as an Apache, a tribe to which he, in common with most of his countrymen, bore the most deadly and unextinguishable hatred.

" Waugh ! " said the Indian, with much satisfaction, shaking his fist in the direction in which the fugitives had just disappeared ; and with this one word he advanced into the centre of the open space, and presently strode up towards the rock, where he stood beside the dying embers of the fire.

He was now but eight feet distant from Pietro, who lay hid behind a projection of the rock to the Indian's left. The young Mexican, however, was too experienced a woodsman not to know that, in the present instance, continued concealment was hopeless ; and accordingly he determined to have the advantage of a surprise, before the Indian could retreat a step, rushed forward, and gaining a position beside the enemy, in one bound, he grappled with the huge Apache.

Pietro's hands were encumbered with his rifle, as were those of the Indian with his musket, and in the hurry exhibited by each to gain a hold upon the other, their weapons met, crossed, and were blended into one, each clutching his own and that of his enemy with terrific force.

The Indian gave vent to his never-failing " ugh ! " and then the combatants paused, face to face, gazing intently one at the other.

Pietro was shorter than his foe, but he was muscular, and full of strength ; still, had not the other been enervated by drink, there would have been little doubt as to the superiority of the man of the woods.

Neither spoke, each striving to wrest the murderous weapon from his opponent's grasp.

They writhed, they jerked, they seemed about to tear their very arms from their sockets ; now Pietro cast the Indian half to the ground, and now the Apache would dash the Mexican from his feet.

Again they struggled, their hands hurrying themselves,

P 2

in appearance, in the iron barrels, until at length they slipped together, and came tumbling headlong to the ground, both guns exploding at the same moment.

The Indian sprang to his feet, and waving his heavy cutlass, rushed upon the Mexican; but Pietro, coolly cocking a heavy horseman's pistol, shot him through the heart, and he fell dead, with a yell that waked the dying echoes both of the forest and the rocks.

Seizing his own arms and those of his enemy, the young and victorious Mexican plunged at once on the trail of his master and mistress, whom he speedily overtook.

"Pietro, much fatigued, indeed completely worn out with his struggle and subsequent pursuit of his friends, mounted his horse, and having regained his breath, related what had passed.

"Those reports will bring the whole party to the camp," exclaimed Don Juan, "and our trail will be the next object of pursuit."

"We are much ahead of the ruffians," said Pietro, "and will gain the shelter, I hope, before they can catch us. See! yonder is the settlement!"

CHAPTER VI.

THE ATTACK.

WHEN Edward and Alice were left alone, a momentary embarrassment ensued. Alice seemed subdued and mournful, while the young sailor, much struck by the gentleness, beauty, and seemingly graceful mind of his companion, began to feel somewhat doubtful as to the precise nature of the feelings which were, even at that early stage of their acquaintance, rising in his bosom with regard to the guardian bud of the Eagle's Nest.

"Do you intend remaining long in Texas, Mr. Brown?" said Alice, first breaking the brief silence which followed the departure of Philip Stevens.

"I left England, and came to Texas with the intention of remaining altogether," replied Edward.

And do you still adhere to so rash a determination? said Miss Stevens, with the faintest shadow of a smile.

"At home I have no friends," observed Blake, somewhat sadly. "I have lost all—parents, friends, and by some strange chance, fortune itself. I am now a species of adventurer, a soldier, or rather a sailor of fortune, and, therefore, where my subsistence is to be obtained, there is my country?"

"But do you not regret England, your real home?"

This was said curiously, and with some degree of anxiety.

"Every Englishman does, who is worthy of the name," answered Edward. "Circumstances may render his native land an undesirable residence; he may find an easier living elsewhere; but no matter what his foreign success, he will ever find a moment to give to memory, and it will be of home that memory will be busy."

"Ah, Mr. Brown," said Alice, warmly, "I that know little of my country, that was a mere child when I left it, still yearn for England—for that land that my imagination paints as little short of a paradise. I see the beauty of this wild and romantic position ; I enjoy to the full the luxury of its pure air, its delightful scenery, its glorious mornings, and alas, as in life, its still more glorious evenings. Its sunrises and sunsets charm and delight me, but I ever feel some secret want here, which, I fear me, never will be supplied."

"And this want——" said Edward, despite himself, eagerly.

" Is companionship ; I know not why. I that live and have my being among hunters, trappers, and wild Indians, should by rights assimilate myself unto them, but I cannot do so. Their ideas and mine do not harmonise ; their conversation is distasteful to me ; their thoughts and feelings are foreign to my nature, and I feel alone."

"I comprehend you fully, Miss Stevens," replied Edward, after a pause ; "and can only ascribe your sensations to an innate appreciation of female dignity ; and to the fact that neither birth nor education originally fitted you for the wilds."

Edward Blake kept his eyes fixed keenly on the countenance of the young girl as he spoke, with a view to gather from its expression if his ideas were correct or not. Alice changed colour rapidly, and for a moment made no reply. Some chord had been touched, which vibrated to the heart of the listener.

" We are very new friends, Mr. Brown," said she, at length, with some little more of distance in her manner, " to be thus cross-examining one another's feelings. Supposing that, instead of thus speculating, I were to show you the secrets of the Eagle's Nest."

" With pleasure," replied Edward, not, however, without some slight evidence of pique in his manner, and rising at the same time ; " this romantically named habitation should have many curious features. But, believe me not impertinent if I have cross-examined you ; it has been because I have taken an interest in one whom I see removed from all fitting society."

"Impertinent! oh, no!" said Alice, turning, and giving her hand to the young sailor; "but I am peculiarly circumstanced, and you must not always ask me to explain either my acts or my words."

"In me, then, find a friend in whom to trust," said Edward, warmly.

Alice replied not, but turned again towards the door, and led the way into the courtyard. On a little rising mound that reached nearly to the summit of the stone battlements of the Nest, stood the whole party connected with that locality, gazing out upon the vast prospect that lay in front. Of these Miss Stevens took not the slightest notice, though Philip glanced with an approving smile towards the young couple, but opening a little wicket to the left, another courtyard, or rather division of the surface of the rock, was gained.

It was about ten yards square, and had been covered with a thin layer of mould, divided into beds by paths of shingle and pebbles, and was dignified by the name of Alice's garden.

The prominent building alluded to above, and which appeared the keep of the castle, formed one side of the young girl's garden, and towards this Alice led the way into the lower room. It was a small apartment, and, for the locality, well furnished with many a little feminine luxury. To the surprise and great gratification of Edward Blake, several books and a guitar lay prominently on a table.

"You have many things here, Miss Stevens, to which in the wilds one is usually a stranger," said the young Englishman.

"They are remnants of the past, of which some day you may know more," replied Alice. "The books are at your service, and, if you play, so is the guitar."

"I do play a little," said Edward; "but would, if you object not, converse of this wild spot."

The young sailor unconsciously took up a book, and it opened at the flyleaf.

A name had been in it, and more, an engraved one, surmounted by a coronet ; but much pains had been taken to erase and efface all sign of what had once existed. Struck with surprise, Edward, forgetting that the girl's eyes were upon him, fixed his glance curiously upon it, and endeavoured to decipher the name which had been blazoned on the page.

Blake thought he could faintly trace the arms and words, and as he did so he turned faint, while a deadly pallor overspread his face.

"You are unwell," said Alice, who had been a strangely interested spectator of this little scene.

"It is nothing," replied Edward, recovering himself, and laying down the book ; "but methinks, I hear a bustle without ; my assistance may be wanted."

"You will be summoned fast enough," said Alice, "but that you may see all that is going on, let us ascend to the roof of this block."

The sailor, whose ideas were in a complete whirl, obeyed, and preceded the young lady, knowing that all over the word that it is etiquette in going up a ladder.

It was a level esplanade, with four guns, one commanding each side of the Eagle's Nest. To mask their presence the port-holes were closed. Each taking one us a seat, the new friends sat down. Neither appeared much inclined for conversation. Edward was pondering on a long forgotten subject, brought forcibly and painfully to his mind, he knew not why, while Alice was dwelling on the somewhat strange manner of her countryman.

Blake was leaning over the parapet—his eye wandering carelessly down the slope towards the forest—when the Mexican party burst from the woods, making hastily for the Eagle's Nest. Both Alice and he rose with some anxiety, as the manner of the fugitives sufficiently explained the reason of their hurry.

"Look out, Mr. Brown," said Philip Stevens, turning towards the block, "warm work is commencing."

"Shall I join you ? " replied Edward.

"Nay ; you can work one of those carronades, I expect."

"With pleasure," cried Blake, all his energy and love of adventure at once effacing any other impression from his mind; "give the word, and I will serve them with a vengeance."

"Bravely spoken," replied the master of the Eagle's Nest, who seemed much struck with Edward's spirit; "and you, Alice, give the rogues a bit of bunting. We will fight for our lives under good colours."

Alice quietly turned to a huge ammunition-box, and taking therefrom a large bundle, proceeded to attach the colours to the halyards. Blake was so intently engaged in watching the progress of the fugitives, as they hurried towards the refuge which appeared to offer them protection, that he hardly noticed the young girl's proceedings. Presently, however, a rustling and fluttering over his head made him look up, and there on a red field waved the arms of England.

A slight tremor of pleasure came to his heart, such as we feel ever, when, in a strange land, a memorial of that country which gave us birth is brought before our eyes.

"You see, Mr. Brown," said the daughter of the outlaw, for such Philip Stevens appeared, "that we have not lost all memory of home."

"Indeed I do, Miss Stevens," he replied, warmly; "and if anything could add to my willingness to meet so foul a foe as that we have to contend with, it is the sight of that gallant, proud, and time-honoured flag."

At this moment, the fugitives being half across the prairie, the band of pursuers came whooping, yelling, and rushing from half-a-dozen different points of the forest; and from the quickness of their movements, compared with the slow progress of the heavily laden mules, they appeared certain to overtake them. Blake's heart leaped within him, for he saw that a woman was amongst the flying party, and the native gallantry of his character tempted him to risk all, to save her from the gang in pursuit. The Mexicans were evidently urging their beasts to the very utmost, but Blackhawk and his party were coming up apace.

"Stand by to lower the gangway," said Philip, in a voice which rang through the Eagle's Nest, and bespoke that now he was in his element; "get ready your gun, Mr. Brown; and when the Mexicans turn into the narrow path, give it to the rogues behind."

"Pray, Miss Stevens, go below," said Edward.

"Nay, Mr. Brown, while one of my own sex is in danger, I will remain. Ah! they are close upon them. Heaven preserve the poor lady."

As she spoke, Don Juan de Chagres and his party had reached a narrow beaten trail, which led directly to the entrance of the Eagle's Nest, and to enter which, they left what had formerly been the track of a ball from the gun which Blake had levelled at the pursuers. Next instant a loud report and a flash drew all eyes to the summit of the block, and a ball went ploughing up the earth in the very centre of the wild and ferocious band of the renowned Blackhawk. The whole party halted, and next moment the Mexicans were under cover of the rifles of Philip Stevens and his men.

"Served like a true man," cried the outlaw, approvingly; "that ball killed no man, but it saved one or two lives. They will now think twice before they attack us, so e'en come down and aid me to receive our new guests."

Alice had thrown a shawl round her shoulders, and assumed a straw hat, having added which slight features to her costume, she accompanied Blake towards the portion of the Eagle's Nest through which the Mexicans were, no doubt with heartfelt satisfaction, hurrying. Hearty congratulations were passed; and while Alice led the young Mexican away to her private chamber, there to seek quiet, and to recover from the severe fright which she, in common with the whole party, had undergone, a conference of the men was held, and various numbers were suggested as being the numerical force of Blackhawk. As, however, Pietro and Chinchea, who alone had seen them, agreed pretty well in calling them fifty or thereabouts, this was received as that against which they would probably have to contend; while twelve, including Don Juan and

Chinchea, comprised the utmost force of the woodland garrison. As the Eagle's Nest was well protected, and supplied in abundance with food and ammunition, while water could always be drawn up in buckets, the numbers would not have been so very disproportionate, had it not been for the desperate and reckless character of the men who composed the beleaguering force.

CHAPTER VII.

THE LIVE OAK CREST.

REPULSED once, the gang, which lay in the woods seeking the destruction of the Eagle's Nest, was little likely to attempt a renewal of the attack, until favoured by the dark canopy of night ; and the garrison of the stronghold having, as stated in the previous chapter, taken every important precautionary measure, occupied themselves in the minor details of backwood warfare—casting bullets, preparing patching, filling powder-horns, &c. As Edward had none of these duties to perform, and was, moreover, anxious to continue his acquaintance with Alice, he strolled towards the little garden, and stood at the gate.

Edward paused when about to raise the latch, as he heard voices, but recognizing them as those of the fair Mexican fugitive, whose dazzling beauty had not escaped his notice, he hesitated no longer, but pushed the gate open, and entered.

As he caught sight of them, Edward hardly knew which to admire most—the gentle, fair, and lovely Alice, all retirement, modesty, and blushing beauty ; or the proudly handsome and womanly Mexican, who moved with majesty, which, on paper, is usually given to queens, but which belongs, without regard to station, to peculiar form, figure, and feeling. They were conversing in Spanish, a language which, in its corrupted form, is familiar to every good Texan.

"I hope, signora, I do not intrude?" said Edward, approaching.

"Say rather that you feel you are doing us a favour, in deigning to throw away your time upon two forlorn damsels," said Margaretta—such was the Mexican's name—in a gay and open manner, such as an Englishwoman would scarcely have assumed after seven years' intimate acquaintance.

"Mr. Brown is a visitor like yourself," interrupted Alice, quietly, at the same time making way for him upon the seat, "and hospitality requires that we make him free of our castle; the favour, however," she added, with a smile, "is on our side, as this garden is rarely open to visitors."

"Perhaps I am intruding now," exclaimed Edward, rising, with a slight crimson flush on his face.

"Nay, you are quite welcome; indeed I am very glad you have come," replied Alice, laughing; "for we were just talking of the strange chance which had made the silent Eagle's Nest suddenly become so gay and bustling.'

"Gay, I should hardly say, since we are in a state of siege, which I can scarcely see the end of."

"Indeed," said the Mexican, somewhat eagerly, "shal we then be kept here so long? Do these terrible outlaws seem so determined?"

"Were we beleagured a week, ay, a month, it would little surprise me," replied Edward.

"Nay, perhaps, three months," exclaimed Alice, "fo though the gang may not be in sight all the time, they may prowl about until the depth of the winter drives then to the lower settlements."

Margaretta took no notice of these replies, and it wa impossible to tell whether she was pleased or not at the prospect of being shut up for so long a period in this wile and sequestered spot.

"But," said she, after a pause, desirous to change th conversation, "what of my party, where is Don Juan?"

"The old gentleman, your worthy father," replied Edward, "was taken very unwell just now. He has, apparently, over-exerted himself."

"Then, show me where he is, I will go to him," said Margaretta, rising.

"Nay, he sleeps, and 'twould be a pity to disturb him. Let us rather discuss how we are going to employ ourselves. I suppose, if not fighting all the time, we may manage to have one or two dances, and as you ladies sing, and there is a guitar, a little concert may be expected. I, faith, do not think we shall do so very badly. We poor sailors are exposed to much more hardships than that."

"You are naval, then?" said Margaretta.

"I hold a commission in the navy of the young republic, for which I was foolish enough to give up one in the British service."

"A—a—an officer, of course?" remarked the Mexican, hesitatingly.

"Of course," replied Edward, rather glad, in his somewhat rough costume, to be able to explain his rank. "I have the honour to be an officer, and a gentleman, though but a poor one."

"In Texas, that is the case of too many, to be any drawback," observed Alice; "and as long as you can sport, hunt, and fish, for your own existence, you rank equal with the president himself."

"But we are wandering from the question," said Edward, gaily, "I was planning amusement for you, and you run off to discuss the economy of Texan life."

"Allow me to run a little farther," added the Mexican. "I wish to understand the probabilities of our sojourn, and, in the first place, would ask who is Blackhawk?"

"Ah! who, indeed," said Edward, gravely.

"I can give little explanation," answered Alice, who saw that she was appealed to, "save that less than a year ago, a band, composed of the refuse of the white and Indian population, appeared on the frontiers of the country, doing deeds of robbery and murder. This chief, whose name is Blackhawk, is said to be a terrible fellow, without heart or conscience."

" Have you ever seen him ? " asked Edward.

" Nay, heaven forbid," exclaimed Alice.

" I have twice," added Edward, sadly.

" Where ? " cried Margaretta.

"Once a year ago, and again last night. On the first occasion, as Captain Harry Coulter, he robbed me of all I had, while insensible, and in the felon chief I recognized the same personage."

"Captain Harry Coulter !" said Alice, in a faltering voice. I have heard him spoken of. When we were in New Orleans, Mr. Stevens, that is, my father, had some connexion with him ; but they quarrelled, for he tried to rob my father. I never saw him, however.

" Strange fatality," exclaimed Edward ; but that man's face is as familiar to me as a youthful dream. I know not why it is, but I often catch myself dwelling on his face, in your presence more than at any other time."

" Surely I am not like the monster ? " said Alice, with a laugh.

" Mr. Brown is very gallant," added Margaretta, merrily, to say that the presence of a lady reminds him of a bandit."

" Mr. Brown," exclaimed the full rich voice of Philip Stevens, "dinner is ready ; if the ladies be at hand, tell them as much."

The summons was obeyed, and the whole party were speedily congregated together, with the exception of Don Juan ; but Cephas Doyle and Jones stood apart as Blake entered, eyeing him with a scowl which showed how little favour he had found in their sight. He heeded them not, however, being fully occupied in seating his fair companions. The dinner was profuse and excellent, as usual in the backwoods—indeed it was more so than seemed wise with a siege before them.

" I think, Mr. Stevens," remarked Edward, " that considering we are likely to be confined here some time, it would have been better, had this ample store been somewhat husbanded."

"Nay, you would not have me stint my guests," rejoined the other, gaily, "especially with such a store as I have to back me. Think not that I have been taken unawares; I have foreseen some such contingency, and have provided for it."

"There! there!" cried Jones, with a scared countenance, "what business have the gentlemen to know that you expected anything of the kind?"

"Don't talk at random," replied Philip, with ill-disguised irritation; "mind your dinner, and leave us to converse as we please. You must excuse him, Mr. Brown, but in his youth he had a fright which he has never recovered. It has rendered him timid ever since."

Alice turned pale at these words, which were said with a calm and bitter sarcasm, before which Jones quailed.

"To the walls!" shouted a sentry from without, at this point of the meal, which cry being followed up by a discharge of gunshot from half-a-dozen commanding points, the whole garrison rushed to defend the works, leaving the women sole tenants of the apartment.

On reaching the open air, Blackhawk and his gang were found to have occupied every available position round the Eagle's Nest. Behind the smouldering trees— on rocks around, seemingly inaccessible, it was clear they had crept; for though, after the first discharge, not a living being could be seen, yet the body of a sentry riddled with musket shot, showed how near and how numerous must have been the volley.

Blake gazed with horror on the bleeding corpse. It was his first sight of blood, and his impression was of a character which at once raised his feelings to a pitch of wild excitement that he had never known before.

"Keep close every man," said Philip, sternly; "this bloody work is begun in good earnest, and with the extermination of one party, it will alone end."

"You, Jones and Doyle, keep the block," he added, after a pause, "and let not a head be seen without firing. They must be met warmly, or we shall have them charging to our very gates. You, William," addressing a tall youth with a huge rifle, "take the Mexicans, and scatter them at the loops around the gate. The rest of you, except Mr. Brown and Chinchea, post yourselves as best you may. First, however, remove the body where the women may not see it—we will bury it to-night."

" With others, perchance," said Brown, in a low, but firm voice.

" Perchance not one may remain to do it," answered Philip, with emotion ; but come, I will take you to my council-chamber ; and there, while we guard that side, we can discuss our plans of defence."

Creeping cautiously along the wall of the Nest, Philip Stevens, followed by Edward and Chinchea, passed the door of the room where they had been dining, and entering a passage, they soon found themselves in a rude bed-chamber—that in which Don Juan slept.

It had two doors, while as many had been passed in the passage. One to the left led into the garden, and could be seen from the common room, while the other, which opened into a small apartment, was entered by the party, and Blake now found that he had reached the very edge of the cliff on that side, and that a small and narrow window looked out upon a singular and striking scene.

" Here we are, Mr. Brown, on the summit of the Eagle's Nest," said Stevens ; " look out and you will gaze upon a view rarely surpassed in this part of the world."

And at the first glance Edward grew dizzy. Sheer perpendicular down, almost two hundred feet, went the rock, with a piece shelving outwards, about a dozen yards below ; while a gushing stream came tumbling from the opposite side, and fell in white mist into the depths beneath, running round the Nest in two branches, like a ditch.

About a hundred yards across, but towering fifty feet above the little fort, was the summit of the opposite rock, crowned by a covert of live oak and pine, that waved majestically in the breeze.

Scarcely had Edward put his head outside the loop, and taken a hasty view, than Stevens called him away.

"A rifle carries far and true," said Philip, "and if the vermin are not already on yonder rock, they soon will be."

"A lovely scene, truly," mused Edward ; "pity that it should be marred by crime and the struggles of man against man."

"Blackhawk on rock," said Chinchea ; "him gun point at Nest."

"Say you so !" exclaimed Stevens, and running to the side, he threw open a window overlooking the garden. "Jones," he cried, "stoop low and keep so. The vermin are on the Live Oak Crest—make it too hot to hold them."

"I see you are fully prepared for every contingency," observed Edward ; "but, seriously, the contest grows warm, and to be candid, are we strong enough to keep this place against so many ? "

"We are not," replied Stevens, coldly.

"Then you expect defeat ? "

"Were we all men, I would defy the rascals. We would fight to the last gasp, and then blow up the Nest, and escape by the stream below. But there are women here."

"Then what propose you ? " asked Blake, eagerly.

"I propose to gain assistance   We can hold out some days.   Camp Comanche is within thirty miles, and if they but knew our position, we should next day be free."

"But how is it to be done ? "

"Chinchea will go," said the Indian quietly.

"Of course," replied Philip, still addressing Brown, "the Indian alone could be of use. This, however, must be a secret with us. At nightfall Chinchea will depart, and on the third day we shall see him return backed by a hundred warriors."

"But how can he escape ? "

"By this window. Until black night he would be discovered. At an hour after dark we will be here to aid him, until then he will remain here alone."

A loud report, a second, then a third, now proved that the carronades were at work, while the crashing of boughs

Q

and the falling of stones, dirt, and fragments of wood, proved that the balls struck the summit of the Live Oak Crest. As fast as they could load, Jones and Doyle kept up their volley, making the echoes rise from every nook and cranny round about. They ceased, and all was still as night, and not a sound or trace of the enemy could be heard or seen.

CHAPTER VIII.

A NIGHT WITH DEATH.

It was two hours after sundown, and Philip, accompanied by Edward and Chinchea, stood again in the chamber described in our previous chapter, preparatory to the departure of the latter, who was stripped, and stood erect in his hideous war-paint, while a short knife and tomahawk were suspended from his waist. In his hand was a short and light fusil.

His demeanour was calm and passionless ; not a motion, not the faintest contraction of a muscle, betrayed his sense of the perilous enterprise in which he was engaged. In that dim light he was rather the motionless statue of au artist's hand, than a human being.

Near him stood Philip Stevens, holding a dark lantern, with the light so directed as to stream upon the ground, without showing any sign to those without, while Edward Blake knelt at his feet, knotting firmly together the ends of two coils of rope.

"You are an apt hand, Mr. Brown, I perceive," said Philip, with a smile.

"I should be, having been a British sailor," replied the other.

"And you are sure it will bear his weight ? "

"It will bear many times as much ; and did you not

want me here, I would gladly make the trial by descending with him."

"No," said the Indian, bluntly, "pale face like bear in the dark—no use."

"I knew you would rather not have me, continued Blake, with a laugh ; "but I would gladly share your peril. Believe me, Indian, I shall have a load off my mind when I see you return in safety."

The Indian made no reply, but holding out his hand, he took that of the young man, and clutched it with a gripe like that of the animal he had just compared him to.

"Now to see that the coast is clear," said Stevens, as Blake followed him to the window.

The night was dark and tempestuous. The wind whistled round the building, as if about to commence operations for the evening ; the fitful gusts which bowed the trees on the crest of the opposite rock were frequent and violent, while the whole sky formed one huge canopy of black vapour.

About twenty feet beneath the Live Oak Crest, however, there was one evidence of cheerfulness and animation. A faint tracery of light arose from behind a ridge of rock, betraying the presence of a fire. It looked like the mouth of a witch's cauldron ; though not a flame was to be seen. Now and then a shadow passed before it ; some one was slowly walking up and down.

"This is unpleasant," said Philip Stevens ; "the Indian must pass yonder by that fire, and how he is to do so unobserved, I cannot tell.

"Cinchea will go—he is ready," said the Indian.

Without remark, Edward and Stevens proceeded to attach the rope by a loop to the Indian's waist ; who, as soon as this operation was performed, quietly walked to the window, and commenced his perilous descent. His fate was not trusted to one rope alone, for Blake and Stevens each held one, which they gradually lowered.

The rock shelved slightly inwards at the summit, and the young warrior, therefore, swung wholly in the air,

Q 2

oscillating fearfully, and performing gyrations which would
have turned the head of many a less-nerved man.   Those
above were carefully to lower him as slowly as possible ;
but presently Stevens, who was looking out to catch a
glimpse, nearly overbalanced himself, and for a moment
Blake felt the rope running through his hands with fearful
rapidity.

"Pull back," cried Stevens, "or he will be dashed to
pieces.   Curse the rope ; if he had trusted to me alone,
he would have required no Blackhawk to finish his
career."

Both now proceeded with the utmost caution ; and
after the lapse of about ten minutes, they came to the
end of the two ropes ; but the weight was as great as
ever.   The Indian had not reached the shelving rock before
mentioned.

"He must be drawn up again," said Stevens moodily ;
"we can never let him hang there while I find another
cord."

"I will look and endeavour to see how far off he is from
his journey's end," replied Blake.

The night was still dark, though a few breaks in the
dismal wreaths of cloud permitted a faint ray of light to
pass ; and, straining his eyes to the utmost, Blake could
nearly discover the Indian's position.

"His feet are about a yard from the shelf, and were it
wider, we might trust to his fall."

"Not there," cried Stevens, "the shelf slopes downwards,
and he would fall a hundred and fifty feet into the black
abyss."

"Merciful God," exclaimed Blake, as the rope hung
loose in their hands, "he is off."

Both thrust their heads through the narrow aperture,
listening, with blood that iced in their veins, for the sound
which should bear tidings of the Indian's destruction.   No
sound came ; but a second glance showed him standing erect
and motionless on the very edge of the terrific precipice.
Next instant he disappeared.

Drawing a hard breath, like men who had witnessed

a providential escape, they drew up the ropes, and found the ends cut by the Indian's knife.

"I have seen many an act of Indian courage and sagacity," cried Stevens, with earnestness, "but never did I see that surpassed. On the brink of a fearful gulf, he preferred risking all, to delay."

"He is a bold fellow, truly," replied Blake, "and this beginning augurs well for the result."

For about an hour they kept their now silent watch, listening with keen and practised ear for any sound which might guide them as to their envoy's progress, but in vain. Not the faintest footfall could be detected. At length, after straining their eyes and ears to the utmost, they caught sight of a dark form, which for an instant showed itself near the fire on the opposite rock, and then, high on the night air, rose an awful sound, to which nothing human could be compared. It was a shriek, and yet so mingled with the howling of a panther as to be scarcely distinguishable. They listened again. But all was still.

The two men then retired from the window; but, anxious to know the fate of Chinchea, we prefer following in his footsteps.

We take up our narrative at the moment when, by those above ceasing to pay out any more rope, he discovered that by that means he could descend no lower. Casting his eye down, the Indian saw that the shelf of rock below him sloped downwards, and that though its surface was uneven, and afforded purchase to the foot, yet that a fall would almost of a certainty precipitate him into the gulf beneath.

The smooth face of the hill against which he swung was, however, broken in one or two places, and jagged. A rapid glance showed him a hole within reach, at which he grasped with his left hand, and, quick as lightning, severing the cords round his waist with the knife which he held in his right, he stood securely upon the shelf; for though the rock he grasped crumbled and gave way, it still sufficiently broke his fall to enable him to rest his feet in security.

A natural path, narrow, sometimes almost imperceptible, sometimes a mere shelf of shingle, now led downwards; this path the Indian slowly and calmly followed, taking every precaution against any false step. The descent was laborious and fatiguing, but it was at length accomplished, and Chinchea was at the foot of the diminutive Niagara which formed the stream running round the Nest.

Without a pause, except to drink a draught of water, he commenced an ascent as painful and full of danger as the descent, but which, continuing with that indomitable perseverance so native to his character, he completed, so as to stand within a few yards of the fire beneath Live Oak Crest, in less than an hour after his departure from the window. Dangers, however, appeared to multiply rather than decrease.

The fire was built on a platform near the mouth of a cavern, with a screen of rock protecting it from the gaze of the Nest. It was composed of small branches of the live oak, which emitted a crackling sound, with much smoke, thus aiding the Indian in his stealthy progress towards the solitary man who now occupied a seat near at hand. His occupation was somewhat singular for one alone in the wilds. He was busily engaged in cooking, not such a meal as one man could reasonably be expected to consume, but a supper for a whole platoon.

Half-a-dozen ducks upon a ramrod, a huge earthen pot, from which something sent forth a most savoury odour, a pile of sweet potatoes cooking in the embers, with a vast turkey turning upon a rude spit, formed the groundwork of the repast.

The cook, whose face was plainly visible to Chinchea, was an Indian of his own tribe, and in whose utter absorption in his task, in his vacant eye, luxurious chuckle, and heavy air, the half idiot was plainly to be traced. His nostrils snuffed the steam, which owed its origin to his own gastronomic ability, with intense satisfaction, while his large eyes glistened with an almost irresistible longing to fall to. Prudence or fear seemed, however, to restrain him, and he pursued his task with patience and gravity.

Suddenly Chinchea was upon him, with a howl like that of a famished panther ; the other, in his terror, emitting a shriek which filled the air, and, though smothered by the wind to any one above, it was plainly heard at the Eagle's Nest. Chinchea had wound his arms round the startled cook, and cast him to the ground, ere he was scarcely aware of his enemy's presence, and in a moment stood over him, with waving tomahawk, and a mien which froze the very heart of his victim.

"The Leaping Panther," said the other, who was not so great a fool as he was cowardly and gluttonous—qualities which had caused his expulsion from his tribe— "is very brave ; he will not take the blood of a slave."

" Ugh !" said the other, with ineffable disgust, " Chinchea wants not his blood, he would not stain his axe with so muddy a stream ; the Leaping Panther is a man, and takes the life of men. But Anton must be dead until morning."

He then explained to the trembling cook that he must enter the cavern, where, gagged and bound, he was to pass the night ; while he, the Leaping Panther, assuming his costume and mien, took upon himself also his duties and office. Anton, or Antonio, as the other had been called, finding that his life was to be spared, freely acquiesced, and after greedily devouring some food, he entered the cavern, at the very mouth of which he lay, gagged and bound, Chinchea having given him plainly to understand that, on the slightest sign from him of mere existence, though he himself perished, he would first meet his reward.

This done, the Wacco proceeded to conceal his arms, and so to disguise himself, as by that light to deceive those for whose eating the sumptuous woodland supper had been prepared. On seating himself, he assumed even the very look and expression of the unfortunate cook. Scarcely had he done so, ere several footsteps were heard descending from above, by the rude path which led to the

summit of the Live Oak Crest. Chinchea gave a guttural
hiss, to remind Anton to exercise prudence ; and then
busied himself in laying the well-cooked viands upon the
rude dishes.

"Well, Anton," said the foremost of the party, the renowned Blackhawk himself, "are you quite ready, for I am?
This besieging is hungry work."

"Ready," replied Chinchea.

"Be seated, gentlemen," said Blackhawk, addressing
two white men and a young Indian chief.

"I do think, Pedro," remarked the chief, "that after
the busy cares of the day, nothing is more delightful than
to retire from one's position as a chief, and, with a
few friends around, to enjoy the sociality of the supper
table."

"Si ! si ?!" replied the Mexican bandit, with a grin :
"supper is a very pleasant meal. It has one great merit;
that as there is no exertion required after it, one can eat
one's fill, without fear of its incommoding him."

"Ma foi !" said the third, a Frenchman, "quality, not
quantity, for me—though I must say I have never had
better fare than in Texas."

"Because, Carcassin, in Texas one lives in the open air,
one takes ample exercise, and, thunder !—why one can eat
anything, from prickly pears to a wild mustang."

"Horse very good," said the young Indian chief.

Chinchea quivered in every muscle.

"Why, that is as men think, Long Arm ; for myself,
I never could try it, though you savages are partial to the
animal."

In conversation such as this, about an hour was consumed, during which the greater part of the fare provided,
followed the example of time—Chinchea contriving to
come in for his share, despite his wonder and anxiety at
the presence of the young Wacco chief, Long Arm. At
length, however, even Pedro the Mexican seemed satisfied.

"Now, Anton, the whisky, and we will initiate our
friend, Long Arm, into the mysteries of punch."

This was a puzzler, as Chinchea was quite ignorant of the place where the liquid fire was kept. He acted, however, with his usual decision, and clutching his knife, with which he never parted, he advanced to the mouth of the cavern.

"Where ?" said he, in a low moaning whisper.

"Inside," replied Anton.

Chinchea groped his way along, and following a passage some twenty yards long, he suddenly came upon a kind of room dimly lighted by an oil lamp, and in which were deposited several jars of various sizes, stolen from neighbouring planters and settlers.

But why pauses Chinchea! Why does his gaze become fixed, impassioned, stern? Why does he clutch his knife, and grind his teeth ?

On a rude pallet, having cried herself to sleep, lay a young, beautiful, and exquisitely formed Indian girl. The tears were yet standing on her cheek, while her swollen features showed how violent had been her sobs and grief.

Chinchea took one glance, and snatching up a jar, he hurried back towards the festive party.

CHAPTER IX.

AFTER SUPPER.

WHEN the Indian regained the fire, the company had
armed themselves with the usual after-supper pipe, and
were apparently quite ready to enjoy the bacchanalian
hours. Indeed, Chinchea received a polite intimation
that if he did not make haste, he should go more rapidly
down hill, and alight in a warmer region than he had any
taste for ; threats and menaces were, however, alike to the
Indian, who rapidly prepared the required beverage, and
handed mugs all round, taking care that very little water
entered into the composition.

"That's a regular stinger," said Blackhawk, having
drained his goblet ; "but go on, Long Arm, don't be
afraid of it, it will do you a wonderful deal of good."

"Ugh!" replied the young chief, who appeared to
entertain considerable doubts on that point, having caught
a violent fit of coughing, the consequence of his inexperience. Determined, however, to be nowise behind the
other, he forced himself, though with an ill grace, to
swallow the fiery decoction."

"Now, Long Arm," said Blackhawk, with an almost
imperceptible wink at his companions, "about this love
affair of yours—are we to hear the story ?"

"Ugh," grunted the Indian, savagely, "you have heard.
The Rose of Day is the fairest girl in all the wigwams of
the Waccos, and Long Arm loved—he would have given
his life for her. He said in her ear, that he would hunt
the bear to bring her furs, the deer to supply her with
venison and mocassins, the mountain sheep for cloaks—
but all in vain. She was betrothed, and the face of him
she was to marry was ever before her."

"And who was this fellow ?"

"The Leaping Panther, a great warrior."

"A braggart whom I long to punish, for filling the world so much with his impertinent name."

"He is a bravo," replied the Indian, with a smile of pride, which he could not forbear, though speaking of a rival.

"Well, and where is he?"

"He is gone to see the land of the pale-face; his mother died on the field of battle, and he found friends in the whites."

At this point in the conversation Chinchea, having replenished the mugs out of which the party were drinking, rose and left the platform, making his way along the path by which he had arrived. On his upward journey he had seen the bright shining leaves of a plant, the stalk of which was invaluable to him now, and he was determined to seek it.

In ten minutes he returned, and passing the merry party—none of whom, wrapped in their calumets and drink, noticed his proceedings—he moved on one side with the whisky jar. He had stripped the stalk of its leaves, and bore the plant, like a cane, in his hand. Taking his knife he made several incisions in the side of the weed, and gently pressing it, a light frothy liquid poured in a little stream into the spirit.

It was a deadly poison, but, mixed with the alcohol, it became merely a powerful and rapidly-acting narcotic.

This done, Chinchea rose, and as he did so he met the cold grey eye of his rival fixed upon him.

The recognition was mutual, but by no outward sign did Long Arm betray his discovery, though it was clear that he was much the worse for the quantity of drink he ad imbibed.

"More drink, Anton, my boy," cried Blackhawk, "more drink. Fill high. Long Head---Arm, I mean---pull away, the liquor is immense. It is nectar, ambrosia "—

"Never heard of those names before, signor; what are they?" asked the Mexican.

"They are Greek for gin and whisky," replied Blackhawk

in a rich Hibernian accent, though he could assume Indian
and Yankee at will.

"Now Pedro and Carcassin, and you, Long Arm, ready
with your bumpers, while I give a toast. You, Anton,
blow your cloud a little further off."

Chinchea had lit a pipe, and was calmly smoking,
and gazing on the scene with certainty as to the result.

"Fill, I say, and I'll conclude to give a toast, which
you're all bound to drink."

"Its *diablement fort,*" said Carcassin, who had sipped.

"So much the better, the subject is a strong one."

"Ready!" cried Blackhawk.

"Ready," replied Pedro.

"*Bon,*" said Carcassin, making a desperate plunge
forward, and in the act of picking himself up, half spilling
his glass.

"Ugh," observed the Indian.

"Here's to The Rose of Day, and he who wins her."

"Hurrah!" cried the two whites, and the toast was
drunk with bumpers.

Chinchea ground his teeth, and swallowed a pint of
tobacco smoke.

"Ugh," growled Long Arm, exhibiting sundry signs of
drunkenness, which were not far from precipitating him
into the arms of the god.

"It works," whispered Blackhawk.

"Good," thought Chinchea.

Long Arm rolled backwards, gave a huge sigh, and was
fast asleep.

"He is got rid of," muttered Blackhawk. "Did the
fool think to bring that sweet girl among us and keep her
to himself? Pshaw!"

"Certainly not," growled the Mexican, who could
scarcely keep his eyes open."

"*Parbleu non!*" muttered the Frenchman.

"Carcassin, you are drunk!" said Blackhawk, who was
unsuccessfully endeavouring to insert the end of his pipe
into his own mouth.

"*Et vous?*" asked Carcassin, slily.

"Oh, me, I am all right, by St. Patrick, *mavourneen*," said Blackhawk, whose eyes were half shut.

"And what is the meaning of *mavourneen* ?" asked Carcassin.

"It's Latin for my dear," replied the outlaw, raising himself, "and that puts me in mind of my little dear that's waiting for me in the cavern yonder. Tell me Carcassin, why it is that when, hardened as we may be, we are about to commit a great crime, we feel a physical pain here—a dilation of the heart, a swelling of the muscles of the *throat* !"

"It is the working of conscience," said the Frenchman drily.

"Of what ?" inquired Blackhawk, as if he had never heard of any such appurtenance.

"Of conscience," replied Carcassin, who had been educated for a priest ; "which never departs from even such men as you and me, Blackhawk."

"You think, then," continued the outlaw, moodily, "that our acts are of such a black die ? Why so ? We are free men ; we roam the world, and take what chance gives us ; what more ?"

"But chance neither gives us the lives of others, nor woman's honour," said Carcassin, sarcastically ; "and we take both."

"You are growing moral," sneered the other.

"Not I ; it is the whisky," replied the Frenchman ; "it opens the heart, and wrings truth from the bottom of the well."

"Hear the philosopher, Pedro, what think you of him ?"

The Mexican was fast asleep.

"The drink works potently to-night," mused the outlaw : "it stupefies Pedro and the Indian ; it weighs on my spirits, makes me sad and gloomy, and takes all heart away ; the Frenchman it sets philosophizing. Egad, there's something in it, after all."

"So there is," muttered Anton.

"Who spoke?" said Blackhawk, looking towards the entrance of the cavern.

"I," replied Chinchea, waving his hand menacingly at Anton.

"I say, Carcassin," continued the chief, "will you have another glass? Gone, too!"

Carcassin lay beside Pedro, both seemingly vying with each other in their attempts at nasal music.

"Well, sleep your fill. One more glass, and I go;" and Blackhawk, despite himself, shuddered.

"You have had enough," said Chinchea, gruffly.

"Speak for yourself, Anton—by the way, does the Rose still weep and deplore her fate? Does she still refuse the honour of mating with the Wolf of the Prairies?"

"She sleeps," said Chinchea.

"Thank St. Patrick," replied Blackhawk, drawing a long breath; "and now, Anton, fill high another bumper, and mind you what I said about Long Arm—pitch him over the rocks; everybody will believe he stumbled in a drunken fit. I say, Anton, I feel as if I were at home; my eyes shut of themselves. It's very dark; ah!"

The outlaw had fallen beside his companions.

Up rose Chinchea, his arms in his hands, and a stern purpose in his eye. He clutched his knife, and approached the robber. He knelt and gazed on his sleeping countenance.

"Bad paleface," he muttered; "the Manitou has given me your life; but Chinchea scorns to take it away from a sleeping man," and he took in his hands a long tress of the robber's hair, cut it, and laid it on his breast."

"Chinchea," hissed a voice in his ear.

The warrior turned slowly round.

The Long Arm stood before him, pouring out upon the ground the drugged liquid which his rival had given him.

"Chinchea is a great brave," said the young warrior, sadly, "and Long Arm is a boy, a squaw. The Rose of Day loves the Leaping Panther—the Leaping Panther has saved her; let him keep the life which is his."

" And Long Arm ? "

" Will Chinchea call him friend?" continued the youth, thoroughly humiliated at the risk which his inconsiderate conduct had caused the woman he loved to endure, simply because she could not return his affection.

The hands of the two warriors were at once clasped in amity, and they entered the cave, from which, in ten minutes, they again emerged, leading forth the bewildered and half-sleeping Indian girl, whose joy and delight on being reunited to him she loved, was plainly visible in her whole demeanour.

With a parting warning to Anton, Chinchea turned into a narrow way which led round the bottom of the Live Oak Crest ; and about two hundred yards distant, he lay down with his companions, to snatch a few hours' rest, in a thick and almost impassable grove of trees, where a bubbling spring burst forth, which by many a winding way —some secret, some open—went to swell the cataract below.

CHAPTER X.

THE CONFERENCE.

On the evening of the escape of Chinchea the storm continued its violence for some hours, and yet Edward, from causes which will hereafter be explained, preferred the open air in the little garden to which Alice had introduced him, to the comforts of the parlour of the Eagle's Nest, where Jones, Philip, Cephas Doyle, and the other tenants of the locality, solaced themselves for some hours in conversation over the usual Texan evening amusements.

At length, the Mexicans and the usual inhabitants cf

the Nest, wearied with the excitement and fatigues of the day, retired to rest, leaving Stevens and Jones alone in the chamber. They, however, moved not; but after closing the doors, they drew near the huge and cheering fire, refilled their glasses, loaded a fresh pipe, and made every preparation for a private carouse.

"For some time neither spoke. Their thoughts were evidently busy on some subject which was deeply interesting to their minds; and there they sat drinking and smoking, but holding no communion. At length, after about half-an-hour had elapsed, Stevens spoke rather in an audible whisper, addressed to himself, than with a view to be heard by his companion.

"It must be ours."

"At any price," added Jones, with an approving nod.

"What?" said Philip, raising his head, and gazing fiercely at the dwarf.

"Of course you know. If men will tempt their fellows, why they must pay the penalty."

"Who is tempting, and who is tempted?"

"Don Juan de Chagres comes here for shelter; nobody asked him to. His servants let out that he has a mine of wealth with him; nobody asked them to."

"Well?"

"Why, of course, he having brought this money here, here it must stay."

"Jones, I shall blow your brains out one of these days."

"No you won't," replied the dwarf, sneeringly.

"Why?"

"Because you are afraid."

"I afraid——?"

"Afraid of ill-using a friend who speaks for your good. The fact is, Philip, I am tired of this wild life. It doesn't suit me at all, and I would have you think with me. Break up the Nest, realize all we have, and with as much as we can make, retire into the centre of Mexico, and there live among our fellows."

"I, too, am weary of this life. It is too lonely—it leaves too much time for thought—too many memories are stirring in the stillness of the night. Yes! could I see Alice but mated, I would gladly leave here for ever."

"As to Alice," said Jones, with his usual hesitating manner, "I have often told you."

"Then tell it not again. You! by whose hand ——"

"Well, what?" said the other, fixing his little grey eyes on the speaker.

"Nothing—but you are the last man who should dare to have such a thought. This young sailor, now——"

"You think so," replied Jones, savagely. "I hate the fellow, from his very face, and this would be another reason."

"I know not why," half mused Stevens, "but I feel an irresistible longing towards that youth. His face softens me as I look upon it."

"He is the very image of——"

"Jones," thundered Stevens, rising and grasping the other by the throat, "breathe but that name, and I cast you dead at my feet."

"Fool that you are," cried the dwarf, who was half choking. "I will drop the subject."

"Jones," continued Stevens, loosening his hold, "I have warned you before; let me not have to warn you again."

"Enough. Let us speak of the Mexican's gold."

"Go on," said Stevens.

"Well," said Jones, speaking slowly, firmly, and distinctly, "this money must be ours. We take it; there is at once an outcry; Don Juan insists on searching the premises; his followers join him; Cephas Doyle and your young English friend join him, and so will our own people."

"Perfectly true," replied the other; "and by your own showing, it is best left alone."

"Not at all," continued Jones, coldly.

R

"What then?" said Philip Stevens, his face half livid with emotion, while avarice glistened in his very eyes, as he spoke.

"If Don Juan were dead, no outcry would take place against us. He is near the outer window, he leans out, he overbalances himself, and is killed."

"Speak plain," sneered the other.

"Then I say, he must die," said the dwarf.

"Who is to kill him?"

"We must."

"We! why not you?" insinuated Stevens.

"Because, my friend, it is necessary that in all matters of this kind we should both be fully equal."

"Idiot," said Stevens, "why should I betray you?"

"Why not?" replied the dwarf; "the reward is tempting."

"Jones, this man shall not die. He has claimed my protection, and he shall have it.

"You grow moral," said Jones, sullenly.

"No!" cried the other; "but enough blood has been shed. Sleeping or waking, the gory flood is before me. When I rise at morn, and gaze out upon the sky, I see blood in the very tints of dawn; the setting sun crimsons all nature with gore. I sleep, and I swim in oceans of the accursed—"

"I never dream," drawled the dwarf.

"'Tis well for you—but I do, and voices, as of the past, come peeling to my ears; and *he* cries, 'Give me back my life.'"

"*He* is very troublesome to you, Philip."

"'Tis twelve years ago, and I have seen and endured much since that day, but not one moment, one second, has he been from my side. At meals, he sits by my side; walking, he walks behind; hunting, he runs to the death; fighting, he shields me from harm, that 'my torture may be longer. Jones, if I could recal that day, if I could be what I was up to that hour—though then not innocent —I would gladly suffer every misery of poverty, of starvation, of woe."

"Regrets are useless. All we can do is to try and make life as pleasant as possible while it lasts."

"How?—by repentance and restitution?"

"I have no wish for a trial and halter," replied the dwarf, with a contemptuous scowl.

"Then how?"

"By adding to our means of enjoyment."

"And what means are there left us?"

"Gold," said Jones, calmly; "gold, that buys every enjoyment."

"We have enough."

"Enough for here, but not enough to hold our heads high in towns among our fellow-men. Come, Philip, be advised; listen to an old friend."

"I have listened too often."

"We have sunk ourselves deep enough in guilt; we can go no deeper. Blood is on both our hands; but we have been scarcely repaid for the trouble. A mine is now within our reach; should we not be fools to refuse acceptance? Besides, recollect how we were compelled to leave New Orleans for want of money. There we were happy, joined in every amusement, and held our heads high. But money failed, and we were compelled to fly."

"We were, and I hope yet to be revenged on those who shunned us when our poverty became apparent."

"You can at once. Possessed of this Mexican's gold and jewels, we return to New Orleans, no longer with a mere paltry pittance, but with a fortune. What pride to overtop those who turned us from the hazard table, who shunned us in the streets, and called us adventurers and poor devils."

"Curse them. Remind me not of those days; I would give years of my life to punish those scoundrels."

"Money will do it," said the dwarf.

"It will."

"And money alone."

"This Mexican is rich?" enquired Stevens.

"Very rich," replied Jones.

R 2

"He is old."

"But a few years, perhaps months, to live."

"He will be missed by nobody," added Stevens.

"No man that dies is. A nine days' grief is all the best of us get from widow, children, mother."

Too true, in part. We grieve for the absent, but not for the dead. We do for a short time, for a few months, perhaps a year; and then one who was perhaps the living joy of a vast circle, the cherished soul of near and dear ties, is forgotten, is unremembered, unchronicled, except upon a cold stone. Death effaces memory. His place is empty, and his name is known no more. Perhaps in a mother's heart a corner, ever-during, everlasting, may be found for a departed child, but nowhere else. The sorrowing widow, choking with grief—the grieving brother —the pitying friend—alike, in this busy world, forget, forget, forget.

But he who has taken life remembers for ever.

For an hour the conference was continued, and after almost giving way to the insidious persuasions of his friend, Philip suddenly exclaimed, "I will decide nothing to-night. All shall depend on this young Englishman. If he shows any signs of paying earnest attentions to Alice, and there be a prospect of their union, my fate is decided. We part. I go to live in peace—where they dwell, for heaven will have taken pity on me, and Alice will——"

"Never consent," added Jones.

"We shall see," and with these words they parted.

CHAPTER XI.

EDWARD AND MARGARETTA.

Two hours previous to the interview recorded between Jones and Philip, Edward Blake, according to agreement, wandered into the garden of the Eagle's Nest, to spend a quiet hour with Alice and Margaretta. The young sailor was actuated by various and strange emotions ; he knew not why, but his mind foreboded ill. In reality, he was in that state of uncertainty and doubt which, of all sensations, is most disagreeable.

He had hitherto never loved ; he had heard and read of this passion, of which it has been truly said, that " it breathed the breath of life into poetry, and elicited music and voice from the coldest human clay," but he had never experienced either its joys or its sorrows.

Young, sensitive, full of the quick passion and tenderness that seem inseparable from the educated and high-minded sailor, Blake was now placed in a strange position. Beside him were two women, both attractive, both lovely, both possessed of every charm which could soul-entrance him, and yet he hesitated.

On one side, the gentle charms of the fair Alice subdued his heart, and filled him with quiet and radiant hope; on the other, the fiery beauty, the energy, and commanding mien of the Mexican involuntarily filled his thoughts, and he entered the garden prepared to drink deep the intoxicating draught, but as yet ignorant which would gain the day.

He found Margaretta alone.

Now, had the blind god selected any means of entrapping the susceptible hero of this narrative, he could not have chosen a time or place more favourable to the triumph of her who first presented herself to Edward's notice. It is true, he was already much disposed in Alice's favour, but hers was one of those natures which grow upon our affections by degrees, but which, once rooted, are not to be cast aside; while the Mexican was of a beauty and character likely to strike the eye, to induce an immediate surrender—as likely, however, to be followed by a speedy rebellion.

The moon was faintly glimmering in the sky, as Edward approached the seat on which Margaretta, in a pensive mood, sat smiling, as the young man came near.

" Good evening, cavalier," said she, gaily.

" Good evening, signora," replied Edward; "but where is our hostess?"

" Alice is with Don Juan," she said; "he has been unwell, and she has taken him some refreshment. I sat with him awhile, but the room was close, and I came out here." Then, as if anxious to change the subject, she said—

" Have you such evenings in your country?"

" Rarely," he said, " but as I am not of those who find only faultiness in their own land, I will say, that I have seen as beautiful a night there as in any other part of the world."

"I should like to see your country, signor," she continued, gravely; " I have heard much of its power, and would fain know the truth."

Blake's heart beat quickly.

"It is a great country," he replied, "and though less grand than some of its compeers, it can yet show front with the most picturesque."

" There is enough of native beauty here," said the Mexican; "it is not that I seek. I would find a land where my soul was free, where a woman is not a slave, to be given away at will; where parents, or proud relatives, have not the power to make a heart miserable for life."

"Can they do it anywhere?" said Edward surprised.

" Can they?" replied the Mexican, with an hysteric

laugh. "They can, and do it in my wretched country. There a woman, ere she be married, is a mere puppet without will, a thing to be tossed about with so many wretched dollars, as a make-weight; a peg to hang a scheme upon.

"Two families are united in the bonds of friendship or interest, and this friendship or interest she is made the mere instrument for consolidating. If her partner be hateful, aged, a fool, it is no matter—she has no voice, no will. Tell me, signor, of a country where such things are not, and there is my home."

This was said with terrible vehemence, and Edward Blake let into his heart a powerful ingredient of love—pity.

"Signora, you speak warmly," he said, in tender tones.

"Because I feel," she exclaimed. "I am a Mexican, but I am a woman, and I know the day might have come when I might have loved, when I might have felt the affection which should bind me undyingly to a fellow creature; and I know, too, that by the fearful power of custom, because I own a fortune, that I am doomed, and it cannot be."

Edward Blake scarcely knew what to reply—his mind was so filled with varied and tumultuous thoughts. Could it be that, affianced to some hated one whom policy and family arrangements bound her to, she now, on seeing him, had allowed tender thoughts to arise, and in the dawn of her love for him, cursed the cruel fate which had promised her to another.

Blake, young, inexperienced in the world's ways, knew not woman's heart, and that though she might love him, yet too, all this while, be but conjuring up imaginary ills to excite his pity, and thus command his tender interest.

"Doomed!" he exclaimed, with an effort at gaiety, "you, so young, so beautiful, talk of being doomed ——"

"So young, so beautiful, you say," she replied, with a transient gleam of satisfaction, which she effectually pre vented him from seeing ; "here lies the evil. Were I not young, this ill might sóon pass ; were I ugly, I might less repine."

"Madam," said Edward gravely, "I do not pretend to know your secret history, but I surely cannot tell why one, with native charms like yours, with many and happy years before you, with wealth and fortune, should repine. Were I, a poor devil, to do so, I should scarcely think it out of place."

"And are you poor?" inquired Margaretta, fixing her large eyes pityingly upon him.

Poor Edward, his heart was escaping him every minute.

"I am poor, madam, very poor ; but I have my sword and my honour, and I fear nothing."

"No ! you may look around and choose where you will. You are poor ; well, success waits for the brave, and then a rich and lovely wife may repair what fortune had before churlishly denied."

"A rich wife, if I could love her," said the young man, his face crimson with emotion, "would be a good gift of fortune ; but if, when I choose, I love truly, I shall not ask her wealth."

"You would love her for herself alone ?" said Margaretta.

"I would."

"Happy woman !" muttered the Mexican, in faint tones, which, if not meant for his ear, reached it, and made his heart leap.

"Why happy woman ?" he timidly inquired, fixing his eyes anxiously on the young woman's face, beside whom he was now seated.

"Did you hear me ?" said the other, with a sigh ; "because a woman who is loved for herself, whose fortune never tempted, whose lover cares but for her, is happier than a queen."

"Doubtless you may be as happy," remarked the young sailor.

"Never !"

"Why ?"

" It is impossible," said Margaretta.

" Lady, you speak in enigmas."

" I speak the truth. But this is idle talk. I know not why I have indulged in it."

" It may not be so idle," replied Edward, with a swelling heart.

" How so ? "

" Forgive me, lady," he said ; I am as yet a stranger to you ; we have been cast together by accident ; we may in time know one another better——"

" What mean you, signor ? " exclaimed the young Mexican, starting back in affright.

" I mean," said Edward, trembling with anxiety, " that I know not what to say—I would fain hope ——"

" Hope what ? "

" Madam," he exclaimed, " I will not say I love you, because I know you not enough ; but this I cannot refrain from uttering, that I know I shall."

"Sooner love hell itself," cried the girl, starting from her seat, pale with anguish, for heaven knows whether she responded to his feelings or not ; " sooner go and cast yourself headlong from the top of yonder block—sooner do any mad and terrible thing, than let your heart say you love me."

" Why, lady ? "

" Signor, I felt wretched to-night, and I spoke freely, more freely than I should to you, a stranger; had I known that there was the bare chance of such an ending to our speech, I had not said one word. Young man, this is the last time we speak together. It might rob you, it would rob me for ever of peace."

"Gracious heavens, lady ! why this terror ? "

"You speak, signor, to the wife of Don Juan de Chagres. Yes ! it was my own wretched fate, being bound by force, to suit the will of a rich family, to wed a man nearly fifty years older than myself, that I foolishly complained of to you."

Edward Blake, pale, trembling, horror-struck, leaned against the wall for support.

"The wife——"

"Yes," said Margaretta, with assumed gaiety, "you see before you the wife of the man you took so gallantly to be my father. This should I have said before, but own I am ever ashamed to say. So come, signor, your pretended passion, for surely it must be pretended, will have no excuse now. Had I been a maiden, you might have feigned a sudden fit of love, and have kept up the joke ; but as it is, excuse me if I remind you that, in our country, such jokes sometimes end seriously. Jealousy is the passion of old men."

It would be difficult to tell if Margaretta felt or not as she spoke. But Blake was as yet unable even to hear what she said.

"The wife of Don Juan de Chagres ?" he muttered, half incoherently.

"Good God !" mused the Mexican ; "and does he love me, then ? Is it come to this so soon ? Oh, wretched fate is mine. But though his forced bride, though dragged by violence to the altar, though I spat upon the ring, and called God to witness I was not his wife, yet in the world's eyes I am Donna Juanna de Chagres,"

This was said with a proud and swelling mien, as if she remembered herself.

"Madam, I thank you for reminding me," said the young man. "I had hoped differently, when I thought you free. But," he added solemnly, taking her hand in his, "fear me not, madam. I now am armed against myself. So quickly born, this love will as quickly die. With me, I feel there must be hope for love to feed upon. There is none here, and I shall think of this evening as a dream."

In truth, so simple, and yet so right-minded, was the character of the young sailor, that with him the discovery he had made, as a matter of course, at once erased even the shadow of love from his heart, though it left that heart sorely vacant.

"Here comes Alice," said Edward.

"Welcome, our hostess," said Margaretta, half gloomily.

"I am sorry not to have met you here before," said Alice, addressing Edward ; "but as madame wished me to remain awhile with her husband, while he dozed to sleep, I thought it a duty to comply."

Margaretta bit her lip. Why, it was difficult to tell.

"At length, however, you are come," said Edward, endeavouring to rouse himself ; and as 'tis said better late than never,' I think I have a promise to perform."

"I think you have," replied Alice ; but as it is growing late, and Norah yonder points to tea—which remnant of civilization I indulge in—let us into the house, and then I will hear you with pleasure."

Edward Blake willingly acquiesced, though he observed as he came into the light, how Alice gazed curiously at his pallid countenance. Determined that she should have no cause for suspecting his untoward feelings, he at once roused himself, and began the narrative of his ship-wreck, which he had promised to detail.

There is always eloquence in truth ; and when, there-fore, a man tells of things which have happened to him-self, he possesses a power of description, an animation, of which he is before scarcely cognisant. Thus was it with Edward ; for, rising with the occasion, his language became rich and glowing, his eyes beamed with light, his colour came and went, and forgetting all but the event he was narrating, he swept on in a perfect hurri-cane of scenic power. His listeners heard him with rapt attention, and, as he ceased, from actual want of breath, they sat silent and anxious for the termination. So minute, however, was the young man in his details, that it was midnight ere the party broke up.

CHAPTER XII.

FAIR and sunny was the morn, when Chinchea and his party prepared to brave the perils which surrounded them on their departure towards Camp Comanche, whither it was now doubly necessary he should arive, both to bring the promised succour, and to place the Rose of Day in the safe keeping of her parents, until he was prepared to unite her fortunes to his for ever.

Chinchea led the way, erect, proud, in all the prelude of savage dignity. Long Arm, humbled by his own act, that of the forced abduction of the bride of another, walked behind, while the lovely Indian girl, all roses like the dawn, which she greeted merrily—more merrily than for many past days—came meekly in the rear.

At any other time, even the Indian might have been disposed to revel in the beauty of nature, but now all his energies were devoted to the task of extricating himself from the difficult position in which he was placed. Clutching his rifle, and treading with almost noiseless footsteps, he skirted the thicket which had served to shelter him and his friends for the night, and brought himself thus facing the Eagle's Nest. He listened now with eager attention for any note of preparation on the part of the besiegers, within a few yards of whose position on the summit of the Eagle's Nest, he was about to climb, that being the only route by which he could hope to gain the plain.

"The pale faces sleep," said Long Arm, with an uneasy contraction of the face, as if the memory of the past night were unpleasant to him; "the fire water has filled their heads with dreams."

"Good,"-muttered Chinchea; "but they are snakes;

they hide themselves in the grass, and may bite and not be seen."

"Ugh!"

"Let Long Arm go," said the chief, pointing to the path which led upward to the camp of the banditti, "and see what the white men do above. He will be safe ; the chief of the pale faces sleeps yet in the cavern mouth."

"Ugh!" replied the other, and losseuing his tomahawk, he obeyed.

With this monosyllable, Long Arm, concealing under a careless mien his anxious feelings, moved slowly up the rugged path which led to the summit of the Live Oak Crest, in an opposite direction to that by which Blackhawk had descended to his woodland supper.

"The Rose will wait yonder," continued the chief, tenderly, pointing to a huge sycamore, which could, behind its vast umbrageous head, shelter and conceal her.

"The Rose will wait," said the girl, with a smile—a smile which went manna-like to the heart of the warrior.

"Good."

This was all he said, and then treading softly, so as not to be heard, he moved towards the scene of the previous night's debauch, in order to discovery if any movement, dangerous to his own plans, had as yet taken place in that quarter.

As he neared the spot, silence brooded over all. Nor voice, nor sound of life was heard, and when reaching a spot whence, without being seen, he could overlook all, the whole party presented the same aspect as when he had left them on the previous night. Blackhawk lay near the extinguished fire, his head thrown back, his arms stretched as if in a deep and heavy sleep, while Pedro and Carcassin were near at hand in a similar state.

Presently, however, the chief of the outlaws moved uneasily ; the chill morning air seemed slightly to affect him, and he gradually gained a sitting posture. His eyes opened slowly and with difficulty, and he gazed around as one who believed himself in a dream. After a while, the senses gained their sway, and he discovered the severed lock upon his breast, and Anton sitting upright at the entrance of the cave, his arms and legs bound, but the gag removed from his mouth.

"Anton," said the outlaw, "what means this?"

"Ugh!" grunted the Indian.

"Why, methought I went to sleep in the cave, and here, at cock-crow, I wake and find myself on the stony platform."

"Ugh!"

"Where is Long Arm?"

"Gone."

"And the Rose of Day?"

"Gone."

"Thunder!" said the outlaw, springing up, and rushing at the throat of the unfortunate cook, "gone! how—when—where?"

"Chin——"

"Chin me no chin!" exclaimed the bandit, striking the crouching Indian furiously as he spoke, "where are they?"

"Gone with Chin——"

"Dolt! idiot! knave!" cried the Blackhawk, more furiously, "who told you this?"

"Chin——"

"Fool! who waited on me last night?"

"Chinchea!"

"Who is Chinchea?"

"The Leaping Panther."

"The Leaping Panther!" thundered the outlaw; "he here last night! Bearding me in my very den. But he and Long Arm are enemies!"

"They have buried the hatchet."

"And the Rose of Day?"

"Is with her own warrior—the flower of the Comanches."

"And am I to be tricked thus with impunity by a brutish red skin? My very soul thickens at the thought. How they will laugh and jibe."

"Ugh!" said the sullen savage, scowling at the bandit,

his soul writhing beneath the blow which the other had most unwisely inflicted.

Blackhawk had roused a lion which he would have some difficulty in putting down.

"But this is all idle," cried the chief; "action, not talk, will serve our turn. Pedro, Carcassin, awake."

"*Buenos noches*," muttered the Mexican, "*caramba ! nuestra demonia ;* who calls ?"

"I."

"Who's I ?" said the sleepy lieutenant, opening his eyes.

"Blackhawk," thundered the outlaw.

"Oh! what's the matter, that one cannot sleep ?"

"Matter! hell is the matter. Wake that brute Carcassin."

"Carcassin, my boy !" said Pedro.

"*Plait-il garçon*," replied the Frenchman, "an omelet and a bottle of Burgundy."

"Why, what does the fool say ?"

"Oh, I was dreaming, *mon dieu*, that I was in the *Café Royal*, supping with the devil."

"You were not far wrong," said Blackhawk.

"I think not," said Pedro, slily.

"No jokes," continued the chief, furiously; "that devil Chinchea, the Leaping Panther, was here last night, bound our cook in the cave, took his place, drugged our liquor, laughed at us in his sleeve, and stole away with Long Arm and the Indian Girl."

"The Rose of Day," said Pedro, drily.

"I say, Blackhawk," asked Carcassin, maliciously, "what was that toast of yours ?"

"What toast ?"

"'Here's to the Rose of Day, and he who wins her.'"

"This is no time for folly such as this, thundered the outlaw. Away above, alarm the. camp, let the whole country be scoured, but they must be found."

"*Bon !*" said the Frenchman; "here's some warm work."

"I like it," said Pedro.

"Which way went they?" asked the chief, addressing Anton.

"Ugh?" answered the sullen Indian, inquiringly.

"I say, idiot, dost hear, which way went they?"

"Down!" replied the irate Comanche, pointing in the direction whence the Leaping Panther had ascended on the previous night.

"Go," said Blackhawk, "bring down the whole band; if they be there, the foxes are caught in their own trap."

The two lieutenants sped upwards on their errand, secretly delighted, as bad men ever are, at the annoyance which one of their own party was subject to.

"Good," muttered Chinchea, "now is my time."

With these words he turned to go; when glancing at the platform, a movement on the part of Anton at once riveted his attention.

Blackhawk was leaning on his gun, his back turned from the cave, near the mouth of which stood Anton. The bandit chief was musing on what had passed, and by the expression of his countenance, he was planning revenge upon those who had baffled his criminal designs.

Anton had in his hand a tomahawk, a huge, heavy thing, with which an ox could have been brained.

A scowl was upon the Indian's face; the rankling of the blows that he had received was still at his heart.

"Blackhawk is gone," thought Chinchea; "Anton will take his life."

The outlaw remained motionless where he stood, gazing vacantly upon the Eagle's Nest.

Stealthily, with serpent tread, on sped the Indian. Murder was in his eyes, revenge flashed from their glare.

"Good," said Chinchea, breathing heavily; "the bad man of the pale faces will lose his scalp."

Still the Indian advanced, and still the chief remained motionless.

"Pale face," whispered Chinchea, solemnly, "the happy hunting-ground now awaits you. The Manitou has stayed his course."

Still the Indian advanced, and now stood within a

couple of yards of the outlaw, while in his right hand the avenging weapon was held, prepared for the blow.

"Take that, fool," exclaimed the white, who had seen all.

With these words he wheeled round; a sheet of flame, a report, and Anton was dead, falling without cry or groan.

"Idiot," muttered the bandit, turning again, and resuming his former position; "it was of your own seeking."

"Ugh," said Chinchea, letting his short rifle fall into the hollow of his hand, and taking aim at the cool and reckless ruffian. But at that moment the picture of the young Rose of Day presented itself, and prudence whispered that the fate of his party would certainly be death, if he avenged the slaughter of his countryman.

With a heavy heart, but a light and cautious step, he turned away to rejoin the Rose of Day, with whom he found Long Arm, who reported the path difficult but practicable. Chinchea at once led the way in the direction of the summit, taking the Indian girl by the hand, and aiding her in her ascent of the rough ground. A few moments brought them upon the camp of the enemy.

To their right was a dense growth of brushwood, thick, black, and impenetrable; in front, the sloping hill, leading to the vast illimitable prairies; to their left, the position of the outlaws, who had just been alarmed by the arrival of Pedro and Carcassin.

At a short distance, tethered and hoppled, grazed the horses of the bandits.

"Now, my lads, follow," cried Pedro; "the dogs are not far distant. We shall have rare sport."

"Turtle hunting," suggested Carcassin.

"And if we catch them?" said Pedro.

"A deep tragedy," answered Carcassin.

And all the banditti laughed in chorus.

"But the captain," said Pedro; "oh! oh! it was too good. He had smuggled the lass so nicely into the cavern;

S

he had got Long Arm so gloriously drunk, and then, ah! ah! ha! he—got—drunk—himself."

"A perfect vaudeville," said Carcassin.

"Good as a play," laughed Pedro.

Again the robbers roared in chorus.

"And this morning, when he woke us," added Pedro, "if you had seen his face, black as night; and his rage, perfectly sublime."

"Ah," said the Frenchman, "he was like poor Robert Macaire, when he would have robbed the mayor; he tried, but he could not."

"He's a capital captain," said Pedro, seriously; "but I am afraid he is no philosopher."

"Never read Voltaire or Rousseau," said the Frenchman, with infinite pity.

And again the robbers laughed, for though they did not understand the joke, they knew a hard hit was meant at somebody.

"But I say, the captain all this while. *Santa Maria,* just now he was in a devil's hurry; I heard him blaze away a signal with his gun.

"Let us go," answered Carcassin.

"Let us go," repeated the whole body of thieves.

"And yonder pass," suggested Pedro.

"Well, I conclude I'll just guard this fixin," said Ben Smith, a huge Yankee.

"Do so, and keep with you your company," replied the lieutenant. "Now away, boys."

Without further parley, the robbers then vanished from the camp, pouring down the narrow path which led to the platform and the cave.

Behind remained Ben Smith and three Comanche Indians, young men, who had accompanied Long Arm in his ill-advised flight from the camp of his people. As soon as the rest were out of sight, Ben Smith, placing his arms near at hand, drew forth a pipe, and loading it, invited the Indians to follow his example. They, nothing loth, readily complied, and in a few moments were deeply immersed in discussing the mysteries of the exhilarating weed.

" Well, I conclude," observed Ben Smith, in a serious tone, " this are better nor a wild goose chase, I guess."

" Ugh," grunted the Indians.

" Now, Ingins, don't ; you cut a huckleberry above me : I don't reckon on grunting ; that's a style of conversation suited to hogs and them like. There ain't no sociality about yer."

" Ugh," repeated the Indians, as if they did not understand him.

" Now, Ingins, if you grunt at that rate, I'll fancy myself in an Alabama piggery, and I'll bust. 'Cause hogs don't generally smoke, I expect, and I *do* think I see three swine now with pipes."

" Ugh," said the Indians, with a broad grin of genuine astonishment.

" Now, red skins," exclaimed the Yankee, laughing, "that Ooo! will be the death of me. I'm bound to bust, I reckon. Now, do jist for variety, say something. I'm the yaller flower of this forest, ain't I now?"

" Ugh," said the Indians, all in one breath.

" Ingins, do you never talk in your part of the world? don't you larn any lingo ? "

" Red skin talk when him understand," replied one of the group.

"Ah! there it jist is; it's all along o' that Tower of Babel, I'm concluding. Well, if I was a king, I'd just make a law agin any lingo but what I could clearly understand.

" Indian talk good for Indian, white talk good for white," replied another.

" There now," said big Ben, with a chuckle, " I know'd you could if you would. That's sociable, I reckon ; I wish I may be shot, if I ain't larnt something in these diggins."

" What has the big white man learnt ? "

"Larnt to know that there is some locrum in an Ingin."

" And what is locrum ? " said the Indians.

"Wake snakes and walk yer chalks," said Ben Smith, starting; and in his eagerness he nearly swallowed his short reed pipe; "what's that? A bar, I'm thinking."

"At the same time an angry growl was heard to emanate from the adjoining thicket.

"It's a bar," continued Smith, sententiously, laying his hand on his gun at the same time.

The Indians never moved, but continued smoking with even greater energy than ever.

"Well, that's cool, anyhow you fix it," observed the Yankee, annoyed at being outdone in calm courage, and laying down his gun; "but it's a bar, I'll swar."

A still more angry growl, much nearer to the group, aroused Smith's ire to the utmost.

"Well, I'm bound to say them Ingins is right away cool; but I'm not a-gwine to be made a meal for monsters. So here goes at the bar, slick!"

"My brother is wrong," said one of the Indians, calmly; "it is not a bear."

"Not a bar; well, I conclude you're cool; darn my old grandmother, tell Ben Smith *he* don't know a bar from——"

"A panther!"

"A painter?" cried Ben, moving uneasily; "no, it ain't a painter, is it?"

"The Leaping Panther," replied the Indians, rising simultaneously, and disarming and casting the American to the ground, almost ere he knew he was assaulted.

The keen ears of the Comanches had recognised the favourite signal of their beloved war chief, and had, at his call, at once returned to their allegiance, and owned the power and tie which, in all parts of the world, is connected with the words "my country."

Ben Smith was so astounded at the assault which had been operated upon him by his three companions, that he suffered himself to be thoroughly overpowered without resistance. At length, however, as the Leaping Panther and his two companions emerged from the thicket, his tongue became loosened.

"Well, if you can't talk, Ingins, you can cheat above a bit, I reckon, I do ; may I be etarnally sucked up into a waterspout, and come down again in a frog shower, if ever I believe a Ingin agin. If I do——"

The remainder of his speech was too thoroughly in the backwood style, to bear being recorded.

"Away, brothers," said Chinchea, calmly, "pick the six best horses belonging to the white men. They can lend them to an Indian whose feet are sore."

Away darted the warriors, obedient to the command of their leader, and eager to cover their former bad conduct by assiduity on the present occasion.

"And you're a-gwine to take them horses, are you ?" said Ben Smith, with nonchalance ; "you're quite welcome, for they ain't mine, I conclude."

Chinchea made no reply, waiting in a dignified, but keenly attentive attitude, for the horses to be brought up.

"Tell Blackhawk," said the chief, as six of the choicest horses—selected with keen and practised eyes—were brought up, "tell him he is a coward and a knave. The Leaping Panther says so, and the Leaping Panther never lies. Tell him that when he killed the poor fool Anton, the eye of the Manitou was upon him, and that the Leaping Panther will avenge him."

"Oh my," cried Ben, with no little astonishment, and at the same time with infinite disgust. "He ain't killed Anton, I reckon."

"The Blackhawk stoops low ; he beats a poor Indian without a soul, and then kills him because he feels the blows. Go! he is a coward."

"He is," thundered Ben, in genuine disgust, "and if ever I foller a fellow as ain't more of a man any longer, I'll turn nigger, and that's about the last thing any Christian man 'ud wish to be."

"Good !" said Chinchea, "the pale face speaks like a man."

"A man too without a cross," replied Ben, " who ain't agwine to stand by and see a dark Indian murdered. Jumping Panther, I'm one of your'n, I swar."

"Let the pale face loose," said Chinchea.

"Well, that's kind," cried big Ben, stretching his hugo limbs with infinite satisfaction; "and I'm bound to say that I'm a deal more light-hearted than when I owned the bloody-minded Blackhawk for a leader."

The party were all rapidly mounted, and then giving loose reins to the fresh and champing steeds, they coursed o'er the prairie in the direction of Camp Comanche.

CHAPTER XIII.

A NIGHT ATTACK.

ABOUT an hour before midnight, on the evening after the interview between Margaretta and Edward Blake, Alice sat alone in her chamber, ruminating on the passing scene. The young sailor had that evening been unusually gay and lively, had told merry tales of his adventures at home and abroad, and had made himself, in fact, exceedingly agreeable. He had, however, retired early, and his example was followed by the Mexican. Alice had been left alone, or at all events with the quiet, silent, and unpretending negro girl seated on a chair at some distance from her side.

It was a lovely night—calm, sweet, and serene. She lingered on the past, she dwelt upon the present, and then came the future, dim and undefined to all, and to none more than to herself. Where would she be, when another cycle of the sun came gently round? In this dreary solitude, surrounded by beings so little akin to her nature; or far away in the land of civilization with——?

With whom?

Alice blushed rosy red, as she asked herself this question;

and then, she knew not why, came to her mind the thought that she liked not the Mexican. Why did she not like her? why did she shrink from her presence, and wish that she were not there? Why had she found them so solid and so stern on the previous evening in the garden, and why had Edward so suddenly brightened up?

These were perplexing thoughts, and yet did Alice, in her simplicity of heart, wonder why they occupied her mind, for she had yet to learn how the events of these few days were bound up in her destiny. What was Edward, or Margaretta to her? And yet she could not refrain from thinking that the young sailor who had so strangely come into the solitude of the Eagle's Nest, must be that perfection of mankind which girls are apt to consider to exist, and a feeling of real regret came upon her as she remembered how short was likely to be his stay.

"Come, Norah," said she, rising, as if anxious to drive away unwelcome and annoying thoughts, "let us out upon the block; it is a shame to be indoors on such a lovely night."

"Him berry cold, him 'spect," replied the negro girl.

"Cold," responded Alice.

"Him always cold arter dark," continued Norah, who was just then not romantically inclined.

"Well, if it be cold, we will not remain out long."

"Berry bell, Miss Als, him Norah quite ready."

With merely a deer-skin cloak thrown over their shoulders, and a broad-brimmed and loosely flapping straw hat, they then went out into the garden; and ascending the ladder which led to the summit of the block, they seated themselves upon the carronades, and relapsed into silence.

Presently Alice sighed deeply.

"Alas!" she cried; "such typifies my fate. Across my path, sad, dark, and weary, has come a momentary gleam, to fade away as sadly, as wholly, as yon truant meteor that has just fallen to earth. Why is it so? Yesterday I was at peace with myself, my hopes were bounded by the fate which so strongly seemed to be

mine, and I crushed within myself those aspirations which
my birth, my family, my name——but that is gone ; and
now *he* has come here to show me brighter things, as the
picture in a mirror, to fade and die."

Again was Alice silent.

" But," she continued, at length, " this is idle. I must
school my foolish heart to think of him as I would of a
stranger ; I must laugh at his tales ; and remember not
the gentle voice, the impassioned gesture, of his being ; I
must remember that never—no, never—can I mate my
fate to any—never ! "

" You call, miss ? " said Norah, starting from a slumber
in which she was already indulging.

" No."

" Den sartin, me dream you call Norah ! "

" Hush ! " whispered Alice. " I see a movement on the
cliff facing the portcullis. Stoop low, girl, the robbers
will make a night attack, and we have no power of
moving."

" Oh my ! "

" Stoop low, girl, I say ; if we be seen, we shall be
picked off by these bold and bad men.

" Dem debbles," muttered Norah, trembling.

" Would I could alarm the Nest ; but to descend the
ladder were fatal."

" Him be killed, sure as I'm a nigger."

" But see ! they have a plank to throw across the narrow
chasm ; they will enter the courtyard, and we shall have
dreadful work here, anon."

" Him Norah faint."

" Faint, child, when 'tis over," said Alice, whose firm,
but feminine soul, forgetting self, grew bold and courageous,
in the cause of the sleeping dwellers of the Nest ; "they
must be alarmed.   Would I could fire one of these carronades."

" Dat berry easy," said Norah.

" How girl ? "

" Him ole rope burn all night," replied the negress,
pointing to a thick old rope, well tarred, which hung

smouldering, in readiness for any emergency, and which would last many hours.

"Use it, girl," said Alice, turning away.

"Him nebber could, Miss Als," half shrieked the negress.

"Then give it me," replied the young girl, who, however, trembled as she took it ; "it must be done. Good heavens ! they are placing the plank across, and will enter the courtyard in a moment. How can I do it !—but I must."

"Oh, Miss Als."

"Remove the cover from the gun," cried Alice.

Norah removed it.

"Now, stand away girl," exclaimed Alice, with an hysteric laugh ; and turning her head on one side, she applied the match, and fell, half fainting, on the block, while Norah gave a shrill scream.

A dozen rifles, aimed at the summit of the block, answered the report.

"Bravely done, Alice," cried the thundering voice of Philip Stevens ; "awake, my lads, and drive back this hungry crew ; give them their own again." The Nest was soon alive with its garrison, and the assailants at once withdrew, leaving their bridge as a trophy of their defeat.

"Come down, girl," said Stevens, as soon as the uproar was over ; "your courage saved us."

"Good heavens, Miss Stevens," said Edward, assisting her to descend, "How came you on the block ?"

"Why, I was sleepless, and somewhat contemplative, and so went up to gaze upon the night."

"When I left you, Miss Stevens," said Edward, "methought you were weary, and going to rest."

"Would you have a woman of the same mind for two minutes together ?" replied Alice ; "fie, you would have us reasonable !"

"Indeed would I," continued the sailor, "especially in regard to ascending blocks within the reach of an enemy's rifle."

This was said so naturally, and in so friendly a tone, that nothing could have been thence construed ; but to

Alice, unused to such care, the young man's evincement of thoughtfulness was pleasing, and she was silent.

"I must really suppose," said Blake, after a brief pause, "that my rambling adventures must have set your thoughts roaming. I must be more chary of my tales of travels, or 'that I did steal away this old man's daughter,' in as far as her sedate habits are concerned, will be as true of me as of Othello."

Alice remembered that Othello stole away the old man's daughter's heart, and smiled.

"You smile," said Edward, who had taken her arm, and was walking up and down the garden, while a faint streak of dawn illumined the sky; "but you may not find it a smiling matter. I have known more than one stay-at-home lass made crazy for foreign travel, by the 'yarns,' as we call them, of a travelled sailor."

"My mind led me to wish for travel only to my native land, and I do not think you will alter that wish, Mr. Brown."

"But your native land is England."

"It is."

"Near what part?"

"Mr. Brown," replied Alice, "I have told you before, that I have secrets—and that is one of them."

When they sat down to breakfast Edward met Margaretta, who observed (with a smile full of meaning, and at the same time with a shade of sadness on her brow), that the young sailor was almost exclusive in his assiduous attentions to the fair daughter of their host, whose gratification, though silent and subdued, was however, apparent.

"A *pleasant* night you have had of it," said the Mexican, with sufficient emphasis on the word to make it to all but Edward seem a gibe.

Edward grew grave, and scarcely answered.

"Pleasanter than you would think," said Alice, innocently enough; "for after the attack was over, the hours until morning sped swiftly along."

"Indeed!" exclaimed Philip Stevens; is our friend's converse so very gay and pleasant?"

Alice blushed, and then laughed to hide her blush, and looked so pretty in her sweet and innocent confusion, that Edward thought her far more lovely than ever.

" Miss Stevens is complimentary," he said ; " though knowing the fright she had received, I did my utmost to amuse her."

Philip, seeing that Alice was annoyed, here interposed, and adroitly drew attention another way.

CHAPTER XIV.

HOW BIG GRIDDLE VISITED THE NEST.

UNTIL the arrival of the looked-for succour to be brought by Chinchea, there was little hope of the attack diminishing in violence. The whole garrison, therefore, remained on the alert, and even Alice and her negro attendant, accompanied by Margaretta, kept a constant look-out. During the remainder of the day there was no further sign of the presence of an enemy. It wanted some two hours of sun-down, and the whole party were collected on the raised terrace which commanded the drawbridge.

" Your promised visit to the Comanche Indian village will be delayed, I fear," said Alice, " if not prevented."

" I hope not," said Blake ; " for I have a great wish to see this famous tribe, of which I have heard such great things. You have seen much of them."

" Nay, not much," continued Alice. " Chinchea often wanders hither on a hunt, and the Nest people go and stay weeks beyond the Canon de Uvaldi ; but I have never seen more of them."

" Let us, then, form a party," said Blake eagerly ; " and when these robbers have been repelled, we can make an excursion to the camp Comanche, and witness its wonders."

" Am I to be one of the guests?" enquired Margaretta.

" Of course," replied Edward quietly.

" Well, I reckon that are a queer start," suddenly exclaimed Cephas Doyle.

What?" said Edward, turning round half fiercely, as if
he thought the Yankee were commenting on his plans.

" Darn my old granny," continued Doyle, "if there
ain't big Griddle, the New-town pedlar!"

" What mean you?" said Philip, while the whole party
gazed eagerly out upon the pirarie.

" I *do* say, that yonder's big Griddle; if it ain't, I'm
bound to be a liar, that's all."

Mounted on a tall horse of more bone than flesh, and
which wheezed perseveringly as it came along, sat a man
who, in his whole attire, presented a strange and anomalous
appearance. His steed seemed fitted to the rider, and the
rider to the horse. The master wore a tall, steeple-crowned,
white felt, bedizened with tags and tatters. On the rider's
shoulders was a variegated mantle, that had saved all the
stray patches, which otherwise had been undoubted rags;
while his steed had a saddle-cloth of multifarious hues.
The rider's boots were quite six inches above his knee,
and had seen many a year of service—in this the horse's
legs resembled their master, being encased in a thick
coating of mud, of much similar colour to his rider's
splatter-dashes. On they came, so glued one to the other,
so compact, or completely one, so Centaur-like, that all
who looked on, without knowing the man, were amazed
and puzzled.

Whiz went bullets from the nearest cover. But the
horse increased not his pace one jot, appearing to treat the
hostile missiles with philosophic contempt.

" Who in the name of wonder," said Blake, "is this
stranger, who appears so anxious to gain shelter here?"

" Which he shall have, and welcome; down with the
drawbridge," said Philip.

" Are you quite sure he is no enemy?" said Jones,
with much caution.

"Faugh!" replied Philip; "an he were, why fear a solitary man? a dozen might alarm you."

"A dozen?" said Jones, slightly pale; "heaven forbid. I would not have a dozen——"

"No, not a dozen rats," interrupted Philip; "they would fright you more than a dozen men would me."

Jones replied not, but turned sullenly away.

"And you ain't hearn tell o' Joe Griddle, Big Griddle, Griddle the pedlar?" said Cephas Doyle, answering Edward's question; "why he's a nataral born carakter. He is the best hand at a yarn in all the west country, and will whip more cats, tell more lies, and eat more pork, than any fellow in Texas."

"He must be a curiosity," observed Edward, with a smile, in which he was joined by Alice and Margaretta.

"Ain't he jist, though?" continued Cephas; "why, he'll swar he can smell a hog a mile off; he's rare—jist the chap, and no mistake. *He's* seen the elephant, I imagine—and a little more nor twice, I expect."

By this time the object of this lucid description had reached the Nest, and was in the act of crossing the narrow bridge, without dismounting.

"Roast pig in the larder, good people," said he; "just what I smelt, inviting me to dine, as I came through the wood. It's a fact, but I swear them thieving vagabones have sucked bacon for *their* breakfast, and I had—nothing for mine."

"There is plenty here," replied Philip, helping him to dismount, and bidding a man take his horse to the coral, where the cattle had almost consumed every article of food; while Jones eagerly looked to the closing up of the entrance.

"Well, I reckon you're above a bit soft," said big Griddle, whose saturnine visage somewhat belied the merry, hearty tone of his voice, "to tell me there are plenty. Bnt as you don't disguise it, just hand it out yar, for I jist want to enjoy the open air, a rare sauce for appetite, good people."

"Why, big Griddle, my boy, are you been in the wars,

that you look so black, or are you catched a cold, that
your voice is so almighty soft?" inquired Cephas Doyle,
looking curiously at him, and bent it seemed, on drawing
him out.

"What brute speaketh?" replied the pedlar, irately,
and even impatiently. Big Griddle ain't in the habit of
wars; no, nor of catching cold, neither. He would like
to see a cold catch him, that's all; he'd be like a dirty, sneak-
ing pig-faced Yankee I know, and pretty glad to let go."

A roar of laughter greeted the pedlar's reply.

"Who *are* you speaking to?" asked Cephas Doyle,
somewhat angrily.

"To you, my sharp-eyed, butter-eared friend."

"Do you know who I am, or have you forgotten me?"

"What! big Griddle forget the bandy-legged tailor of
Houston; who made him a waistcoat out of seventeen
pieces, each big enough for a coat?"

"Tailor!" thundered Cephas Doyle, amid another volley
of mirth; "I, Cephas Doyle, a tailor! Big Griddle, I am
a free-born American, I am; and I ain't no tailor."

"Many free-born Yankees is, I expect. I do conclude,
howsomever, that if all tailors were like you——"

"Big Griddle, you're drunk," said Cephas Doyle.

"You're another," replied the pedlar, nodding at the
same time to Norah, who had placed before him a wooden
tray, covered with eatables and drinkables—roast pork and
spruce-beer forming the principal ingredients.

"Big Griddle!"

"Yes."

"You are a liar!"

"Don't be alarmed, I've got a job for you," said the
pedlar with a laugh; "and you shall do it, as sure as my
name's Griddle."

"But it ain't," said Cephas Doyle, in a cold sardonic
tone, which drew the whole party, including Edward and
the two women, hitherto standing aloof, round the tonguy
combatants.

"What are the fool arter now?" replied the pedlar,
still eating his meal, but casting a wary eye around.

"I tell you," said the Yankee, with a gleam of horrible satisfaction, "you may have robbed, most likely have murdered big Griddle, but you ain't him, though you are in his clothes, and *do* about a bit make him up."

"Then, who am I," said the other insolently.

"One, I expect, everbody will be very glad to see," exclaimed Cephas Doyle, tearing, at one grasp, wig, beard and hat from the false pedlar.

"The BLOODY BLACKHAWK!" said one or two of those around.

"Harry!" cried Philip.

"Murder!" cried Jones, turning quite livid.

"Captain Coulter!" said Edward Blake, coldly.

"Heaven have mercy on him!" faintly exclaimed Alice, who nearly fainted and fell to the ground, while the bandit chief fixed a look of peculiar meaning and sneering familiarity upon her.

"So I am found out," said the bandit, with a cold sneer; "I must say I thought myself a better actor. That blundering fool Doyle must betray me, too. Well, it cannot, I suppose, be helped. Glad to see you, Philip; and you, Jones; and you, Alice, dear; ah, my little water spaniel, whom I picked up on Lake Sabine, Mr. B——B——"

"Brown," said our hero, biting his lip.

"Brown, was it?" replied the bandit; "I thought not. But of course you know best."

Philip and Jones had retired slightly from the group, while this colloquy took place, and for the first time for days they spoke together with anything like confidence. They appeared, by the glances they cast at Blackhawk, to be discussing the prospects of some proposed measure with regard to the bandit. The face of Philip was stern and pallid with passion; that of Jones white with fear, and scowling with hate.

"Harry Markham," said Philip, advancing, "alias Coulter, alias Blackhawk, for it appears you are that bloodthirsty hound, who has been thirsting these days past for our blood; you are now in our power."

"I rather think I am," said the other.

"And as surely as you are in our power, so surely must you pay the forfeit of your folly."

"Why, what the deuce are you prating about?"

"In New Orleans I owed you a grudge; there you robbed me at the hazard-table——"

"Fair play—fair play, by Jove," said the bandit.

"Here you have, though I knew it not, stolen my cattle and horses, and killed one of my men," continued Philip Stevens, sternly; "am I to let you live?"

"You won't kill me," replied the other, quietly.

"Nay, take not the law into your own hands," said Edward Blake.

"There is no law here, young man," exclaimed Philip, "but the law of self-preservation. It is he or I. If he lives, he will take my life; to prevent that, I must take his."

"Yes, *his*," repeated Jones; "he's a raging wolf; kill him." And the arrant coward crept behind Cephas Doyle, as he uttered these menacing words.

"He's a bloody varmint, he is," put in Cephas Doyle, with a solemnness of manner which was strongly in contrast with his usual levity; "for if he ain't murdered big Griddle, and stole his fixins, my name ain't Cephas, I'm bound to swar."

"You'd swear a man's life away mighty cool," replied the robber, quietly. Big Griddle's better off this minute than I am. I tell you, Yankee, I never kill unless to serve a purpose, and then it's in fair fight. The pedlar will ride on his way as soon as he finds his horse and trappings, which, it seems, I have been foolish enough to borrow."

"Well, if big Griddle ain't dead," said Cephas, much mollified, "and how so you'll send him up yar, why I don't care if I swap you agin him, which ain't quite fair neither, seein' he'd make three of you."

"But I have *nay* to say to this, Cephas Doyle," exclaimed Philip; "for the present, he stays with us. Yonder wood-hole will be his prison, until better men than he decide his fate."

"Thanks!" said Edward, who, in this middle course saw a submission to his influence ; let him at least have a fair trial."

"He shall have a fair trial before all here," replied Stevens, solemnly ; "here, on this spot, in an hour hence, I, Philip Stevens, will arraign him as a thief, and a murderer."

"*Murderer !*" repeated Blackhawk, fixing his now cold and impassive glance on the other's face.

"If not," said Philip, cowering before his glance, "at least one who has killed many."

"None in cold blood, Philip Stevens, save one who would have brained me yester morn," replied Blackhawk, quietly.

"Cease this parleying ; away with him to his cage," cried Stevens, hoarsely.

"Yes, away with him," said Jones in a shrill voice, the voice of fearful but terrible passion.

Cephas Doyle and the rest seized the bandit, and dragged him to the small block-built out-house which was to serve for his prison, into which having thrust him they left him to his meditations.

Pale, with eyes resting fearfully upon the daring outlaw, with bosom heaving, and hands clenched convulsively, Alice had remained a spectator of the above scene. To a casual and unobserving looker-on, her emotion would have appeared nothing more than the natural terror of a maiden, brought suddenly into contact with so notorious and daring an outlaw. But a careful observer (and on the present occasion Edward Blake was one of these) might have noted something of more painful interest in her manner. There was terror at the man, but still greater terror was manifested at the idea of his punishment—an inexplicable look of sympathy, which the young sailor vainly endeavoured to explain to himself.

"Thank heaven ;" she muttered, as she lost sight of him, when he entered the cell.

"Now," said Stevens, "we have work fit only fo

T

men. Alice, take your guest to your chamber ; this is no place for women."

Edward Blake was standing with his back to the speaker, and he noted a scornful smile on Alice's lip as she advanced to obey the mandate. To reach the garden, she had to pass between our hero and his host, and the young sailor, expecting a word of salutation, had turned to receive it. What was his surprise to see gentle Alice standing, with sparkling eyes and menacing mien, before her father.

"Philip Stevens," said she in whispered tones—tones clear and distinct, which, however, reached the ears of one more than they were intended for—"lay one finger on him at your peril. I, Alice——

"Hush, not that name, girl !" replied Philip, who was ghastly pale.

But she had said it, and Edward Blake, who alone had heard it—for Stevens turned away too abruptly to catch the words—stood, as if rooted to the spot, chained, as it were, by some mysterious fascination. All was now clear to him as noonday sun, and the blood ran cold and chill in his veins, as he walked to the walls to hide his deep and awful emotion.

The blood-made orphan, the fortune-robbed child, stood in the presence of the secret of his life ; to fathom which, he felt that considerable coolness, courage, and even dissimulation, were necessary ; and, though one week before he might not have been equal to the task, yet now he felt he could perform it. The undefined dreams of his first night in the Eagle's Nest, the strange visions of his sleepless couch, now took body and shape, and Edward Blake vowed in his inmost heart to detect and unravel the mystery.

Alice, meanwhile, had left the terrace, and had betaken herself, with Margaretta, to the solitude of her own chamber.

Philip Stevens then sternly addressing the whole party, summoned a council of war, or rather of death.

CHAPTER XV.

THE PRISONER.

" BLACKHAWK is now in our power," observed Philip Stevens, as soon as the whole party, Edward Blake excepted, had congregated round him ; "and it is for us to consider how we may best rid ourselves of one who is the scourge of the frontier ; who steals our cattle without mercy, and who makes the woods not only unsafe for the women, but for the hunter in search of game. Jones, what say you ? "

" Dead men trouble not the living," replied the coward, who believed in no safety from an enemy but death; "let him die. We may never have another chance."

"I thought as much," said Philip, with a sneer ; "and you, my hearties ? " addressing the men.

" Kill him ! kill him !" was the unanimous answer.

" Cephas Doyle, what advice give you ? "

" Why seein' he ain't an Ingin nor a nigger, I ain't for cuttin' him off in this 'yar cool style, if so be as he ain't killed big Griddle. If he have, I'm bound to strangle him, I say. Only think of the varmint, with his roast pork ; but he was out. He warn't a gwine to take in Cephas Doyle, not by no manner of chalks."

" Then you are not for his death ? " said Philip.

" Sartin not."

" Nor am I," said Philip, emphatically.

Edward Blake turned full round, and gazed in surprise on his host, near to whom he advanced.

" You look astonished, Mr. Brown."

"Not at all. I heard what *she* said."

"Who?" whispered Stevens, hurriedly; "my daughter?"

" Miss Alice," said Edward, with emphasis.

" What mean you ? "

" Nothing. My words are very clear," replied Edward,

T 2

with a cold shudder as he spoke ; for he could, that instant, willingly have raised his hand, and struck dead to the earth, the man whom he addressed.

" Well, whatever it means, we can discuss it anon ;—in the meantime Cephas Doyle, how purpose you finding if big Griddle be dead or not ? "

" I'm bound to go and see," replied Cephas.

" What, venture out among the vermin ? "

" I tell you, Capt'n Stevens, if so be Blackhawk have killed big Griddle, I'm bound to kill him ; and when I says it, I reckon I mean it. You know as how I don't poke fun in these locrums."

" I do know."

" Well, it ain't in natur' to believe on his own word, that he ain't killed big Griddle, seein' his word ain't above a bit good. So I say, Cephas Doyle will go and spy for his-self."

" Be careful, Doyle," replied Philip ; "once in the hands of these knaves, it may be hard to get out."

" It will soon be dark, I guess ; and I'm sartin the varmint will be on the look-out for signals. Blackhawk ain't slipped his head into this noose for nothin, I expect. Well, I leave these diggens, and I go to the wood ; and if I don't ferrit out big Griddle, if he are alive, he never smelt roast pork, that's all."

" A wilful man will have his way, Cephas," replied Philip ; "and since you will, you will. Meantime, do you, Jones, see that Blackhawk is safe ; and if he have killed this pedlar in cold blood, he shall die, though he were twice her——" This was said in a low, muttered tone, of which Edward alone caught the import.

" Her what ? " said Edward, hastily.

" You seem deeply interested in the girl, and watch with marvellous care all she says and does," continued Philip Stevens, with a smile, as they moved apart.

" I do," replied Edward, deeply gratified to find the other on the wrong tack, when his own indiscreet words might have led him on the right.

" You are frank, at all events, Mr. Brown," said Philip,

with a quiet smile; "and Alice may well be proud of
such a suitor."

"I said not that I was her suitor; I could not be,
while so much of mystery hangs about herself and you."

"Mystery, Mr. Brown?"

"Mystery."

"In what way?"

"She is not your daughter, tho' she passes as such."

"Not my daughter, sir?"

"She said as much just now," replied Blake, firmly.

"True! true! poor thing, she never knew a parent's
care," said Philip, mournfully; "but if she be not my
child, can you blame me for taking a parent's place?"

"Certainly not," replied Edward, with a choking sensation in his throat, a tingling of the eyes, and a stern
dilation of the nostrils; "but why call her Miss Stevens,
when her name is——"

"What?" asked Philip, in a low, hushed, sad voice,
while his face for a moment borrowed the fearful and
terror-stricken expression of Jones.

"Blake," replied the young man, in as careless a tone
as he could assume, and pretending to light his pipe in
order to conceal his intense emotion.

"Blake!" said Philip, in hushed whisper, glancing
fearfully around into the nooks and corners of the building, "how came you to know that?"

"Said she not so?" replied Edward, calmly; though
what was hid beneath his calm, he alone could tell.

"Ah! did she say so? But, young man, why these
questions?" asked Philip sternly, almost menacingly.

"Said you not I was her suitor, sir? If so, excuse my
questions; they have a meaning."

"Mr. Brown, I know little of you, save that you carry a
letter of good recommendation in your face, which, I know
not why, excited, at the first glance, my sympathy."

Blake shuddered fearfully, and, only by a violent effort,
curbed his tongue.

"You appear to like my ward;—I dote on her. Yes,
sir, though, as you may one day learn, she be no relative

of mine, and though from reasons between her, myself, and our God——"

" And me," thought Edward to himself.

" She likes me not, I fain would see her happy. It is my one hope—and to bring that about I would peril my life and fortune. She has, perhaps, to blame me for much suffering, mental and bodily. No sacrifice, therefore, that I can make shall be too great to atone to her for whatever fault she has had to find in me."

Edward gazed in surprise on the owner of the Eagle's Nest ; and a glance of pity stole upon his face, followed, however, on the instant, by a look of scorn and undying hate, which Philip Stevens, wrapped in gloomy thought, saw not.

" Did she love you, and you her, you should know the history of my fortunes—you should be my confessor, and in your hands should be the means of reparation."

" There is, then, guilt ?" said Edward, sternly.

" Are we not all guilty, Mr. Brown, in this world ? "

" Aye, but some much more than others."

" Of these," said Philip Stevens, speaking more to himself than to the other, " I have been ; and yet *'twas he that urged and did the deed.* But Mr. Brown——"

" *Mr. Blake !* " said, or rather hissed, the young sailor, in his ear. " I, Edward Blake, or rather, Sir Edward, son of Sir Hugh, who by your hand——"

" God of heaven!" cried Philip—pale, white, trembling —"have mercy on my guilty soul."

" You said just now 'twas *he* that did the deed. If so, there is yet pardon. But, mark me, Philip Stevens, this secret is between you and me. I have reasons for concealing my real name for some time longer. You have yet time to think of what to do. If you be not wholly guilty —if the accursed deed were not yours—you can clear yourself."

" How ? " asked Stevens, horror-stricken.

" Let me, as a stranger, win her confidence ; let me hear from her lips the story of *that night.*"

" *That night !* Oh, God of mercy."

"And if, from mere confidence in one she loves, she tells me all, and you are exculpated, the guilt falls on other heads."

"Sir Edward, you shall hear it from her lips—she best of all can clear me—not of guilt, but of the damned, accursed deed."

"Until she does, I must look upon you as guilty."

"So be it," groaned the other, whose resolution had wholly forsaken him.

"Then let us be as before. I, Mr. Brown, to you and all. You my host."

"As you will."

"Here comes Cephas, bound on his wild expedition. My brain is on fire, action is needed, and I will accompany him," said Blake.

"Just as you will."

"Captain Cephas," said Blake, "I am curious to see this pedlar, who must be quite a character."

"Rayther, I calculate," replied Cephas; "spry and active as a *painter*, and cute as a Albany needle."

"When start you?"

"In about ten minutes. Lord, Lord, won't I and Griddle have a talk, I expect, when we two gits together. Darn my old skin, but it will be no mistake."

"Have you known him long," said Edward Blake, while Philip Stevens walked away towards the room where the party usually congregated at night.

"I reckon he seed me first; for I warn't above a fut high, and he wur the doctor as assisted me into this univarse, I'm bound to say, seein' my old grandmother has told me so ever so many times."

"Doctor!" said Blake, endeavouring to be amused, in order to draw his mind from the wild and startling thoughts that filled his soul; "why, he has many professions."

"As many, I reckon, as there are hairs in a bull's tail," replied Cephas; "an' considering all things, that's a deal, I reckon."

"What is he, besides a doctor?"

" Well, I guess he'll tell more fortunes in a day, nor a Spanish pedlar would in a month."

" What else ? "

" Why, thin, he's a mighty tall clockmaker ; most as good as Sam Slick, as you Britishers has bin poking fun about."

" So Sam Slick is a real character ? "

" Real ! ain't he jist ? Why, he's in a book."

" That is no proof ; many men invent characters."

" Well, I hearn tell of that afore ; but I ain't availed it can be true.   There are so many busters of raal characters —riglar good uns—as ud kill a crocodile with laughing, that I can't account it true any man ud be such a Rhode island jackass as to invent one."

" Certainly, if there were many big Griddles," said Edward, smiling in spite of himself, " I expect romancists would require little invention.   They would only have to copy nature.

" As I see'd a born fool doin down east.   He showed me a daub of paint jist like a broom, and swar it was a tree. Lord, I could see with half an eye he was poking fun.   I reckon nobody ever seed a tree sich a size.   Why, my hand was bigger."

" Much amused with Doyle, and perceiving that there was stuff in the man worth bringing out, Blake, whose mind was of that elastic character that could accommodate itself to circumstances, went to his room ; and, arming himself, he prepared to accompany the Yankee in search of big Griddle, from whose acquaintance he promised himself much satisfaction.

CHAPTER XVI.

BIG GRIDDLE, THE PEDLAR.

In the very heart of the forest, facing the Eagle's Nest, and near to a purling and pellucid stream, where at night-fall the sandhill crane or stork came to water; and where tasteful deer, wandering through the woods, during noontide heat, would slake their thirst; and where all travellers, who wended their way through the neighbourhood at night, were wont to camp, there was an aged tree—a sycamore—whose huge branches made pleasant shade in sunny weather. Its roots, gnarled stumps, peeped forth above ground, as if scorning to be buried beneath the green sward. Some even, more disdainful of mother earth than common, peaked their points a foot higher than others; and to one of these, tied with stout cords,—the tether of his own horse,—was attached a man of somewhat colossal dimensions.

Six feet high, thin, gaunt, and yellow as any guinea, or as his own leathern breeches—his only garment save and except his boots and red flannel shirt—he sat up in the twilight, the very ghost of the tree against which he leaned.

Near his right hand was a bottle, whence escaped at the same time a faint odour of recent brandy—and a secret worth knowing. To that huge vegetable excrescence—for it was a gourd that had served its turn as brandy case—the delinquent owed, in the first place, that he went to sleep in a strange place, without keeping one eye awake; secondly, that being thus asleep, he suffered the loss of his hat, coat, waistcoat, and cloak, to say nothing of his jargon, which men could only borrow, and that further loss which was common to himself in Upper Texas, and to Sancho Panza in the Sierra Morena—the stealing away of his beloved "dapple."

Big Griddle—for it was this renowned pedlar—had,

during his tour out west, heard tell, sometimes as a thing doubtful, that the Eagle's Nest was inhabited by a bold squatter, and a numerous family. Now, as men and women were, in big Griddle's eyes, but so many animated hedges whereon to hang peddling ware, or big eyes to look at his clocks, or as persons who might want his attendance—for he regarded all mankind medicinally, as mere viaducts for the conveyance of his medicines—he determined that the in-dwellers of the habitation that bordered on the Cross Timbers, should no longer suffer from the want of his visit.

Strapping upon the back of his faithful animal, an extra bale—taken from some well-contrived *cache*, known only to his beast and himself—doctor, *alias* pedlar, *alias* big Griddle, started accordingly in the direction of the region which he supposed likely to turn out a good investment.

As he went, his bale became lighter and his purse heavier, for no corner, no nook, nor cranny, where house or hut could perch, or sit hen-like, and hatch melancholy in the shade, was too remote for him.

His nose was as acute for a customer, as it was sharp for roast pork—sharp enough, as he would often playfully and facetiously remark, for vinegar sauce to his favourite dish, a pig at nurse—or rather unnaturally deprived, of its lacteal nourishment.

Months, therefore, ensued between Griddle's coming to the decision, and his being able to carry it into effect—months which rendered necessary three distinct voyages to replenish his bale. He had reached the very verge of the prairie in which was situated the spot it was his ambition to gain ; when, fatigued with his journey, and having mercy on his beast, towards which he entertained a perfectly pyladian friendship, he halted at the spring to drink, and perchance to discuss his morning meal, when his nose and eyes were at the same time irresistibly assailed, and the double garrison of sight and smell were carried by storm.

"By my father's old huckleberry stump, sweet pork by——; a remnant, a fag-end, a sample, the leavings of some dainty mortal, more nice than wise, though I say it that shouldn't, who am benefited by it ; but still roast pork, by the head of the immortal Van Buren, General Jackson, and the army of *the* U—ni—tid States," continued he, using his favourite oath—or expletive, as the moderns have it—and dismounting, he opened a carefully corked gourd, accidently left by one of the banditti ; " brandy, by——."

This was a *nasal* asseveration, in a double sense, because he judged by the odour, and spoke through the nose ; but before he proceeded to make assurance doubly sure, by the employment of any other faculty thereupon, he acted in some particulars with his accustomed circumspection.

Tying the bridle of his horse to a long rope, and having removed saddle and bale from its back, he allowed it the range of the lasso. The bale and purse were hoisted, by a leathern thong thrown over a branch into the very thick of the boughs of the tree, which thong was then concealed behind the parastical plants that crept up the huge trunk of the sycamore.

" Now I reckon I can eat," said big Griddle, with a frightful grin, quite ogrian in its intensity. " Gen'ral Jackson and *the* army of *the* U—ni—tid States, but this pork is good. By my mother's distaff—poor Mrs. Griddle —but it is not long enough, though—talking of old Mrs. Griddle, puts me in mind of my Mrs. Griddle, she did used to fry a pork chop spry. Darn my old horse's sackcloth, but I should like to know how she gets on in the north. She must have increased the population of New Jersey since I left ;—— and I not there. I suppose they sent that for darned old Whiffles, the quack—Ugh ! the brute. There's a state of things ; one's own family supporting the opposition ! But these women are so obstinate. I told her I'd be home on purpose, if she'd wait until next Christmas."

" Oh, my ! that brandy *is* first chop ; French, I *con*—— clude. Well, I do think that ere tree's winking at me. Gen'ral Jackson and the army of *the* U—ni—tid States."

In this mumbling, incoherent manner, the old pedlar

went on until he had consumed the whole of the animal portion of his supper, undiversified by any of the vegetable. He then applied himself to the brandy bottle, and to that universal *weed*, which King James hath counterblasted with such determination and vigour. Speedily he found himself in that delightful state, when a man begins to have an acute perception of his being first cousin to royalty.

In this agreeable state was big Griddle found by the rambling Blackhawk, when scouring the woods in search of Chinchea and the other fugitives ; and knowing the pedlar well—having cheated him more than once—he resolved to purloin his clothes and horse, and thus to obtain an entrance into the Nest. As he felt convinced the pedlar had money and goods near at hand, he bound him fast to the tree; determined, as soon as the capture of the Eagle's Nest was effected, to return and force from the unfortunate huckster the confession of where his pack was concealed.

Big Griddle, when introduced to the reader—as evening was drawing in—had just awoke ; the somniferous and stupifying effects of the quart and more of brandy he had imbibed, having hitherto bound him in heavy durance. Uttering a volley of oaths—Griddle was, if a Christian at all, a cast-iron one—he struggled violently to get loose.

"Darn that old horse," he cried—at first half inclined to laugh at his mishap—"he's bound to have walked round me until he's fixed me to the tree ; I'll swar this brute was brought up in a mill, I du. Joe, you varmint, won't you walk back agin ? Gen'ral Jackson and *the* army of *the* *U*-ni-tid States, but thar knots, I'll go bail. Oh ! old hickory, I'm cotched. What coon's in the woods, too deep for old Joe Griddle ?

Darn that brandy, as my poor old father used to say— oh, his old huckleberry stump—its the fertile river whence many sources of evil spring. But whar's my horse ? Oh, Billy Power, where are ye ? Joe, Joe ! namesake, whew ! And my pack, oh, by the head of Martin Van Buren—and considering all things that's a big oath—that's safe, anyhow.

But Joe Griddle, my boy, this sarves you right, for drinking that catankerous brandy. Darn it's old stockin. Well, I'd give the best clock out of Maine—though that ain't offerin' much—to git loose from this here state of moral petrifaction, I would. And my coat, lud! there's all the pieces I've carried about as samples for this twenty years in that old coat; and the hat, my go-to-meetin' hat, though go-to-meetin's neither here nor there. And old Joe, my poor horse, here's a fixin. I only wish I had the varmint, the unchristened coon, I'd make him suck his fingers without molasses. Talking o' 'lasses puts me in mind of pork. Pork and 'lasses is a rare drink. I smell pork; ah, it's only the odour."

"You're right, Griddle, my boy; I knew I was bound to find you. Well, I never did expect to see you taking it cool arter this fashion."

"Jist look out. I'm savage. If you've bin poking fun at me, you're bound to pay for it," said Griddle.

"I," cried Ceyhas Doyle; "why, you're drunk."

"No," said the pedlar, "I ave bin, but I ain't jist now. But I smell a rat about these diggins; you're Captain Cephas Doyle as was at Saba."

"I am."

"Thin jist operate."

Cephas Doyle, assisted by Edward Blake, who could not repress a smile, now quickly loosed the knots that bound the pedlar, during which operation they gave an account of the way in which the Nest had been imposed upon. Cephas Doyle, who loved a joke dearly, made the most of the scene, and Joseph Griddle was wondrous irate at the use made of his person.

"Gen'ral Jackson and *the* army of *the* U-ni-tid States, but I'll pound his jacket, I will. To ask for roast pig too; why, he might have deceived poor Mrs. Griddle herself," and the pedlar's hair actually stood on end at the bare thought of such an enormity.

"But I think we had better regain the Nest," observed Edward, quietly.

"Young man, I expect you're right;" and, whisking his

pack upon his shoulders, having removed it from its elevated position, the gaunt pedlar, walking side by side with
Edward and Cephas Doyle, went on his way rejoicing,
towards the Eagle's Nest, to reach which spot had cost him
so adventurous a three months.

Walking along, the eccentric huckster excited the risible
faculties of Cephas to the utmost, by the droll account of
all his wanderings, which he narrated with infinite relish
and humour.

" That Blackhawk's a rare brute, I expect ; I should
like to have his portrait taken, and send it to Mrs. Griddle, I do think."

" Perhaps she would fall in love with it, Joe ? "

" Fall in what ?   Martin Van Buren squeeze me into
etarnal atomy, but you're poking fun at an almighty big
rate, Mr. Cephas."

" Women are mortal," said Cephas, drily, " and there's
no accountin' for taste."

" Gen'ral Jackson and *the* army of *the* *U*-ni-tid States,
you're about right, I guess," replied big Griddle, with a
huge grin, " or else you'd never git a wife."

" What, you're at that game, are you ? "   said Doyle.

" What game ? " replied Griddle.

" Why, a makin' an almighty big donkey of your own
private self," responded Cephas.

" Captain Cephas Doyle," said big Griddle, solemnly,
"du you reckon who I am ? "

" I conclude, big Griddle ; Griddle the pedlar."

" You do ? I'm glad to hear it ; because pedlars ain't
generally called donkeys without speaking their mind."

" But we were calculatin' about that fellow, Blackhawk,"
said Cephas, who saw that Griddle was a slight degree
offended.

" Oh, he'd smell roast pork, he would," replied Griddle.
" I expect you'll hang that chap."

" No ! " said Doyle.

" Not hang him ? " exclaimed Griddle.

" Sartin not."

" Then, Cephas, you're a brute.

" A brute !" shouted Cephas.

"" Yes ; ain't that plain ? You want something stronger, I expect."

" No !" said Cephas.

" Then perhaps you'll jist explain the reason why you don't want to hang that varmint."

Cephas Doyle accordingly, with many a hearty laugh, gave an account of the trial ; during the progress of which narration the whole party reached the Eagle's Nest, and the true and false Griddle were brought into familiar proximity.

CHAPTER XVII.

THE WAR CRY.

THE Leaping Panther and his six companions were unable to perform the whole extent of the journey they had expected to complete during the day, on account of the inferior character of their horses, and the many tangled thickets and muddy streams which intervened. It was dark night even, when they reached the proposed camping ground which was made the goal of their wishes for that day, instead of the picturesque and romantic village of the Comanche Indians.

About an hour after sunset, the Leaping Panther, who rode at the head of the party, drew rein, and halted by the edge of a pine grove that offered both fuel and shelter.

"Camp here," said Chinchea, addressing himself to the white man, the loquacious Benjamin Smith, who was introduced so unceremoniously to our readers.

"First—chop," replied Ben, with a huge grin ; " it 'ave got jist all four wants—wood, water, sky, and airth,

Only lug out somethin' a feller can jist dig his teeth into, and I'll swar it immense."

"Look," continued the Indian, pointing with his outstretched arm to the other side of the diminutive lake, where a black mass of rock rose perpendicularly; "good camp, no eyes see fire."

This was true.

The trees formed a crescent round a little bay, completly shutting out all observation of the camp, except exactly on the opposite side, and there, by the light of the pallid moon, could be discovered a perpendicular rock, rising from the water.

The Indian knew it well, and had selected the position because least likely to attract the wandering Towachani on so cold a night.

Every necessary disposition was rapidly made, much to the satisfaction of Ben Smith, who appeared once more in his element; for camping out was as natural to him, as sleeping in a bed of down is to the luxurious dweller in towns, who knows not the pleasure and delight which are experienced by the woodland fire, with no roof save the heavens, no walls save the surrounding trees, no bed save mother earth, and the green sward above her.

The fire was lit, the supper was being prepared by the hands of the lovely Rose of Day, and all proceeded eminently to the satisfaction of the whole party.

"This are pleasanter than outlying with the bloody Blackhawk," remarked Smith; "he's a varmint I don't half like."

"Then why did the white man join him?" said Chinchea, drily.

"Don't rile me," replied Ben warmly, "for I can't jist say. I'm a real fevert boy, I am, and no mistake; and, somehow or another, I fell in with thim fellows— but I have found 'em out in time."

"Ugh!" said Chinchea, laying his finger on his lips.

All was still as death in an instant. Ben listened with all his ears, but could catch no sound.

"What is it?" he whispered, in cautious tones.

The Indian made no reply, but pointed to the lake with his raised finger.

"I can see nothing," said Ben.

"Did my brother ever see two moons?" asked Chinchea, after another brief silence.

"Never," replied Ben, indignantly, "nor no other man."

"But he will see two lights streaming on the lake."

Ben now clearly perceived the reason of the Indian's caution. The halo cast by some blazing fire, spread its influence on the lake, and seemed to cross the rays of the moon, which poured its light towards the party.

"It moves," said Ben, after some minutes of careful observation. "It's thim Towachanies fire-fishing."

"Good," observed the Indian, approvingly.

"Thin, we may expect raal warm work," said Ben

"Ugh!" replied the Comanche, sententiously.

The whole party now moved silently away from the fire, and concealed themselves within a few yards of its glare.

Chinchea and Ben skirted the edge of the little bay, and discovered the exact position of the cause of alarm.

"Raal jam," whispered Ben.

"Towachanies!" said Chinchea, after a moment of quiet examination. About two hundred yards distant, on the pellucid waters of the lake, there were some dozen bark canoes, filled with Indians engaged in fishing.

"What is to be done, Injine?" said Ben.

"Hist!" replied Chinchea; "they come this way."

At the same moment, the tiny fleet was impelled forward to within less than half their former distance.

A low and angry growl—that of the panther—again startled Ben, but a moment's reflection made him aware of whence it proceeded.

One by one, cautiously and stealthily, the whole party collected round Chinchea.

"Must we fight?" said Ben, calmly, at the same time cocking his long Tennessee rifle.

"Ugh!" replied Chinchea.

"Jist pass the word, then," said Ben.

U

"Hist !" again said Chinchea, with a low laugh; "Chinchea has lost his eyes—he cannot see."

And he said a few words to his companions.

A combined yell, fearful and horrible beyond all hope of description, rent the air. It was the awful Comanche war whoop. The effect was magical.

Again did the party on shore raise their voices, but it was in song; the cadence they sang was the war-cry of the Leaping Panther. Up rose the Indians all; cheerily burned the lights; on came the canoes, for the combined party of Comanche and Towachanie fishers recognised the presence of the favourite warrior of the former tribe !

CHAPTER XVIII.

THE ESCAPE OF BLACKHAWK.

A DEEP and heavy silence had for hours hung over the whole of the Eagle's Nest; trusting to the watch-dogs, not even a sentinel had been placed upon the walls.

About an hour after midnight the door of Alice's room opened, and she herself came forth, followed by the ever-faithful Norah. In her hand was a small lantern, the light of which she shaded as much as possible, anxious, it seemed, not to attract observation.

A few steps brought them to the door of the wood-house, where Blackhawk was imprisoned.

" Hold the light," said Alice, "while I unbar the door."

" Berry well, miss, berry well," replied Norah.

" Hold it up high," continued the fearless girl.

" Oh !" sighed Norah, as she saw Alice gradually remove the barrier between her and Blackhawk.

" Now give me the light, and follow," said Alice, as gently pushing open the gate, she entered the wood-house. " Speak not a word, lest you wake him suddenly."

"Oh!" groaned Norah aloud, in the full conviction that her last hour was come, and that she was about to become a martyr to her domestic devotion.

"He sleeps," said Alice; "wretched man! with such a fate before him, and such crimes upon his head. Can he know the reality of his position?"

"Him just say," whispered Norah, "him desp'rite coon, and him massa say him look a right down bad un. Him not so berry ugly do; 'most ansum as one color genl'man."

"Silence, Norah; bring the light, and hold it over his face. Let me see, and know that it is he."

On a pile of Indian corn husks, and wrapped in an old Mexican poncho, lay Blackhawk.

"Harry," said Alice, in a low but distinct whisper.

"De debil!"

"Hush, Norah," exclaimed her mistress, sternly.

"Good;" and Norah, with a sigh, retreated into a corner.

"Harry," repeated Alice—this time laying her hand heavily upon the unconscious man.

Still no answer—no motion on the part of the sleeper.

"Strange," said Alice, musingly; "innocence itself could hardly sleep more soundly.

She shook him again.

"Him wake dis time," said Norah, retreating in considerable alarm; "him wake, and den lud hab mussy!"

"Silence!" said Alice, raising her finger menacingly. "I tell you, girl, I will have no word spoken."

"Hist! hist!" said the waking man, "where am I?"

"Not a word above your breath, if you value your life;" said Alice laying her finger on her lips.

"Alice!"

"Yes, Alice; Harry Markham, Alice is here for once."

"For what?—why are you come?" exclaimed the bandit, rising.

"To save you from a death, I fear, richly deserved."

"To save?" cried the robber. "Good, kind, generous Alice; ever the same."

"Much changed," said the girl, quietly; "but not so changed as you."

U 2

"Changed in what?" said Markham.

"Changed in heart," cried she; "changed from a little prattling child, as you knew me once in the old country, to a stern and resolute woman."

"You are not twenty, Alice," said he, with a smile.

"Young in years, but old in heart," replied she, sadly. "The few summers which have passed over my head have been bleak and stormy—time and trouble have laid a heavy hand upon me."

"Not worse than upon myself," said Markham.

"Ah! but your ills have been of your own seeking, Harry; and to you, chiefly, I owe the troublesome scenes which have chilled and blighted my bright hopes—hopes, perhaps, by far too bright to be realised."

"Then why seek to save me?" said he, with a sneer.

"Because I do not wholly forget what once you were to me, and to all those who knew you."

"But you no longer look upon me, then, as little Harry, who once called you his——" and the robber gave a meaning smile.

"One word of that," said Alice, sternly—though a rich blush mantled on her cheek—and to your fate I commit you. It is not womanly weakness that brings me here; but I told him he should not slay you, and slay you he shall not."

"No matter why I am saved, Alice, if saved I am to be," exclaimed Markham, with levity.

"Now, then, to the block," said the girl, sadly. "You must escape through my room; it is your only chance."

"As you will."

"Lead the way, Norah," exclaimed her mistress.

"Eess, mess," replied the astonished negress.

"Philip Stevens has well chosen his lair," said the bandit, looking round the Nest as he proceeded, "although it must be but a dull place for you, Alice."

"There is a bright day coming for us all," replied the girl, in tones that somewhat belied her words.

"From whence?"

I know not," replied Alice.

"Perhaps mine may come too—who knows?"

"When you will."

"How?" exclaimed Markham.

"Seek repentance, and with repentance will soon come peace," said Alice, gently.

"Folly!" cried he; "'tis too late, I fear, for me."

"Tis never too late," whispered the young girl, as she turned and faced her companion.

"There is but one thing that could tempt me to repentance and a change," said Blackhawk.

"And that is——?"

"You!" said Blackhawk.

"Me?" shrieked Alice.

"Yes, Alice, you;" and the robber spoke in sad and solemn tones.

"Harry Markham, when I was a mere child, some nine years ago, you called me wife. I laughed at you then. Were you now as innocent as in those days, I should laugh at you still; but, as you are——"

"Say no more," exclaimed the man, moodily; "it is but justice. Let us part."

"To meet no more, I hope," replied Alice.

"That depends on fate. But how am I to escape?"

Alice, at once led the way, and the bandit soon succeeded in effecting his escape.

Alice then returned to her chamber, to meditate on the consequences of what she had done.

CHAPTER XIX.

A WELCOME ARRIVAL.

IT was somewhat late on the morning after the escape of Blackhawk, ere the garrison was on foot; and as the young sailor happened to be one of those who overslept themselves, he found that Alice, Margaretta, and he had to breakfast alone. Alice was pale; while her eyes showed signs, either of much weeping, or of a long and sleepless vigil. Blake, who, for many reasons, now watched Alice with more attention than formerly, remarked the circumstance.

"You seem unwell," he said, tenderly.

Margaretta looked fixedly at him, while her colour came and went.

Alice, without noticing this, smiled languidly.

"Truly this unhappy state of things presses on my spirits. I was not formed for war and bloodshed."

"No," interposed the Mexican; "but this bold, bad man they have taken,—will not his death put an end to the struggle?"

"They will not take his life," replied Alice sadly; "they dare not, and they cannot."

"Why?" asked Edward, curiously.

"He is far beyond their reach, Mr. Brown. I told Mr. Stevens—that is my father—that it must not be; and in the night I opened his prison-door."

"You have acted more boldly than wisely, I think, Miss Alice," said Blake; "but may I ask, why such interest in this robber ruffian?"

"I take little interest, Mr. Brown, in the bandit. He deserves death, I fear; but not at *their* hands. But excuse me if I am not confidential. I own I have other reasons. They will be spoken—they must—but not yet."

A loud cry from without now caused the trio to rise from the table.

"Catankerously cleared out, I snore," cried, above all, the voice of Big Griddle. "A riglar coon, I *conceive.* Sloped like a Kentucky John—behind a pretty consider-able sleek set of keepers; he has, I expect, played 'em possum, and no mistake. Never waited for papers, I'll be bound; but cleared out like a corsair, I calculate, and no mistake. Won't there be doins down in the lower parts! I pity the pigs, I do. Ha! ha! roast pork in the wind, by thunder."

"Treason," squeaked the shrill voice of Jones· "treachery ! Find it out, and hang the traitor ! No mercy, I say ; no mercy ! "

The whole party were standing round the open door of the robber's prison. On the threshold was Stevens—his eyes flashing with passion, his face colourless, his thin lips quivering with emotion. His hand clutched his gun, and he was wrapped in thought.

" Gone ! " said he, without paying attention to the exclamations of Jones.

Before this man Alice paused, and turning to him with a firm, but stern and menacing brow, she touched him lightly on the shoulder.

" Well ? " said Jones.

" Would you hang me as well as kill my——? "

" Hush, in the name of God ! " cried Jones, reeling, and nearly falling ; " who would hang you ? "

" I gave freedom to Harry Markham ; and I, therefore, am the traitor."

" You, girl ? " cried Stevens, on whom Blake fixed his eye with warning.

" Well, I *am* steel-strapped, chawed up, and ain't got a leg to stand on," said Big Griddle, " if you ain't the very spirit of Mrs. G.—By Jove, if I only wanted pig for breakfast, I had it for supper. It's jist the way of the gals. You'd have made a corpse of Blackhawk, darn his skin, but the gal saved his bacon. Ha ! ha ! good idea that. Ha ! ha ! jist kick me, or I'm bound to bust alarfin. Well, that *is* pokin fun and no mistake."

" Well," said Stevens, who had caught the expression of Blake's eye, " perhaps 'tis all for the best. This man's blood, at all events, will not be on our hands."

" So ho, there ! " cried a look-out from the summit of the block.

" What news ? " replied Stevens.

" Injins," continued the look-out.

The whole party rushed towards the terrace, which overlooked the prairie, and there, on the edge of the forest, in the rich panoply of war-paint, and mounted on their small but sturdy nags, came a hundred warriors of the Comanche tribe, with Chinchea in advance.

"Give them welcome," shouted Stevens ; "quick to the block, and up with the red flag of England ; and you, Jones, hoist out the white one here ; open the gates and lower the bridge."

The whole garrison received their welcome deliverers with alacrity.

The greeting between Blake and Chinchea was sincere and hearty, and the Indian related his many adventures on the road towards the camp of his friends.

" And what has happened to my white brother ? "

" Many things, Chinchea ; more than I can tell you now.   But I shall soon want the advice of a brave "

" Chinchea is ready," said the Indian.

" His brother knows it," continued Blake, "and will tell him all when the time comes."

" Good," said Chinchea,   " My brother likes not this place.   Will he go to the wigwams of his red friend ? "

Now Blake knew that Chinchea was trying to find an excuse to return to the side of his dusky love, to celebrate the wedding he so long desired.

" Chinchea is right.   I like not this place.   To me, the air is close and unwholesome ; it smells of the charnel-house," replied Blake, gradually growing excited.   " For days, doubts and fears have filled my mind ; now there is no doubt ; I must, therefore, stay and find out the secret of innocent blood being foully shed, and most base wrong being done.   Chinchea, the secret of my life is here.

" Who has taken the scalp of a friend of my white brother ? " said Chinchea ; "the tomahawk of the Comanche shall take his in return."

" No, no, Chinchea, I will not have his life taken.   In the hands of those who have a right to judge, will I place him, if my suspicions prove just."

Philip Stevens approached.

" Well, Mr. Brown, are you for a sally ?   We propose scouring the woods in search of the enemy, who will now doubtless beat a retreat."

" I am ready at a word," replied Blake.

" The white man is hasty," said Chinchea   "let the

scouts move first, and see that the enemy be not hid in the grass, to fly up and bite like snakes."

"You are quite right, Redskin," said Stevens, "Whom will you dispatch?"

"None yet. Chinchea will wait until the night is come, and then he will go himself."

"Will you take a white man with you?" asked Stevens.

"Yes, him," said the Indian.

"I am quite agreeable," responded Blake—the person selected; "but let us go at once. Your cavalry can easily pour down to our rescue at the least alarm."

"Good—my white brother is very wise, and Chinchea will go."

The party was now arranged in proper order. The whole body of Indian horse were drawn up close to the Nest, while the whites were dispersed amongst them; leaving Big Griddle, Pietro, and the Mexicans with the women, to guard the cattle in the fort. The next requisite was for the two spies to gain the wood, without being detected by any of those who might be watching their movements from the edge of the forest.

Chinchea at once devised a plan, and having given full directions to Blake, he proceeded to put it into execution. Selecting a dozen of the very fleetest horsemen, and those most gaily caparisoned, Blake and he, having stripped themselves of every unnecessary article of clothing, mounted behind two of the horsemen in the rear of the troop, and placed themselves so as to be unseen. These men, properly instructed, then swept madly down the slope, taking various directions, and skirted the wood, as if in search of enemies. The two who bore outlyers behind them, constantly darted in and out of the thick brushwood, as if suspecting proximity to those they sought, but presently the whole gang, at a given signal, darted back and rejoined their companions.

CHÁPTER XX.

MASSACRE OF THE BLACKFEET.

MAKING a sign to Edward to follow him, Chinchea entered a stream, whose pellucid water, however, but slowly hid their trail as it swept over their footsteps in the sand. In this way they advanced some hundred yards, when Chinchea halted.

"Ugh," he said. "Good—they are found."

"What is it?" said Blake.

"Blackfeet," said Chinchea ; "the squaws of the hills have joined the white thieves. A foot comes ; we must hide."

Quick as thought the two friends disappeared behind a bush, just in time to avoid being seen by three Indians, who were returning to the boat with a fat buck on their shoulders. Two were full-grown warriors—the third a lad of some twelve years. Ere the Blackfeet could throw down their load, their enemies were upon them, cutlass and tomahawk in hand—to avoid the discharge of fire-arms. Taken thus by surprise, the struggle lasted not a minute. The warriors fell lifeless ; the lad was a prisoner.

Blake and Chinchea leaped into the boat.

The chief stood up in the stern of the frail craft, while Blake and the youth propelled it. The warrior's eye surveyed every point. No discovery, however, for some time rewarded his diligence, and at length, entering a small but deep basin, where the water lay in a natural cavity of rock, with a small island in the midst, they halted.

"My white brother will stay here until night," said the Indian; "we shall then find the enemy. We will burrow like prairie owls."

The island was a mere tufted stone of large dimensions, on which a little stray earth sufficed to support a few thick bushes, which sufficiently served the purpose of concealment. Several huge pieces of rock, piled up in rough confusion, made, on one side, a kind of rampart; and a small inlet, a few feet in width, between these and the main stone, served to draw the boat out of sight. Blake remained in the canoe as sentinel over the lad, whose arms, as a further precaution, were bound behind him, in case of an attack, when their attention might be drawn off.

About an hour before sunset, a trampling sound was heard below the diminutive lake, proclaiming the presence of both horse and foot. Blake and the Indian raised their heads. They saw at once the mistake they had made in selecting camping place. The enemy they sought were about to camp within twenty yards of their position.

"It's all over with us this time, Chinchea," said Blake, sinking beside his friend in the canoe.

"We will escape," replied Chinchea," calmly. "The Blackfeet are squaws; they will smell a warrior, and think it but the resin from the pine-trees."

"We shall have a heavy storm, said Blake.

"Thunder," was the calm reply.

A splash in the water made them both start. Their captive, though bound, had, while they had been examining the signs of the night, rolled himself out of the canoe, and was making for the shore. The Indian, with a stern brow, at once seized his rifle, and prepared for the deadly struggle which he saw must now ensue; Blake did the same.

A sudden idea seemed to strike the Indian; for, seizing his tomahawk, he drew up the bark canoe on the rock, and, to the great astonishment of his companion, began hacking it to pieces. Placing these where a blaze of light would not fall upon themselves and betray their position, Chinchea added some dry bushes, and the paddle broken into bits. Beneath all he placed a little loose powder, and dry moss torn from the rock, as well as a small piece of paper.

Scarcely had these preparations been concluded, when a sudden bustle in the two camps proclaimed that the news was spreading; and lying low upon the rock, the two friends saw dense masses collecting on the nearest shore, which was about eighty yards distant, while the other was two hundred; but the water was too deep there, to permit the chance of the enemy wading.

"My white brother will shoot after me," said Chinchea, quietly, "then the Indian will load. Watch the water; they will swim if they dare."

"I will," said Blake, who could not forbear a bitter smile at the idea of their combating two hundred men.

But the Indian himself was not more determined. At this instant a very low and irregular sound came from the opposite shore. Chinchea started, and raising himself, he gave, as lowly, the well-known growl of the panther.

Four dark figures at once plunged into the water, while the Indian, quietly turning the other way, discharged his rifle at the crowd who stood in council on the strand. A shrill cry and a dozen balls flying over their heads, showed that the shot had told, and several of the enemy, pushing out a canoe, made furiously towards the rock. The night was clear enough to distinguish ten men in this boat, besides the lad who had betrayed them.

"Shoot one of the rowers," said Chinchea, quietly, "and then load."

Edward Blake did as directed, and the canoe, the oarsman being wounded, whirled half round.

Ere they could again start fair, the four dark figures stood in the narrow gap, beside the Indian and Blake. It was Smith, Cephas Doyle, and two Comanche warriors, who, having left the Eagle's Nest at nightfall, had penetrated to the enemy's camp, and overheard their discovery of the fugitives, whom they immediately determined to join. This reinforcement gave renewed courage; and Chinchea resolved to avail himself to the full of the advantage thus gained.

Every gun was levelled at the boat, but ere they were discharged, the Comanche fired the train leading to the fire-beacon, and then the united volley was poured upon the canoe. Petrified at the unexpected force on the rock, and the greater part wounded—two being killed—the boat's crew fled, and landed amid furious outcries at the deceit which they accused the lad of having practised upon them. He protested that he had told the truth; but he was not credited, but was killed by his revengeful country-men, after lingering tortures.

Meanwhile the bark fire sparkled high, and the blaze, unimpeded by the wind, rose curling and wreathing, as if about to follow the upward flying smoke ; so that the little band knew it must be seen at the Eagle's Nest.

To distract, therefore, the attention of their enemies, they kept up a constant and running fire of three, which was answered as steadily, the artillery of heaven soon joining in the action.

After a short conference, the besiegers divided themselves into six columns; and seeking various spots where there were fords, they entered, and advanced steadily—in all cases headed by white men.   Stern and steady was the fire of the little band of the besieged, as they crouched upon the sand, back to back, and side to side.

They were calm, though their fate seemed sealed; and they awaited the approach of their enemies in sullen silence. But they came slowly.   Six times they reached the centre of the stream, and six times they fell back before the steady and coolly delivered fire of its defenders.

Suddenly this ceased, and all was still.

Believing that the powder of their enemy was exhausted, on came the whole gang ; gaining, unopposed, the much wished-for goal, barely in time to see the figures of the retreating garrison rising from the water-way by which they had fled.

" Back, every man of you !" shrieked Blackhawk, plung-ing, with an almost superhuman leap, into the depths of the lake—" back, or ye are dead men."

All obeyed, or sought to do so : but at that instant, the match, burning nearly at a level with the water, and de-pendant from a hastily closed up cavity which had alarmed the outlaw chief, took effect—and the contents of six large horns of powder sent the rock in ten thousand fragments into the air, with a terrific and awful report.

Shrieks and yells arose upon the night air, and then

all was still as death. Hastily surveying the damage done, it was found that more than twenty men had been killed, while as many more were wounded. Meanwhile the bold knot who had thus terribly punished their enemies, were too far off to make attempt at capture of any avail.

" Stand to your arms, lads," cried Blackhawk, "and come round me quick." His gang congregated close.

" Listen, and act. In five minutes the Comanche hawks will be upon us. Let the Blackfeet bear the brunt. You disperse secretly, as if gaining your camp, and meet me at the blasted cedar, on Skull Creek."

In another instant the survivors of the robber gang were, apparently, dissolved into thin air. Not one was to be seen. Scarcely had this base desertion of their allies been effected, when, bursting like the black riders of some demon clouds, down came the Comanche band upon the devoted Blackfeet.

Retreating slowly, the thinned band of Indian warriors reached the edge of the lake, fighting all the way, and leaving many a mark of their redoubtable valour.

But the God of battles was against them, and overpowering forces broke every hope of escape.

Blake was the first white man to withdraw from what was becoming a massacre, and his example soon led his countrymen away. But the redskins had no such feelings; their glory was not so much in victory as in the extermination of their enemies, and not one Blackfoot escaped to tell the tale, except one or two prisoners saved by the interference of the whites. This interference had, however, an object in view.

CHAPTER XXI.

EDWARD BLAKE AND ALICE.

By a low and carefully concealed fire, sat the gang of Blackhawk, which, by desertion and death, was now reduced to twenty men ; but the leader was not among them. For hours had they awaited his arrival, yet he came not ; at length, as they began to fear that some misfortune had befallen him, he made his appearance.

"Where have you been, captain," said Carcassin.

"At the Eagle's Nest," replied the bandit, moodily.

"Ha ! and have you made a prize?" cried Pedro.

"I came as I went—empty-handed," continued Black-hawk ; "but come, let us to council. Something must be done. These wild Comanches are raging through the forest for our blood, and are in too great numbers to be defeated. They have slain every man of the Blackfeet."

"Every man ! the *sanglant* varmint."

"Santa Maria," cried Pedro, "but they *are* pagans."

"True, they are not such Christians as we are," said Blackhawk, with an involuntary shudder.

The ex-priest laughed, but made no reply, and the bandit council continued.

Next morning, not a trace of Blackhawk or his gang was to be seen in or near the Nest.

The mission of the Comanche warriors ended with the defeat and slaughter of the Blackfeet, and the dispersion of the gang of Blackhawk ; therefore after receiving a suitable reward, they returned to Spanish Peak.

Two days afterwards, Philip Stevens called a council of his companions.

"My friends," he said, after a short pause, "I have not called you idly together, but to learn what you will do to render me some assistance in an important matter. I am about to abandon the Eagle's Nest for ever."

A murmur of surprise arose, in which all joined, save the Indian and Jones.

" Yes, I cannot any longer hope to remain here in peace;
many of you are shortly about to depart, and, once the
garrison is weakened, the relentless Blackhawk will attack
the fort, and not only rob us, but put everyone to the
sword. I have, therefore, determined to pack up all my
traps, and, turning my back upon the wilderness, to seek
once more the settlements. It will be far more suitable
to one no longer young, besides, I must think something of
Alice."

" What I assemble you for," continued Stevens, " is to
learn who amongst you are willing to accompany me. The
Brazos river is within ten miles, and on that I have a
skow well enough concealed to make sure of our finding it
still. In this matter how will *you* act, Mr. Blake ? "

Our hero started at hearing his real name thus inadvertently mentioned, while Jones looked scared and
horror-struck. Alice, too, was agitated at the mention of
that name. _ "I for one," said Blake, coldly, "am ready to
accompany you."

" Thanks," replied Stevens; then, turning to the others,
he received answers equally encouraging ; so that in half-
an-hour the departure was fully arranged.

Edward had in five minutes concluded all that he
had to attend to ; and, wandering out upon the terrace,
he was about to give himself up to dreams of the past,
when a graceful form glided to his side, and, looking up,
he beheld Alice.

" You, too," he said, " feel sorry to quit this place ? "

" Ah no !" replied Alice, shaking her head ; " but I
wish to speak to you for a moment."

" On what wish you to speak, Alice ? "

" I scarcely know why; but a few simple acts or yours—
your starting so strangely once when you saw certain
armorial bearings in a book of mine, and your coldness towards Jones and Mr. Stevens, combined with your having
been addressed by him as Mr. Blake, have determined me to
confide to you the mystery and secret of my history. I have
powerful reasons for what I do, and no second opportunity
may occur. In justice to one criminal, not so guilty as
others, I must be explicit.

"I was born, I believe, in a remote part of the north of Ireland. My father owned much property ; but, having lost his wife in early days, he retired to his country seat, and, dismissing nearly all his servants, he lived on the tenth part of his income.

"The house in which we lived was situated in a lonely corner of open land, at no great distance from some hills, over which came, occasionally, riding on his shaggy pony, a little cousin, a lad of about ten, while I was about eight; he was my constant playmate. Son of my father's only brother, who was a poor country parson, my father,"—here Alice blushed violently—" always encouraged the prospect of an union between us, and often spoke of it, though we were mere children.

"Suddenly, however, he fell ill ; and so severe was the sickness, that it in some degree impaired the powers of a naturally strong mind. Taking advantage of this, some distant relatives of my father contrived to gain his favour, and they even ventured to relate to him reports injurious to my mother. So vile were their arts, that they succeeded in getting him to make a will entirely disinheriting me, and constituting them his heirs.

"Gradually, however, his health and strength returned, and with it his soundness of mind, and that love and confidence in her he had espoused, which made him dismiss the calumniators, and revoke the will by another, which made me his sole inheritress. Unfortunately he still kept the extorted will in his possession, quite content with the existence of the one of later date which revoked it.

"A year passed away, and my father's malady returned more violently than ever, and the physicians pronounced that he had not more than twenty-four hours to live. I slept in a room close to him, and about nine o'clock, after I had been in bed an hour, I rose to go and look at my dying parent. I crept softly near his bed, and hiding behind the curtains, near the wall, between which and the bed I squeezed myself, I gazed with awful and agonising interest, child as I was, on the ebbing life that was to leave me an orphan.

x

"Suddenly, in the moonlight, I saw a shadow fall on the floor, and then another, as if two men were entering by the window.

"I held my breath, and perceived that two men—armed with knives and pistols, and their faces covered with crape —had taken advantage of the unfastened window, to ascend into the apartment. One of the men was much taller than the other, who was short even to dwarfishness. Dreadfully alarmed, I would have shrieked out, but my tongue refused its office, and I saw the two men approach the bed.

"'Is that you, dear Hugh?' said my father, in a faint voice—he thought it was his brother—'You will soon be *Sir* Hugh, I fear!' I forgot to mention that my father was a baronet.

"'No,' growled the dwarf; 'it is not Hugh.'

"'Who is it then?' said my father, rousing himself.

"'Harkee!' hissed the dwarf, standing close by the bed, while the other gagged and blindfolded the sleeping nurse; 'our business is short. You have in your possession two wills. Where are they?'

"'What want you with them?' said my father. 'Ah, I see; you come from those vile Parkers, who hope to rob my child yet!'

"'Now, Sir William, no palaver,' said the dwarf, savagely, and holding his pistol cocked. 'We have come here to earn a thousand pounds. We risk our lives—but the bait is tempting—the wills or death.'

"'Pshaw,' replied my father, faintly, 'I am dying; you can but send me an hour sooner before the judgment seat of God.'

"'Fool,' said the dwarf, in a bitter and sardonic tone, 'do not tempt us.—Ah, Stevens, see what is behind there!' and the dwarf trembled like a leaf.

"The tall man darted to the end of the bed, and dragged me forth, placing his hand coarsely on my mouth to prevent my shrieking. Despite my struggles, I was securely gagged and brought to my father's bed-side.

"'Sir William,' said the dwarf, with a grin, drawing me within my dear father's sight, 'the wills in five minutes, or I put this child to death before your eyes.'

" My father looked inquiringly at the man, and in his cold, savage, and brutal, but cowardly face, he saw that he *could* murder an innocent child.

" ' Better let her be robbed,' he groaned, 'than deprived thus of life so young ; besides, Hugh will protect her.' He then directed them to a drawer in a room near at hand, where the wills were deposited.

" ' Go, Stevens, I will keep guard,' said the dwarf.

"The tall man, who was all along silent, and seemed little to relish the affair, moved slowly away.

" The dwarf sat by the bed-side, with me closely clutched, while his eye wandered round the room in search of plunder. Suddenly his glance fell on a mirror opposite, where plainly could be seen my father's hand rising to the bell which hung by the bedside, and which communicated with the servants' hall.

"Like a tiger he turned upon his prey, and rage and fury, I suppose, acting on his ferocious nature, he sprang at Sir William's throat, and the wretched daughter saw her father murdered before her eyes."

" At this moment the taller man entered ; and, discovering what had been done, a scene of violent altercation ensued. The tall man declared that he washed his hands of the deed.

" ' I joined in this foul business at your temptation, fiend ! to gain a rich reward. But I engaged only to frighten an old man, while you have shed his blood.'

" ' He would have alarmed the house, idiot ! ' said the dwarf; ' but have you the will ? '

" ' Yes ; but I will have no more of this.'

" ' Stevens,' muttered the dwarf, ' if you retreat and betray me, you will betray yourself. The old man is dead, and Harry Markham is outside, who, if I but say the word, can *prove* that you alone entered.'

" Harry Markham ! " said Edward ; " the son of Mary Markham, who nourished you at her bosom—your foster-brother ? "

" Yes," continued Alice, whose pale and agonised face denoted her self-inflicted suffering ; " it was of him they spoke. But let me conclude.

x 2

"The taller man seemed to think of this, and a conference was held. I discovered by this, that they were to receive one hundred pounds, on condition that the will of Sir William, in favour of his vile relations, was alone found; and two hundred pounds a year as long as they lived— they keeping the will in my favour as security for the payment. The murder having been accomplished, their plans were much changed, and they at once determined to take me with them.

"They accordingly lifted me up, half insensible, and lowered me into the arms of Harry Markham. His meeting with them was curious. Lurking about on one of his lawless expeditions, he saw them attempting to enter the house, and cried 'shares of the plunder.' They at once agreed, and he kept careful watch, smiling at his own good fortune.

"Leaving behind them the will in favour of my enemies, they brought with them that which secured me, besides carrying off much money and jewellery.

"One night, about ten days after the awful event, they took me by the hand, and, after warning me, at the peril of my life, not to breathe a word, they led me down towards the beach. A boat waited for them. I was placed in it; then the taller man entered, and Jones was about to follow, when a dark figure sprang forward and seized him by the throat.

"'I hold you—murderer—assassin!' cried the stranger —It was my uncle.

"'Let go,' said Jones, trembling in every limb.

"'Never,' shouted my uncle.

"'Then take it, since you will,' said Jones, and his murderous knife pierced the bosom of my uncle.

"For—oh—for a long, long time, I had no sense of what had happened. When I recovered consciousness, we were in a French emigrant vessel, bound from Havre to Texas. I had been a whole month delirious. I would have exposed the villains, but no one spoke a word of English, and even the tall man threatened my life, if I dared to betray them.

"We arrived in Texas, and at once proceeded here. Their money enabled them to have great assistance, and they erected this fort. The tall man, after my solemn pledge to reveal nothing until he gave me leave, always treated me kindly; he bought me books, music, a slave; and when we visited New Orleans, he did everything in his power to compensate for his fearful wrongs. But the assassin was ever before me.

"At New Orleans, where the two hundred pounds was regularly sent, they quarrelled with Harry Markham, who, not being in the secret of this remittance, cared not much for their company. For two years he has—having passed through every stage of crime—exercised the trade of an open robber, associating with the vilest of the vile, the refuse even of Texas.—You know the rest."

"And Jones it was who killed my father."

"Yes, Sir Edward," said Stevens, who now discovered himself; for, unseen and unnoticed, he had heard all, so wrapped were both speaker and listener. "It was Jones who killed your father. My hands are free from blood. May I dare to hope for pardon?"

"Edward, was I then right?" exclaimed Alice.

"Mr. Stevens," said Sir Edward Blake, "you shall be forgiven—nay, rewarded; and you may, in penitence, ask pardon of God for your own sins, on one condition."

"And that is—— ?"

"The blood of my father must be avenged; the murderer of my uncle and my parent must die by the law, and you must be the witness."

"I ?"

"Yes!—But you need have no apprehension. Arrangements can be made for your pardon, on your turning king's evidence."

"It shall be done!" exclaimed Stevens; "and this wretch who tempted my poverty to crime, and who made me the part accomplice of his fouler deeds, shall receive no mercy at my hands."

"And the will of my uncle?"

"Is safe."

"You must appear against these still viler fiends, who, to accomplish their foul ends, paid for murder."

"Any atonement, I am ready for," said Stevens.

The young baronet advanced rapidly towards the large party, which was only waiting for a signal to mount, and selecting Jones at once, he seized him by the collar, while Stevens dexterously disarmed him.

"What means this violence?" said the ruffian.

"I, Sir Edward Blake, son of Sir Hugh, and nephew of Sir William, arrest you for the murder of my father and my uncle. Struggle not—it is vain."

Jones, trembling, horror struck, his whole coward soul revealed, made no answer for a minute, and even suffered himself to be bound before he spoke. During this interval Stevens rapidly narrated the crimes of which he had been guilty.

"Citizens!" exclaimed Jones, glaring with tiger hate at the young baronet, "I am in a free country, and I appeal to you all to release me from this maniac."

"Well, I do expect it are about *the* freest diggens I know of," said Captain Cephas Doyle ; "but still it ain't free enough for a varmint like you. I do convene to a fair stand-up fight, and ginrally carry the documents to do it, I du ; but a cowardly sneak as kills a dying man in his bed ain't no better nor a catamount. So, do you see, Sir Edward, if you're agreeable, the first oak we come to we'll string this crittur up."

"By the immortal smash," cried Big Griddle, "I do think I'm about as active a friend to liberty as any man, and always vote the Locofoco ticket, I du ; but thar's no liberty in taking two old men's lives in cold blood, so I'm ready to lend a hand, as Captain Doyle has it."

"Thanks, my worth friends," said Sir Edward, warmly ; "but this man must have a fair trial in his own land." ·

Jones at these words bowed his head. He saw that his hour was come.

All arrangements being now complete, the long stream of horses and mules left the Nest on their journey. Philip Stevens, did not start till fully five minutes after the rest of the party. Just as he joined them, Blake, turning round, saw by the smoke which curled along the side of the block, that Stevens had set fire to the place.

" Sir Edward," said Philip, " I have so arranged wood and straw, that in half an hour the whole of the Nest will be in flames. I was determined it should never serve as a retreat for Blackhawk and his gang."

CHAPTER XXII.

CONCLUSION.

ABOUT sunset the retreating children of the wilderness found themselves within 100 yards of the Brazos river. Some at once began to prepare the evening meal, during which interval Stevens took the rest down to the water's edge, and after loosening a padlock that bound a chain to a tree, the skow was drawn forth upon the muddy waters of the long-flowing Brazos.

It was a long and wide, flat bottomed boat, drawing but little water, and a hundred men could have found place and shelter in it.

As soon as supper was concluded, the Mexicans and the men hired by Stevens, began loading the boat, while Jones was placed beneath a small deck in the very bows of the vessel.

Every care was now taken to avoid a surprise; the men lay round the fire, at a sufficient distance to avoid being seen, and the women retired to their cabin. Doyle mounted guard on deck, concealed by the unshipped mast and sails, while Chinchea, calling Blake to his side, entered the small bark canoe which belonged to the skow, and departed on a scouting expedition. It was a still, dark night, and everything was wrapped in the thickest gloom.

The course of the two friends was up the river. For about a mile their progress was unrewarded by any discovery, and Chinchea determined to sweep downwards, when the crackling of some dry sticks on the bank—the bank occupied by Stevens' party—made the Indian gently urge the canoe into the deep shadow of some overhanging boughs.

"I could swear I heard a paddle," exclaimed, in a low tone, a voice on the other side of the river.

"A fowl, a canard," replied Carcassin, for it was he.

"I suppose it must have been," said Blackhawk; "but as caution is necessary, I shall keep along the bank, as we descend, while you continue to lead the party."

As soon as they saw that Blackhawk and his party were moving down the river towards the skow, Chinchea and Blake at once started to return, and soon reached their own encampment.

Presently their eyes, fixed on the movements of the enemy, discovered Blackhawk and his gang collected within pistol shot of the encampment, which lay in the stillness of death. At this instant the low and angry growl of the panther was heard; and next moment, a head—that of Doyle—was slowly raised from the skow, and a hasty sign was instantly exchanged with the Indian.

"Now," said Chinchea, taking aim.

The rifles of Blake, Doyle, and the Indian, spoke simultaneously, and a yell from the robbers told the fatal effect of the discharge. Revenge, however, seemed the uppermost feeling; for, darting forward, they were about to advance to a hand-to-hand conflict, when a heavy discharge from the bank, near the skow, damped their impetuosity, and drove them to cover.

"We shall have a hot night of it," said Stevens; "though I fancy they will scarcely dare to charge us here, Still, unless destroyed or weakened thoroughly, the wretches will lay us all along the river, and cut off some of our best men, from some close ambush. I am, therefore, for attack, not defence."

"Good," replied the Indian; "let us go."

"I must stay to guard the women and my prey," said Sir Edward.

"I am glad you keep the castle," said Philip; "I will leave the Mexicans and two whites. With those you can keep the ruffians at bay."

Without another word, Chinchea, Stevens, Doyle, Smith, Big Griddle, and four other white men, dropped over the side of the boat next to the river, and gained the forest in the opposite direction to the enemy.

With his rifle firmly clutched, Blake stood leaning against the cabin which contained Alice.

"Dear Edward," said Alice, "is that you?"

Ere Blake could answer, he received a blow upon the head, which made him reel; and a second would have followed, when close behind the young man was poured forth the hot flame, and the intruder fell headlong into the river. Blake, whose fall was only momentary, crying to Alice to close the cabin door, levelled his gun and fired, just as a crowd of ruffians ascended the deck, and prepared to inundate the vessel. They were more than thirty in number, and came tumbling furiously down the steps which led from the short upper, to the lower deck. Blake, however, was now surrounded by his five dauntless comrades, three of whose guns were loaded, and sent forth their murderous discharge from behind a rampart of bales.

A dozen muskets and double-barrelled guns were at their feet, all loaded, and next minute the whole party fired, amid yells of fury from the assailants, who immediately sprang to the summit of the cabin, as if about to fly.

Fresh arms were seized by Blake and his men, only one of whom was wounded, and again the air rang with the awful volley, this time followed by a discharge as terrible from the land. Taken between two fires, the bandits turned; but blood had been shed, and even Blake rushed forward to cut off their retreat. Every rifle was again loaded, and the contents poured upon the fugitives, not three of whom escaped from what now became a massacre.

The victors then sternly turned to examine the results, while Chinchea glided about like the Spirit of Evil, proudly collecting the awful trophies of success. Eighteen dead men were found, and seven so severely wounded as to leave no hope. Among these were Blackhawk and Carcassin—the Mexican had perished. Not one of the other party had escaped without a wound; and so dreadful had been the power of superior arms, and the attack on the robbers in the rear, while Blake and his men were hid behind a breastwork, that the victory had been earned without one death on the part of the defenders, though Big Griddle vowed that he was maimed for life.

The dead bodies were tumbled into the river, and when the vessel had been hastily washed of the bloody stains, only three men remained alive of the wounded; the other four had died in the brief interval.

"Where is Alice?" said Harry Markham feebly, "if indeed she will speak to him whom, as Blackhawk, she has so much dreaded."

"You are dying, wretched man," replied Alice, stepping forth from the cabin; "and death is too awful not to make us forget even crime."

"Mine has indeed been a sad career," groaned Markham.

"You are, I think, fully avenged, Sir Edward," muttered Stevens; "there is but my death wanted to have all the three destroyers of your early hopes crushed."

"Who speaks of Sir Edward?" said Markham.

"I am Sir Edward Blake, nephew of him you aided to rob and murder," replied the young man.

"Ah!" cried the other, gazing with terror upon him by the light of the glaring pine torches, "something whispered to me you were no stranger. But murder—no, I had no hand in it; that was all Jones' doing."

"It was all me—all me," shrieked Jones, in a thick voice. "But here I am, dying; give me water."

Blake, accompanied by several others, rushed to the end of the boat; and there, lying on the floor, lay the dwarf, bleeding to death from wounds received from the rifles of the bandits. On examination it was, however, found that no one wound was mortal, and Blake sternly insisted on their being bound up.

In another half hour not one of the bandits remained alive, and at the earnest request of Alice, a grave was dug, in which her foster-brother was placed, far away from the land which gave him birth, without stick or stone to mark the lonely and desolate spot.

This solemn duty discharged, the whole party, wearied, fatigued, and exhausted, lay down to snatch that repose which they so much needed.

A sentinel was of course placed, but no sound again disturbed the stillness of the night.

At dawn of day, ere the morning meal was taken, the skow moved from the scene of so much carnage. Jones had received such a shock that it was evident he could not long survive.

The wretched man seemed aware of his awful state, and volunteered a full confession, which was carefully taken down in writing, all witnessing it. He lived, however, to reach Galveston, where the document was read to him in the presence of the several consuls; and, having been acquiesced in by the murderer, the officials affixed their signatures. At the end of a month Alice and Sir Edward sailed for England, accompanied by Philip Stevens, and every document necessary to eject the unjust and unprincipled family who had robbed the orphan of her inheritance.

The parting of Blake and Chinchea was hearty and sincere.

The voyage of the cousins, though long, was not wearisome, and in nine weeks they were in London.

The next day, Sir Edward Blake visited a lawyer, and within ten days a letter, fully explaining all, with copies of all documents, was deposited with the utterly astounded family, who had defrauded Alice, and caused the murder of her father.

Sir Edward was stern. His terms were awfully severe, for he wished to punish them as well as to right Alice. The terms were : the restoration of the property, one half of the annual revenue for eleven years, in a lump, and a public confession, in the public press, of their fraud and crimes.

They resisted. But the alternative of a trial was too much, and they at length consented to all; leaving the country for ever, under assumed names, almost ere the terrible advertisements, which, far and wide, proclaimed their shame and the mercy of the injured, appeared.

Stevens, who had atoned for his guilt, as far as in his power, and whose penitence was sincere, still lives.

Alice and Edward were then united; and, taught in the great and trying school of adversity, their union was happy indeed.

THE END.

SAMUEL COWAN AND CO., STRATHMORE PRINTING WORKS, PERTH.

THE SELECT
LIBRARY OF FICTION.

The Best, Cheapest, and most POPULAR WORKS published, well printed in clear, readable type, on good paper, and strongly bound.

Containing the writings of the most popular Authors of the day.

TWO SHILLING VOLUMES.

LONDON : CHAPMAN & HALL, 193, PICCADILLY.

THE
SELECT LIBRARY OF FICTION.

The best, cheapest, and most POPULAR WORKS published, well printed
in clear, readable type, on good paper, and strongly bound.

Containing the writings of the most popular Authors of the day.

TWO SHILLING VOLUMES.
When ordering, the Numbers only need be given.

SELECT LIBRARY OF FICTION.

VIRGIN CORK FERNERY

FROM THE

al World & Garden Guide.

is sold by the Company at a remark-heap rate, and is unsurpassed for form-a inside lining to summer-houses and s; indeed, for this purpose it is impos-u say too much in its praise."

VIRGIN CORK

is easily fastened with nails or wire to framework or boxes, and, if desired, can be varnished with oak varnish. pieces to cover crevices, or little naments, can be secured with icks gutta-percha, melted in the of a candle or gas.

Sold in Bales of 1 cwt., ½ cwt., ¼ cwt.

ders by Post, with remittance, will be punctually executed, and arded by e Railways, as directed. Every information forwarded on app tion. st-Office Orders may be made payable to Mr. A. H. OLDFIELD.

Virgin Cork, sold by the London & Lisbon Cork- Co (limited) 28 Upper Tham London

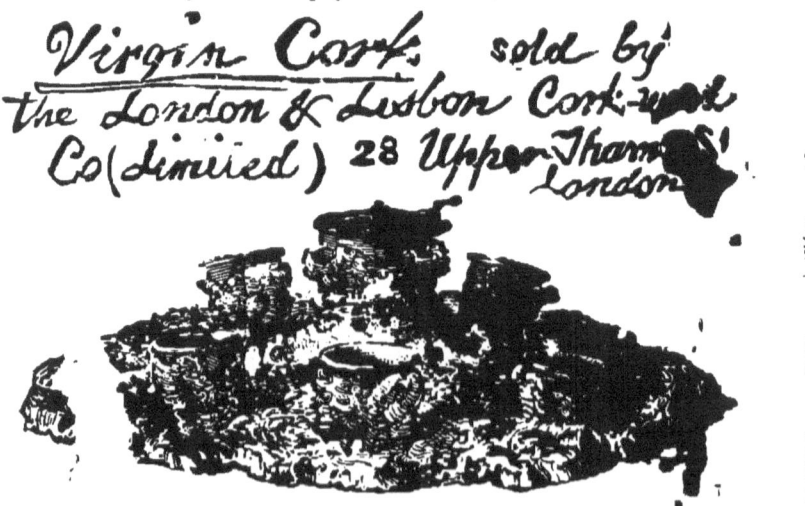